The Edge of Dark

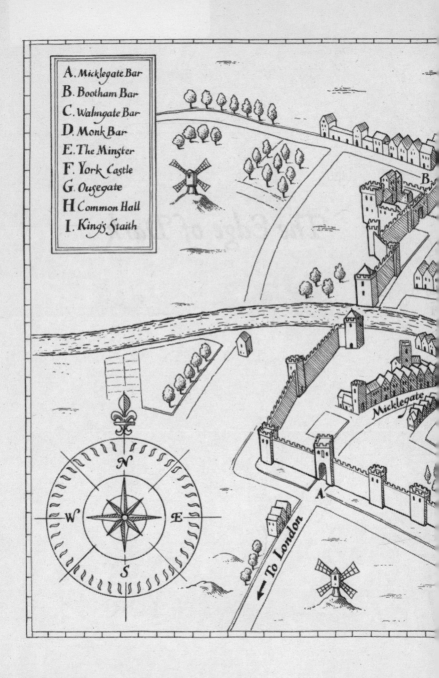

A. Micklegate Bar
B. Bootham Bar
C. Walmgate Bar
D. Monk Bar
E. The Minster
F. York Castle
G. Ousegate
H. Common Hall
I. King's Staith

Micklegate

To London

N
W E
S

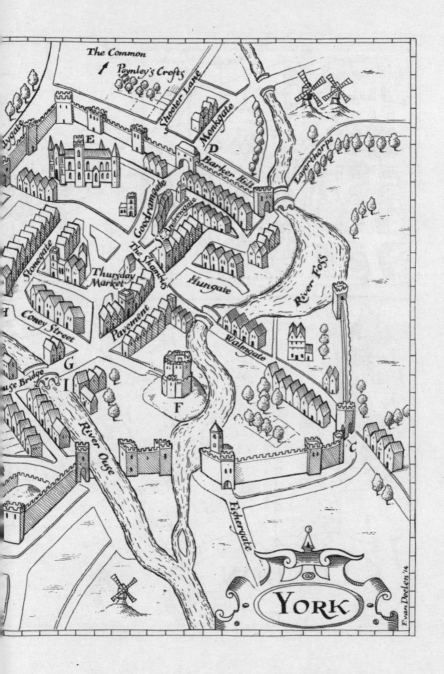

The Common
Paynley's Crofts
Shooter Lane
Monkgate
D
Barker Hill
Layer-thorpe
E
Goodramgate
Undergate
Stonegate
The Shambles
Thursday Market
Hungate
River Foss
Coney Street
Pavement
Walmgate
G
I
F
use Bridge
River Ouse
C
Fishergate
YORK

F. van Deelen '14

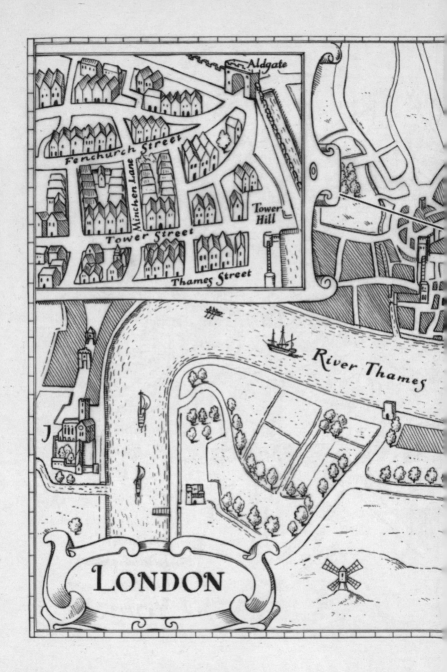

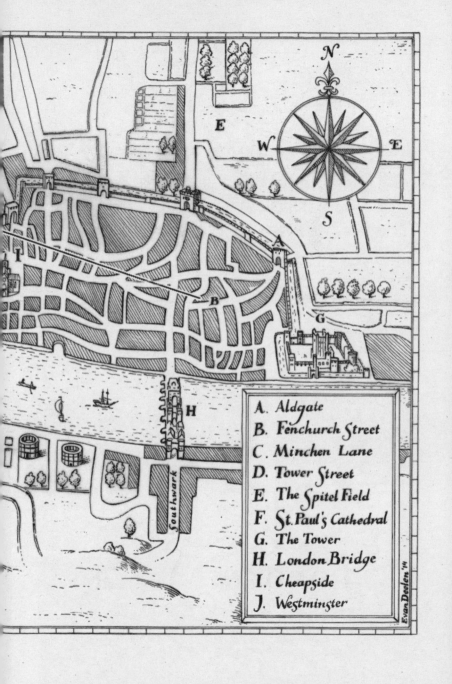

A. Aldgate
B. Fenchurch Street
C. Minchen Lane
D. Tower Street
E. The Spitel Field
F. St. Paul's Cathedral
G. The Tower
H. London Bridge
I. Cheapside
J. Westminster

Prologue

October 1986

Urgent hands scooped her out of her bed. She murmured in protest but she wasn't afraid. Her mother's smell was familiar, and she slumped over her shoulder, ready to slide back into sleep. But then they were running, running down the stairs, the way her mother said she never should in case she fell, and she woke properly, alarmed by the jolting and her mother's harsh, jerky breathing.

'Oh-god-oh-god-oh-god . . .' Her mother kept saying the same thing over and over, the words running together in a stuttering gasp. She felt like her mother, and her hair smelt the same, but she sounded like a stranger, a stranger who was trying not to cry, and Rosalind began to struggle. She didn't like this. The night was for sleeping, not for running through a darkness thick and foul and swirling with a horrible smell that made her choke and stung her eyes.

'Mummy . . .' she whimpered. 'Mummy, stop.'

But her mother didn't stop. She didn't cuddle Rosalind on

her lap and stroke her hair and say that it was just a bad dream, that she was to go back to sleep and everything would be all right in the morning. She just kept on lurching and stumbling through the darkness, still muttering 'Oh-god-oh-god-oh-god-oh-god' under her breath as if she didn't know she was saying it at all.

The horrible smell was stuck in Rosalind's throat and she coughed and coughed as her mother stumbled into the kitchen. Rosalind barely recognized it in the dark. Before she went to bed she had sat at the table eating macaroni cheese and peas with Emily and Amanda and the room had been bright and cheerful. Mikey had squirted tomato ketchup all over the table so there was none left for anyone else, and her mother had sent him to his room, but apart from that, everything had been normal.

Now nothing was. The breath tearing from her mother's throat was shockingly loud in the silence. The kitchen units were humped black shapes in the darkness. They seemed to be watching Rosalind as her mother blundered through the room. It was as if the table and chairs had deliberately put themselves in their way, and were trying to grab at them. Rosalind clutched her arms around her mother's neck and buried her face in her shoulder.

There was some fumbling at the back door, and then they were outside. It was dark and damp and the wind gusted through the trees, making them heave and sway, their leaves shivering and rustling and protesting as they were tossed against each other.

For a moment her mother sagged against the door frame to draw great rasping breaths of the clean, cool air. She was trembling, her eyes darting around from side to side, and Rosalind wriggled against the tightness of her grip, confused and frightened.

'Mummy . . .' Her voice rose precariously and her mother pressed her back into her shoulder.

'Shh . . . shh, Boo . . . *please.*'

A last shuddering gasp and they were running again, across the grass, past the trees and the slide and the plastic chair that lay on its side, past the washing line and Mikey's bicycle, to the shed.

Rosalind hated the shed. It was mouldy and full of cobwebs. Her father kept the lawnmower in there, and the shed smelt of old grass cuttings. There were tools hanging on the wall and plastic boxes full of bottles and cardboard for recycling, and a tottering pile of junk that her father kept saying he would take to the dump and never did. Everything was dirty and old. Mikey had shut her in the shed the weekend before and whispered through the door about spiders and earwigs, and then he had run away and left her. She had trodden on a snail by mistake and squashed it, and she had had to bang on the door until Amanda heard her and let her out.

Her father had made Mikey apologize, and he had said he was sorry, but Rosalind knew that he hadn't meant it.

So when her mother shifted her onto one hip to wrench at the shed door, Rosalind began to struggle in earnest. 'No!'

'Boo, please . . . I want you to stay here and be very quiet.'

'Where's Daddy?' she whimpered.

'I'm going to get Daddy now. And Emily and Amanda.'

'And Mikey?' He was mean to her, but he was her brother.

It was too dark to see her mother's expression, but she felt her flinch as she lowered Rosalind to the floor and tried to loosen her daughter's grip on her neck. 'I'll find Mikey too,' she said after a moment. 'But first you have to stay here. You mustn't follow me back to the house, do you understand?'

Rosalind didn't. She didn't understand what was happening, but she nodded her head miserably because she knew that was what her mother wanted her to do.

'You must promise me.' Her mother's voice wavered with desperation and she kept looking over her shoulder through the shed door to the house where a strange orange light was flickering in the bedroom windows. 'Look at me, Boo.' She took Rosalind's face between her hands and made her look into her eyes. Even in the darkness, Rosalind could see the intensity of her mother's expression, so fierce and so frightening that she tried to squirm away but her mother wouldn't let her go. 'Look at me!' she commanded again. 'You know what a promise is?'

This time Rosalind's nod was more certain. 'Daddy told me.'

'It means you do what you say you're going to do, doesn't it? And you must never, ever break a promise or something terrible will happen. I want you to promise to stay here in the shed and be quiet as a mouse, and don't come out until I come and get you.'

There's spiders in there as big as saucers. And beetles. And earwigs. Rosalind could still hear Mikey whispering through the door, the way he had sniggered as if he was glad she was frightened.

Her lower lip trembled. 'I don't want to,' she said, trying to cling to her mother. 'I want to go with you.'

'Promise!' her mother shouted, and Rosalind shrank back, appalled by her anger. Her mother never raised her voice. She was gentle and kind. She didn't shout or scold. Rosalind didn't want her to be cross with her. 'Promise you'll stay very quiet and you won't open the door.'

'I . . . I promise,' she whispered tearfully.

'Good girl.' She was rewarded with a hug so tight it hurt. 'See, I brought a blanket for you.' She pulled the rug from Rosalind's bed off her shoulder and shook it onto the dirty shed floor, over the dust and the dried snail shells and grass cuttings and dead earwigs and all the things Rosalind didn't want to see. 'And here's Pook.'

Pook was a toy dog that had been Rosalind's constant companion since she was a baby. Mikey had pulled off his eyes and he had been sucked and crushed and washed until he barely looked like a dog any more, but Rosalind couldn't sleep without him. She clutched at him for comfort and buried her face in his soft fur.

'Be a brave girl for Pook,' her mother said, her own voice unsteady. 'You know he doesn't like you to cry.' She touched Rosalind's hair. 'I'll come back as soon as I can, all right?'

Unable to speak, Rosalind nodded wordlessly into Pook's head, and after a moment's hesitation, her mother drew a ragged breath. 'Remember your promise,' she said, and turned away, only to slump in exhaustion as she saw the orange light spreading gleefully from window to window upstairs.

'Oh God . . . oh God, Mikey, what have you done?' she whispered.

Pushing herself upright with an effort of will so great that even Rosalind could see it, she pushed the door of the shed closed behind her and stumbled back up the garden towards the burning house.

Rosalind was plunged back into darkness. Her heart was thumping painfully and there was a rushing in her ears. She mustn't cry. She had to be quiet. She had promised. She squeezed Pook tightly to her, seeking comfort in his familiar smell, but her throat was tight still with the effort of not crying.

'You're five now,' her father had told her on her birthday the week before. 'You're a big girl, too old to suck your thumb.' Rosalind had been trying not to, but now her thumb slid into her mouth without her realizing it was going to. She stood very still in case there were spiders on the blanket, and she held onto Pook. She had been given a special doll for her birthday that she had called Emma. Emma had big staring blue eyes, golden hair and a rosebud mouth, and she was dressed like a bride in a long white dress with lace and a veil. Rosalind thought she was the most beautiful doll she had ever seen, but right then she was glad she had Pook with her instead.

She wanted her mother to come back. She wanted her father to lift her up into his arms and carry her back to her bed so that she could wake in the morning with Emma beside her and the sun shining through the curtains. She wanted to go next door and clamber into bed between her parents, and then afterwards maybe Amanda and Emily would play with her. Mikey would be hunched obsessively over his models. He never joined in any more, but Rosalind wouldn't mind, as long as they were all there and she wasn't left alone in the dark shed.

A sob pushed into her throat and she sucked hard on her thumb, her brows drawn fiercely together to stop herself crying. Pook didn't like her to cry. She wished her mother would come back. She wished she knew what was happening, but she mustn't open the door. Her mother had told her not to, and she had promised.

You must never, ever break a promise or something terrible will happen.

Rosalind didn't sit down. She didn't dare, not with the spiders and the earwigs, but she did stay in the shed. She didn't open the door. She waited for her mother to come and get her.

Her mother never came. Her father didn't come either. Nor did her sisters. Nor did Mikey. The fire engines came. When Rosalind peeped through the shed window she could see their blue lights swooping eerily over the house. The police came and the neighbours gathered in appalled groups, but nobody came for Rosalind. So she stood in the dark and she sucked her thumb and she held onto Pook and she stayed very quiet, just as she had promised.

Chapter One

York, present day

Her case was heavy. Roz put it down and flexed her fingers as she studied the sign. York. She'd wondered, of course, if coming back would trigger some memory of her early life, but there was nothing. It was just a word, barely that, more a collection of lines and curves against a white background, the 'O' a fat contrast to the spiky 'Y' and 'K'.

'Promise me you won't go to York,' her aunt had begged when Roz had been applying to university. Sue had been fragile then, still shocked by her husband's sudden death. There had been other places Roz was considering anyway, and she hadn't wanted to upset her aunt, who had brought her up since she was five. She'd promised, and applied elsewhere. She hadn't bothered to ask why.

Now she knew.

Roz hoisted her laptop bag back onto her shoulder and bent to pick up her case once more. Knowing didn't make any difference. She wasn't in York to pick over the past. She was here to do a job. This was her big break, and she couldn't afford to turn it down, even if she had wanted to.

'You've got to face it sometime,' Nick had said the night before. He was lounging on the bed, watching her pack. 'You can't pretend that you don't know what happened.'

'I'm not *pretending*.' Roz shoved another jumper into her case. Everyone knew it was colder up north. 'I'm just not obsessing about it, like you.'

'I'm just saying, it's a big deal to find out that your whole past was a lie,' Nick said. 'Somewhere along the line, you're going to have to deal with it.'

'My family weren't killed in a car crash as I always thought, they were burnt to death. Yes, I'm shocked.' Roz was grabbing handfuls of underwear from a drawer and cramming them into the case that lay open on the bed next to her husband. 'Yes, it was a bit of a surprise to discover that after years of thinking I had no siblings, it turns out that I've got a sociopathic brother who is apparently alive and well and living in York under an assumed name. My aunt lied to me for years, presumably because she thought she was doing the right thing. I'm not pretending none of that is true. How else am I supposed to deal with it?'

'You could find out what really happened.'

She slammed the drawer shut. 'I don't *want* to find out! Oh God, I haven't packed any shoes yet . . .'

Snatching open the wardrobe doors, she began scrabbling around in the bottom, throwing shoes and boots behind her as she found them. 'I don't remember anything before I went to live with Aunt Sue and Uncle Keith, and I'm guessing there's probably a good reason for that. Why bring back memories of something that must have been so traumatic my brain went to a lot of effort to blank it out? I can't change the past, Nick. Nothing I do will bring my parents or my sisters back, so why keep picking away at it?'

'You can't change the past, but you can understand it.'

Roz straightened, exasperated. 'When did you buy into all this understanding the past crap anyway?' she demanded as she swooped down on the shoes that scattered the floor, matching pairs and either tossing them into the case or back into the wardrobe.

'You know when,' said Nick evenly. 'And you know why.'

With a sigh, Roz threw the last pair of shoes into the case. What else did she need to take? The top of the chest of drawers was littered with necklaces, the bold pieces that she favoured. She'd been to a seminar once on power dressing, and a striking necklace was part of her professional uniform now. 'Fine,' she said, sorting through for her favourites, meeting Nick's eyes in the mirror. 'You want to spend your time trying to work out how you suddenly acquired a fourteen-year-old son, that's up to you, but what's the point? He's not going to disappear just because you've understood why Ruth didn't tell you she was pregnant.'

'And you wish he would.' Nick's voice was flat.

It was true. Roz wasn't proud of it, but Nick seemed to have forgotten how stubbornly he had resisted the idea of starting a family. *I'm not ready for sleepless nights and nappies. We're too young. We're having too good a time. We don't need a kid to keep us together.* Roz had heard all the arguments while her body clock clicked and whirred and the urgent tugging in her uterus twisted into an ache and then a rawness that flared every time she saw a baby or heard about another friend who was pregnant.

And then, *then*, when she was raw with grief and shaken by the discovery of her family's terrible death, Daniel had turned up, and suddenly Nick was converted to the joys and responsibilities of fatherhood. He'd said he was going to tell her, of course, when she was less distracted, but Roz had found out by accident, and his secrecy, coming on top of her aunt's lie, had knocked the foundations of her world askew.

Roz knew she should have been more understanding about Daniel. She *wanted* to be, but resentment was lodged like a burning coal in her throat and she couldn't force the words out. For years she had wanted a child, and all Daniel had to do was track Nick down on Facebook and bang, they were supposed to be a happy modern family. Roz couldn't do it. She couldn't pretend to be okay about the situation. She just couldn't. She wanted to yell and cry and drum her heels on the carpet but instead she had barricaded herself behind a mask of composure that cracked only in the occasional snappy, scratchy skirmish over loading the dishwasher or exactly what kind of rice was best. She found herself taking a stand over issues that didn't matter, and their arguments over the small things took on an increasingly vicious edge.

They could do with some time apart.

Nick didn't want her to go to York. He thought she should stay in London and confront her past, or some such nonsense. Roz didn't have time for that. She held up two necklaces, weighing their advantages, then chose one to add to her case.

'Look, I'm just saying I want to concentrate on my career for now. The York job is a great opportunity for me. I can't throw it away just because our pasts have turned out to be not quite what we thought they were.'

Nick swung his legs down and sat on the edge of the bed, dangling his hands between his knees. His face, normally so alert and mobile, was set in stern lines.

'What about us?' he asked.

'Nick, we've been through this,' she said tiredly. 'It's only for a year, and I can come home most weekends.'

'You said you wanted to start a family,' he reminded her.

'And you said you weren't ready,' Roz retorted, unable to help the bitter edge to her voice. Their arguments always ended up going round and round like this. 'I accepted that, and started to build a career as a freelancer, and suddenly you want me to drop all of that because, oh yes, you know about being a father now and you've realized it's not as bad as you thought it was. Well, I'm sorry, but now it doesn't suit me.' Angrily, she yanked on the zips of her suitcase. The zipping noise scraped on her nerves. It sounded too much like hopes being ripped apart. 'Given the circumstances, I don't think it's a bad idea for us to have a bit of space, do you?'

And Nick had said no, he thought she was probably right. It was all very civilized.

She had done the right thing coming to York, Roz reassured herself, labouring down the steps with her case. This wasn't about the past; it was about doing a job, and doing it well. And that was what she was going to do.

'Micklegate, please,' she said as she climbed into a taxi. 'Holmwood House.'

The taxi driver pursed his lips and regarded her in his rear-view mirror. 'Holmwood House . . . is that a hotel?'

'It's a restored Elizabethan house,' said Roz. How many of them could there be in York?

'Oh aye, I know where you are. With all the scaffolding?'

By the time she had finished with her marketing plan everybody would know where Holmwood House was, Roz vowed.

The traffic was heavy, even this early in the afternoon, and it took an age just to get out of the station. At last they were on the road, although stuck in another queue, and Roz could see York Minster looming over the other buildings in the distance across the river.

Surely she must have seen the Minster before? Roz stared at it, straining for a glimmer of recognition, but there was nothing. From this distance it was just a building, impressive for its size and its age but a cathedral like any other. There was no sense of déjà vu, no flash of familiarity, no sense of coming home.

It was a strangely colourless day, with a milky light that blurred every outline. Even in mid-September the pavements seemed to be crowded with ambling tourists. Roz rubbed her thighs with the heels of her hands, impatient to be up and moving forward, to be doing something instead of sitting in this taxi not being able to remember or recognize anything.

She was not impressed by her first sight of Micklegate. The street rose up the hill in an elegant curve, lined with an odd mixture of nightclubs and dark old churches, of body piercing clinics, tanning parlours and second-hand bookshops. The taxi rumbled over the cobbles and pulled up outside a building hidden behind scaffolding. Green netting festooned the scaffolding and made it impossible to get a proper look at the house.

No sense of foreboding made Roz pause as she paid off the taxi. Adrian had told her that the facade of Holmwood House had been stripped away to reveal the original Elizabethan timbers, but the adjoining buildings in the terrace retained their Georgian elegance. A discreet brass plaque was affixed to the door of the house on the left: The Holmwood Foundation. This must be the office Adrian had told her about. Anxious to get inside and look around, Roz knocked briskly.

The woman who opened the door was about Roz's age but dressed as if she was much older. She had a blouse tucked into a sensible skirt and shoes so dowdy that Roz had to look away.

'Can I help you?'

'Hi. I'm Roz Acclam. The new events director,' she added when the woman's brows only rose.

'Oh. Yes. We weren't expecting you until tomorrow.'

Well, thanks for the warm welcome, thought Roz, but she kept her smile pinned to her face. 'I know, and I hope I'm not disturbing you, but I've just arrived and I thought I'd come and say hello to Adrian.'

'I'm afraid he isn't here at the moment,' the other woman said stiffly. 'I'm his PA, Helen Cox.'

'Oh, hello, Helen.' Clearly she had erred somewhere, but Roz persevered. 'We've been in touch by email.' Although you would never have guessed it from Helen's closed expression. She had a doughy face and short brown hair with a tight, resentful mouth. Roz had never seen anyone more in need of a makeover, or more determined to revel in her plainness. Still, she kept smiling. Perhaps Helen was just having a bad day. 'It's nice to meet you at last,' she said, and held out her hand, leaving Helen no choice but to take it, although her handshake was limp with reluctance.

'Adrian said I should pick up a key to my flat here too,' she said.

'*Sir* Adrian. That's how we all refer to him here at the Holmwood Foundation,' Helen pointed out.

'Really?' Roz kept her voice pleasant, although Helen's naked hostility was beginning to irritate her. 'He insisted that I call him Adrian.'

Helen's face darkened. 'I'll get you the key.'

Leaving Roz on the doorstep, she turned and went into her office to find the key, but by the time she came back Roz was in the stone-flagged hall with her case and her laptop and her expensive-looking handbag. She was unbuttoning her coat as she glanced around at the portraits of various Holmwood ancestors and she looked as if she was about to make herself right at home.

He insisted that I call him Adrian, Helen mimicked savagely to herself. Sir Adrian hadn't stopped going on about Roz Acclam since he had come back from London a few weeks ago. How attractive she was. How clever she was. How she was exactly what was needed to put Holmwood House at the top of York's visitor attractions. Even Roz would have a hard time topping the Minster, Helen had thought sourly to herself.

She had been dreading the arrival of such a paragon. Helen had seen her CV, and she knew all about Roz's degree, her master's, her background in swanky London institutions and latterly in the museum world. Roz was everything Helen had dreaded, and more. She wasn't pretty exactly, but she had a lively, interesting face with strikingly pale eyes and thick dark hair tied up in one of those artfully messy styles that Helen had always found deeply irritating. Why couldn't she brush it neatly back from her face? No, it had to look as if she had twisted it up and pinned it carelessly.

Helen's lips tightened. She was prepared to bet that Roz Acclam never did anything carelessly. She combined the glossy assurance that Helen was only too aware that she lacked with a fine-drawn quality that made fools out of men. It wasn't quite fragility – Roz looked sturdy enough – but there was a hint of strain around her eyes that clearly had Sir Adrian aching to be her white knight.

'Here's the key,' she said.

Roz took it. 'Thank you,' she replied, but she didn't put it away. She stood turning it between her fingers.

'The flat's in St Andrewgate, on the other side of the river,' said Helen, turning away. 'I'll call you a taxi.'

'Actually, I think I'd like to look around the house first, since I'm here.'

Helen sucked in an irritable breath. 'It's not a very good time,' she began, turning back to Roz with a forced expression of regret, but before she could finish, the door opened as Sir Adrian returned from his lunch.

As always when he appeared, Helen's heart stumbled. His hair might be silvering at the temples but Sir Adrian was still the most handsome man she had ever seen. He was a true gentleman, too: courteous, charming, with an old-fashioned gallantry, too often wasted, in Helen's opinion, on women who didn't deserve it.

Look at him now, fawning over Roz Acclam. 'You made it!' he cried, swooping down and kissing her extravagantly on both cheeks, which Roz, of course, took as her due. 'It's marvellous to see you!' Anyone would think she had achieved some extraordinary feat just by turning up inconveniently a day early and throwing out everybody else's plans, thought Helen. 'Have you had a look around?' Adrian asked Roz.

'Not yet. I gather this isn't a very good time,' she said coolly.

'Nonsense, of course it is! Come and I'll show you the house and you can meet everybody.' He rubbed his hands together in anticipation. 'Let me take your coat . . .'

As if Roz couldn't take off her own coat. Tenderly, he

helped her off with the coat, and dumped it in Helen's arms. 'Helen will look after your bags, too, won't you, Helen?'

Helen set her teeth. 'Of course.' Her arms were full of soft cashmere and she could smell Roz's fragrance, something subtle and expensive.

She watched as Adrian ushered Roz through the door that led into Holmwood House, his hand resting fussily at the small of her back. The door closed behind them with a dragging swish. Helen carried the coat back into her office. She spread it over her desk, inspecting it. It was a beautiful coat, soft and supple and light, with striking buttons. Roz had looked good in it. She probably liked it a lot.

Helen picked up a pair of scissors, and very carefully snipped off a button. Brushing the stray threads away, she hid the button at the back of a drawer and hung up the coat, pleased. It was enough.

'We've put in a door here, behind where the buttery and pantry would have been.' Adrian pulled the door to behind them and Roz took the opportunity to step out of his reach as unobtrusively as she could. She couldn't bear the way men like him seemed to think they could *handle* you. Adrian was constantly touching her elbow, her arm, the small of her back, as if she were a fragile flower that couldn't make it from one side of the room to the other without male guidance.

'It's convenient to be able to go between the two houses, and of course we've put in a state-of-the-art kitchen next door which means we can use Holmwood House for catered events.'

He talked on, leading her through the small dark rooms into a large room so magnificent that Roz stopped and gaped.

'Wow,' she said inadequately.

'This was the great hall.' Adrian looked around proudly. 'The buildings archaeologists were able to tell us how big it would have been, and we've used the latest research to restore the room to its former glory.'

'I can see,' said Roz. The walls were panelled with glowing wood, and the ceiling was an elaborate mass of intricate plaster decorations. She craned her neck to one side to look at it. 'The ceiling is amazing!'

'Yes, it's been well done, hasn't it?' Adrian's voice was plummy with satisfaction. 'We brought in specialist craftsmen to restore the house using original techniques and materials as far as possible. And of course it will look very different once we've got the furniture and wall hangings in place.'

Roz hoped it would look more welcoming. The room definitely had the wow factor at first glance, but after that initial gasp it struck her as cold and the air had a strange dense quality to it, closed and unyielding. She put it down to the scaffolding that covered the windows and filtered the meagre light through the green netting. It was chilly, too, and she wished she hadn't left her coat with Helen. Absently, she rubbed her arms.

'Where will the visitors come in? The way we did?'

'No, there's a passageway at the side of the house which leads into a yard at the back. Visitors will be able to buy entrance tickets in the shop, which will be in what would have once been the kitchen range, we think. We haven't developed the back yet,' Adrian told her. 'That's something to think about for the future.'

Roz glanced at the massive wooden door. 'You're not using the front door then?'

'I don't want to spoil the hall with computers and credit card machines.' Adrian's nostrils flared with distaste. 'The whole point is that the house is completely authentic.'

'With electricity,' Roz couldn't resist pointing out, with a nod at the discreet sockets set into the wall, and his lips tightened.

'Sadly, the fire risk means that we can't rely on candlelight,' he said. 'You wouldn't believe the health and safety regulations we've had to deal with. Bureaucracy run mad! But as far as possible I want everything to be as it would have been in Sir Geoffrey's day.' Stubbornness crept into Adrian's voice. 'It was Sir Geoffrey who established the Holmwood fortune and we've been able to establish that this was his house, so I want it to be one he would recognize. A kind of tribute to him, if you like. That's his coat of arms over the fireplace. See the red boar?' he said, leading Roz over and pointing as if she couldn't tell a coat of arms by herself. 'That was his personal emblem.'

Dutifully Roz admired the fireplace, which was magnificent, but the coat of arms gave her the shivers. The boar's expression was mean, its head lowered aggressively, its tusks vicious. Roz's skin was shrinking against her scalp and she had the oddest sensation that the room was tightening around her. She wriggled her shoulders and rubbed her arms, hoping Adrian would take the hint that she was cold. When she felt someone come up behind her, she turned gratefully, hoping that Helen had realized how cold she would be and had brought her coat, but the hall was empty.

Odd. A frown touched Roz's eyes. She could have sworn there had been someone there.

She forced her attention back to Adrian, who was determined to tell her all about his illustrious ancestor.

'Holmwood House was Sir Geoffrey's residence in York,' he said, with a grand gesture to encompass the room. 'The family seat, Holme Hall – where I still live, in fact – is in the Wolds, but records show that the Holmwoods had a house in Micklegate as far back as the early fifteenth century. When they found the Holmwood crest carved into some of the timbers, we were able to identify this as the house.' Adrian's patrician features were alight with enthusiasm. 'Of course, we don't know exactly how it would have been decorated, but it's inconceivable that Sir Geoffrey wouldn't have refurbished his town house in the latest style, so Lucy has been sourcing the kind of furniture and hangings that we know were used by noble families during that period.'

'Lucy?' Roz leapt on the chance to interrupt his flow.

'Oh, I should have explained.' To Roz's relief, Adrian led the way across the hall to a passageway at the far side. 'Lucy is our curator, so she's in charge of the displays. She's out chasing up some tapestries today, but she'll be back tomorrow.'

'Who else is on the team?' Roz asked, glad to hear that she would have colleagues.

As director of the Holmwood Foundation, Sir Adrian

Holmwood was a major supporter of museums and art galleries around the country, and his personal wealth was said to be enormous. Even so, Roz had dismissed him as a bit of a buffoon when she had met him in London. He had probably been very good-looking when he was younger, and he still had a thick head of hair, greying at the temples, but there was a jowly look about him now, and the air of self-importance he radiated didn't quite disguise the portly stomach or the extra chin. He made a huge effort to be charming, but all that olde-worlde gallantry struck Roz as phoney and unnecessary, and it was a relief to know that there would be other professional members of the team.

She would just have to hope that the others were friendlier than Helen.

'There's only a small team at the moment working specifically on Holmwood House,' said Adrian as he led the way up the stairs. 'Lucy is responsible for the displays, Mark is going to head up the front-of-house team, and you're in charge of the marketing and publicity side. Obviously there's administrative and IT support at the Foundation next door. Once things are up and running, we'll be bringing in people to help you, but I'm afraid we're not very organized yet.'

'Well, that's why I'm here, isn't it?' said Roz with a professional smile.

'It's *marvellous* to have you.' Adrian beamed at her from the top of the stairs. 'I'm *so* pleased you decided to take the position,' he said. 'I've been telling everyone what a wonderful job you did for the Godincourt Museum, and I know you're going to be just what Holmwood House needs to put it on the map.'

'I'm glad to have the opportunity.' She kept her smile neutral. Adrian's effusive compliments made her uncomfortable, but she mustn't forget what a good deal she had here: she had been lured from London with a hefty salary and free accommodation, and the chance to really establish her reputation in the field as a freelance events manager. Nick might not think it was a good idea, but she was committed now, and she would make the best of it.

Chapter Two

The first floor smelt of new wood and dust. 'We're still at the snagging stage,' Adrian said, pointing out the sawdust and curls of wood shavings. 'The contractors are working through the house again, finishing off and fixing all the inevitable niggles, but they know they have to be finished before the launch on 31 October.'

Above the hall was a large room Adrian called the great chamber, as well as several smaller rooms. 'We think one might have been used as a parlour, and there would have been further bedrooms, and this one was perhaps a closet or a study.'

No. The word was so clear in Roz's head that she jerked in surprise, and Adrian broke off to look at her enquiringly.

'Sorry,' she said. 'It's nothing.' But she was glad when he moved on.

Her office was on the top floor, under the eaves. 'We knocked two smaller rooms together for you,' said Adrian. 'Lucy has an office next door, and there's a third room along the passage for when your team expands.'

The ceiling sloped almost to the floor on one side, and a casement window was set into the roof to add a bit more light. The room had been freshly painted and equipped. There was a desk, three pale-wood filing cabinets ranged against the wall, and a couple of easy chairs under the window.

It should have been a charming room, but it had an oppressive atmosphere that Roz couldn't put her finger on. There was a heaviness in the air, as if something was mouldering and festering behind the clean paint, and her nose twitched at the acrid smell of smoke, of burnt wood.

'Has there been a fire in here?'

Adrian looked puzzled. 'Not as far as I'm aware.' He looked at her, sensing her reluctance to step further into the room. 'Is this okay as an office for you, Roz? We could rearrange, perhaps, and put Mark up here if you'd rather be next door in the Foundation.'

What could she say? She wasn't going to be the prima donna who insisted on moving rooms the moment she arrived. Roz prided herself on her ability to fit into a team.

'It looks lovely,' she said firmly.

'Excellent.' Adrian rubbed his hands together. 'Now, let's go down and get some tea, and we can talk about your plans.'

Roz was more relieved than she wanted to admit to leave the office. She could feel herself hurrying towards the narrow stairs that led down to the floor below, and made herself slow down. For once she was glad of Adrian's old-fashioned gallantry as he gestured to her to go ahead of him, and the sound of her heels on the wooden steps exploded into the silence like gunfire. All at once her heart was beating hard, and when she collided with a large body as she turned out of the stairwell, it was all she could do not to scream.

As it was, she gasped and fell back, a hand clapped to her throat. 'Oh, I'm sorry,' she said breathlessly. 'You startled me.'

'Ah, Jeff,' said Adrian, coming up behind her, as she took in a man dressed in green overalls, looking almost as startled as she felt. 'Roz, this is Jeff Jones,' he said, introducing her, and Roz cringed slightly at his condescending tone. 'Jeff does a marvellous job as the caretaker here, and he can turn his hand to almost anything, can't you, Jeff?'

'Hi.' Roz stuck out her hand before Jeff had to frame an answer to that. 'I'm Roz Acclam.'

After a moment's hesitation, Jeff took her hand and then shook it briefly, muttering what might have been a greeting in return. He seemed to have recovered from his surprise at their collision, and his expression was shuttered. His eyes slid away from Roz's and she had the feeling that he was working to keep his face deliberately blank.

'Once the events are up and running you may need to liaise quite closely with Jeff,' Adrian went on, 'but until then, if you need a light bulb changing or anything lifting, just give Jeff a call, right, Jeff?'

'Right,' said Jeff in a flat voice.

'Roz, we'd better get on.' Adrian nodded dismissal to Jeff, who stood aside with what Roz was sure was mock deference.

'Nice to meet you, Jeff,' she said.

'He's awfully competent,' Adrian confided in an undertone

as they went downstairs. 'And really rather intelligent, considering.'

'Considering?' Roz echoed coolly.

Adrian lowered his voice further. 'One of the things the Foundation does is offer opportunities to ex-prisoners, who often find it hard to find employment. Jeff came to us several years ago after his release. I must say, I thought he would have wanted to move on by now, but he seems to like it here, and he looks after the house extremely well.'

He held open the door into the Foundation. 'Now, let's get Helen to make that tea.'

His chest was hurting. The pale eyes, the mouth with its slight overbite, the way she had smiled, all had come at him like a fist driven hard under his ribs. He'd known she was coming – he'd heard Sir Adrian talking about her, drawling her name in that affected way of his, and he'd whitened with shock the first time he heard it. Rosalind Acclam, coming to York. He remembered his knuckles tight around the mop handle, a roaring in his head. He'd wanted to lift the mop and strike Sir Adrian with it . . . But he hadn't. He was proud of that, proud of his control.

He'd learnt that here, when the hall had been a model shop. He'd crept in one day, a shy, snivelling child, to buy a kit with his birthday money, and he'd left fearless and strong. A coldness and a power had fallen over him as he watched the trains rattle round the track, and when he lifted his head and saw the kits he wanted just sitting there on the shelf, he was filled with the certainty that he could take whatever he wanted. Why should he have to pay? He hadn't even hurried as he picked up the kit and slipped it under his jacket. He was entitled to it.

He took a model car the next time, some paints the time after that. Nobody ever stopped him. It was as if he was invisible. Invincible.

Sometimes, at home, when his mother was cooking and his baby sister was making everyone laugh, he would think of the stolen boxes in his room, and feel sick. He hated those times, when he could almost stand outside himself and see how cruel and deceitful he had become. But then he'd look at himself and see that pathetic little boy who'd let himself be bullied, who actually cared what other people thought of him, and he'd be filled with contempt. He wasn't that boy any more. He'd learnt that it was easier not to care, not to feel.

It was a lesson that had stood him in good stead in prison, too.

Nice to meet you, *she had said. She had a nice face, lively, with quizzical eyes. Quizzical was his favourite word; he thought it meant she was intelligent and humorous, ready to laugh at herself as well as at others.*

She hadn't recognized him.

There was no reason she should, he started to tell himself, before the coldness that lived in this place dropped over him once more, so familiar now that he didn't question the bitterness that rose in his throat and choked him, or the fury that boiled out of nowhere and insisted that she should remember.

She would remember. She would. *He had not forgotten, and neither should she.*

*

'Meet Sir Geoffrey.' Adrian drew Roz's gaze to the portrait over the mantelpiece in his office. It showed a man in a ruff with red lips and cold, cruel eyes, and looking into them, something unpleasant travelled down Roz's spine.

'You're cold,' cried Adrian as she shivered. 'Helen, a pot of tea, please!'

Roz chose a chair in which she didn't have to look at the portrait, but even so she could feel that mean, boar-like gaze pricking between her shoulders. Adrian's study was predictably old-fashioned, with a vast, leather-topped desk and bookshelves lined with weighty tomes that looked as if they had never been opened. There was a lot of leather, a lot of gilt lettering, and the room smelt opulent and faintly oppressive. She wished she hadn't agreed to tea.

Helen brought in a tray and set it down on the coffee table between the chairs. She didn't look at Roz. 'Will there be anything else, Sir Adrian?'

'I think Roz would like to see our latest find,' he said, steepling his fingers and looking pleased with himself.

Roz saw Helen stiffen. 'The necklace? But it's in the safe.'

'So I should hope.' Adrian's smile held a hint of steel. 'We'll put it back, of course, but I'd like Roz to see it. She needs to know just what a treasure we have here.'

'Of course, Sir Adrian,' said Helen after a tiny moment's hesitation.

She came back a couple of minutes later with a flat box which she handed to Adrian. 'Ahhh . . .' he said on a long breath as he pulled off the lid and set it aside. Then there was a ripple of gleaming black as he lifted something out of the box. Roz's first thought was *snake*, and she shrank back in her chair as horror streaked through her without warning.

'We found it wedged under the floorboards when we were refurbishing the top floor,' Adrian said, oblivious to her instinctive recoil. 'In your office, in fact. It was blackened and charred when we recovered it, but we had it cleaned and look how beautifully it's come up!'

Roz made herself look again, surprised to see that the necklace wasn't black as she had first thought but a gleaming gold, and hung with tiny exquisite flowers made of rubies and pearls which trembled in the electric light.

'It's . . . very pretty,' she said, but her mouth was dry.

'Here.' Before she could protest, Adrian had leant forward and was dropping the necklace into her lap. Roz had to open her hand quickly to catch it, and it slithered into her palm like a living creature. Involuntarily, she closed her fingers around it and the feel of it sent a shock up her arm. Sucking in a startled breath, she looked up to find Helen watching her with a hard, intent gaze.

'We puzzled over what such a valuable piece was doing on the top floor,' Adrian said as, unaccountably shaken, Roz dropped her eyes back to the necklace. She opened her fingers cautiously, half afraid it would skitter off her palm, but it lay there, lustrous and heavy, warm against her skin. She could see every pearl in the dainty flowers, the voluptuous glow of the rubies. 'Those rooms would have been used by servants and no servant would have owned a necklace like this.'

'It was probably stolen,' said Helen flatly.

'No!' Roz's protest was out before she knew she was going to say anything. It was only when Adrian and Helen looked at her in surprise that she realized she had spoken at all. It felt as if the shout of denial had come from the necklace itself . . .

Which was obviously a ridiculous idea. 'I mean . . . perhaps we could use the mystery somehow,' she improvised weakly. 'We could let visitors decide or propose alternative theories about how the necklace could have got into the attic room.'

It was the best she could think of, but Adrian nodded sagely. 'Nice idea,' he said. 'I've already arranged to have a copy made, as this is far too valuable to have on display, but it would take an expert to know the difference.'

I would know, Roz thought involuntarily, and she could have sworn the necklace throbbed an agreement in her hand.

'Has it been dated?' she said instead.

'It's late sixteenth or early seventeenth century, so it fits into Sir Geoffrey's period very well.' Adrian nodded at the portrait. 'He may even have bought it himself.'

Roz flinched as the necklace seemed to stir in her hand.

'It's very beautiful,' she said, meaning it this time.

'Would you like to try it on?'

'Oh no, I couldn't,' Roz started to protest, but Adrian was insistent. He plucked it from her palm and unfastened the catch.

'A necklace like this was made to be worn by a beautiful woman,' he declared, getting to his feet.

In spite of herself, Roz caught Helen's eye. The other woman was watching her with something so reptilian in her gaze that Roz felt a chill go through her.

'It's too valuable,' she said to Adrian.

'I insist,' he said, urging her to her feet. 'I've been longing to see this as it was meant to be, not as an exhibit.'

She could hardly refuse without making an even bigger fuss. Uncomfortable, avoiding Helen's gaze, Roz got up and let Adrian turn her to face a mirror on the wall.

Biting her lip, she lifted the stray hairs at the nape of her neck and bent her head so that Adrian could drape the necklace round her throat.

'There,' he said when he had fastened it carefully.

Roz lifted her head and stepped away from him, spreading her hand over the necklace to adjust where it lay against her skin. The gold felt warm to the touch.

'I've never worn anything so valuable before,' she confessed.

'It looks wonderful on you, doesn't it, Helen?'

Unwillingly, Roz found herself meeting Helen's eyes in the mirror again, and she saw such malevolence there that her breath caught in her throat and the necklace itself seemed to pulse against her skin.

'I wonder if we should get a photo of you modelling it?' said Adrian, but Roz had stopped listening. She was sure the necklace was growing warmer. How was that possible?

'What was the name of that photographer we used?' he asked Helen while Roz touched the necklace, puzzled.

'Oh,' she said. It was definitely hotter. She twisted her

fingers around the gold chain. Yes, the metal was glowing. 'Oh,' she said again, confused, and then, 'Ow!'

'Roz?' Adrian broke off his discussion with Helen to look at her in concern.

'The necklace . . . it's burning me!' The gold was searing into her skin, the pain doubling and redoubling, while Adrian just looked blank.

'What do you mean?'

'It's *burning* me!' Frantically Roz tried to lift the necklace away from her skin. 'Please . . . take it off!'

'A necklace can't burn you,' he said soothingly, but that only increased her panic. She *knew* that a necklace couldn't heat itself, but with a collar of vicious pain around her throat she was in no mood to discuss what was and wasn't possible.

'Please . . .' she begged, almost in tears as she struggled to protect her neck and the gold burned into her fingers instead. One hand fumbled for the catch while the other attempted to protect the delicate skin on her neck. 'Please help me! *Please!*'

'Roz, my dear, calm down,' said Adrian as her voice rose, but it was Helen who stepped forward in the end.

'Oh, for heaven's sake,' she said, briskly unfastening the clasp. 'What a fuss!'

'Thank you . . . thank you, Helen,' said Roz gratefully. As soon as Helen pulled the necklace away, her panic subsided into short, jerky breaths. Her hand was at her throat still, and her eyes were wide and dark with horror as she stared at the necklace gleaming and glittering in Helen's hand.

'There's absolutely nothing wrong with it,' said Helen with

a disgusted look. She handed the necklace back to Adrian, who turned it over between his fingers.

'I have to say, it feels perfectly normal to me,' he said.

'It was hot,' Roz insisted shakily. 'It's burnt me.'

But when she looked in the mirror, expecting to see the flesh around her neck red and blistered, her skin was smooth and unmarked and there was no sign that the necklace had been there at all.

A dull throb had started behind Roz's eyes and she was glad in the end to let Helen call her a taxi. Adrian had wanted to take her to the flat, but before Roz could demur, Helen had reminded him about a meeting, and Roz sent her a grateful look, which she met with a stony glare. It was a shame Helen seemed so hostile. They were of a similar age and Helen was from York too. They might have been at a toddler group together. If things had been different, they might have gone to the same school. They might have been friends.

As Adrian had explained at length, the Holmwood Foundation was all about preserving the past, and Roz had somehow expected to be given a little flat in one of the historic houses they owned around the city. Instead she found herself in a modern apartment on the second floor of a purpose-built block, surrounded by similar blocks with the kind of faux Georgian facades that Nick so loathed.

Inside, the proportions were meagre and the décor bland: beige carpets, beige furniture, blank cream walls. Roz left her case by the door and unbuttoned her coat as she went to explore. It was only then that she realized one of the buttons was missing. She'd been in too much of a state when she'd left to notice that she'd lost a button somewhere along the line. It was a shame as the coat was one of her favourites and the buttons were particularly striking. She inspected the gap more closely. How had the button come off without leaving so much as a thread behind?

Roz frowned. Just one more odd thing on this odd day. With a sigh, she threw the coat over a mean-looking armchair and touched her fingers to her neck. It wasn't painful exactly, but her flesh shrank just thinking about that searing agony. Clearly Adrian and Helen thought she had made it all up, but why would she want to make a fool of herself? Roz wriggled her shoulders uncomfortably at the memory of her panic, the way her voice had risen to a shriek. So much for impressing them with her professionalism.

It didn't take long to investigate the flat: it had a living room with an open-plan kitchen at one end, a windowless bathroom and a bedroom, all decorated in the same bland colours. Roz tried to talk herself into a more positive mood. So it wasn't the most characterful flat in the world, but it was dry, clean, central; that was all she needed. She'd be going home to London at weekends, and for a moment the thought of the flat she and Nick had bought and decorated together stabbed her in the belly with such intensity that she covered her stomach with her hands.

Enough. Roz scowled at her own weakness. She could make this boring flat more homely. It would be fine.

Wandering over to the window, she pulled down the slats of the venetian blind – a pale grey plastic – and peered out to see if the view was any more inspiring.

It wasn't. No charming higgledy-piggledy medieval houses met her gaze, just a courtyard paved in brick with some neatly parked cars and more pseudo-traditional apartment buildings.

Unimpressed, Roz was turning away when a drift of smoke below caught at the edge of her vision. *Weird. Who would be having a bonfire here?* She craned her neck anxiously to see where the smoke was coming from in case she needed to make a run for the stairs. Even before she'd understood why, she'd had a phobia of fire, and the idea of being trapped in a burning building was the worst fate she could imagine. Just thinking about it made her palms sweat.

But all was as it should be. She relaxed when she saw that the smoke was puffing out of the kitchen chimney. The narrow yard beneath her window ran past the kitchen, past the wood-store and the henhouse, past the apple trees and the scrubby patch of herbs to the thatched stable and the back gate that opened into –

Kitchen? Stables? Roz blinked as her mind caught up with what she was seeing, and the scene vanished. There was no smoking chimney. There were no trees, or outbuildings, just the cars parked in their slots and the bland block of flats behind.

Roz jerked back from the blind, and the snap of the slats rattling into place sent her heart lurching into her throat. 'What . . . ?' Puzzled, uneasy, she stared at the blind. Through the slats she could see the top of the building opposite and some bruised-looking sky. There couldn't be a yard below, but she could picture it so clearly: the way the smoke had drifted in the damp air, the grey-green lichen clinging to the tree trunks, the trampled path to the woodstore, the hens pecking in the mud. The stable door had stood ajar.

'What stable?' Roz said out loud, her voice echoing queerly in the empty room. 'How did I know that was a woodstore?'

Her head was aching, a dull steady pounding inside her skull, and she dropped onto the sofa, pressing her fingers to her eyelids. She must have imagined that scene. She was tired as she hadn't been sleeping well, and it had been a strange day. Perhaps it had been a hangover from a long-forgotten dream? It hadn't been real.

Lowering her hands, Roz lay back against the cushions and opened her eyes. She looked up at the plain white ceiling. Of course it hadn't been real. How could it be real? There was nothing there. She should get up and unpack, make a cup of tea. Do anything other than sit here and wonder about what she had seen through the window.

Still, her eyes kept sliding sideways to the blind. From the sofa the slats looked secretive and enticing at the same time. *Come and look*, they seemed to whisper into the air. *Come closer. You won't be able to see unless you come really close. What do you think you'll see if you do?*

Roz knew what she would see. A car park. She didn't need to look. She was going to put the kettle on instead. But when she got to her feet, the blind shifted at the edge of her vision.

'Oh, this is ridiculous!' she said at last. Now she was going to have to check.

She stomped over to the window, ignoring the wild warning cry of instinct at the back of her mind, ignoring the throb of her neck where the necklace had lain. There was nothing there. She was going to pull up the blind and look out of the window, and when she found herself staring down at the car park, she was going to feel an idiot. There was no reason for the heavy thud of her heart, or the fear squirming through her belly. Good God, she wasn't going to be able to hold down a job in York if she didn't dare look out of a window!

Even so, she paused with her fingers on the cord. She'd meant to jerk the blind up, but instead she found herself side-stepping to the edge of the window so that she could ease the slats cautiously away from the glass and look outside once more.

Chapter Three

November 1570

The hens pecked unconcernedly out of Jane's way as she hurried down to the herb garden. A petulant drizzle cast a sheen of damp over everything and Jane rubbed her fingers together, wishing that she had stopped to put on a gown. There was little enough growing at this time of year, but she might be able to find some thyme, some rosemary, a leaf of bay, enough to make a faggot of sweet herbs. Ellen was going to show her how to stew a fillet of beef for dinner and Jane had consulted her mother's cookery book, running her finger carefully along each line to make sure they had all the ingredients.

Her father had been in a black mood all morning, thumping his meaty fist on the table and shouting until the wainscot rang with his booming voice, and it had been a relief when he stumped out of the house to attend a council meeting. The stewed fillet was his favourite and Jane was hoping it would sweeten his temper. If he was pleased with his dinner, Juliana would be able to wheedle a new gown out of him, and then *she* would be happy for a while.

'You must look after your sister,' Jane's mother had said. Her voice had been rasping with effort and she had stopped after every few words to lick her cracked lips. 'Her passions are so violent, I fear for her. She is not strong in spirit like you, dear Jane. Promise me that you will care for her. Keep her safe.'

'I promise.' Jane took her mother's hand. She could hear Juliana weeping hysterically in the other chamber. Jane wanted to weep too. She wanted to throw back her head and howl like a dog, but her mother had taught her to be modest and quiet, so she sat very still, lips pressed firmly together, and she held her mother's hand until she died.

Afterwards, her father told her that it would be for her to run the household now.

'Ellen will help you,' he said roughly. 'She's been servant here long enough to know how to go on. You are twelve, old enough to take your mother's place and care for your sister.'

Jane was doing her best, but she missed her mother. Juliana was their father's pet. Her hair was a glorious gold, tumbling in curls to her waist, and her eyes were as blue as a summer sky. Small wonder Henry Birkby was besotted by his beautiful daughter, and irritated by Jane, who was thin and plain and whose eyes were the murky green of a hedge ditch, and who had not had the decency to be born a boy. Juliana knew to a nicety how to cajole her father into a new gown. The merest hint of tears sparkling on the end of her lashes was enough to have him reaching for his purse. Once or twice Jane had ventured that it might not be good for Juliana to be quite so spoilt, and was accused of being jealous and a killjoy for her pains. Her mother had known how to manage both her husband and her daughter, but it was harder for Jane without the authority of a wife or a mother.

It wasn't that Jane didn't love her sister. How could she not when Juliana was so very beautiful? When Juliana was in a sunny mood, she was as enchanting as a kitten and impossible to resist, but her moods were so changeable that Jane never knew how she would react. One minute she would be laughing delightedly, the next cast into despair and weeping herself into a state of misery that could take days to lift. She had feverish enthusiasms that died overnight, and was so ruthlessly self-absorbed that sometimes Jane could only gape at her lack of concern for others.

She had promised to look after Juliana, but it was no easy task, and there were times, faced with hysterical weeping, when Jane felt overwhelmed by the charge her mother had laid on her. She took refuge in keeping house, in the practicalities of making sure that her father was fed and Juliana comfortable. Jane knew that she was dull and plain, and she would rather be in the kitchen with its comforting smells of bacon and spices than sitting in the parlour. She took more satisfaction in casting the accounts than in tales of knightly quests, and she tied on her apron with as much pleasure as Juliana did in smoothing down the skirts of a new gown. Away from her father's vicious rages and Juliana's extremes of emotion, Jane was glad to beat the carpets and dress the meat and polish the silver goblets her father flaunted until they reflected her homely face back at her.

Henry Birkby was a butcher whose wealth eclipsed many a gentleman's, or so he liked to boast. Jane was hopeful that one day she would be married, if only for her dowry, and while she would never be a beauty, she would have practical skills to offer in place of a fair face. Sometimes Jane dreamed of it, when she was on her own, and absently plumping up cushions or folding linen; she would have a kind husband, children, and she would be able to lavish on them the same care she gave her father and her sister, but with greater reward. Her husband would appreciate her and commend her, and her babies would clutch at her hair with fat little hands, and nestle trustingly into her bosom the way she had seen her neighbours' babes do. Jane sighed a little mistily whenever she thought of it. It did not seem so much to ask, to be loved, just a little. She didn't need extravagant declarations of passion the way Juliana doubtless would. She didn't need a knight to slay a giant for her. She only wanted to be needed and appreciated. Just a little.

So she dreamt of a future home of her own, and she listened to Ellen and she learnt how to go on. 'We'll make a housewife of you yet,' Ellen sometimes said approvingly.

Jane liked Ellen. She was not so old, nineteen or twenty, but Jane's mother had trained her from a girl, and she knew the kind of things Jane wanted to know: how to make a remedy for a rheum or how to make a tart of an ear of veal. Ellen could be brusque, and her temper had been shorter than usual lately, but she was a good cook, and it showed in her round figure.

Where *was* Ellen, anyway? It was not like her to be away from the kitchen for so long. Jane frowned a little as she bent over a straggle of thyme. She had been looking tired and puffy-eyed earlier, and Jane had seen her rest her hand on her ample stomach and wince. Jane glanced down at the privy at the end of the garden. Perhaps Ellen was in there? She would leave her be and start stewing the fillet herself. She would read the recipe and it could not be so hard. Already she had set out her ingredients: raw beef from her father's shop, oozing blood, some claret, some mace, a precious lemon. The lemon was somewhat wizened, but it would serve.

A restless gust of wind blew the branches of the apple trees about, splattering dampness and drizzle in Jane's face. She wiped it off with her knuckle. Just a few leaves more and she could go back to the warmth of the kitchen. Shivering, she crouched to pick over more twigs in search of some green, and that was when she heard it.

A groan, as if ripped out of a belly, a whimpering gasp. Jane jerked upright and spun round. Had it come from the jakes? What if Ellen was ill in there? She took a step towards the wooden privy, only to stop when another cry came from the stable.

Her father was out on his horse, and his servant, John, had gone with him. Tom, the apprentice, was minding the shop in the Shambles. The stable should be empty.

Jane hesitated, her hands full of thyme leaves. A stable would be a fine hideout for the vagabonds and rogues her father said were thronging the city. She tiptoed down to the privy. 'Ellen,' she whispered, but there was no reply, and when she tentatively pushed at the door, it swung open to release the familiar stench.

Should she go back to the house and find her? Or she could pretend that she hadn't heard anything. Half of Jane wanted to do just that, to run back to the kitchen and warm her hands by the fire, to slice the beef half as broad as her hand, as the recipe said, and set sweet butter sizzling in the frying pan. But there had been real distress in that muffled scream. Someone was hurt, and Jane couldn't walk away.

The stable door stood ajar. Hesitantly, Jane laid down the thyme and pulled the door wider so that she could step into the opening. 'Who's there?' she called, trying to sound like the mistress of the house and not a scared twelve-year-old maid.

The only answer was another wrenching cry.

'Who is it? Who's there?' One cautious step after another, Jane advanced into the stable. It smelt of straw and horse and wet leather, and of the apples wrinkling in the loft above. The meagre November light through the open door barely penetrated the shadows, and Jane paused, blinking as her eyes adjusted to the dimness. A pitchfork was leaning against the wall, doubtless where John had left it, and Jane picked it up. She was but a poor squab of a girl, as Henry Birkby was always pointing out in disgust, and the pitchfork was taller than she was, so Jane was not at all sure how she would be able to use it to defend herself. But it would make her look as if she was not to be trifled with, surely?

'Who's there?' she said again, comforted by the weight of the pitchfork in her hand.

A stifled gasp came from the stall. She could see more clearly now, and she picked her way around a splatter of dung

44

towards it. Taking a firmer grip of the handle, she stepped around the end of the stall to confront the intruder inside. Only then did she see who was crouched in the straw, clutching onto the manger, her face contorted with pain.

'Ellen!' Jane dropped the pitchfork. It clattered to the stable floor unnoticed as she fell to her knees beside the servant. 'Ellen, what has happened?'

The tendons in Ellen's neck stood out and her eyes were rolling wildly. 'You shouldn't be here, Jane,' she managed between gasps. 'Get back to the house!'

'I can't leave you! You're sick!'

Ellen gritted her teeth against a grunt of pain. 'I'm not sick, you simpleton! Arghh!' Hoisting up her skirts, she slumped back into the corner of the stall while Jane watched in horror. 'Go on, get out of here,' she snarled at Jane when she had the breath.

Jane scrambled uncertainly to her feet. 'I'll get help.'

'No,' gasped Ellen. 'No, there's nowt anyone can do now. It's too late for the midwife.'

'Midwife?' Jane gaped at her and Ellen barked a laugh between the mighty twists of pain.

'God's bones, what did you think was happening? Did you think I'd just grown fat these last few months?'

She *had* thought that. Jane flushed. 'I am sorry,' she said in a small voice. 'I did not know.'

Unable to bear the innocence in the huge eyes, Ellen looked away. 'Well, now you do.'

'What . . . what of the baby's father? Does he know?'

Ellen stared at the knots in the wooden stall, exhausted

by the pain that had her in a savage grip. 'Oh aye, he'll know.'

'My father will speak to him. Put him in mind of his obligations.'

Ellen's laugh was bitter. 'You reckon?' She broke off with a scream as another contraction, more powerful than the others, shook her. 'You shouldn't be here,' she panted when she could. 'You're just a lass, Jane. Go on, begone with you.'

'No.' The soft mouth set in a stubborn line. 'If I cannot get help, then I cannot go. Tell me what to do.'

'Sweet Jesus, do you think I know?' Ellen buckled under another onslaught of pain, and Jane crept up to take her hand.

'Does it hurt very much?'

Tears oozed down Ellen's face. The cap had slid off her head and her wiry hair was damp and dark with sweat. 'What do you think?' she managed with a twisted smile before her eyes rolled back once more and she bellowed as if her body was being ripped apart.

Jane looked around frantically. There had to be *something* she could do. Spying the cloth John used to rub down the horses, she snatched it up and dipped it into the water trough, so that she could wipe Ellen's face. 'It will be all right,' she said in her firmest voice, and a faint smile twisted across Ellen's face.

'What would you know?' she managed, but she groped for Jane's hand once more. 'I'm frightened,' she confessed in a hoarse whisper. 'I'm right glad you're here, lass.'

Jane was frightened too. She wished she knew how to help, but childbirth was women's work, and she was just a maid. Her mother had died giving birth to a brother who had never lived at all, but she had had her midwife and her sister and her gossips around her, all of whom had babes of their own and knew what she was enduring. She had not been alone with a poor, scared dab of a girl for company.

'You're strong,' she told Ellen, trying to sound confident. Trying not to wince at Ellen's painful grip on her hand. 'All will be well.'

At first it seemed that it would be. The pain was terrible and Ellen screamed and panted and cursed, but all at once a bulge appeared between her legs and then a baby slithered out onto the straw.

One moment there had been just Ellen and Jane in the stable; the next there was a child too. Jane's throat closed at the wonder of it. Awed, she reached to pick up the babe, careless of the blood and the slime.

'Oh Ellen,' she said, and her eyes filled with tears. 'You have a fine boy!' Entranced, she stared down at the baby's red, wrinkled face. His eyes were screwed tight, his tiny fingers curled into fists. From his belly ran a dark, pulsing cord, and as Jane watched, his mouth opened and he let out a thin wail, barely more than a bleat, and flailed his arms and legs. 'He is beautiful,' she said, belatedly turning to place him tenderly in his mother's arms. 'I will go and find a cloth to swaddle him in.'

'Don't bother,' said Ellen. A spasm crossed her face as the baby squirmed against her but she didn't look at him. Instead she struggled grimly up, tipping the baby so that she could hold him by his ankles as he wailed in protest. The navel string was attached to a bloody mass.

Still on her knees, Jane watched Ellen lumber over to the trough. Perhaps she thought Ellen wanted to wash herself or the babe. Afterwards Jane couldn't be sure. All she knew was that she knelt there and watched as Ellen shoved the baby into the trough and held it under the water.

To Jane, staring uncomprehendingly, everything seemed to happen very slowly but with excruciating clarity. She saw Ellen's face twist, saw her arm curve up and then down. She heard the baby crying, then the muddled splash cutting off his wail, but none of it made sense, and when it did, it was too late. Scrambling to her feet in horror, Jane stumbled over to the trough, but she was too slow. It felt as if she was floundering through a quagmire of invisible mud that clung to her skirts and dragged her back.

'Ellen! Ellen, what are you doing?' Desperately, Jane grabbed at Ellen's arm as it held the baby down, but Ellen shoved her back with her free hand.

'Leave it!'

'Ellen, no!' Jane leapt forward once more, flailing at the maid, beating with her fists when Ellen barred her way. She could see the baby's leg kicking feebly, and as she watched one tiny hand bobbed out of the water as if reaching for help. 'Ellen, please, stop,' she sobbed.

But Ellen didn't stop until she lifted the baby out of the water and dropped it, dripping and lifeless, onto the straw, and the stable was filled with a silence so enormous that it drummed and roared in Jane's ears.

Chapter Four

'Best thing for the little bugger.' But Ellen's hands trembled as she plucked a handful of hay from the manger to wipe between her legs.

Jane stared at the baby that lay limp and silent in the straw. Her hands were still red from his birth blood. 'You killed him,' she said, her voice hoarse from screaming at Ellen to stop.

'What else was I to do with him?' Ellen demanded, wiping her nose with the back of her hand. 'Your father would turn me out if I have a child.'

'No . . .' Jane couldn't think clearly. She was buckling under the shame of having let the babe die. If she had been stronger, if she had fought Ellen harder . . . 'No, he wouldn't.'

'He would, and there would be no one to take me in. I have no kin in York. I would starve and so would the babe. It is better this way.'

'But the father—'

'You nodcock.' Ellen cracked a harsh laugh with no humour in it at all. 'Who do you think the father is?'

Jane tore her eyes from the pitiful body in the straw to stare at Ellen. 'No,' she said, shaking her head from side to side. 'No.'

'I tell you, yes.'

'Then . . .' Slowly Jane looked back at the baby. She remembered the way he had flailed his arms, the tiny hands struggling to find a grip on life. She remembered the feeble wail, the way he had reached out of the water to her, to anyone who might save him. 'Then this is my brother?' she said dully. Her kin, a babe she might have raised with love and kindness, who might have loved her back. Murdered before he had a chance to know any care at all.

She turned and vomited into the straw.

When she lifted her head, Ellen was grimly forking the soiled straw into a pile in the corner of the stable. 'Come,' she said. 'You must help me clear this.'

'Should I get a priest?' Jane whispered, wiping her cheeks with trembling fingers.

'A priest?' Ellen echoed incredulously. 'Of course not! We cannot tell anyone!'

'But we must bury him.'

'Fire would be better. Or we'll give him to the swine. There won't be much left when the pigs have finished.'

Jane's hands crept to her mouth. 'You cannot!'

'What choice do I have?' Ellen's face was ravaged as she threw the pitchfork against the wall and staggered back to the stall. 'You do not have to watch. I told you to leave, but no, you must stay, and now you know.'

Reaching down, she plucked the baby's body from the straw and held him by his heels. He dangled from her hand, still bloody from her womb, still dripping. A piece of rotten straw from the trough clung to his crumpled face. Jane felt vomit rise in her throat once more, and she retched.

'Listen to me!' Ellen took her arm in a vicious grip with her free hand and shook it until Jane lifted her head wretchedly. 'No one else must know, do you understand? You must promise that you won't tell anyone. You must swear on your life.'

'But the babe . . .' Jane was gulping back sobs. 'You have denied him Christ!'

'Do you think I wanted to kill him?' Ellen spat. 'Do you think I wanted your father heaving on top of me? He was rutting with me while your mother lay dying, and now I must bear the bairn, and I must dispose of it, or he will dispose of me. There must be no evidence, Jane, or they will hang me. Is that what you want?'

'No,' said Jane, but she kept seeing Ellen's expression, the grim set of her mouth as she held her baby under the water.

'If they find the bairn, they will hang me,' said Ellen brutally. 'You must help me. If you cannot stomach the pigs, go into the kitchen and stoke up the fire, as hot as you can, and when it is ready, come and call me.'

Jane dragged her forearm across her mouth. 'All right.'

'Do you promise not to tell anyone?' Ellen caught her by the arm again as Jane turned to leave. 'Swear to me, Jane, that you will not tell a soul. And if you break your oath, know that you will burn in hell for it.'

'I will not tell,' Jane managed shakily.

'Go then, and be quick.'

A lifetime had passed since she had stepped out to gather thyme. As if in a dream, Jane walked unsteadily back through the amiably clucking hens and let herself into the kitchen. The fire glowed in the grate, and the smell of pottage simmering in the cauldron turned her stomach. Lifting it from its hook, she set the cauldron aside and added more logs to the fire. Dully she watched as the fire sucked greedily at the wood. The flames flickered, caught, leapt higher, and the logs crackled and spat as they settled, and she threw on more and more and more until the blaze roared and her face burned from the heat.

Then she went to call Ellen, who was squatting in the straw, her child limp and lifeless by her side like so much offal. 'The fire is ready,' Jane said.

Stiffly, Ellen got to her feet. 'There's no one around?'

Jane shook her head. Her father was still out, and anyway, he wouldn't come to the kitchen. Nor would Juliana, who had no interest in cooking and preferred to sulk in the parlour.

'Come, then.' Ellen made to pick up the baby, but Jane stopped her. She couldn't bear to see him dangling from Ellen's hand like a piece of meat hung from a hook in her father's shop window.

'I'll take him,' she said.

He was so small he weighed almost nothing. Swallowing hard, Jane wrapped him in the clean cloth she had brought from the kitchen and carried him to the house. She had worn away a path by now, and her clogs squelched through the mud. Ellen followed, her face set like stone.

She nodded when she saw the fire, how fiercely it blazed. 'Good,' she said. She glanced at Jane. 'Burn him,' she said.

'I . . . can't.' Instinctively, Jane took a step back. This was wrong. The child should have a Christian burial. There must be some way to arrange things. She would pretend that she had found the babe. Something. He mustn't burn.

'Then I will. Don't look at me like that!' Ellen cried savagely as she snatched the body from Jane's arms and, turning, threw the baby onto the fire.

'*No!*' she cried out, starting forward to rescue him from the flames, but there was something between her and the fire, something solid blocking her way: a wall, a window. Then a clatter of plastic slats rattling into place, and shock jolted her back to herself.

Trembling, Roz sank to the floor and covered her face with her hands. The sour taste of vomit was raw at the back of her throat. 'No,' she said again, shaking her head in her hands.

She must have fallen asleep. *Standing at the window?* a small, uncomfortable voice in her head queried, but Roz pushed it aside. It had just been a dream; what else could it have been? But so stark and vivid a dream that she was still disorientated and nauseous. A blinding headache was pounding behind her eyes and she tipped her head back against the blank cream wall and took a deep, shuddering breath.

A nightmare, that was all. Her senses were still jangling with the smell of damp straw and blood, with the spit and greedy suck of the flames, the way their heat had battered her face. She could still hear the squelch of her clogs in the mud, the cluck of the hens.

The sound of the baby dropped lifeless in the straw.

Roz pressed her knuckles against her mouth as her stomach heaved at the memory of the child so casually killed before it had a name or a chance to know the comfort of its mother's breast. What dark corner of her mind had produced an image that horrific? It disturbed Roz to think that she was capable of even imagining such a thing.

But it hadn't felt imagined. It had felt real. That was even more disturbing. It was as if she had really been there in that stable, had held the baby and felt it warm and slippery from Ellen's womb. Roz lowered her hand from her mouth and held both palms out in front of her. They were shaky but clean. Carefully, she turned her hands over. Not a trace of blood beneath her fingernails, or engrained in the lines over her knuckles.

Of course there wasn't, because it had been a dream. Irritated with herself, Roz struggled to her feet and staggered into the bathroom. Splashing cold water on her face, she groped for a towel and pressed it against her nose and mouth for long minutes while she kept her eyes squeezed shut and concentrated on breathing slowly, in and out, in and out, until her heart rate slowed. When she lowered the towel at last, she opened her eyes to stare at her reflection in the mirrored cabinet above the basin. She was very pale, and her eyes were huge and dilated, but she was unmistakably Roz Acclam. She was not a twelve-year-old girl, and she hadn't just witnessed the birth and brutal murder of a baby.

Then her eyes dropped to her throat and her heart stuttered, for around her neck, like a necklace, lay a circle of blistered red marks.

Roz reeled back from the basin with a stifled scream of shock, her hands going instinctively to her neck as if she were about to strangle herself. She couldn't catch her breath, and darkness roared at the edges of her mind. She thought she was going to pass out but after a moment the feeling disappeared, leaving her light-headed and nauseous, and she dropped her hands to clutch the edge of the basin and lean over it, breathing very carefully.

There was a logical explanation for this. There had to be.

'What's wrong?' asked Nick the moment he heard her voice.

Roz held the phone away from her ear and frowned at it. It had taken a considerable effort, but she had pulled herself together. She had rationalized the whole incident: she was tired; it had been a disturbing dream, but a dream nonetheless. Quite why her subconscious had chosen to act out various issues in costume had been harder for Roz to explain away. She remembered the feel of the linen smock against her skin, the warm weight of the wool skirt that hung to her ankles. Her feet had been thrust into sturdy wooden clogs that kept her out of the mud. In the dream, of course, she had been barely more than a little girl. Her figure had been childish and unformed, but the bodice fit snugly around her chest, and there had been a plain frill around the collar, something that was not quite a ruff.

So in her dream she had been wearing Tudor costume. That was hardly a surprise given that she had spent the afternoon in an Elizabethan house, was it? As for the burn marks on her neck, they were clearly psychosomatic. She was obviously more anxious about coming to York than she had thought she was.

Roz had convinced herself it made a kind of sense. She had taken her case into the bedroom and unpacked briskly. She had arranged her moisturizers in a line in the bathroom. She had found a supermarket nearby and bought tea and milk and a ready-made salad for supper, although her stomach still churned with distress and she couldn't imagine ever wanting to eat again. She had let herself back into the flat and made a cup of tea and taken some aspirin to ease the headache that thudded against her skull. She had practised speaking out loud so that her voice didn't wobble and Nick wouldn't guess how desperately she wished that she could go home.

And after all of that, all she had had to say was, 'Hi, it's me,' and he was asking what was wrong.

'Nothing,' she said automatically, turning her back to the window, which nagged at the edge of her vision like a toothache. 'I'm just a bit tired. You know what it's like starting a new job. I went to Holmwood House, and it's quite something. I can see lots of potential for some fabulous events,' she rattled on. 'I don't think Adrian's assistant likes me very much, though.'

She could picture Nick, the phone tucked under his chin as he sat at his computer. His narrow face would be intent, his brows drawn together, and homesickness gusted through her. She wanted to be there, letting herself into the house, taking

Nick a glass of wine. He had a chair in his office and she liked to toe off her shoes and curl up in it and tell him about her day, and Nick would forget about his deadline and swing his chair round to sit with his back to his blinking cursor so he could focus his attention on her.

But that was before her aunt died, before Daniel, before Adrian offered her the job in York. Before everything she'd always believed to be true had started to crumble, and their marriage with it.

'You sound . . . strained,' said Nick.

'Do I?' Roz forced surprise into her voice, but even she could hear the frenetic edge to it. Her fingers were rubbing at the arm of the chair in small, obsessive circles and she made herself stop.

'Come on, Roz. We've been married for eight years. I can tell when something's up.'

She gave in. 'I just had a bad dream,' she said. 'I fell asleep when I got to the flat and it was . . . nasty.'

'What was it about?' Nick asked.

'Oh . . . there was a baby . . . and it died . . .' Roz's throat closed at the memory of Ellen's bloodied skirts and the tiny, slippery body in her hands. 'You can never explain a dream, can you? It doesn't matter, anyway. But it was horrid.'

Nick was silent a moment. 'You know I thought you should have some counselling about your family history,' he said carefully. 'Maybe dreams are another way of dealing with it?'

It had been an ordinary Sunday. They had wandered along

the South Bank and had a late breakfast overlooking the Thames before taking the Sunday papers home.

'You should do something about your aunt's papers,' Nick had said from the depths of the sports section. 'You can't keep putting it off.'

'I don't want to,' Roz confessed. 'It feels like invading her privacy.'

Aunt Sue was the only mother she remembered, and it had been a shock when she had dropped dead of an embolism. Roz had been organizing a treasure hunt for 150 primary school children when her mobile rang, and still the sound of children shrieking in the background could plunge her into confusion and grief. Her uncle had died years before and there had been no other children.

'You're all we want,' Aunt Sue used to tell her when Roz wished for a brother or a sister. 'We don't want to share you.'

They had been open about her adoption from the start. Roz had grown up knowing about the terrible accident that had claimed the lives of her parents and her sisters. She had seen the photos of herself when she was small, at the centre of a happy, smiling family. It was sad, but she loved her uncle and her aunt, and when Sue died, Roz grieved for the only mother she had ever known.

'Come on, I'll help you,' said Nick. He carried down the big box of papers Roz had taken from the house the day her aunt died, and they sat on the floor, sifting through years of cards, letters, photographs, old bills, newspaper cuttings, and assorted official papers and certificates.

'"Rosalind tries hard and plays enthusiastically,"' Nick read out from one of her old school reports. 'Nothing new there, then.'

'Look at this.' Roz handed him a photograph of a smiling woman with a baby. 'That's me.'

Nick studied the photo. 'You look just like your mother.'

'That's what Aunt Sue used to say.' Roz dug out some photographs and shuffled quickly through them before passing them over. 'These are all of my parents and sisters. I should keep them.'

'Have you noticed what an odd edge some of these photos have?' said Nick, looking through them. 'It's almost as if somebody's been cut out of the picture.'

Roz took one back to study it. 'I see what you mean. Odd,' she said, but she didn't think much about it. Not then.

It was a sad business sorting through her aunt's life. So much that must have seemed important at the time, important enough to keep, was now tired and trivial. 'I mean, why keep newspaper cuttings about a factory fire?' Roz sighed, adding another piece of paper to the recycling box.

'Perhaps she was a pyromaniac on the quiet,' Nick suggested flippantly.

Roz thought of her quiet, conventional aunt and she was smiling as she pulled a letter from its envelope, not realizing that her life was about to change. 'I don't see Aunt Sue playing with matches,' she was saying as her eyes skimmed over the letter. She was halfway through before she stopped, frowning, and went back to the beginning. 'This is weird.'

'What is it?'

'It's from . . .' Roz turned the letter over to read the signature on the back. '. . . Jim Hebden. He says he's a retired police officer and that he worked on the Acclam case. I didn't realize my parents' accident was a case.' She flipped the letter back over and reread the first part of the letter. 'It's dated 1995 and he's talking about somebody called Michael . . .' Her voice trailed away as foreboding stalked down her spine.

Nick leant forward. 'Let me see.'

Wordlessly Roz handed the letter over. She felt thrown without quite knowing why. It was as if the floor had tilted slightly, and she put one hand flat on the carpet to steady herself.

'"Dear Mrs Miller,"' Nick read out. '"I don't know if I'm doing the right thing in contacting you, but I thought you ought to know that I saw Michael in York recently. There must have been a risk assessment before he was released on licence and I am very surprised that they would conclude that he was no longer a risk to society. I was a police officer in York for many years, and the Acclam case was the most disturbing one of my career. I was there when Michael was arrested and I do not believe that he showed any remorse at all for what he had done."'

Nick stopped and raised his brows. Like Roz, he turned the letter over and then back. '"He was the most manipulative interviewee I ever encountered,"' he read on, '"and was able to switch at will between different personas. It is my belief that people don't change and that Michael is more than capable of pretending to be anything that he wants to be. Had it not been for the incontrovertible evidence, he might never have been convicted at all.

'"I am very concerned that he may try to contact you or his sister now that he is free . . ."' Nick trailed off. 'His sister?'

'Do you think that's me?' Roz's voice sounded odd in her own ears, as if it was coming from a distance.

'I don't know. This is very weird.' Nick turned the page. '"I shouldn't be speaking to you about this, but I think you should be warned that he will have been given a new identity. He will have had the opportunity to start afresh and the fact that he has chosen to return to York makes me anxious that he still has unresolved issues to do with his family and the way they died. I hope you don't mind me writing to you, but I just want to know that you are both safe."'

Nick lowered the letter and stared at Roz. 'What the hell is that all about?'

'I've got no idea,' she said. She took the letter back and smoothed it on her leg, conscious that her fingers weren't quite steady.

'Do you think you're the sister he refers to?'

'I don't know,' said Roz, 'but if I am, that means I have a brother.'

All those years of longing for a sibling. Had she had one all along? 'Why didn't Aunt Sue tell me?' she burst out. 'She brought me up to be straight. She knew how important honesty is to me. How could she lie to me like that?'

Nick looked uncomfortable. 'Maybe she just wasn't telling you everything. Maybe she was trying to protect you.'

'It was lying!' The more Roz thought about it, the more devastated she felt. Her uncle and aunt had been steady, straight-as-a-die people. Realizing that they hadn't practised the honesty they preached knocked askew the foundations of everything that had been certain in her life.

'There may have been a good reason for her not telling you everything,' said Nick after a moment. 'This Michael . . . the letter doesn't say why he was in prison, does it?'

'No.' Roz felt sick.

'What are you going to do?'

'Do?'

'Well, you can't just leave it there,' said Nick, and it was only later that she realized how neatly he had moved the conversation on from honesty. 'You need to find out what really happened.'

Roz bit her nail. 'I'm not sure I want to know.'

'Roz, there's a big question mark over your past. You can't just ignore it.'

Nick insisted that she ring the number on the letter, but it turned out that Jim Hebden had died five years earlier. His widow was sorry, she didn't know anything about a letter.

'There must have been something in the papers.' There was no stopping Nick once he got the bit between his teeth, and as a freelance journalist, he was determined to ferret out what he could online. Roz left him to his computer and went to ring her aunt's best friend.

'Oh God, I *told* Sue she should tell you the truth!' Karen interrupted before Roz had finished explaining about the letter. 'We had a huge row about it when they first adopted you.'

'Karen, what happened? What didn't they tell me?'

'Your parents didn't die in an accident. They'd both been married before, did you know that?'

'I knew Emily and Amanda were my half-sisters.'

'That's right. Your father was widowed when he met Amy, while she'd been married to an abusive man – Sue said he was awful. He had the girls, and she . . . she had a son.'

'Michael,' said Roz with a sickening sense of certainty.

'Mikey,' said Karen. 'They called him Mikey. When Amy and Patrick got married, she and Mikey moved in with Patrick in Millingham Road. Amy loved that house, but Mikey wouldn't settle. He was an odd little boy, Sue always said, and I suppose it was understandable that he was a bit jealous of Patrick, but nobody ever expected him to do what he did.'

'What did he do?'

'He set fire to the house one night, and he killed them all.'

Roz went hot and then cold. For a moment she couldn't speak, but hadn't she been expecting this ever since reading that letter? People didn't get shut away in secure units for an accident.

'Were they sure it was him?' Her voice sounded as if it was coming from far away.

'Absolutely sure. Oh, it was terrible! Sue was distraught. She adored Amy and she couldn't bear to see Mikey again, not knowing what he'd done. She wouldn't have anything to do with him.'

Roz was silent, trying to reconcile her memories of her quiet, kind aunt with an implacable resentment. She rubbed her temple where a headache was nagging.

'I don't understand. Why didn't I die too?'

'They found you in the garden shed. They think Amy hid you there and then went back to try and rescue the others, so she must have known what Mikey had done. Such a tragedy,' Karen remembered. 'I sometimes wonder if Sue ever really got over it.'

'But why don't I remember any of this?'

'You were very small, Roz. When it was clear that you either didn't remember or had blocked the memories out somehow, Sue and Keith decided it would be kinder not to burden you with the truth. You didn't need to know, Sue said, so they told you your parents and sisters had died in a car crash instead, and they moved away from York so that Mikey would never find them – or you.

'I thought it was a mistake,' said Karen, 'not telling you once you were old enough to understand. The truth will come back to bite you, I said, and now it has.' She sighed. 'Don't judge Sue too harshly, Roz. She did what she thought was right, and she loved you very much. I think she felt guilty sometimes because she'd always wanted a child, but she didn't want her sister to die so that she could have you. Be careful what you wish for, she used to say to me.'

'That's it?' Nick had said when Roz reported this conversation to him. 'You're just going to leave it at that?'

'What more do you expect me to do?'

'Don't you want to find out *why* your brother killed your entire family?'

'Understanding why won't bring them back. I just need to accept it.'

Nick had disagreed. He wanted her to have counselling.

Roz refused. 'I'm not traumatized,' she'd said indignantly. 'How can I be traumatized by something that happened twenty-eight years ago that I don't even remember?'

'Just because you don't remember something doesn't mean it can't have huge consequences,' said Nick, and she hadn't realized what he meant. Not then.

Now Roz sat in the flat in St Andrewgate, holding the phone long after Nick had said goodbye and cut the connection. She turned it absently in her hands as she thought about what he had said. Was it possible that the horrific dream was some bizarre way of dealing with the accumulated stresses of the past few months?

She supposed it did make a kind of sense, Roz decided reluctantly at last. Ellen could represent her confusion about her feelings towards her aunt, the mother figure who had turned out to have lied. Roz still found it hard to accept the way her aunt had hidden the truth from her, so yes, there might well be some hidden resentment looking for an outlet. As for the baby . . . Horror roiled in her stomach as she remembered the way its body had dangled lifelessly from Ellen's hand. She was afraid she knew only too well what the baby signified.

Daniel.

It had been one deception too many.

'Of course I was going to tell you,' Nick had said when she confronted him. He said he hadn't wanted her to deal with anything else after her aunt's death. She'd had too much on her plate already, he said, and besides, he was still coming to terms with the shock of becoming a father himself. He was waiting for the right moment to sit Roz down and tell her that he had a fourteen-year-old son.

It was Daniel who had tracked him down on Facebook. His mother, Ruth, had always been open about the fact that he hadn't been fathered by the man she had married. She'd made the decision not to tell Nick that she was pregnant after their brief fling. They had only got together while she was on the rebound from Tony, Nick said. According to Ruth, she and Tony had agreed to take a break, but when they got back together and she realized that she was pregnant, Tony had been happy to bring Daniel up as his own. All had been well until Daniel had reached adolescence and had started kicking over the traces. Demanding to know about his biological father, he had tracked Nick down, and Nick, faced with a boy who looked exactly as he had done at fourteen, had found himself plunged into fatherhood at exactly the same moment as Roz was coping with the shock of Sue's sudden death.

'I didn't want a child,' Nick said to Roz, 'but now that I've got one . . . I can't explain it, but it changes everything. Tony's always going to be Daniel's father, but I want to be part of Daniel's life.'

Roz had tried to understand, but she was hurt by the way Nick had kept the truth from her. She'd only found out about Daniel when he had posted a photo of himself and Nick on Nick's Facebook page. *Me and my dad*. Roz remembered reading the words again and again, unable to make any sense of them. Nick wasn't a *dad*. But it was unmistakably him, and his face changed the moment she mentioned Facebook, so she knew without him saying any more that it was true.

Nothing had been the same since then. Nick had lied to her. Her aunt had lied to her. It felt as if the two people she loved most had turned on her, and Roz couldn't find a way to push through the resentment that blocked every way she turned. She tried pretending that everything was okay, that she understood, but it was an effort to squeeze the words past the great lump in her throat, and Nick knew that she didn't mean it.

The distance between them that had opened while Roz had been preoccupied, first by her aunt's death and then by the discovery of her true history, had widened steadily. Standing on one side of the abyss, Roz looked yearningly at Nick, but she didn't know how to reach him any more. It felt as if they had been going through the motions for too long. But surely it meant something that she'd been feeling so homesick since she arrived in York? It was still Nick she wanted to talk to at the end of the day.

So perhaps that horrifying dream about the baby was her subconscious trying to shock her into getting past her resentment at the way she'd found out about Daniel. He might not be a baby any more, but he was still a child, and he couldn't be disposed of in a convenient water trough.

If she wanted to save her marriage, she would have to be prepared to cope with Nick's child. Was that what the dream was all about?

Roz tested the idea gingerly, turning it over in her mind. It *seemed* to work.

But why dress it all up in costume? an insistent voice at the back of her mind countered. What was *that* supposed to symbolize?

Well, there was no point in trying to rationalize a dream, Roz told herself firmly. It was enough that she had an explanation that satisfied her. She could forget about it now, and let the dream fade the way dreams were meant to do.

'It's not fair!' Juliana pulled petulantly at her bottom lip, as she watched Jane walking up and down the table, adjusting a glass here, straightening a trencher there, moving the pepper box a little to the right.

The table was covered with the best damask cloth and the silver chafing dishes gleamed in the candlelight. A basin and a ewer sat at either end of the table, with a towel neatly folded beside each. In the kitchen, Mary was keeping an eye on the roast meats and putting the finishing touches to the salads. Jane wished that she could be there to oversee the sending forth of the first course, but for once her father had insisted that she be there to greet their guests.

For tonight was her betrothal supper.

Henry Birkby had called her into his closet three days before. He had been in an uncharacteristically jovial mood. 'Well, daughter,' he had said, rubbing his palms together. 'You are to be a lady and live in a fine house in Micklegate. How do you like that?'

'Father?'

'I have made an excellent match for you,' he boasted. 'They laughed at me when I swore my grandchildren would be gentry, but now let them laugh on the other side of their faces!'

'I am to be married?' asked Jane cautiously, and he scowled.

'Have I not just told you so? The Holmwoods have barely two farthings to scratch together, but they are a gentry family, and not so nice that they will turn their noses up at a butcher's brass.

'Old Hugh Holmwood must be turning in his grave,' Henry went on with satisfaction. 'It took him long enough to sire a son, and when he did, it didn't take him long to get the measure of him. A fine, finicky gentleman young Holmwood might be, but he don't have an ounce of business sense. He'd have squandered it all if Hugh hadn't been canny enough to truss him up and skip a generation. The estate's invested in a son, which is why yon Holmwood's so eager for a bride.'

He gave a crack of laughter. 'I don't say they like the smell of the Shambles overmuch, but the smell of money is sweeter. Aye, a fat dowry did the trick. Not that I'll be played for a fool, mind,' he added. 'I'll not have hard-earned brass tossed away on idleness and fancies. Your dowry's tied up tight so he can't put you off and if you die, it will revert to me.'

Henry paused, evidently waiting for Jane to congratulate him on his far-sightedness. 'Thank you, Father,' she murmured, keeping her eyes downcast so that he wouldn't read the irony in her expression.

Her feelings were mixed. It might grate to be disposed of in marriage without so much as a by-your-leave to a man whose father hadn't trusted him to manage his own affairs, but she was fortunate, Jane knew, to have the option of marriage at all. She had always assumed that Juliana's beauty would mean that she would be married first, and Jane had resigned herself to the bleak prospect of keeping house for her father.

But now it seemed she was not only to be married, but to a gentleman. Henry's aspirations were a poorly kept secret in the parish. Jane knew that their neighbours laughed behind their hands at him. Henry Birkby might be wealthy, but he was a butcher and a butcher's son. He would never be the equal of the merchants and mercers who arranged matters in the city to suit themselves.

'They have asked for *me*?' she said carefully, just to check. Dowry or not, a butcher's plain daughter would not be much of a match for a gentry family.

'They'd heard about Juliana's beauty, but you're the eldest,' her father said largely. 'I make a gentlewoman out of you, and there's no saying how high I might look for my pretty Juliana. I might wed her to a nobleman, and then let my Lord Mayor look down his long nose at me!'

His doublet, already straining over his substantial stomach, expanded perilously as he puffed up with satisfaction at the prospect.

'And Juliana?' said Jane.

Henry Birkby didn't pretend to misunderstand her. 'Aye, her nose will be out of joint, I don't doubt, little puss that she is,' he said indulgently. 'But she is so fair I will have little trouble in finding her a fine husband. I had to drive a harder bargain for you.'

Chapter Five

He ran a critical eye over his elder daughter. Jane had ever been the plain one. Oh, she was well enough. She had no cast in her eye or warts on her face like some, but she was thin and sallow-skinned and quiet-faced, just like her mother had been, and you could never tell what she was thinking, not like Juliana. Henry's mouth softened at the thought of his pet, a daughter so beautiful he could only marvel that she had sprung from his loins. Jane was harder to read. She never gave him cause to chastise her, but there were times, like now, when her expression held a gleam of humour that he didn't understand, and he would find himself blustering under her cool gaze.

'The Holmwoods will come for the handfasting on Friday next,' he said. 'We'll have witnesses so all is tied up tight, and then do you serve a noble feast with everything of the best for your betrothal dinner.'

'Very well,' said Jane. 'May I ask who I am to marry?'

Henry scowled. 'I've been telling you!'

'I just wondered if I might know his name,' she said.

That was just like Jane, Henry reflected. She looked right at you and there was nothing in her words or demeanour to suggest that she was anything less than respectful, but somehow he found himself pulling uncomfortably at his girdle.

'Robert. Robert Holmwood. He won't expect much of you,' he added. 'I've told him you're no beauty. She sets a good table, though, I said to him, and you won't find a better housekeeper.'

A faint smile touched Jane's mouth. 'Why, thank you for the compliment, Father.'

Juliana was furious when she was told. 'Why should you be married and not I? I am seventeen.' Tears trembled in her eyes. 'I am old enough to be wed!'

'Our father explained it all,' Jane said patiently. 'You are so beautiful, he must get me off his hands first.'

Juliana was not to be consoled. 'A gentleman is wasted on you,' she said sullenly. 'You will never make a lady. You will put on your apron and spend your days in the kitchen with the servants instead!'

'Indeed, I am sure you are right,' said Jane, smiling faintly.

'You do not take anything seriously.' Juliana flounced over to the window and hunched a pettish shoulder. 'I hope your fine husband is fat and looks like a toad,' she added spitefully.

Jane said nothing. She didn't want to admit that she was wondering what her betrothed would look like. Not that it would make a difference. The marriage would go ahead no matter how toad-like her bridegroom. And after all, she told herself briskly, she was no beauty, so she could hardly complain if her husband was less than handsome. But oh, she hoped he would not be a toad! She would have to sleep in his bed, and let him do what he would with her. Jane's knowledge of what that involved was hazy as yet. She had seen couples out under the hedgerows, grunting and bucking, and once had come across her father's servant hard at work with one of the maids under the stairs. They had been so intent on each other that they hadn't noticed Jane, and her face had burned when she had realized just what they were doing. Now she would be firm enough to chastise them both soundly, but then she had been very young still, and rather than say anything she had turned on her heel and tiptoed away, as if she was the one who was in the wrong.

She was going to be married. The truth of it hit Jane all at once and her stomach hollowed as if at a blow. She would be stripped to her shift and put into bed with the faceless Robert and she would learn just what they all did. Jane didn't know if the thought of it excited or terrified her, and she put her fingers to her lips, wondering what it would be like, how it would feel. Her blood set up a slow pounding and there was a roaring in her ears and a disturbing, squirming sensation in her privy parts.

She might have a child. A babe of her own. It was a thought that filled Jane with hope and longing, mixed with guilt. For she could not see a baby still without thinking of that terrible day in the stable. Jane looked down at her hands, where the scars remained pink and puckered seven years on.

She hadn't thought when she leapt forward and reached into the fire for the baby. She had just acted, and the pain had been so intense that she had been unable to prevent a scream, which had brought the neighbours running, the busybody Eliza Dawson at the front of the mob. They had seen Jane sobbing over the charred baby, seen Ellen grim-faced, and they had sent for the constable, who took Ellen away to prison to await the assize courts.

When he heard what Jane had done, Henry Birkby had roared at her for a simpleton and a busybody worse than Eliza. He called Ellen a whore and ordered Jane to tell him exactly what Ellen had done and said, and he had beaten her until she confessed. Yes, it was Ellen's babe, she admitted at last, weeping from the pain in her shoulders where her father's belt had laid great raised welts. No, Ellen hadn't said who the father was, Jane lied. She'd hoped her father might be moved to help Ellen if he believed that she had kept their secret, but she might have spared herself the untruth. Henry could not wash his hands of Ellen quickly enough.

For Jane, it was a bitter lesson. She tried to visit Ellen in prison, but she had no money to bribe the gaoler. She took baskets of food instead – some bread, some cheese, some ale, a pie – but had no way of knowing if they ever reached Ellen.

They tried Ellen in the assize courts. They said that she had given birth to a child which she threw onto the fire in the kitchen of her master's house. They did not ask who had got her with child, or what she was to have done if she had been turned out.

They sent her to hang.

You must promise that you won't tell anyone, Ellen had said, her eyes burning into Jane's. *You must swear on your life.*

But Jane had told, in the end, and Ellen had died. She had broken her promise, and her belly tightened painfully whenever she remembered what she had done. She did not forgive herself for being but a little maid. She knew only that she had promised, and then she had told, and the shame of it sickened her.

Never again, Jane had vowed to herself. Never again would she break a promise.

Wrapped in her thoughts, Jane did not register at first that Juliana was weeping, taut, gasping little sobs that would escalate into a full-blown tantrum if not stopped soon. And Juliana in a tantrum could make life unendurable for everyone. Jane had learnt early that it wasn't worth the risk of leaving her to cry herself out.

Mentally squaring her shoulders, she went over to her sister. 'Come,' she said, 'you do not want to make your eyes all red.' Briskness tended to work better than sympathy.

Juliana turned and threw her arms around Jane's neck. 'I am a vixen! Do not listen to me, dear Jane. I don't want your husband to be a toad, I don't! I just hate the thought of you leaving me. What will I do without you?'

'You will be mistress of our father's house,' said Jane, patting Juliana on the back, hiding a wry smile in her sister's golden hair. When her sister was affectionate, she was very hard to resist. 'You will be able to do exactly as you choose without me scolding you to get up and get dressed. Think how comfortable you will be!'

'But who will manage the servants? I do not know how!'

Because you have never troubled yourself to learn. Jane bit back the words. 'Mary is very capable,' she said instead. 'You will have nothing to do.'

'But it will not be the same.' Juliana drew back, her bottom lip trembling. 'You make us all comfortable. I still do not see why my father does not marry me to Sir Robert and keep you as his housekeeper.'

Jane had wondered the same thing herself. 'He plans an even greater marriage for you,' she assured her sister.

'Greater?' Brightness glimmered in the beautiful blue eyes. 'Oh, I wish it might be so!'

'Why should there not come a time when you scorn to associate with me?' Jane suggested artlessly. 'Who are the Holmwoods, after all? Mere Yorkshire gentry! With your beauty, Juliana, you may look much higher for a husband. A lord, perhaps, or an earl.'

Restored to smiles, Juliana twirled away, holding out her skirts. 'I may be a duchess!'

Privately Jane marvelled that her sister could really believe a butcher's daughter could rise to be a duchess, but then, was her own marriage not nearly as remarkable? Money, it seemed, could buy anything nowadays. Still, from St Andrewgate to nobility seemed a large leap indeed to Jane, but she knew if she said as much she would be vilified for her dullness and lack of ambition. It hardly seemed fair to encourage Juliana in such dreams, but to introduce a prosaic note of reality would plunge her back into the sullens.

Juliana clapped her hands together, all smiles now at the thought of her glorious future. 'We must have new gowns!' she announced. 'Your betrothal is but the first step in our family's progress. When the Holmwoods come for the handfasting, they must see that we are worthy of them.'

For herself, Jane had no desire for a new gown. She disliked being turned and prodded and measured, and was quite happy with the blue taffeta kirtle she wore on holidays. It lay in the chest in the chamber she shared with her sister, tucked about with musk balls she had made herself from nutmegs, mace, cloves, saffron and cinnamon. But to cross Juliana at this stage would be unwise, Jane knew.

'I will ask our father if you may have something pretty for the betrothal feast,' she said. Henry Birkby was close-fisted with his money, but if approached at the right time would usually open his purse for his pet Juliana.

This time, however, he insisted that Jane had a new gown too, in spite of her protests that it was unnecessary. 'You cannot meet the Holmwoods looking like a milkmaid,' he said, eyeing Jane up and down critically. Her wool kirtle was plain but serviceable, and her hands were calmly folded over her apron. 'God's bones, can you not at least try to make a lady of yourself?'

Did he expect her to oversee the house in a silk gown? Jane's lips tightened, but she kept her eyes downcast.

'There is much to do in the kitchen to prepare for the feast,' she pointed out. 'My sister will be happy with a new gown, and it will keep her occupied, but I have little time to spare.'

'Then make time,' snapped Henry, irritated as always by her calm good sense. 'Else you shame me before the Holmwoods. Take Juliana and buy the costliest fabric, and then take it to

John Harper in Stonegate. That rogue owes me a favour, and he will make both gowns up quickly.'

So Jane went with Juliana to Stonegate, where they bought a length of red mockado at the draper's, with some velvet for the trim, and Juliana chose a glossy satin in a blue that the draper's apprentice said matched her eyes. He carried the cloths down to John Harper's shop and handed them over to the tailor with a barely concealed sniff of distaste.

Not that John Harper cared for anyone's opinion but his own. He greeted Jane and Juliana with a bow, but there was nothing polite about the way his heavy-lidded eyes ran over them, as if he could draw the pins from their sleeves just by looking and see right through to their shifts. Jane shifted uncomfortably beneath his gaze, but Juliana was delighted by the suggestive smile that curved his mouth as he turned her backwards and forwards and sideways, flattering her out-rageously, and she chattered about him all the way home, how handsome he was, how polite, how polished.

Jane shook her head, marvelling anew at her sister's ability to see only what she wished to see. Jane could admit that Harper had a certain brutal appeal, but he was not polite, no. There had been lewdness lurking in every glance, insolence in every word, and she worried that Juliana could not see it. Left to her own devices, her sister was wilful. She tossed her head when Jane lectured her on the need for modesty, and Jane was afraid that she would fall into wildness when there was no one there to steer her towards a more careful path. Their father had dismissed her concerns, though.

'You always pull a long face about Juliana,' he complained. 'She is as capable as you, would you but give her a chance. You think no one can go on without you,' he said sourly. 'Once you are married, you will see my little Juliana come into her own. The world does not revolve around you, daughter.'

You must look after your sister . . . promise me that you will care for her, her mother had begged as she lay dying, and Jane had promised, but how could she care for her sister if she was not there?

Perhaps her father was right. Perhaps Juliana just needed to be left to manage the house by herself. Still, Jane worried for her. Between her anxiety for her sister and the thought of marriage and leaving home and everything that was familiar, Jane was uncharacteristically nervous as she bustled around the house, making sure that the wood gleamed and the silver was polished and that there were no cobwebs clinging to her father's expensive new tapestries. In the kitchen, she set Mary and the maids toiling over a feast fit for the Queen's Majesty herself. Her father had slaughtered a fine cow, and there would be baked venison and a shoulder of mutton as well. There would be roasted coneys and a goose, a pie of pigeons and a dish of larks. A dozen quail. Pigs' feet boiled with verjuice and dates, and seasoned with cinnamon and ginger. Duck boiled with turnips. Custards and gingerbreads, fritters and a tart.

Jane chopped and scraped and seasoned, trying to forget about the hollowness in her stomach. The closer she came to leaving her father's house, the more affection she felt for it. It wasn't just Juliana she would miss, she realized. She would miss

Mary and the other servants, and the gossip in the warm kitchen. She'd miss her neighbours and her father's old mastiff, Picard. She would miss the chamber she shared with Juliana, with the window that looked out over the yard, and the little herb garden her mother had planted and which she cared for still.

But so it was for all women, Jane reasoned briskly. She would have a new home and a new family, and soon, God willing, they would be as familiar to her as her life in St Andrewgate.

All in all, Jane was glad when the day of the handfasting arrived. At least now she would meet her bridegroom and be able to imagine her new life. It was hard when at the back of her mind she kept wondering if he would be as toad-like as Juliana had envisaged. It was no use asking her father, and when in York, the Holmwoods lived in Micklegate, on the other side of the Ouse. They didn't entertain the likes of the neighbours in St Andrewgate, or go to church in King's Square or shop in Thursday Market. They might as well live on the moon for all Jane would have encountered them and seen for herself what Robert Holmwood looked like. He might have a wet mouth like Percival Geldart, or a bulbous nose that dripped all the time like Eliza Dawson's son. He might have a cast in one eye, or a club foot, or have hairy hands like John Harper.

There was nothing she could do about it if he did, Jane reminded herself, so there was no point in worrying about it. Still, she was more nervous than she wanted to admit as she checked the table one last time.

John Harper had delivered the new gowns that morning, and Jane was tricked out in red and velvet skirts that hung over her farthingale. She had a freshly starched collar and lace cuffs, and pearls at her waist. Her bodice was decorated with silver buttons, her sleeves fashionably slashed. Her hair hung obstinately straight down her back in token of her virginity.

She wished she had on her old kirtle and her apron.

Her father grunted his approval. 'You'll do,' he said, and then his expression softened as his eyes rested on Juliana, whose pleasure in her new gown was offset by the realization that she would not be the centre of attention that night. 'Now, now, my pretty, do not take on so,' he said, eyeing her trembling lips with foreboding. 'I will marry Jane off and then look around for a nobleman for you. What say you to that?'

Before Juliana could say anything, her father's old mastiff lumbered to its feet and began barking at the door.

'Aye, that will be them now,' said Henry. 'You must hide yourself away, pet,' he said to Juliana. 'We do not want Sir Robert to be so dazzled by you he passes over Jane, do we?'

Jane barely heard. She put a hand flat on her stomacher with the sudden, dizzying realization that life as she knew it was about to slam to a halt, and nothing would ever be the same again. She wanted to cry out to her father to stop, to not open the door, but it felt as if a stone was lodged in her throat and she couldn't speak, she could only stand rooted to the spot while her vision blurred with nerves.

Henry Birkby threw open the door and welcomed his guests into the hall himself. They came in with much stamping of feet, much slapping of shoulders. Jane had an impression of assurance, of richness and colour. Their doublets were velvet, their gowns trimmed with fur, their boots buckled with silver. Gold gleamed around their necks. Her father must be mistaken, Jane thought. These men were not poor. But it must be true. Why else would they be here, marrying their son to a butcher's daughter, and a poor dab of a girl at that?

Her blurred impression resolved into four men and a woman. Three of the men were her father's age, and the woman much the same. She was coldly beautiful with a hard mouth and eyes that flickered dismissively around the hall that Jane's father had furnished at such expense. That must be Sir Robert's mother, Lady Margaret Holmwood. Jane could not imagine calling such a woman mother, and she thought with a pang of her own mother, so long dead, who had been plain and sensible and kind, and who would at least have smiled at her child's betrothal.

The older men were witnesses for the Holmwoods, Jane gathered as her father greeted them, but her gaze was already moving on to the other man, where it stopped in disbelief.

This was her husband?

He was not old. He was not fat. He was not a toad. He was golden-haired and handsome, with wide-set eyes and a red mouth, and his beard was barely more than down on his jaw. He could have been a knight at King Arthur's table, a prince. He belonged in a storybook, not in a butcher's hall.

He could not be for her, thought Jane, dazzled. There would be some mistake. She was plain Jane, the dull daughter, the dreary, sensible one. Girls like her did not have handsome husbands.

But her father was beckoning her forward, and gesturing to the young man. 'So, Sir Robert, this is my daughter Jane,' he said. 'She is modest, as you see, and dutiful, and qualified in all the household skills. I have told her what I have done for the preferment and advancement of your marriage and she has agreed to be ruled and married by my good counsel.'

Jane dipped a curtsey and tried not to notice the dismay in Robert's eyes as her father passed her hand to him as he might a pig's trotter across his shop window. Robert held it limply. His fingers were cold and flaccid, and when he looked from Jane to his mother, his desire to be released from the betrothal was writ large on his face.

But Margaret Holmwood nodded firmly, and he turned back to Jane. 'I bring you gold as a token of my goodwill,' he said woodenly, releasing her hand to dig in his purse, and without thinking Jane wiped her fingers against her skirt as if his reluctance was a slime she could rub away.

From the purse Robert produced a ring, which he dropped into her palm rather than touch her again. Jane had to pick it up and slide it onto her finger herself.

Well, what had she expected? That a man so fair should delight in finding himself yoked to a plain bride?

No, not delight, but some courtesy, perhaps, would not have been too much to ask for. Jane sighed inwardly, and then chastised herself. If she was not careful, she would be as tragical as Juliana. She was no simpering miss wanting a lover's adoration.

She should count herself fortunate that she was not to be married to a man with lips that slobbered like her father's mastiff beneath the table. Robert might not want to wed her, but she would be his wife anyway. She would share his life and bear his children and make him comfortable, and perhaps in the end he would not mind her lack of beauty so much. All might still be well. It would be up to her to make sure it was.

So she smiled as she settled the ring into place on her finger and looked straight into Robert's strangely blank eyes. 'With this ring I submit myself to be your wife before these witnesses here.'

Robert looked back at his mother. 'Kiss her, Robert,' Margaret said, and her voice brought a chill to the warm spring air. 'Kiss her and plight your troth. It cannot then be undone.'

Dutifully Robert lowered his head and pressed his lips to Jane's. His mouth was hot and moist, the kiss perfunctory, but Margaret was right, it was done. They were betrothed.

Handfast, they turned to receive the stiff good wishes of the witnesses, and of Juliana, who pressed her cheek to Robert's. Jane had been dreading this moment, to see the yearning in his face as he realized that he had missed out on the beautiful sister, but his expression didn't change.

Perhaps there was some courtesy in him after all.

'He is very handsome,' Juliana whispered in Jane's ear when she came to kiss her. 'You are so fortunate, Jane.'

She was, Jane knew. Why then did she feel like weeping?

Her father was rubbing his hands together in satisfaction. 'Now we will have some friendly cheer. My daughter has prepared a feast to mark the betrothal. Come sirs, sit you down,' he said, gesturing the guests to the table. 'Jane, is all prepared?'

'It is. I will send for Mary to bring in the first course.' Over her father's shoulder, she could see Robert standing close to his mother, who stroked his cheek tenderly with her hand.

'She is a doting mother,' Henry Birkby said, following her gaze. 'But you will be his wife. It will be up to you to earn his affection in the bedchamber,' he said roughly.

'I understand,' said Jane.

Her quiet reply seemed to make Henry uncomfortable. 'Well, you are a sensible lass,' he said. 'You won't be moping and pining if Robert doesn't dance attendance upon you. Make him comfortable and give him an heir, and you will do well enough.'

She was to be married. It was her first thought when she woke, and she rolled over in the bed, surprised to find that it was empty. It wasn't like Juliana to be up before her.

It was dark still. She pulled herself up against the pillows, pushing her hair back from her face only to pause, struck by how different it felt. It was thicker, softer, shorter. Unbraided. How strange.

Puzzled, she let her hand fall onto a sheet far finer than any she had slept in before, and she blinked into the darkness. Was she married already and disorientated by waking in a strange house? But where was her husband if that were so? A memory of Robert's blank expression rose before her eyes and she frowned. Surely she would remember her marriage? Unless she had been ill?

Her fingers crept to her throat; they encountered only warm flesh. No linen nightgown. She felt along her shoulder. A thin strap. Following it down, feeling her way, she discovered that she was wearing a scandalously brief gown in a slippery, silky fabric she didn't recognize. It barely covered her breasts, and her cheeks burned.

Could she be dreaming? It didn't feel like a dream. She dug her fingernails into her leg to test herself and winced – and woke up properly.

With a shaking hand, she reached for the bedside light, relieved when the room sprang into focus, and she stared around her, desperate for something that would prove that she was Roz Acclam, not Jane Birkby. That this was the twenty-first century, not the sixteenth.

Her phone. She fumbled for it on the bedside table and clutched it, needing its sleekness, its lightness, its now-ness in her hand. The icons glowed up at her, and there was the date and the time: 03.19.

No wonder she was disorientated. The middle of the night, sleeping in a strange bed and in a strange city, after a strange day. Under the circumstances, it was hardly surprising that she had dreamed.

She had dreamed before, of course she had, but nothing like this. She dreamed of being carried through the night sometimes, although that was so vague that it hardly merited being called a dream; it was just a remembered sense of darkness and panic and wrongness, a feeling that only meant something now that she had learnt the truth about the night her family had died. It was a memory, not a dream.

That was how this dream had felt too. A memory. But how could it be? She couldn't remember a life that wasn't hers. But it had been so vivid that it was waking that felt unreal and insubstantial. It was the here and now that felt like the dream.

Roz's heart was slamming hard and low against her ribs, every thud reverberating through her and booming in her ears. There was something she should know, something that was just out of reach, but the more she strained for it, the more elusive it became. She made herself breathe slowly instead, staring deliberately around her.

The overhead light. Her iPod dock, its light glowing blue. The tub of hand cream by her bed. Her trousers, folded neatly and hung over the back of a chair. There was nothing of Jane's world here, so why suddenly should this room seem strange and alien? She couldn't shake the conviction that it would have felt more familiar to have woken in a chamber, in the feather bed she shared with her sulky sister, with a bolster under her head.

The duvet which had seemed so light and insubstantial when she went to bed was now heavy. As heavy as the embroidered coverlet Jane slept under. Stifled, crushed by the weight of another world, Roz realized that her legs were tangled up in it and she panicked, snatching back the duvet and scrambling out of the bed, her breath coming in short, sharp little gasps.

She sounded like Juliana on the verge of hysterics.

'Stop it,' said Roz, but her voice trembled in the silent room.

In the bathroom she ran cold water over her hands and held

them to her face for a long time. When she lowered them, she made herself look straight at her reflection in the mirror. 'I am Roz Acclam,' she said clearly, as she had done earlier that day. 'I am not Jane.'

The grey eyes that looked back at her were nothing like Jane's hazel ones. Her hair was a rich chestnut colour, Jane's a honeyed brown that fell straight and fine to her waist. They had nothing in common at all.

'I have a career,' Roz said out loud. 'I have choices. I do not need to be married off to a man I do not know. I have a husband I chose for myself.'

Nick. A longing for him gusted through her. His thin, intelligent face, the humorous eyes, the way his mouth quirked. He was lean, almost whippy, but more solid than he looked. Roz would have given anything right then to turn and burrow into him, to hold on to him and let him reassure her that it was all just a dream, that nothing was wrong, that the past had magically resolved itself and everything was as it had been before. When there had been no weird dreams of life in Elizabethan York. No murderous brothers. No Daniel.

No bitterness or resentment. No crumbling certainties.

Enough, Roz told herself as she padded into the kitchen and put on the kettle, not really wanting any tea but needing to do something normal, something real. If Jane could make the best of a marriage to a charmless stranger – the thought of Robert's blank eyes set something twitching beneath Roz's skin – then she could certainly survive a couple of strange dreams.

She'd been feeling sorry for herself, that was all, but perhaps it was time to get a grip. These dreams of Jane seemed to be a weird way of her psyche reminding her that she was more fortunate than she had realized, Roz decided. *Really?* countered an inner voice, a prickle at the back of her mind, but Roz ignored it. Clearly she had been working herself up into a state and this latest dream of being betrothed to a stranger was obviously a reminder of how much she had loved Nick. How much she still did.

Roz poured boiling water over a teabag and rummaged in a drawer for a teaspoon. She badly wanted to call Nick, but it wouldn't be fair to wake him in the middle of the night. He would think it was an emergency, and Roz wasn't the kind of person to ring because she'd had another bad dream. She'd already confessed to one earlier. She could picture how Nick would frown, listening to her; how he would carefully suggest that she wasn't herself and should think about coming home.

Fishing out the teabag, Roz dropped it in the bin with a clang. She was a little homesick, and yes, a little spooked, but she couldn't go running back to London after a day. She had a job to do. Setting up the events programme at Holmwood House was her chance to make a name for herself. She had given up her existing clients for this. She couldn't leave before she had started just because of a couple of dreams.

What about that necklace? That pesky inner voice was back, scratching in her skull, undermining her best attempts to make sense of it all. *How do you explain those burns?*

Roz put a hand to her throat and peered into the shiny surface of the kettle. The burning sensation had gone while she was asleep, and the ugly marks had vanished.

Psychosomatic, she told herself firmly.

'I miss you,' Nick had said before he rang off earlier. In spite of the angry words they had thrown at each other like stones before she left, in spite of their stilted conversation and the gap that seemed to yawn between them lately, he was missing her, and that knowledge had warmed Roz as she got ready for bed.

Perhaps that was why she had dreamt of a betrothal.

Perhaps that was all it was.

The greyness had lifted the next morning when Roz set off for Micklegate. The brighter light through the blinds she'd forgotten to close had woken her early and in spite of her broken night, she showered in a positive mood. It felt as if she had passed some kind of test. Determined to make up for her hysteria over the necklace, Roz had dressed carefully in her best suit, the one she had hidden from Nick when she took it home from the sales the year before. Her money was her own, but still, she felt sick when she thought about how much it had cost, and she'd known Nick wouldn't have thought it was worth it. It did wonders for Roz's confidence, though, and if ever she needed a boost it was that morning. She smoothed down the skirt before she left, and had an incongruous flash of memory, of nervously smoothing her new red gown while she waited for the Holmwoods to arrive.

Roz shook it aside, irritated. Dreams were supposed to fade in the morning, not stay crystal clear in your mind. Besides, she had no time for dreaming today. She was going to impress everyone at the Holmwood Foundation with her professionalism.

She pulled the door behind her with a snap and stepped out into a bright morning. The dampness that had clung oppressively to everything the day before had vanished, blown away by a wind that pushed billowing clouds busily across a pale September sky and shadows swooping across the street in a flicker of light and shade. The air was cooler, sharper, with the unmistakable damp bark and dead leaf smell of autumn. For a moment Roz could swear she smelt woodsmoke, and she looked along St Andrewgate, half expecting to see smoke drifting up from the tenements before she shook herself in exasperation.

There *were* no tenements. There were no jettied houses leaning in across the street, no morning fires being stoked. There were apartment blocks and Georgian buildings, all no doubt centrally heated.

Reluctant to lose her good mood, Roz turned determinedly and walked along the street. She was already regretting wearing her favourite polka-dot heels. They looked good with the suit, but they weren't the most practical for walking across a city, especially not one with as many cobbles as York. But she didn't want to go back and change. She wanted to get to Holmwood House early and spend some time getting a feel for the place on her own before the meeting she had arranged with Adrian Holmwood and the rest of the team. Pinched toes were a small price to pay for looking professional and appearing in charge.

At the end of the street, vans were queuing behind a truck parked half on, half off the pavement, its back doors open. For most of the day the city centre was pedestrianized, Adrian had told Roz, which meant that all deliveries had to be done first thing in the morning, but the streets were so narrow that one wide lorry could bring the rest of the traffic to a standstill.

Hesitating before she crossed the road into King's Square, Roz smiled in recognition of the church she could glimpse between the vans. It was good to see the familiar squat stone tower of Holy Trinity again, illuminated in a brief burst of light before the sun was blotted out by another cloud racing by. She glanced at her watch. She had plenty of time. She would step into the church on her way past and breathe in the long-remembered smell of the nave with its worn floor, she decided as she dodged between the vehicles, but when she reached the other side she faltered, looking around in disbelief. For the church had gone. In its place were benches and litter bins and pigeons clustering in the hope of crumbs. Disquiet prickled over Roz's skin, raising the tiny hairs on her arms and at the back of her neck.

She had been so sure there was a church here. She could picture it exactly, with the stubby tower and the odd, asymmetrical walls. She had seen it, just now.

And she remembered it, remembered the smell of new wood when the pews were put in, and the drone of Sir Thomas's sermons, which went on and on while Juliana shifted restlessly and whispered her discontent no matter how firmly Jane tried to shush her. She remembered the carvings on the rood screen, and the window her grandfather's father had paid for, with St Lawrence and his gridiron and Christ and St Cuthbert. That had been a long time ago, of course, when everyone had belonged to the old religion –

'No,' said Roz out loud, her voice shaky, and an elderly

women tugging a tartan shopping trolley cast her a curious glance as she passed.

Ignoring her, Roz stumbled over to one of the benches and slumped onto it. Her pulse was roaring in her ears and she dropped her head onto her knees. She wasn't dreaming now. She was wide awake and fear tumbled queasily in her stomach. What was happening to her? There was no way she should be able to remember what she remembered so clearly.

Breathing carefully, she lifted her head and made herself look around. The space was called King's Square, she knew that much, but it wasn't a square so much as a roughly triangular space. It was completely the wrong shape for a church. Which meant her imagination was working overtime. There was no church here, and never had been.

Shakily, she got to her feet, and it was only then that she noticed the raised platform area at one end of the space. When she went over, she found some grave slabs laid amongst the paving stones.

Grave slabs from a churchyard.

Gnawing at her bottom lip, Roz stared down at them.

Perhaps she had come here as a small child? Had she seen the church then? This could all be some weird recovered memory from her past. But it didn't look as if anything had been demolished recently. The grave slabs were worn and the paving well established.

Which meant . . . what?

Nothing, Roz told herself fiercely. *It means nothing*.

Chapter Six

She had to get on. Her earlier confidence was shaky now and Roz struggled to recover her positive mood. Enough with the ghostly churches, she decided, and drawing a deep breath, she made herself walk straight across the square, through the wall of the church, across the nave, right under her grandfather's window and out the other side, where she let it out unevenly.

A cluster of tourists were blocking the way at the top of the Shambles. Roz had to sidestep round them. She could hear the guide explaining that in the Middle Ages the street had been known as the Flesh Shambles, where meat had once been sold and where the great hooks that the butchers had used to hang their carcasses could still be seen at some of the windows. The street itself seemed to be clamouring for her attention, and the air was suddenly thick and sickly with the smell of raw meat. Against her will, Roz turned her head to glance down the street, and when the scene wavered alarmingly, she had to jerk her eyes away. Her heart was pounding and she stumbled away in panic, lurching over the cobbles on her heels, past the greedy suck of the street, careless of the tourists she jostled or the tuts of disapproval.

Finding herself in a market by a blessedly modern stall selling camouflage jackets, second-hand books and plastic pet toys, Roz made herself stop and take deep breaths. This was getting ridiculous. She couldn't keep letting her imagination get the better of her, and she couldn't turn up at Holmwood House in this kind of state either, not after yesterday's scene with the necklace. Her neck throbbed at the memory.

She found a coffee bar and ordered a latte, and drank it at a table until her pulse steadied and she could think rationally again. The dreams had been easy enough to explain away, but that memory of the church had been in broad daylight, when she was wide awake. Roz cradled her coffee between her hands. The cup was chunky, mass-produced, reassuringly modern. Outside the window, passers-by talked into mobile phones and wove between another queue of vans. They wore trousers and short skirts and jackets, not doublets or ruffs. It was *now*.

There would be a logical explanation, she told herself. There had to be. But in the meantime, she couldn't tell anyone what was happening, least of all anyone at the Holmwood Foundation. After yesterday's incident with the necklace, Helen had clearly already written her off as neurotic and attention-seeking, and Roz didn't want any suggestion that she wasn't capable of doing the job she had come to do.

*

'Morning!' Roz had her brightest smile at the ready as she put her head around the office door. Helen was there behind her computer, sitting rigid and typing with sharp little pecks on the keyboard.

'Good morning,' she returned coldly, unable to resist a glance at the clock. She had been at her desk since a quarter to eight, and she was disappointed to see that it was only just nine. Roz looked the type to swan in after ten at the earliest. That was when Sir Adrian arrived, of course, but it was different for him, Helen thought loyally. He was the director of the Foundation. Roz was just a floozie brought up from London because she could flick her hair back and simper effectively.

She had another over-the-top outfit on too, Helen noted sourly. A short skirt in a mock tweed and a matching boxy jacket with an extravagant pea pod brooch on the lapel. And – good grief! – high heels covered in polka dots. All very well in some glossy magazine, but totally inappropriate for York, unlike her own sensible flatties.

'Did you walk here in those shoes?'

'I did,' Roz said. 'They're not exactly practical for the cobbles, are they?'

Helen had been about to say precisely the same thing. You'd think Roz would be embarrassed at wearing such ridiculously impractical shoes, but no, she was smiling as if inviting Helen to join her in the joke. She swivelled one foot backwards and forwards to show off the shoe. 'You've got to admit they're gorgeous, though, aren't they?'

Helen had no intention of getting into girlish chats about shoes with the likes of Roz Acclam.

'You won't be able to wear them in the restored rooms,' she said dourly. 'Heels ruin the floors.'

'Oh,' said Roz, and Helen was pleased to see some of the glossy confidence fade from her face. 'Oh well, I'll take them off then.' She held up a briefcase and her coat, the one missing the button that was secreted in Helen's drawer. 'I'm just going to dump my stuff in my office, and then I thought I'd go round the house again and familiarize myself with the rooms.'

'There's a meeting at half past ten,' Helen reminded her sharply, drilling a finger into the diary where Sir Adrian had marked the time.

'I haven't forgotten,' said Roz, coolness creeping into her voice. 'I think an hour and a half ought to be more than sufficient. The meeting's in Adrian's office, isn't it?'

'*Sir* Adrian's office.'

Roz didn't even bother to acknowledge the correction. She just smiled slightly as she turned to go, and Helen eyed her with dislike.

She couldn't bear Roz's lack of respect, that awful smug certainty that she was Sir Adrian's equal instead of an employee like everyone else. She didn't even have the decency to look embarrassed about that appalling scene she had made the day before. What a hoo-ha about the necklace! Helen hadn't been able to *believe* the way she had carried on. Sir Adrian, of course, had fussed over her as if Roz really was burnt instead of just demanding attention.

'How are your burns today?' she asked snidely, letting her eyes rest on Roz's unblemished neck, and at last had the satisfaction of seeing that oh-so-cool expression tighten.

But instead of stuttering an apology for the ridiculous fuss she had made, all Roz said was, 'Fine, thank you,' and walked out before Helen had the chance to say any more.

She shouldn't let Helen get to her. Roz stomped through the Great Hall of Holmwood House, barely noticing its splendour, and up the stairs to her office, too irritated to remember how uneasy the room had made her the day before. Throwing her briefcase onto her desk, she dropped into the high-backed executive chair, pushed it away from the desk, and swivelled three hundred and sixty degrees. She had always wanted a chair like this, an office like this. She should be raring to get going on the next challenge, not grinding her teeth because of a jealous PA. It wasn't Roz's fault that Helen was in love with her boss. That much had been obvious, and just as obvious was the fact that Adrian was oblivious to her feelings. She should feel sorry for Helen, Roz told herself, not exasperated. Still, lovelorn or not, it wouldn't have killed Helen to be a bit friendlier, would it?

It was quiet up in the attics. Nobody else was around yet – apart from Helen working virtuously next door, of course – and Micklegate with the cars rumbling over the cobbles and people on the pavements seemed very far away. Roz wriggled her shoulders, feeling suddenly isolated and vulnerable.

Vulnerable? Where had that word come from? Roz frowned

at her briefcase. She wasn't *vulnerable*. She was perfectly safe up here on her own.

But she stopped swinging the chair around and found herself sitting very still instead, only her eyes darting around the room. The walls looked back at her, painted plain white, and yet somehow secretive and sly, as if they knew something she didn't. Outside, the morning breeze had grown more aggressive and was banging officiously at the dormer windows. Inside, the silence was dense, spongy. Roz felt as if she could push her hand through it.

She could hear her own breathing, not quite steady. The burning sensation was back around her neck.

And there, haunting the air, the smell of smoke.

The chair slammed back against the wall as Roz jerked to her feet, both hands flat on the desk, danger drumming in the back of her mind, but when she sniffed again, the smell was gone.

'Enough.' Her voice sounded raspy in the room's dead air but she made herself open her briefcase, scowling at the tremble of her fingers. She wasn't going to let herself be spooked again.

She found her tablet with its stylus and held it in her hand, reassured by its sleekness. Nick rolled his eyes whenever she got it out to make notes, and insisted on using paper and pen as a matter of principle, but Roz thought it was important to keep up to date with technology. '*I'm* not afraid of progress,' she would jibe when she wanted to annoy him. She prided herself on being forward-looking, cutting-edge. The past was over and done with, she'd insisted to Nick.

Which made these dreams of farthingales and ruffs doubly disturbing.

Taking only the tablet and stylus, Roz left everything else behind in the office and headed down the narrow stairs to the great hall on the ground floor, more relieved than she wanted to admit to have a good excuse to leave her office so soon. But she had planned to take notes room by room. She wasn't running away, Roz reassured herself. She wasn't frightened by her own office.

The great hall was shadowy, with a green pall cast over it from the netting swathed over the scaffolding. Roz paused in the passageway entrance and for a moment the air seemed to swirl and stir and solidify so that she sucked in a sharp breath, but even as her heart tripped, she saw that someone was moving from the shadows.

The caretaker she had met the day before, carrying a broom. Roz searched her memory for his name. 'Oh . . . Jeff . . . it's you,' she said, wincing inwardly at the high, precarious note in her voice. 'Hi.'

Who had she been expecting to see? he wondered. She looked startled. No, frightened. He could see the quick rise and fall of her jacket, the pulse hammering in her throat.

'Morning,' he said. He was prepared this time, and able to look at her more closely without his head ringing.

Little Boo, all grown up.

She looked like their mother, but sharper, smarter, not as soft. The mother he longed for and hated for abandoning him.

'I wasn't expecting anyone to be here,' she said. 'It's so quiet, I thought I was the only one here.'

'The house is bigger than you expect,' he agreed. 'You can get lost in it.'

'Yes.' He saw a shiver race down her spine, but then she smiled. 'How long have you worked here, Jeff?'

Jeff. He'd chosen the name – or it had chosen him – but it sounded odd in her mouth.

'I've been with the Foundation more'n ten years now, but only in this house since the contractors finished.'

'*Have* they finished?' Roz looked dubiously out at the scaffolding. 'It looks as if they've still got a lot left to do.'

'Nah, it's just snagging now,' he said, pleased to know more than she did. 'They'll come back and fix the little things – doors that stick, boards that creak, that kind of thing – but it'll all get done before the launch.'

'I hope so,' said Roz. 'It won't be much of a launch if we've still got the scaffolding up.' She walked into the middle of the hall, looking around her. 'It's got a definite atmosphere, hasn't it?'

So she felt it too. He had wondered. But he could do stolid when he wanted to. 'Atmosphere?'

'I mean, it's hard to believe that this is all basically new. It's recreated, rather than restored, but it feels old.'

He shrugged. 'The fittings are new, but the house has been here a long time. Since the fourteenth century, they reckon.'

'I thought it was a sixteenth-century house?'

'It's been recreated as it was in the time of Sir Geoffrey, but there was a house here long before that. He was the one who made the Holmwood fortune, and he transformed the house, but they were an important family in York long before that.' In spite of himself, he couldn't keep the note of pride from his voice, and Roz noticed.

She looked at him, her head cocked on one side, the way their mother had used to do when she was interested. Jeff was used to people's gazes sliding over or away from him, but Roz looked right at him, as if she saw everything about him.

But not quite everything.

'You know a lot about the history of the house,' she said.

He shrugged. 'Just what I've picked up working here.'

'Would you be interested in being a guide?'

Out of nowhere, rage surged through him. He, a guide? Reduced to showing doltish strangers around his house? And then, just as suddenly, the feeling was gone, and Jeff shook his head to clear it. It happened like that sometimes. He'd be minding his own business and then without warning his muscles would clench with fury and there would be a grip like ice around his mind, and he'd find himself staring into a terrifying darkness. He didn't tell anyone about it now. Schizophrenia, they'd said at first. A bad reaction to the drugs. They didn't know. It was best not to mention it, he'd learnt. It never lasted long and he could control it.

'I'm happy doing what I'm doing,' he said. Because it was all right having a murderer sweeping your floors and cleaning your toilets and clearing up your messes, but engaging with the public? Jeff didn't think so.

Roz wasn't bothered anyway. She was already walking away, her heels clicking on the new oak floorboards. The sound made her stop in consternation. 'Oh, I've just remembered I'm not supposed to be wearing these shoes in here.'

'Why not?'

'Helen said they would damage the floorboards.' She looked ruefully down at her shoes and Jeff snorted.

'Helen! What does she know? The only problem is with stilettos – and that's more health and safety than anything else – in case you get your heel stuck between the boards and go arse over tit. Them shoes you've got on are okay.'

'Are you sure?' Roz lifted first one foot then another to inspect the heels. They were high, but not needle-fine like some Jeff had seen. 'That's a relief. I'll try and wear something more practical tomorrow.' She smiled at him, a flash of sunlight in the gloomy hall, and the smile was so familiar that his gut twisted painfully and his breath stumbled in his throat.

But she was already moving away once more and pulling out some fancy gadget. 'I wanted to go round all the rooms to get a proper feel for them,' she told him, and he saw her tap something into the tablet she held in one hand with a stylus. 'This was the great hall, so it's the natural place for the launch,' she said, turning slowly to study the room. 'But we could have a range of events in here.' She shot him one of her disconcertingly direct looks. 'How do you imagine the hall being used?'

Jeff held on to his broom as he looked around. He could see the hangings, glowing in the candlelight, the long table set with goblets and basins, with silver and pewter. With jugs of the finest wine and, ah, the food! Dish after dish of meat: beef and pork, veal and venison, peahens and partridges and pigeons, baked and boiled and roasted. Pies and tarts, sugar comfits . . . And the air, ringing with voices, rank with sweat and reeking of grease and wine. He lounged in his chair, enjoying the beautiful blaze of fire at the end of his hall, enjoying the admiration and envy of his guests, his contentment only curdling at the memory of how she would have shaken her head and prated of plainness, of decency and modesty and honour – pah!

Jeff started, realizing too late that he had exclaimed aloud, and his knuckles tightened around the broom. *Control*, he reminded himself. He had to stay in control.

'Feasts,' he managed, his voice hoarse with the effort of keeping it steady. Sometimes when he'd watched the trains careering round the model railway, back in the days when the hall had been a shop, they had gone so fast they'd started to blur before his eyes, and he'd glimpsed the hall as it had once been, but he'd never seen it as vividly before. He shifted from foot to foot, dismayed in a way he didn't quite understand. It was as if Roz was changing things, just by standing there. There was an edge to the air, an unease swirling around her. Could she feel it?

She didn't seem to, or at least not at first. 'Feasts. Hmm, yes, banquets would be an obvious money-spinner,' she said. 'You could get, what, a hundred people in here? Say we had a long table here, and one *here* . . .' She stopped, head poised at an angle, listening. 'What's that noise?'

A train, chuff-chuff-chuffing round and round the track. A coldness stole over Jeff. 'I can't hear anything,' he lied.

'We're not near the station, are we?'

'It's not that far.' But already he could see Roz shaking her head, puzzled.

'Weird. It sounds like a steam train. Or, no, a toy train. It's sort of rattly . . .' She fixed Jeff with her eyes. 'What *is* it?'

'I don't know,' he said, but he did.

He could see the model shop now, its towering shelves stacked high with boxes, miniature cans of paint and mock foliage. The long, narrow room was crammed with model boats and cars, trains and planes, with rows of tiny plastic soldiers joined together. He remembered the snap as he broke them off one by one, the little knobbles left where they had been joined, the heady smell of the glue as he laboured over the models he made. There were model houses and stations and miniature plastic people, and plastic animals to stock a plastic countryside.

He'd liked the models right at the back of the shop, where it was dim and quiet. To get there, you had to squeeze past the elaborate train track that filled the middle of the shop. Three miniature trains had circled relentlessly, rattling round the curves, and disappearing into tunnels before emerging again on the other side of the shop. They chuffed through the tiny countryside, complete with farms and little towns and stations where tiny plastic commuters waited rigidly for the trains that never stopped.

A miniature world with no bellowing fathers, no meaty fists crashing through the silence. None of the giggling girls who filled the house once his mother married Patrick Acclam.

Patrick never bellowed. He was kind and concerned and deter-minedly understanding, but he hadn't wanted to be understood. He hated Patrick, hated Patrick's daughters, hated the fact that Patrick made his mother happy.

And in the model shop, he had changed. After that first time he'd shoplifted, he went back again and again. The rattle of the trains was the backdrop to his transformation, and he hadn't even been surprised when he'd heard their echo in the hall when he returned. Nobody else had ever heard them, though, except for Helen, who had stopped once to listen, frowning, before clearly brushing the sound from her mind as if it were a blowfly buzzing irritatingly close.

Roz shouldn't be able to hear the trains. Jeff found himself holding his breath.

She had been straining to listen, but now she shook her head. 'It's gone . . . That's odd, I must have imagined it,' she said, to his relief. She looked as if she was about to say more, but glanced at her watch instead. 'I'd better get on. There's a team meeting at ten thirty. Are you coming?'

What did she think? Jeff's lip curled, his early dismay leach-ing away as a familiar contempt crept over him. 'I'm a caretaker.'

'You're part of the team.'

It was exactly the kind of thing Patrick would have said. Jeff sneered. Who was she kidding? Did she really think Adrian Holmwood would sit around a table with a caretaker and a murderer? 'I just clear up the mess,' he said curtly.

Strange guy, Roz thought as she went up the stairs behind

the hall to look in the room Adrian had called the great chamber. There was a slightly unnerving intensity to Jeff, but something about him appealed to her too. He reminded her a little of Nick, she thought. He had the same leanness, the same intelligent eyes. Perhaps that was why he seemed familiar.

She wondered what he had been in prison for.

She was glad to leave the great hall behind with that disquieting rattle of a toy train nagging at her, too faint to be certain where it was coming from, too loud to ignore. Roz could have sworn Jeff heard it too. *I can't hear anything,* he'd said, but there had been a flicker in his eyes, a shuttering of his expression. He hadn't even tried to listen.

Her footsteps sounded very loud on the wooden stairs. The staircase was newly built and smelt of fresh timber, but the air was thick and musty as if the stairwell hadn't been opened for a very long time. It pressed around Roz's face, stifling her, and all at once the shadows at the top of the stairs seemed to be breathing, beckoning her up. Warning shrilled, a scream of instinct in her head, and Roz paused, her heart jerking, one hand on the wall.

Everything in her told her to go back, back down the stairs, out of the house, but how could she? Jeff would be there. How could she tell him she was too frightened to go up the stairs? And what about the team meeting at ten thirty? What could she say then: *I'm here to do a great job, but I'm scared of the house?*

Anyway, she was being ridiculous. It was just a staircase, and it was only shadowy at the top because there were no lights up there.

Swallowing, Roz made herself walk on up to the top. No ghostly hands reached out for her, no monster grabbed her. There was no whispering in the shadows.

But her heart was still beating hard as she walked across the landing and hesitated in the doorway of the great chamber. The room was empty, waiting for her. Roz could feel it licking its lips in anticipation.

The sense of oppression that had been dogging her all morning solidified into a conviction that she was being watched, and the hairs on the back of her neck lifted in a slow, shivery wave. 'There's no one here,' she said out loud, but her voice came out cracked and dried. 'It's an empty room.'

Deliberately, Roz made herself step inside. Her heels rang on the wooden floor. Jeff would be able to hear her below. The thought of his presence was insensibly comforting. Ex-offender or not, he was a human being.

She got out her tablet and stylus and forced herself to concentrate. The room had been panelled with new wainscoting and the windows were glazed as befitted a wealthy house at the end of the sixteenth century. Adrian had told her that Lucy, the curator, had sourced a great bed dating from that period, and that new hangings and coverlets had been commissioned. Otherwise he thought there would have been little furniture in the room. A chest or two perhaps, a stool, some cushions. A rush mat on the floor. Maybe a chair by the fireplace.

Which meant the room would be uncluttered. Roz turned slowly, trying to envisage the chamber furnished. It could be an intimate venue for a small wedding ceremony, with a feast to follow in the hall downstairs.

Weddings, she typed onto her tablet. *Licence?*

There would be other events where a smaller, cosier space would be more appropriate too. *Poetry readings*, she noted. *Book launches. Parties.*

Séances.

Roz stared down at the word that had appeared on her tablet. She didn't remember writing it.

But that was what happened sometimes, she reassured herself. When your mind was buzzing with ideas, sometimes your fingers got ahead of your brain. The atmosphere of the house was clearly having an effect. It wasn't surprising that the idea of a séance had popped into her head.

And it wasn't a bad idea, Roz thought as she wandered over towards the window. Haunted houses were a big draw. Why not capitalize on the creepy atmosphere?

Tapping the stylus absently against her teeth, she stared out of the window. It would be good when the scaffolding had gone. The windows were surprisingly large and on a sunny day the room would be bright, but the green netting that shrouded the scaffolding made it seem so dark in here. They should light more candles. She looked down to the street below, frowning at the sight of a bare-headed woman. And there was another, walking down the street in her shift!

Startled, she blinked, but the woman had gone, and the street was dark and empty as it should be at this time of night. A cur slunk along the gutter, scavenging for scraps, and the sound of the wedding feast in the hall below spilt out through the chinks in the closed shutters.

'Come,' said Margaret Holmwood, brusque as ever. 'Why do you moon over by the window? We must prepare you for your husband.'

Jane turned obediently. There had been something strange about the street a moment ago, but she couldn't remember what it was. And why worry about what was happening in the street in any case? This was her wedding night, the moment she would be truly married to Robert. She shook off the feeling of sadness. There was nothing to feel sad about. She should be merry, rather. She was a bride and her husband was young, handsome, gently born.

She had barely spoken to him. The wedding feast had been held here in the Holmwoods' house in Micklegate, where the sign of the red boar hung above the great door. It was enough that they would be marrying a butcher's daughter. For all his wealth, Henry Birkby could not be expected to provide a feast fit for Sir Robert's wedding.

Jane's father hadn't argued. He had purchased the Holmwoods' gentility, and he would not tarnish it by insisting that their kin and friends mingled. Nobody asked Jane what she wanted. Nobody thought that as a bride she might like to have her friends about her. Only her father and Juliana had been invited to the feast. The Holmwoods had little patience with the traditions Jane had looked forward to. There had been no bridelaces in Jane's hair, and she had had no maids to gather flowers to strew before her that morning when she walked from her father's house to the church in Micklegate. Juliana, deeply envious of Jane's good fortune, had accompanied Jane and their father, and was even now sulking downstairs at the feast.

Still, she was married. Jane tried to absorb the thought, to comprehend the reality of it, but the idea was too huge, too slippery. No sooner did she think that it felt real than it would slither out of her grasp, like the wet soap Ellen had taught her to make all those years ago.

Jane wished she hadn't thought about Ellen. *Do you think I wanted your father heaving on top of me?* The image of her father's meaty hands on Ellen still had the power to make Jane acutely uncomfortable. She knew what would happen tonight, of course. She had heard the servants talking, and Eliza Dawson, taking pity on her motherless state, had taken it upon herself to give Jane instruction in a wife's duties.

Robert would put his thing inside Jane, she had said, matter-of-fact. 'It will hurt at first, but you'll get used to it.'

It hadn't sounded very pleasurable when Eliza described it, but when the other maids talked about their sweethearts they smiled behind their hands and stroked their throats in a way that made Jane feel envious. She wanted to know what made their eyes dance with remembered delight, what secret memory caused their mouths to soften into curve.

And tonight she would know. Jane's blood fizzed with mingled nervousness and anticipation. Her role had been made very clear. Margaret Holmwood had looked Jane up and down, lips pursed, eyes flinty. 'You are to give Robert a son,' she said. 'I trust you will be a good breeder.'

'I would like to have a baby,' Jane had confided shyly. Even if it did mean she might bellow and scream in pain the way Ellen had done, the thought of holding her own child in her arms warmed her heart.

But Margaret wasn't interested in what Jane wanted. Her hands were brisk as she unpinned Jane's sleeves, lecturing her on the need to please her husband. Jane's new maid, Annis, was silent, but her eyes met Jane's in sympathy as she unlaced her bodice and helped her out of the new white satin kirtle Henry Birkby had given Jane as her wedding gift. White didn't flatter Jane. It drained her of colour and left her whey-faced and lustreless. Robert had barely glanced at her during the marriage ceremony, and had sat silent and resentful at the feast below. Only Margaret, leaning over to whisper in his ear or stroke his cheek, had been able to make him smile.

When Jane was standing in her shift, Margaret nodded to Annis to brush out her straight, fine hair while she stood back to study her critically. 'You're no beauty,' she said, 'but that matters little if you can bear a son. You know what's expected of you?'

The roast meats from the wedding feast rolled queasily in Jane's stomach. 'Mistress Dawson explained it to me,' she said.

'And who, pray, is Mistress Dawson?'

'Mr Dawson is a scrivener,' said Jane, glad to be able to boast a friend with more prestige than a butcher, but Margaret was unimpressed.

'A scrivener's wife?' she jeered. 'What does a scrivener's wife know of pleasuring a man?'

Jane bit her lip. 'She told me I must do as my husband desires.'

Margaret's smile struck a chill in Jane, like her father's cleaver slicing into a carcass. 'Did she so? Then see that you do.'

Nobody had bothered to scatter rosemary on the sheets, and the bridal bed felt cold and uninviting when Jane clambered in. Margaret had left, followed by Annis, who at least sent Jane a sympathetic smile of farewell.

Jane pulled the coverlet up beneath her chin. She was cold and tired and she felt sick from the rich food. She'd drunk too much spiced wine because she was nervous and now her head was thumping. She didn't want to be married, she realized. She wanted to be at home in the bed with Juliana pinching and snatching at the covers.

But it was too late to go home. She was married, and now she had to wait for her husband to come to bed.

He reeled in, laughing and jostling with his companions, a few minutes later, just when Jane had begun to think he wasn't coming at all. She smiled nervously, but Robert barely seemed to notice her. He was too busy slapping his friends on the back and exchanging lewd jokes. Jane might as well have been a bolster on the bed.

But at length the young men staggered out, having stripped Robert down to his shirt and urged him into the bed, and Jane was left alone with her husband. He lay on the other side of the bed and the silence was so heavy it crushed the air and made it hard to breathe.

Chewing her lip, Jane slid a glance at Robert under her lashes. She wished that she had asked more questions of Eliza, instead of ducking her head and muttering that she understood. But the message had been clear: she was to do as her husband desired, so she must wait for him to make the first move.

Robert sighed at last and turned to look at her. 'I will do this in the dark,' he muttered and blew out the candle. For a moment, before her eyes adjusted, Jane was wrapped in a muffled blackness and her mouth was dry with fear. Then her husband was upon her. Without a word, he hauled the coverlet aside and pushed up her nightshirt to her waist. His hands fumbled at her, shoving her legs apart and jabbing at her privy place. Jane tried to help, but she didn't know what to do. She spread her legs wider but she was very uncomfortable.

'Lie still,' Robert hissed at her, still pushing roughly at her. He was heavy on top of her, smothering her, and he started slobbering at her neck, muttering to himself, words that Jane couldn't understand. He smelt of sour sweat and sour wine. Crushed beneath him, she struggled to breathe, and she turned her head to one side on the pillow, sucking in air. Eliza had said the first time was the worst and Jane hoped that she was right. It couldn't be this horrible every time, surely?

Then something was pushing between her legs, and all Jane could think was that it would soon be over. But it didn't go very far. Jane was still wondering if that was it when Robert thrashed and cursed some more before flopping over onto his back.

'I told my mother you were too plain,' he said, his voice peevish. 'Now see what has come of it.'

Tears of disappointment and humiliation stung Jane's eyes. It was her fault. She was too plain.

'I am sorry,' she said.

For answer, Robert turned onto his side with his back to her. Jane lay very still, staring up at the dark canopy. So this was marriage. It was not what she had hoped for. But she would have to make the best of it. She hadn't had a chance to make Robert comfortable yet. He might yet grow fond of her. And while she couldn't do much about her plainness, perhaps she could try harder the next night. Perhaps she wasn't supposed to lie still? Perhaps he would like her to sigh and buck her hips? But he had told her not to move . . . Jane stirred wretchedly. Was it like this for every new bride? Beside her Robert was snoring the way her father did sometimes when he had had too much wine. It had been a long day, and Robert might be as tired as she was.

It will be better tomorrow, Jane told herself. *It must be.*

It will be better tomorrow. The words were clearly typed on the screen. She stared down at them, shame, embarrassment and disappointment still curdling in her stomach.

'*There* you are!' Helen's voice cut across the room, cold as a slap, and the floor tilted sickeningly as Roz jerked back to the present. The tablet and stylus tumbled from her nerveless hands and landed with a crack on the floor, and there was a rushing and a roaring, dark and dangerous, in her head.

Instinctively, she clapped a hand to her mouth as nausea rolled through her.

Seeing her standing immobile, Helen bustled forwards to retrieve the tablet and stylus with an exasperated huff. 'Jeff said you were up here but I couldn't believe it,' she said, thrusting them back at Roz, who somehow managed to fumble them into a grip. 'I've been ringing and ringing your office.'

'I'm sorry, I . . . What time is it?' Roz's voice sounded blurred to her own ears and the words felt unwieldy in her mouth.

'It's ten thirty-five. I thought you understood the team meeting was at ten thirty. We're all waiting for you.'

'I . . .' Desperately, Roz tried to pull herself together. 'I'm so sorry, Helen. I must have lost track of the time.'

Helen blew out an irritated breath. 'Well, if it's not too much trouble, perhaps you could come now?' she said. 'Sir Adrian's a very busy man and he's got a lot of other commitments today.'

Shaken and frightened, Roz followed Helen back down the stairs, across the hall and into the house next door. It was all she could do to put one foot in front of the other at first. The floor might look solid, but to Roz it was precarious, as if the slightest misstep might send her tumbling back into the past.

'Roz, do hurry up,' Helen snapped. 'The rest of us don't have all day.'

Roz sucked in a steadying breath. She couldn't think about what had just happened, not yet. She had to get through this meeting first. She couldn't afford to think about Jane, poor

Jane, crushed beneath her brutish husband, blamed for his impotence, humiliated and abandoned. She couldn't afford to think about what it meant. All she could do was concentrate on breathing and on not being sick.

Putting up her chin, she let Helen wave her sarcastically into Adrian's office.

'Roz, my dear, are you all right?' Adrian leapt up to greet her. 'You're white as a sheet!'

'I'm fine, Adrian. I was in the great chamber and I lost track of the time, I'm afraid,' she said.

'Oh, we've all done that,' said Adrian conspiratorially. 'It's part of the charm of the house.'

Charm? It wasn't the word Roz would have used, but she summoned a smile. 'Anyway, I'm so sorry for keeping you all waiting.'

Chapter Seven

Helen brought in coffee and biscuits while Adrian introduced Roz to Lucy, the curator, and Mark, who would be in charge of the front-of-house team. They were fawning over Roz too, Helen thought contemptuously. To hear them, you'd think she had done them some great favour by keeping them waiting ten minutes!

'We were just talking about the launch,' Sir Adrian said when they had finally given Roz enough attention, and Helen was settled next to him, ready to take notes. 'As you know, we agreed on 31 October, which isn't long to get things organized, but I'm anxious to get the house open to the public.'

Roz poured milk into her coffee. 'That gives us six weeks. We should be able to organize something suitably spectacular by then.' Her voice sounded a little odd to Helen, high and tight, but no one else seemed to notice. She was obviously neurotic, Helen decided, remembering how Roz had dropped the tablet. What her mum would have called 'narvy'. No one had any time for nerves in Helen's family.

'That's where it's so important to have an experienced events manager on hand,' Sir Adrian said and Helen kept her head down so that no one would see her rolling her eyes.

'Mark was suggesting we tie the launch theme in to Halloween,' Lucy put in. Helen didn't mind Lucy. She was a Scot, with a round, pleasant face and none of Roz Acclam's fine-boned nerviness or London affectations. Sir Adrian didn't make a fuss of her either.

'We're going to struggle to get visitors over the river,' Mark explained, picking up on the argument they'd been having before Helen was dispatched to find Roz. 'Most of the major attractions are on the other side of the river, and I think we need to have something unique that will get the punters to make the trip up Micklegate. Ghosts are always a big draw,' he said, and Helen saw Roz's hand jerk, slopping coffee into her saucer. 'Holmwood House could easily be haunted, don't you think, Roz?'

Sir Adrian, Lucy and Mark all looked expectantly at Roz, whose hand, Helen noticed, trembled as she put down her cup and saucer. The woman was a bag of nerves, she thought.

Roz cleared her throat. 'The house certainly has the right atmosphere for a ghost,' she said after a moment. 'It's really quite creepy when you're there on your own.'

'Oh, do you think so?' Sir Adrian sounded surprised, as well he might, thought Helen. There was nothing ghostly about Holmwood House. She had been over there masses of times on her own, and she'd never noticed anything out of the ordinary. Helen's pen stabbed at the paper. This was just Roz making herself interesting again. She wasn't going to write it down.

'Definitely,' said Roz, and Mark looked gratified. The others had dismissed his haunted house idea until Roz came along. 'It's very shadowy in parts, especially in that passage leading to the closet.'

'What passage?' asked Lucy, puzzled. 'There isn't a water closet in the house.'

'No, I meant closet as in study,' said Roz, looking from one blank face to the next. 'You know, the room at the end of the passage leading from the great chamber? Past the parlour . . .' Her voice trailed off as they all shook their heads.

'There isn't a room there,' said Helen with satisfaction, enjoying Roz's evident consternation.

'Oh, but . . .' Roz stopped, frowning uncertainly.

'It's interesting you should think that,' said Lucy. 'The buildings archaeologists did speculate that there might have been another room down there, but later modifications to the house meant they couldn't be sure, so we didn't recreate it in the end.'

To Helen's delight, a mottled flush was creeping up Roz's throat. She didn't look so cool and collected now, did she? 'I must have been thinking about some other house I've seen,' she said, which didn't convince Helen for a minute.

Still shaken by her experience in the great chamber, Roz was struggling to concentrate. Mark was enthusiastic about the haunted house theme. 'It's a pity the house hasn't been continuously occupied,' he said. 'I'm sure we could find someone who's died here, but all the locals only remember it as a model shop.'

Roz looked up sharply at that. 'A model shop?'

'Yes, you know, all those kits to make boats and planes, and toy cars.'

'And train sets?' For a moment she could hear again the thread of sound echoing in the great hall, the faint rattle of the wheels on the track vibrating, needle-fine, in her skull.

Mark nodded. 'It burned down, oh, years ago now. In the nineteen eighties. You were around then, weren't you, Helen? What happened to it after that?'

'I don't know,' said Helen, doughy with disapproval. 'I was only a child. I think there was another shop for a while, and then there was another fire about ten years ago. They thought it was arson but nobody was ever arrested. And when they were clearing up after that fire, they uncovered the original timber framing . . . and that's when we got involved.'

Lucy made a face. 'Not much scope for hauntings in a model shop, unless there was a fight to the death over a toy train!'

'Someone lived there before it was a shop,' Roz heard herself saying. 'We should play up the human story of the house, so it's not just about the furnishings but about the people, the servants as well as the Holmwoods themselves.' She turned to Adrian. 'Do we know anything about who lived there in the sixteenth century?'

'Well, there's Sir Geoffrey, of course.'

'There aren't any records about anyone else who might have lived in the house then?'

'I'll get the archivist to have a look.' It was clear that Adrian was only interested in Sir Geoffrey.

'You know what?' Mark leant forward. 'We should have a séance. Where I worked before, we used to hire out the hall to psychics who'd come and spend the night and do investigations. It was a really good money-spinner. It's amazing what these guys will pay to set up their equipment in a historic building, and we found it was a bonus for us too. The sniff of a haunting brought in a lot more visitors. If we did the same here, I'm sure they'd be bound to find a ghost or two, and then we could market ourselves as a haunted house.'

Adrian wrinkled his nose in distaste. 'It's a bit tacky. What do you think, Roz?'

'I think Mark's right about it being good for publicity,' she said.

'Oh, honestly!' Helen could contain herself no longer. 'I can't believe you're seriously going to hold a séance! There's no such thing as ghosts!'

Roz thought about Jane, about the way time in York had wavered since she had arrived. Three times now she had slipped into the past, and it was getting harder to dismiss it as some bizarre trick her subconscious was playing on her. The first couple of times, yes, it had made a weird kind of sense, but how often did you dream in sequence?

'I used to believe that too,' she told Helen. 'But I think I might be changing my mind.'

*

At last the meeting was over. Roz was glad of Lucy's company as they climbed the stairs to the top floor together. Lucy's office was next door, and knowing the curator was there made her own room feel less threatening.

Letting the smile drop from her face, Roz shut her office door and looked around her. The room regarded her stolidly in return, just a freshly painted, newly furnished office. Nothing to be afraid of at all.

She sat at the desk, her hands flat on the surface as if to anchor herself to reality, and forced herself to think rationally. She had been in the great chamber earlier, but the room was empty. She hadn't *really* been put to bed there, or lain suffocating under a thrashing, hopeless husband. Horrifyingly vivid as the experience had been, it hadn't been real. Helen had come to find her and there had been no bed, no Robert. Of course it hadn't been real.

Which meant there were two possibilities, Roz decided. She might be having a breakdown that involved extraordinarily vivid and coherent hallucinations about a life in the sixteenth century.

She didn't *feel* as if she was having a breakdown, but that might not mean anything. And if she was, what then? Should she go to a doctor? And say what? *The thing is, doctor, I keep travelling through time? I close my eyes and I'm sharing a bed with a drunken, selfish sot who can't get it up?* Before she knew where she was, she would be referred for psychological tests. There would be low-voiced discussions, and hospital appointments. How long before the Holmwood Foundation decided they needed someone a little more reliable to head up their events programme?

This was her big break. Roz couldn't stand the thought of slinking back to London and a chorus of unspoken 'I told you so's. She had made such a big deal of coming to York. How could she give up now? No, she couldn't tell anyone she thought she might be having a breakdown.

The alternative was even worse. Roz made herself consider coolly the possibility that she was somehow regressing to Jane's life in the past. Before she came to York, Roz would have dismissed the idea out of hand. She had been like Helen, certain that there was a rational, scientific explanation for every mystery. The thought of being possessed by a ghost would have made her scoff. Roz was the least spiritual person she knew. She didn't believe in God or ghosts. She didn't even read her horoscope. It was all nonsense.

And yet it was happening. Roz didn't understand how or why, but she wasn't making this up.

So, she was either hallucinating, or possessed by a long-dead woman.

Roz rested her elbows on the desk and rubbed her temples. So much for rational thought. She didn't care for either option, but she couldn't think of any other explanation.

Perhaps she should stop trying to explain it and decide instead what she was going to do about it? Roz sat back in her chair. She'd ruled out getting medical help, but maybe it was time to forget her prejudices and try some spiritual assistance. She had a vague idea that you were supposed to call in a priest to deal with ghosts, but she would feel a fool doing that. The Holmwood connection suggested it was something to do with this house, but she could hardly ask a priest in to exorcize the place without asking Adrian, and how could she do that without him writing her off as a hysteric? Roz didn't even want to think what Helen's reaction would be.

Mark's idea of a séance might be her best bet, Roz decided. If she arranged for allegedly psychic experts to come to Holmwood House anyway, surely they would be able to identify whether Jane was a ghost or not? And if they could, perhaps they would know what to do about her, without Roz herself ever having to admit to her own weird experiences.

Encouraged at the thought of being able to take some action, Roz sat up straighter and pulled her briefcase closer so that she could open her laptop. The Holmwood Foundation had provided a computer, but now that she had a plan of action she wanted to get on with it straight away rather than work out how to use a new system.

So intent was she on googling psychic investigators that Roz didn't at first notice the curl of smoke under her door. It was only when the smell, acrid as resentment, scraped at the back of her throat that she looked up and horror struck her cold to the marrow. Smoke was seeping slyly under the skirting boards, filling the room with a choking haze that thickened with terrifying speed in front of her eyes.

'Oh my God!' After that one frozen moment, Roz pushed back her chair and grabbed the phone. What had Helen told her about an outside line? Dial o first, yes. Her fingers fumbled with the buttons on the phone as she found 0 and then jabbed 999. 'Fire!' she gasped when the operator answered. 'Fire at Holmwood House on Micklegate. Please, hurry!'

She had to get out. Panic clutched at her, made her clumsy as she bumped her way round her desk and stumbled across to the door. The smoke was a living thing, a beast that grabbed gleefully at her, coiling around her ankles and her wrists, wrapping itself around her throat, smothering her, choking her.

Was this what it had been like for her parents, her sisters? Terrified, Roz reached the door and struggled for long, desperate seconds before she realized that it opened inwards. Then she was out in the corridor, retching, her breath hoarse in her ears.

'Fire!' she tried to call, but her throat was too raw, and she groped her way along the corridor to Lucy's office to bang on the door. 'Lucy! Lucy, get out!'

The smoke snuck in behind Roz as she pushed open the door. It swirled around her, dark and vile, but she had to check that Lucy wasn't there. Her arm pressed to her nose and mouth, her eyes streaming, Roz ran across to make sure that Lucy wasn't lying behind the desk, but there was no sign of her, and she staggered back out into the corridor, followed by the smoke, thick as mud, and behind it, she was sure, the dark, malevolent chuckle of flames.

Where was the fire alarm? Roz couldn't remember. Choking and spluttering, she threw open the door to the last office, also empty, and plunged down the stairs, practically falling in her haste to get away from the fire that lunged after her.

'Fire!' she rasped but there was no one to hear her, and she bumped against the walls, blundering in her panic as she checked the great chamber and the smaller parlours. Oh God, so much work had gone into restoring and recreating the house. It couldn't burn down now!

At least there was no one there. Roz clattered down the last set of stairs, so panicky that she didn't see Jeff coming up them until she ran right into him. 'Jeff! Oh Jeff, thank God!' she coughed.

'What's going on?' His hands were hard on her arms as he held her away from him. 'I heard all the running upstairs. Was that you?'

'The top floor . . . fire . . .' she choked out, too terrified to notice how he went rigid at the word. 'Where's Lucy?'

'She went out about half an hour ago.' He stared at her, craning his neck to see past her up the stairs. '*Fire?*' There was a strange note in his voice. 'Are you sure?'

'I'm sure.' Frantically, she bundled him back down the stairs. 'I've called the fire brigade. Please, we just need to make sure there's no one here.'

'There's no one else downstairs,' said Jeff. 'You go and warn the others and I'll get the fire extinguishers.'

'No!' Roz grabbed at him. 'You need to leave as well, Jeff. It's too dangerous.'

She wouldn't let him go, kept dragging him over to the door and into the Foundation house. 'Helen!' She sagged in the office doorway. Her throat was burning, as if the fire itself had lodged there, and she rubbed her neck to ease it as she coughed and retched to rid her lungs of the smoke.

Helen looked up irritably. 'What on earth is the matter?'

'Fire,' Roz rasped.

'Nonsense,' said Helen.

'The whole top floor is full of smoke, Helen. I've called the emergency services.' Even as she spoke, Roz could hear the whoop and wail of sirens approaching. 'Jeff says there's no one else in the house, but I think everyone should leave here too, just in case.'

'Oh, for heaven's sake!'

'I think we should all go, Helen,' Jeff put in. 'Better safe than sorry. I'll pull the alarm, shall I?'

Sighing, Helen nodded. 'Thank goodness Sir Adrian has gone already,' she said, and made a big thing of taking her time to gather her bag while Roz fidgeted, desperate to get everyone outside to safety. It seemed to take ages for the other staff to file down the stairs and out onto the street, where they gathered in a huddle.

Helen narrowed her eyes up at Roz's window in the roof. 'I can't see any sign of fire,' she objected, but Roz ignored her, turning in relief as three fire engines raced past the traffic that had pulled over to let them through, blue lights flashing frantically as they jarred over the cobbles.

An officer was swinging down from the cab almost before the first engine had stopped. 'Who reported the fire?' he demanded.

'I did,' said Roz, stepping forward. Her throat was hot and raw still and her voice came out as a rasp. She pointed up at the roof. 'My office is in the attics and the whole floor was full of smoke.'

'Is there anybody in there?'

'No, we checked.' Roz glanced around for Jeff, but he had drifted to the back of the crowd and was watching the firefighters with a curious expression.

Two firefighters were fixing their face masks on while another man checked the pressure gauges on the breathing apparatus they carried on their backs. They headed towards Holmwood House, purposeful but unhurried. Moved across the road with everybody else, Roz watched them, rubbing her throat as she forced the clean air into her burning lungs. She couldn't imagine voluntarily heading into such horror. The roar of the fire appliances filled the air and she shivered, wrapping one arm around herself.

Helen was muttering impatiently to the rest of the Foundation staff. Roz could feel their curious looks, and she found herself wishing the firefighters would come rushing out and order the turntable to raise the ladders up to the top floor.

But when the men emerged, they were in no hurry. There was a long conversation with the officer in charge, who turned at last to the waiting staff. 'Who's in charge here?'

There was a pause. Roz struggled to think. Adrian and Lucy seemed to be out and there was no sign of Mark. Perhaps that made her the most senior person there? But before she could say anything, Helen stepped forward.

'In Sir Adrian's absence, I think I'm the most experienced person here,' she said with an unfriendly look in Roz's direction. 'Can you tell us what's happening?'

'My men have been through the building and there's no sign of fire on the top floor or anywhere.'

'But that's impossible!' Roz burst out. 'There was smoke everywhere! I could hardly see!'

The fire officer shook his head. 'They didn't see any smoke damage at all.'

'I don't understand,' she said helplessly.

'I knew this was a waste of time,' snapped Helen.

'Wait. Listen.' Roz held her head between her hands as if afraid it might explode. 'There must be some mistake. I didn't make this up. Why would I invent a fire?'

'Well, it's a funny thing no one else saw this fire,' said Helen snidely.

'What about Jeff? He was there.' Roz beckoned him over urgently, but he avoided her gaze, and would have slipped away behind the fire engine if she hadn't gone over and taken him by the arm. 'Jeff,' she said desperately. 'You were on the stairs. You must have seen the smoke. Tell the inspector.'

Jeff's arm was rigid with tension. He kept his eyes on the pavement. 'I didn't see no smoke,' he said.

'What?' Roz gaped at him in dismay.

'I didn't see nothing,' he said, surly, sullen. 'But I smelt it. I smelt the smoke.'

'What's going on?' Sir Adrian came rushing up to Helen, who had sent him a text to let him know that they were being evacuated. She thought she'd made it clear that it was a false alarm, but obviously he'd been concerned enough to leave his meeting.

'Nothing,' said Helen, lowering her voice soothingly and taking Sir Adrian's arm to turn him to one side and reassure him that everything was under control. 'Roz seemed to think it was amusing to waste the fire brigade's time and drag the entire staff out into the cold just because she thought she smelt a bit of smoke that no one else could smell.'

It was a mistake to mention Roz, though. Adrian's eyes widened and he pushed past Helen to grab Roz's hands. 'My God, Roz, are you all right?' he asked urgently.

Roz, Roz, Roz, that was all he could think about! Helen's mouth twisted as she watched Roz pretend to pull away even as she simpered up at him.

'I'm fine, Adrian,' she said and Helen had to admire the way she injected just a touch of impatience into her voice, as if to suggest that she wasn't interested in herself. 'I was just worried about the house.'

Ha! That was a joke. Any fool could see that she was desperate for attention. A wave of dislike surged through Helen, so intense it stopped her breath for a moment. Everything had to be about Roz. Helen had been able to tell that the moment she opened the door to her the day before. Why couldn't men see it? They were such fools for that fragile look. Even that weirdo Jeff, who always gave Helen the creeps, seemed to have fallen for it.

Of course, Sir Adrian's protective instincts were part of his gentlemanly charm, Helen reminded herself, swallowing down the bile that was curdling in her throat. He was just too generous for his own good. Only she ever seemed to understand that.

He didn't realize that he was the one who needed looking after. There were too many women, exactly like Roz, who were ready to take advantage of his good nature.

Now Sir Adrian was urging Roz to take the rest of the day off and Roz was putting up a show of being determined to carry on, like she was the one with the problem. What about the rest of them who'd had their morning disrupted for no reason? Oh no, Roz was the brave little flower who would suffer in silence and make sure everybody knew that it was harder for her than anybody else!

Watching Roz's performance, Helen felt the dislike chill and harden into hatred. It was a strange feeling, like another skin settling over hers, and for a moment it seemed as if she was standing outside herself, looking at her stocky figure in her sensible suit and sensible shoes, at the way she was watching Sir Adrian with naked yearning, and frustration and a kind of contempt surged through her.

Helen frowned and shook away the sensation. She didn't look ridiculous, she looked practical. She wasn't yearning hopelessly for Sir Adrian, she loved him, deeply and truly, and she knew what he needed. She would be there for him when the Rozes of this world were long gone, and then he would turn to her and realize at last that the woman he needed had been right there all along.

Helen had imagined the scene so many times. The look of wonder that would come into his eyes as he stared at her. 'Helen,' he would say, cradling her face tenderly between his hands, 'I've been such a fool. Why has it taken me so long to realize that you're the one? I can't manage without you.' And then he would kiss her and Helen would melt into his arms. 'Come, my darling,' he would say when he raised his head. 'Let's go home. I can't wait any longer to make love to you.'

Helen's nipples hardened and a lust shook her that was so savage it startled her. Normally her dreams were rose-tinted romantic affairs, but this was something different, something dark and feral, a need for a dirty, brutal coupling. Who needed gentle kisses? She wanted him to push her against the wall and shove his cock into her until she screamed and bucked and raked her fingernails down his back.

'Helen?'

Helen sucked in a sharp breath as she realized that Sir Adrian was standing right in front of her. Her mouth was dry, her blood pounding, and dull colour mottled her throat as she recalled just what she had been thinking. That wasn't like her. She loathed vulgarity. She didn't think of Sir Adrian as a man with a cock – a vile word, and one she never used.

'Helen?' said Adrian again and with a huge effort she pulled herself together.

'I'm sorry, Sir Adrian.' Her voice came out deep and husky and she cleared her throat as she struggled to sound her normal practical self. 'I think I might be coming down with something, and standing out here in the cold hasn't helped.'

'That decides the matter,' he said. 'Roz wants to get back to work, but she's clearly had an unpleasant experience, and perhaps she'll accept it if I tell her I'm sending everyone home. The fire officer will let the staff in to collect their things and will then do another inspection, and I think it's better if we start again tomorrow.'

Here was her chance to prove to Adrian that she was the one who could be relied upon. Helen straightened her shoulders. 'That's very kind of you, Sir Adrian, and I'm sure the staff will appreciate it, but of course I'll stay. I want to get those letters finished for you, and we could go over the lottery application. It might be a good opportunity with just the two of us and no distractions . . .'

But Sir Adrian was already turning away to watch as Roz walked over the road in those stupid shoes and disappeared into the house with a firefighter. 'That can all wait until tomorrow,' he said absently. 'We might as well all take the day off.'

Tight-lipped, Roz shoved the laptop back into her briefcase under the eyes of the firefighter who had accompanied her to her office to reassure her that there was no fire. She hadn't wanted to believe it at first, but there was no trace of that thick, malevolent smoke in the air, no insidious crackling of a fire taking hold. She'd stared around the room, at the skirting boards and walls, all pristine, as if the choking, billowing black air had never rolled around her, as if she had imagined it all.

Maybe she had.

But Jeff had smelt the smoke too, Roz reminded herself with a kind of desperation, and her eyes were still red and stinging and her throat still felt as if it were clogged with the horror of the fire chasing her down the stairs. She could barely swallow past it, but how could it have vanished without trace?

She must have imagined it.

The firefighter watched stolidly as she went over to her desk. When she pressed her laptop, the screen sprang into life. She'd left it open on the website of Charles Denton, allegedly the UK's most renowned psychic. Had the firefighters seen that when they checked the room?

The muscles in Roz's cheeks tightened as she imagined them exchanging glances and twirling their forefingers against their temples. They must have written her off as an eccentric, or neurotic, as the rest of the staff obviously thought of her now.

Her head felt as if it were gripped in a vice and there was a blinding pain behind her eyes.

She'd told Adrian that she would work at home that afternoon, and immediately he'd offered to drive her, as if she were some kind of invalid. She'd wanted to snap that being a crazy person who invented fires and evacuated buildings didn't mean that she wasn't capable of putting one foot in front of another, but she'd bitten back the words and refused him as politely and firmly as she could. 'It's quicker to walk,' she'd pointed out truthfully, 'and I could do with the air.' Which was also true.

Outside in the corridor, the firefighter waited for her, shuffling his feet and muttering something into a walkie-talkie. Roz hoisted her briefcase onto her shoulder and threw a quick glance around her office. The room was very still. It felt as if it were waiting for her too. Waiting for her to see something, to hear something, to understand something important.

One hand on the strap of the briefcase, she tilted her head and strained her senses and there it was again, the faint crack

and snap of flames, flicking at the edge of her mind, and coldness rippled through her. The fire was there, behind the wall,
waiting for her. She was sure of it.

'Ready, love?' the firefighter asked from the doorway.

'You don't hear anything, do you?' said Roz.

Patiently, he cocked his head, listened for a moment and
then shook his head. 'No. What am I listening for?'

'Nothing,' she said dully. 'It must have been nothing.'

'You don't sound yourself.' Nick said he was worried about her
when she rang that night. Roz didn't tell him about Jane's marriage, or about the smoke. It was too hard to explain. She just
said that they had all been evacuated because of a possible fire
and that she'd worked in the flat all afternoon. It was the truth,
after all, but Nick knew that she wasn't telling him everything.

'Why don't you come home this weekend?' he said.

Roz hesitated. A part of her wanted to go back to London
more than anything else, but her pride wouldn't let her admit
that she was frightened of York. 'I've only just arrived,' she said.
'Besides, I thought you had Daniel this weekend?'

She heard Nick sigh. 'You can't keep avoiding him, Roz.
He's just a kid. It's not his fault.'

Knowing that just made Roz feel guilty, and guilt soured her
temper and made her scratchy and unreasonable. Intellectually,
of course she understood that the situation was nobody's fault,
least of all Daniel's.

It wasn't Nick's either. He hadn't been expecting to be
tracked down on Facebook by the son he hadn't known he had.

Roz knew all of that too, but something about the ease with which Nick had stepped into fatherhood grated on her. He was so calm, so accepting. It infuriated her. Having been faced with a whole new reality, he had spoken to Daniel's mother and discussed what had happened and why. He'd come to terms with a past that had turned out to be not quite what he had thought it to be.

He had done everything she didn't want to do with her own story, and she resented him for it.

She resented him for not telling her about Daniel straight away.

She resented him for understanding.

Roz could feel their marriage shrivelling. She wanted to get it back, to make it good again, but she didn't know how to push past the resentment that clogged everything. It had been a relief to get on the train to York, but as soon as she got here she'd missed Nick, and now she needed him, and she resented that too.

'I think I'd like to settle in here,' she told Nick. Her skin felt too tight, as if it didn't fit her properly any more, and she wriggled her shoulders, irritated with herself, with Nick, with everything. 'I'll come home next weekend and we'll talk then.'

As soon as she'd switched off the phone, of course, she wished she'd made a different decision, but she was feeling too scratchy to ring Nick back and admit that she'd changed her mind. The flat was very quiet, and the silence seemed to hum, a high, fine whine that vibrated in Roz's head. She found herself moving cautiously, as if the floor was precarious. The feeling of being watched tickled the back of her neck, and several times she whirled round, certain that she would find Jane standing right behind her, but there was never anybody there, just a dense pocket of air, a shift of pressure so subtle that Roz couldn't put a name to it.

There was no way Roz would have admitted it to anyone else, but she was nervous about going to bed that night. In the event, though, she slept dreamlessly, and for the rest of the week she stayed firmly in the present. True, the atmosphere in her office dragged at her, tugging relentlessly at the edge of her consciousness until she stilled with her fingers on the keyboard. She would sit for minutes at a time, listening intently, her eyes moving round the room. Sometimes she could have sworn she smelt smoke, and fear would dart through her, cold and pin-sharp, but the next instant she would decide that she had been mistaken. At other times, the air would be wavery and the walls insubstantial. The more Roz stared at them, the more certain she became that they were just a screen, a stage set that might ripple and slide at any moment, and her pulse would boom and thud in her ears.

But nothing ever happened. The walls stayed still, no smoke slithered beneath the skirting boards. It was just a room. Roz let herself believe that the strange episodes when she had imagined herself living Jane's life were over.

That faint, lurking whiff of smoke made it impossible to relax completely, though, and Roz booked an inspection by a fire risk officer in spite of Helen's objections that Sir Adrian hadn't wanted any trace of the twenty-first century in Holm-wood House.

'We can't have ghastly fire exit notices all over the place,' she had complained. 'They'll completely spoil the atmosphere.'

'Not as much as a fire would,' Roz pointed out, exasperated. 'We don't have any choice about this, Helen. You can't open the house to the public without a fire plan. I'm amazed a risk assessment hasn't been done already.'

'We did get a notice from the council,' Helen allowed grudgingly. 'But Sir Adrian knows the chief executive. He was going to have a word with him about it.'

In other words, Adrian wanted to bypass the regulations. Roz's lips tightened. Clearly, the rules were for other people, not for the Adrian Holmwoods of this world.

Helen's pudgy face was set in stubborn lines. 'You'll need to talk to Sir Adrian,' she insisted, but Roz wasn't prepared to wait.

'I need to do my job,' she said crisply. 'Adrian's employed me to set up a programme of events, and nothing's going to happen until we've got a fire plan in place. If you don't know a risk assessment officer, I'll find one myself.'

A quick google and Roz had identified a fire risk assessment service without any assistance from Helen. She shouldn't have bothered going to the office at all. Helen was determinedly unfriendly, and Roz was getting tired of trying to win her over. She talked to a retired firefighter called Alan Martin, who said he would come and inspect the house the following week so they could discuss an effective fire plan.

Reassured, Roz put the phone down. It was good to talk to someone so sensible. If there was any risk of fire, she was confident that Alan Martin would find it.

Still, the click of the phone sounded very loud in the silent room. Lucy was out, as she often was, and Roz was alone on the top floor. She hadn't seen Jeff at all that day. Not that she needed to know that he was in the house, but the attics were always so quiet. No wonder she got odd fancies up there. The street seemed a very long way away, almost another world.

And here it came again, that insistent, needling conviction that she had forgotten something important, that the answer lay in this room.

On an impulse, Roz set her fingers to her keyboard again and looked up the phone number for Charles Denton, the psychic she had been reading about when the room had filled with smoke.

'Do a psychic reading in Holmwood House?' he said when she had introduced herself. 'Yes, I could do that. What makes you think the house might be haunted?'

'I don't,' said Roz feebly. 'At least, not really. It's just . . . the house has a funny atmosphere.'

Charles Denton paused. 'What exactly is it that you want me to do?'

'I'm not sure.' She was beginning to feel foolish. What was she doing, ringing a psychic? It wasn't even as if she believed in ghosts. She was a sceptic. Or she had been. 'I suppose, could you tell if there's anyone – any*thing* – there?'

'You mean apart from Jane?'

Her pulse spiked, stopping the breath in her lungs. 'What?'

'I'm getting a very strong sense of her,' said Charles Denton. 'Does the name Jane mean anything to you?'

Roz held the phone away from her ear and stared at it. Her mouth was dry. There had been no sign of Jane for the past few days. She had thought it was over.

She had hoped it was over.

'No,' she lied instinctively, not wanting to admit it to herself.

Charles Denton said nothing, but his silence was eloquent with disbelief. Roz's face warmed as if he could see her, but she couldn't go back on the lie now. She didn't believe that Jane was real. Didn't want to believe it.

There was a fine tremor in her hands when she put down the phone after making arrangements for the psychic reading. She had wanted Denton to be a charlatan, so that she could present the idea as no more than a marketing exercise, but it was as if his question was reverberating in the still air.

Does the name Jane mean anything to you?

Coincidence, Roz told herself. A fortune teller's trick, no more. Jane wasn't an uncommon name. He had guessed and struck lucky, that was all.

Chapter Eight

Roz had a drink with Lucy on Friday night, but Saturday found her at a loose end. She was glad not to be going into the office, but there was nothing to do in the flat, and she wished again that she had gone back to London, where there were always little jobs around the house to do, where she and Nick could have gone shopping in Borough Market and then read the papers over coffee, or arranged to meet friends that evening. Where the world was solid and she was never afraid to look in a mirror in case there was someone standing behind her.

Where Nick would be preoccupied with Daniel.

Pain jabbed behind Roz's eyes, and she threw down the paper she had been trying to read in exasperation with herself. She was sick of moping around. She would go for a walk, get some fresh air and pull herself together. She had chosen to come to York, and she had chosen to stay here this weekend, so it was time to get *on* with it, as her aunt had used to say when Roz was a teenager and finding it hard to get motivated.

The memory of her aunt brought another pang of mingled loss and hurt, but Roz pushed it away. She couldn't let her aunt's one lie taint all the other memories she had of the woman who had been the only mother she could remember.

Shrugging on a jacket, Roz let herself out of the flat. It was a soft September day with a glowing, golden light that poured down into the streets like liquid and threw long blocks of shadow. The autumn sun hung low in the sky, making Roz squint and wish she'd thought to bring her sunglasses. She headed for the river at first, walking into the sun, so that people coming towards her were no more than black silhouettes outlined with a hazy aureole of sunlight.

She wouldn't think about anything, Roz decided. She would just walk and enjoy the sunshine. But familiarity nagged at her as she glanced up at the lantern tower of All Saints Church on Pavement or studied the rise of Ousegate before it dipped down towards the river. This was the way she walked to Holmwood House every day, but she had never looked at the church properly before, never wondered why it should appear both strange and familiar at the same time. And the street was the same as always, a little more crowded, perhaps, with Saturday shoppers, but no different to the day before. So there was no reason to suddenly feel this disquieting sense of déjà vu.

Perhaps she had come here as a small child, Roz thought. She had read somewhere that the brain processed and retained every experience, filing the unimportant ones away to avoid overloading the mind, but that none were ever truly forgotten. Who was to say that she hadn't been brought to Ousegate in a pushchair one day? Or hanging on to her mother's hand, perhaps, with her half-sisters beside her, and Mikey scuffing along behind them, none of them knowing how soon or how terribly the family would be destroyed? She might have seen the church then, seen the rise of the road, Roz reasoned. That would explain this uncanny sense that she had been here before.

On Ouse Bridge, she stopped to peer down at the river. Sunlight was flashing on the water, exploding in tiny, flickering bursts of light, like paparazzi bulbs flashing, so bright that it hurt Roz's eyes to look at them straight on. A buzz of laughter and chatter rose from the crowd outside the pub on King's Staith, enjoying the unexpected warmth. Pleasure boats were tied up against the quay, and Roz frowned a little, watching them. There was something odd about those boats, something distorted in the scene that set a memory rising, unfurling, almost there, but just out of reach. The boats. The river. Something missing. Something wrong. If only she could remember . . .

'Mistress?'

She started. 'Oh . . . Annis.' She rubbed her forehead. 'What was I saying?'

'You were talking about them keelboats.' Annis regarded her closely. 'You sickening for something, mistress?'

'No, no . . . at least . . .'

She did feel a bit strange, Jane realized. It was as if there was something tugging at her mind, something that she was trying to remember. For a moment when she had gazed down at the staith, something had stirred at the back of her mind, but before she could remember, she was distracted by the glitter on the water, by a subtle shift in the air, so that it seemed that the river changed before her eyes and the boats clustered by the staith wavered and vanished. But then Annis had touched her arm, and everything snapped back to normal.

'I'm just worried about my sister,' she improvised, and it was true enough. She had met Eliza Dawson from St Andrewgate in the market, and Eliza had shaken her head over Juliana's antics. Jane should speak to their father, she had said, else Juliana would lose her reputation.

Jane couldn't imagine her father listening to her. Juliana was his pet still, and he would brook no criticism of her, but Jane fretted that without her restraining influence, Juliana's wildness was increasing. Her temper, always erratic, swung wildly from dazzling good humour to the black depths of misery. Jane didn't understand how hard things were for her, she complained. How dull it was to live on her own with their father. She needed excitement. She needed attention. She needed rich clothes and jewels and dancing. It was all right for Jane, with her big house and her handsome husband.

Then Jane would think of the house in Micklegate, where her husband barely bothered to conceal his contempt for her and his mother watched her with a face like flint. If Juliana only knew how little Jane's lot was to be envied, Jane thought wryly, but there was no point in trying to explain, and no point in complaining. She was married and there was nothing she could do but endure. But Jane was always glad to get out of the house like she had this morning and escape to the market with Annis. There was a wrongness in the air in the Micklegate house, a sly chill that coiled up from the floorboards. Jane shivered at the thought of it.

Perhaps Annis was right and she wasn't well. 'Perhaps,' she said.

'Or perhaps it's summat else,' said Annis with a grin.

Jane looked at her blankly. 'Something else?'

'My last mistress, God rest her soul, her wits would allus go a-wandering when there was a bairn on the way.'

'Oh.' Hot colour rose up Jane's throat. 'No,' she said sadly. 'It's not that. I don't think so.'

She only wished it were that. She longed for a child of her own. Robert put Jane in mind of a boy forced to pick up a slug, and she burned with the humiliation of his fumbling attempts to mount her, the revulsion on his face whenever she tried to touch him back. The tendons would stand out in his neck and his jaw would clench.

'I need a son, curse you,' he muttered as he jabbed at her with his fingers, but his yard refused to rise. Sometimes in the dark, it grew stiff enough to push a little way inside her, but he had barely entered before it would wilt.

If only she *could* give him a son. Jane clung to the thought. If she gave him the child he wanted so badly, surely he would look on her more kindly? It was hard to remember how astounded she had been at her good fortune when she had first seen him. She knew now that her husband's temper was mean and petulant. He was a man grown tall and handsome, but a child still inside. He ran to his mother whenever he was crossed, and Margaret indulged him. She stroked his hair and cooed to him that he was a good boy, and Mamma would make it all right.

Jane was little more than a servant, for all Annis called her mistress. She ran the household as she had learned to do for her father. She went to the market and she cast the accounts. She cooked in the kitchen and made sure that the silver was polished, the carpets beaten and the rushes swept. She slept in the bed in the great chamber and let her husband grunt with frustration over her before he took himself off to his closet, but she was not a real wife. Not the way she had imagined it.

Margaret called Jane into the little parlour and told her that she was disappointed in her. 'Robert says you cannot satisfy him,' she said, her voice sharp with disapproval, her fingers drumming impatiently on the arms of the turned chair. 'How can you give him a son if he can take no pleasure in you?'

Jane kept her eyes lowered, her hands clasped before her. She was outwardly calm but humiliation prickled her skin. 'I try to please him,' she said after a moment.

'Try harder,' said Margaret. Her lip curled as she studied Jane, standing before her in her apron. 'We should have known that a butcher's brat would be too coarse for Robert's tastes. Robert is a gentleman, and he has a gentleman's desires.'

Her skirts rustled stiffly as she got to her feet and advanced on Jane, who had to force herself not to flinch as Margaret put her face close to hers. 'Do you want to know how to please your husband, plain Jane?'

Jane swallowed. 'Of course.'

'Then I will tell you how you may.' Her lips were at Jane's ear, whispering secrets. Jane could feel the spittle on her cheek, and her face burned. Nothing she had heard from the maids in St Andrewgate had prepared her for what Margaret was suggesting. She was to take Robert's yard in her mouth and suck on it until he was hard. She was to lick him and pat him, and bend over and let him take her like a dog. Jane's throat closed in disgust as Margaret whispered on, perversion after perversion. Such were his gentleman's desires.

'I do not want to,' she said without thinking and Margaret drew back to deliver a stinging slap that made Jane rock back on her heels in shock.

'You do not want to?' she echoed savagely. 'It does not matter what you want, plain Jane. Do you think anyone asked me if I wanted to do that for my father? For my uncles? You know nothing of the world if you can prattle about what you want! Just do as your husband desires.'

Bitterly, Jane nursed her cheek as Margaret swept out. She felt soiled, sick. She could not imagine doing any of the things Margaret seemed to think it was her duty to do to her husband, things Margaret had done to her father and perhaps to her own husband.

But what if Margaret were right? What if that was the only way she would ever conceive a child? Jane was not a fool. She had given up dreaming of a husband who would care for her. Her hope now lay in a babe, a son who would satisfy the Holmwoods and give Jane someone to love. She yearned for it, but whenever Robert clambered petulantly into the great bed at night Jane could not bring herself to do anything Margaret had told her to do. Just thinking about it made her want to scrub herself all over.

'There now,' said Annis, misreading Jane's expression. 'It will happen. You are not long married after all.'

'A year and more,' said Jane.

Annis looked around and then leaned closer. 'They say old Mother Dent out on't common can give you a potion. No harm trying, eh?'

'A potion?' Jane stared. 'What sort of potion?'

'You know, to help you conceive if that's what you want – or not if you don't.'

'You mean she's a witch?'

'Shh, not so loud!' Annis flapped her hand, flustered. 'Some say she is, some say she's a wise woman. She gave my mistress something to stop her breeding, she had that many bairns. She'll give you a love spell for a farthing too.'

A love spell.

Jane turned the idea over in her mind as they carried their baskets up the steep slope of the bridge. She barely noticed the urchins chasing each other over the cobbles, or the two prosperous mercers outside St William's Chapel, trying to negotiate over the snarls of the dogs they held on tight leashes.

A spell.

Could a spell make Robert love her? What would that be like? He might send his mother to the country and devote himself to Jane. Instead of setting his teeth as he climbed on top of her, he might smile tenderly and then . . . well, Jane wasn't quite sure what would happen, but she knew it must be different to what happened now.

She kept her eyes demurely lowered but her mind was working busily. She was sensible and devout. Witchcraft was an abomination. She could not go out and demand a potion from the old woman. And yet . . . what if the spell *did* work? Would it not be worth it?

Jane glanced at Annis, who looked back at her knowingly. She liked Annis. A big, raw-boned girl, Annis had a round, good-humoured face and shrewd eyes and although she was the same age as Jane, she was the older by far in the ways of the world. Jane had seen the way she flirted with men, and the way their eyes rested on Annis's bodice where her breasts swelled; the way they watched her walk away with that provocative swing of her hips. Jane was fairly sure that Annis would know how to make a husband want her without any need for a spell, or for abasing herself in the way Margaret suggested, but she couldn't bring herself to ask. It was too humiliating to admit that you weren't sure if you were still a virgin or not.

But a spell might change all that.

'Annis,' she said, making up her mind, shifting her basket to the other arm so that she could draw closer. 'How could I manage it?'

They went together the next afternoon. Jane had a few coins left from the market, and Annis wrapped up an eel pie and a piece of cheese in a cloth and carried the basket.

Annis seemed to know her way through the labyrinth of footpaths and tracks between the fields and garths outside the city walls, where the grass grew long and lush and the hedgerows rustled with chirrups and twitters. The countryside drowsed in the warmth of a summer afternoon. Out on the common, cattle ambled hock-high in buttercups, and horses stood nose to tail in the shade, tails twitching at the flies.

Nervous about the idea of visiting Sybil Dent, Jane distracted herself by gathering herbs for her still room. She found arsesmart, which she used to drive fleas away, borage for a syrup to cool and cleanse the blood and wild daisies aplenty, to make into oils and poultices for wounds, and she tucked them all into her basket. It gave her a good excuse to dawdle, and nobody seeing her basket of herbs would question what she was doing out in the crofts. Nobody would suspect that a respectable woman and her maidservant would be on their way to visit a witch.

'And this is lady's bedstraw,' she told Annis, stooping to lift the yellow flowers with one finger. 'Mixed with sheep tallow, it is a singular remedy for burns and scalds.' She sniffed at the plant, remembering the smell of the ointment they had put on her hands after she had snatched Ellen's baby from the flames, and the memory of that terrible day rolled over her like a cloud blotting out the sun.

Annis nodded, but she wasn't interested in remedies, and went back to chattering cheerfully about the latest gossip in the street. But Jane wasn't particularly interested in *that*. She brushed her hands along the high grasses in the verge, looking for plants she could use, listening with only half an ear while Annis told her about Jack, assistant to the notary who had moved into the house next door.

'He's from London,' she said, impressed. 'I don't believe half the stories he tells me, but ooh, he's got a look in his eye that makes me come over all melty!' She winked at Jane. 'Maybe I'll get me a love potion too!'

But even Annis grew silent as they left the fields behind and made their way across the scrubby common to a scattering of trees. Tucked away inside, on the edge of a little clearing, looking as if it had grown out of the ground, was Sybil Dent's cottage.

By unspoken consent, they paused. Somewhere in the distance a sheep was bleating, but in the clearing it was very quiet, so quiet that the silence beat at Jane's eardrums. 'Do you think we should be here?' she whispered, eyeing the cottage dubiously.

'We're not doing no harm,' Annis whispered back.

Jane bit her lip and her fingers tightened around her basket. She could hardly believe that she was here, at a witch's cottage. They should go. Witches were evil, an abomination before God. She should run back to Micklegate and throw herself on her knees in the church to beg forgiveness for her sins.

But running back to Micklegate wouldn't make her husband want her. It wouldn't give her a child. It wouldn't change anything, and oh, how she longed for something to change!

The clearing was still as glass. All the way out the country had been teeming in the summer warmth, but here no bees blundered through the air, no swallows swooped, no blackbirds squabbled and sang amongst the trees. No coneys sat up on their back paws, noses twitching, before lolloping back into the grass with a flash of white tail. Only a solitary crow sat on a branch overhanging the cottage, watching Jane so beadily that when it flapped its wings and croaked, she started as if it had shouted at her.

'Look.' Annis dug an elbow in Jane's ribs, and Jane's heart jerked again when she followed Annis's gaze and saw an old woman in front of the cottage, leaning on a stick of ash. Where had she come from? A moment ago Jane could have sworn there had been no one there at all, and Sybil was too bent and gnarled to have run round from behind the cottage.

But there she was, dark and twisted and knotted like an old tree, her eyes bright as a hedgepig's as they settled on Jane. 'You're here then,' she said, as if she had been expecting them.

Jane cleared her throat. 'Good day to you. I . . . I have heard that you have some skill with remedies,' she managed awkwardly.

'Remedies, is it?' Sybil spat on the ground. 'Better come in then, hadn't you?'

Jane and Annis glanced at each other, then both started forward, but Sybil stopped and pointed at Jane. 'Just you.'

'I'll wait for you out here,' Annis whispered, unable to disguise her relief.

So Jane had no choice but to hand Annis her basket of herbs, take the one with the pie and the cheese in return, and go on alone. The little cottage seemed to draw her in across the clearing. Ducking under the doorway, she stood blinking in the dim light. The roof was low over her head, the mud floor covered with fresh rushes. A pot hung over the hearth in the middle of the floor where a few coals burned dully. Smoke drifted up to the hole in the sagging roof, but the air was green and it smelt of the woods.

'Sit.' Sybil jerked her head at a stool, and Jane sat obediently. Now that she was here, she felt strangely calm. She put the basket on the floor by her side, watched unblinkingly by a cat whose green eyes glowed in the shadows.

Muttering to herself, Sybil poked at the coals. 'Tell me what you want,' she said abruptly without looking round.

'I . . . well, I . . . I would like something to make my husband love me,' said Jane in a small voice. She didn't like having to say it out loud. It made her sound like a foolish servant girl, not a married woman. She couldn't believe that she was really there, sitting on a stool in a witch's cottage, asking for a love spell.

For answer, Sybil hobbled over to Jane and took her chin in her hand to force her to look into her face. Her fingers were rough but surprisingly strong. 'Tell me what you want,' she said again. 'What you *really* want.'

Jane looked into the ancient eyes and felt her stomach drop away, as if she were falling, falling. 'I want a child,' she heard herself say.

'Are you sure?'

'I am sure.' Jane's voice grew in confidence. 'I have been

married a year now, more than,' she confided, 'and I still don't . . . I still can't . . .'

'It's not you who cannot,' said Sybil with a harsh crack of laughter. 'You will bear no child while your husband is unmanned with you. You don't need love,' she told Jane. 'You need his yard to rise. But love will help. I can give you something to make him want you.'

Turning away, she began poking around in the bowls that sat on the rough shelves, mumbling to herself again. Jane watched her, wishing she dared ask what Sybil was doing. She had some skill in the still room herself, but her room was nothing like this. Hers was light and airy, while the cottage was dark and dreamlike and strangely powerful.

Jane kept her feet planted on the floor. She felt that if she lifted them, the stool would unyoke itself from the ground and float upwards, and she with it.

'Here,' said Sybil at last, handing her a twist of paper. 'Take this, and give it to your husband and no one else. Put it in a dish and serve him at the edge of dark. It is the most powerful time, twixt day and night, so mark it well. And at night, let him come to your bed. His yard will be hard by then, but remember, he must spill his seed in you if you are to have a child.'

Jane stared down at the paper in her hand, twisting it between her fingers. *If.* She lifted her eyes to Sybil's. 'Can you tell?' she asked with difficulty. 'Will I have a child?'

Sybil regarded her for a moment. 'Show me your palm.'

Jane turned her right hand upwards, and Sybil took it. Her old fingers seemed to burn into Jane's skin anew as she traced the old scars with surprising gentleness. Her toothless mouth worked strangely, and her eyes were glassy.

'Fire,' she said at last, and an expression that sent a fast little jerk down Jane's spine slid over her face. Something almost like anguish. 'I see fire.'

Well, it was not so hard to tell from the scars after all. Jane nodded, trying to disguise her disappointment. 'The fire was a long time ago,' she said firmly. 'I wish only to know if I will have a child.'

'Aye, there will be a child,' said Sybil, giving Jane her hand back, suddenly all briskness once more. 'But be careful what you wish for,' she said.

But the promise of a child had Jane getting to her feet before Sybil had finished speaking, clutching her twist of paper, smiling, not listening. 'I thank you,' she said, and bent to pick out the pie and the cheese and set them on the small table with some coins. 'These are for you, for what you have done for me and for my maid. Can she come in now?'

Sybil hesitated, almost as if she would have said more, but in the end she just turned her hand in a gesture of acceptance. 'If she will,' she said.

'Did you get it?' Annis whispered when Jane went out, blinking in the light.

'Yes . . . yes, oh, Annis . . .' Jane couldn't keep the news to herself. 'Annis, she says I am to have a child after all!'

Annis beamed. 'That's grand! Now for me . . .' She looked at the door doubtfully. 'She didn't have no familiar in there, did she?'

'There's a cat, but it will not hurt you.' Jane could laugh now that she was out in the air and knew that she might have a babe very soon. She took the basket of herbs from Annis and shooed her towards the cottage. 'She is strange, but I think she is kind. Go on, and find out if you will have your Jack after all.'

Annis came out looking disappointed. 'She wouldn't give me no potion,' she complained. 'Just this to hang round my neck.' She held up a piece of paper in disgust. 'It's got Jack's name on it, is all. She said I didn't need nothing but my smile.' Annis's face creased with suspicion. 'I wish I hadn't cut her so much cheese now!'

Jane couldn't help laughing. 'Annis, it is good that you need no help from her. Put that piece of paper under your pillow, and smile at Jack. If Sybil thinks that is all you need, perhaps she is right.' She had tucked her own twist of paper carefully beneath the herbs in the basket. 'Now come, we must go home.'

She must have spent longer in the cottage than she had thought. It was cooler now, the summer warmth leached from the air, and she pulled her gown closer around her, puzzled by the smell of fallen leaves. It was only June. The trees were in full leaf, not lying in yellowing piles. She turned to ask Annis if she smelt it too, but Annis had gone and all at once the world was shifting, tipping, and the herbs and grasses and flowers that thronged the edges of the track slid away, dissolving into brick and metal and a solid lifeless grey beneath her feet. Stumbling in horrified disbelief, she thrust out a hand to stop herself falling, and grazed it against rough bark. The shock of it jolted her into awareness, and she clutched at the tree to anchor herself as the world steadied and settled.

She had no idea where she was. Roz stood frozen, braced against the tree trunk, while her heart thundered and her mind swerved giddily between past and present. A woman walking a dog passed her with a curious look; two teenagers in hoodies and scuffed jeans ignored her as they slouched past in the other direction. Roz didn't dare let go of the tree at first, but when another dog walker approached and looked at her in concern she took her hand away and managed a weak smile. Perhaps he thought she was drunk. It felt a little like that, as if her head wasn't properly connected to her body.

Cautiously, Roz looked around her. She was clearly in the suburbs, on a main road lined with mostly semi-detached houses. How in God's name had she got there? Ice pooled in her stomach at the realization that she must have crossed busy roads without any awareness of where she was or what she was doing. She could have been killed.

She had thought Jane was gone. At least, she had wanted to believe that she was, but she couldn't fool herself any longer. Roz wrapped her arms about herself, fighting a wave of self-pity. For one treacherous moment she felt so lonely and lost that she wanted to weep, and it was that thought that made her pull herself together. She had never been a crier, and she wasn't going to start now.

But what was she going to do?

For want of a better idea, Roz started walking again while she tried to think clearly about her options. Jane's ability to take over her head terrified her, but at the same time she was fascinated, and part of her wanted to be back in Jane's skin, living Jane's life, seeing the world through Jane's eyes. A world that was more vivid and immediate and familiar than the one Roz was walking through now.

Could it be true? Was she really possessed by a ghost from the past? The rational part of Roz's mind wanted to scoff, but the memory of Jane's encounter with Sybil Dent was so *real*. She hadn't dreamt it, she had lived it, she knew she had.

Roz walked along a wide suburban road, remembering the common with its rutted tracks, the lush, lovely grass and the dizzyingly pure air. As if to underline the contrast an old van passed her, billowing fumes from its exhaust.

Digging her hands in her pockets, Roz waited to cross the next main road. Beside her, a mother leant down to tuck a blanket around her baby in its pram, and a familiar envy twisted in Roz's gut like a knife. She looked away. All those years longing for a baby, letting Nick persuade her that the time wasn't right, that he wasn't ready, and it turned out that he had been a father all along.

She thought about the little twist of paper she had tucked out of sight under the herbs, and how her heart had leapt at the prospect of having a child.

Jane's heart.

That hadn't been her, Roz Acclam. She wasn't reduced to hocus-pocus or trapped in a marriage with an impotent bully. Poor Jane, trying so hard to make the best of it. Roz hoped she had the baby she wanted so much.

Anyone would think she wanted to go back.

Roz gathered her jacket closer at the neck, worried by the wistful train of her thoughts. She had to get a grip. She would ask the psychic Charles Denton to come earlier. Ghosts were his business, so perhaps he could help her. Or she would find a vicar. Roz didn't relish the idea of stumbling through an explanation of what was happening to her, but she couldn't carry on like this.

The sun was still bright, and a breeze was hustling the first of the fallen leaves along the gutters. Roz kept walking, as if she could somehow outpace the sense of dislocation that swirled in her head, and gradually the queasy, disconnected feeling faded to be replaced by something that was not quite unease, more a niggling conviction that she was missing something important, a buzzing in her head that was growing inexorably louder.

Her steps slowed and she looked about her more carefully. She was on what seemed a very ordinary suburban street. It was familiar, Roz thought, but only because she had grown up in a semi-detached house in the London suburbs.

But when she reached a junction, and glanced at the street sign, the name jumped out at her like a shout: Millingham Road.

Roz stood looking at it for a long time. Millingham Road, where she was born. Where her parents and sisters had died. The one place in York she had planned to avoid. Roz saw no point in making a pilgrimage. She had had no intention of coming out to see the house.

And yet here she was.

She stared up and down the street, straining for a memory, but no picture slid into her mind. There was just that faint buzzing in her head, that sense of an unseen finger prodding her between the shoulders.

Almost against her will, Roz turned and walked along the road, counting off the houses as she went. All the odd numbers were on one side of the road, all the evens on the other. The houses here were detached, a mixture of bungalows and two stories, unadventurously designed but clearly ideal for families. The side roads were quiet and every house sat well back behind low brick walls and carefully tended gardens. It felt like a safe but not very exciting area, a place where people washed their cars on a Sunday and mowed the lawn and were pleasant to their neighbours.

This was where she had spent her first years. She presumed she had been happy. 'Everyone adored you,' her aunt had told her. 'They used to call you Boo, because you loved playing Peekaboo with them all. You were such a dear little thing.'

Roz had always liked the idea of being adored, but how could she be sure that it was true? If her aunt had lied about something so big, why stop at a little white lie? Perhaps she had been grizzly and whiny. Perhaps her sisters had resented her arrival. Perhaps neither of her parents had really wanted another child.

Because if it had been such a big happy family, how come one member of it had decided one cold night to set fire to them all?

And there it was on the corner, number forty-seven. Roz

wasn't sure what she had expected. Intellectually, she had known that it wouldn't be a smouldering pile any more, but still, she hadn't expected the house to look so exactly like all the others either. Shouldn't there be something fizzing in the air here, some sense of the tragedy that had unfolded marking the stones? But it was just a house like a thousand others.

Perhaps every house had its share of tragedy.

It had been over twenty-five years since the fire, and no sign showed on the freshly painted walls. The PVC windows looked new, and it appeared that the owners had added an attic room recently. She walked past as slowly as she could without looking suspicious. To give herself more time to look, she pretended that she had a stone in her shoe and stooped to fiddle with it by the driveway. The wrought-iron gates stood open. The owners were house-proud, or hoping to sell the house. The garden was neat, the drive well tended.

And none of it was familiar.

Roz looked up at the windows. There was a large one, hung with net curtains, clearly the master bedroom, and what looked like a little room beside it. The kind of room you might put a baby in, so you could hear it in the night.

Where you could snatch it up and carry it to safety if you needed to.

Her room?

A low privet hedge had been planted behind the brick boundary wall. It followed the street, curving round the corner. Roz could see over it and between the trees to the back of the house. A conservatory was an obvious recent extension. Whoever lived in the house now had small children too. Brightly coloured plastic toys were scattered over the grass. A football. A chunky yellow slide. A covered sandpit.

Had the garden looked like that when she lived there? Had Mikey kicked a football around? Had her sisters played with her in the sand? All at once Roz yearned to know.

A fence divided the house from its neighbour, and a concrete path led straight along its edge to the bottom of the garden. Roz's eyes followed it down to a shed wedged up against the privet hedge and a memory reared up so suddenly that her heart lurched and she fisted a hand to her chest to hold it in, afraid that it might batter its way through her ribs otherwise.

She remembered.

Except it wasn't really a memory, more a jumble of sensations: darkness, bewilderment, the smell of damp earth and privet. An orange glow. And a fearful voice: *Stay here, Boo. Stay very quiet. Promise.*

'I promise,' she had said.

Chapter Nine

Alone in her still room, Jane untwisted the paper very carefully. Inside lay the spell, a mixture of seeds with dried shredded leaves and bark and a powdery substance she couldn't identify. Cautiously, she lifted it to her nose. It smelled strongly of garlic and she thought she caught the scent of gentian too, but for the rest she preferred not to guess. Who knew what dark arts Sybil had used to make her spell? Jane shivered a little at her own recklessness. If Robert or Margaret found out that she was putting a spell on him, their anger would know no bounds.

But she had the spell now. Jane closed her fingers around the paper. She couldn't throw it away. She would have to go through with it.

She stood with the spell in her hand, pondering how best to use it. In the end she decided to steep it in a little wine, and add it to one of Robert's favourite dishes. Jane set the maids to readying the rest of the meal and prepared a small dish of capon boiled in a white broth with her own hands. She simmered a capon with prunes, dates and raisins, and boiled up almonds for a broth. In the still room, she strained the spell and carried the wine through to the kitchen and, at the very last minute, when no one was looking, she poured it into the broth. Her heart was jumping in her throat, fast and hard.

It was done.

Now she had to make sure that Robert ate it. Jane had puzzled over how to make sure that only Robert was served the spell, but luck was with her and the Holmwoods were dining alone that evening. She put a small portion of the broth into a bowl and carried it through to the hall where Robert was lounging at the table, cleaning his fingernails with his knife. Margaret sat beside him, inspecting each dish critically as she did every day even though she never cooked anything herself. 'Your sauce is too thin,' she would say. 'Not enough salt.'

That night she looked down her nose at the dishes Jane had prepared so carefully. There was a baked trout, and a spinach tart. Turnips filled with eggs. Stewed fillet of beef and a roast hare. A salad with all kinds of herbs. There were cakes and apples cooked with cinnamon and ginger and then the sweet-meats that Robert loved so.

And the capon cooked with almonds.

'Why is there so little of this?' Margaret demanded as Jane set it on the table in front of her husband.

'I'm sorry, Mother.' Jane kept her eyes lowered. 'The dish was spilled in the kitchen. This is all that was saved, but it is good, I think.'

'Clumsy girl,' sniffed Margaret. 'Robert, dearest, what will you eat?'

'I will take some of the beef.' Robert reached across, ignoring Jane as she took her seat at the end of the table and Annis set the last of the dishes out before dipping a curtsey and retreating to the kitchen. Jane wished she could go with her, but she had to see that Robert ate the potion. She tried not to stare as Robert and Margaret filled their plates, passing dishes between themselves, dipping their fingers in the basins of water and wiping them fastidiously on their napkins. They had the beef, some tart and the trout, while Jane fiddled with her knife and pretended to eat a piece of the roast hare. Why would Robert not taste the capon? She didn't dare offer it to him, though, in case he refused it. It was the kind of thing he would do. She had to sit quietly and behave as normal.

Still, she couldn't help tensing when Robert at last pulled the dish of capon towards him. He lowered his head and sniffed at it. 'Good,' he decided, and then to Jane's dismay, he offered the dish to his mother. 'Do you care for some capon? There is little enough of it.'

'I will take a little, and you may have the rest, sweeting,' said Margaret, who always spoke in a sugared voice to Robert, quite different to the one she used to snap at Jane and the maids. She stabbed a piece of the capon with her knife and spooned some of the sauce onto her plate before passing the dish back to Robert, who tore off some bread and dipped it into the broth before pushing it into his mouth.

'It's good,' he mumbled through the bread, still chewing. He glanced at Jane as if surprised to see her sitting at his board. 'You set a good table, wife.'

Jane was so surprised at the unexpected compliment that she thought at first that she must have misheard. 'I am glad you are pleased,' she said after a moment, but her mind was racing. Was it possible the spell was working already? Could one taste be enough to amend his humour and make him look on her more kindly?

She took a little of the trout but couldn't eat. Her entrails twisted and looped with nerves. Perhaps, she thought, he would start to feel amorous soon. Perhaps he would come to her that night.

Perhaps tonight would change everything.

That night, Jane took extra care as she prepared for bed. She made Annis bring a bowl of water to her chamber, and she washed under her armpits and her privy parts. She rubbed her teeth and Annis brushed her hair so that it fell long and straight and shining down her back.

'Good fortune to you,' Annis whispered as she set the brush back on the chest. She was the only one who knew about the spell, the only one who guessed how much it would mean to Jane to have a child.

When she had gone, Jane was left alone in the middle of the chamber, thrumming with a mixture of anticipation and apprehension. Robert hadn't indicated that he would come to her chamber, but surely the spell would be having its effect and turning his mind to love.

Or if not love, desire.

And if not desire, need.

He needed a son, she longed for a child, to be loved. Surely, *surely*, tonight he would leave his closet and come to her bed?

Dry-mouthed, Jane left the candle burning hopefully, hitched up her nightgown and clambered into the big bed. She lay beneath the coverlet, unable to get comfortable on the bolster, kicking at the weight of the blanket, staring up at the canopy. In the flickering candlelight the red cloth seemed to be moving in and out of the shadows, leaping in the darkness like flames.

Jane made herself lie still and listen to the sounds of the house settling for the night. She was waiting for the sound of footsteps on the boards outside, for the click as Robert lifted the latch. She heard the servants moving around overhead, a cough, a low-voiced grumble about hogging the bedclothes, the thump of a chest lid. She heard a dog barking and a sleepy curse from across the street. A baby's thin wail made her face twitch.

She waited and waited, but the latch never lifted. Spell or no spell, Robert wasn't coming.

A bubble of resentment was blocking her throat. Was she so grotesque? Jane ran her hands over her body through her shift, feeling the curve of her breasts, the dip of her waist, the line of her thighs. Perhaps she was too slender for Robert? He might want a woman with fuller breasts perhaps, or a fleshier body. She couldn't do much about her plain face, but she could try to eat more and make herself fat.

Oh, why didn't he come? She had been so hopeful when she

came home from the common, so sure that one tiny potion would make everything better. This might be her only chance. She had used all the potion tonight. She couldn't go out to Sybil again and say that she had failed. It was tonight, or never.

If Robert wouldn't come to her, she would go to him. She could go and ask what she could do to please him. The idea, terrifying in its simplicity, slid into Jane's brain. She pushed it away at first. How could she? He had made it clear he didn't want her in his closet. She would not dare.

But if she did not dare, there would be no baby.

Jane shifted restlessly in an agony of indecision. After all, why *shouldn't* she go? She was Robert's wife. She had a right to lie with her own husband.

Do you want to know how to please your husband? Margaret's words seemed to bounce off the canopy and Jane turned her face into the pillow as if she could block out the memory. The truth was that she knew what Robert wanted, but she didn't want to do the things that would please him. She didn't understand how they could give him pleasure.

Perhaps Sybil's spell would make his desires different, Jane tried to tell herself.

Ah, she could not lie here any longer! Suddenly, she was tired of waiting. It was all women ever did, Jane thought crossly. Sitting bolt upright, she threw back the coverlet. It was too hot to sleep anyway.

The rush matting was ridged beneath her bare feet as she trod over to the door and hesitated before lifting the latch very carefully and easing it open. The house was dark and quiet.

Behind her, the candle guttered and threw leering shadows around the room, and Jane waited in the doorway for her eyes to adjust to the darkness outside.

Robert would be asleep in his closet. She would sneak into his bed there, wake him with a kiss and hope that the spell would work its magic after all. And if it didn't, she would reach for his yard before he had a chance to push her away. She would do the things Margaret had told her to do to satisfy his gentlemanly desires.

At the thought Jane nearly turned round and went back into her chamber, but she thought of the child she would never see unless she acted, and she drew a deep breath and walked silently through the house and down the stairs.

The house looked different in the dark. The great hall was shadowy and still and strange, as if it had thrown on a different gown over the colourful hangings and cushions. The chests were dark shapes in the dim light, and the table was pushed back against the wall. Beneath her bare feet, the stone floor was cool.

Jane wasn't sure what made her stop in the middle of the hall. A sound, scampering across her hearing, a flicker of some- thing at the edge of her consciousness, something that made her eagerness evaporate. She stood very still and listened, and there it came again, a gasp, a groan, a grunt. Was he ill? She should run and find out, but instead she found herself staring at the corner of the hall and the passageway that led to the closet, and a dull dread began to drum along her veins. She didn't want to go and see what was happening in the closet, but she had to.

She moved jerkily towards the passage, her bare feet making no sound on the floor. It was as if someone else was moving her limbs, making her go forward when her head was screaming at her to turn round and run back up the stairs.

The passage was dark too, but she could see the flicker of candlelight where the closet door stood ajar. Silently, unwillingly, Jane walked up to the door. She could see inside without opening it. The desk where her husband sat and did whatever gentlemen did in their closets. An inkwell and a book. The fine mantelpiece and the burning embers of a fire burnt low. A chair before it. Margaret sat in it, legs lewdly splayed, skirts and smock hoisted high and bunched around her waist.

And Robert, on his knees before her, his face buried between her thighs, slurping at his mother's privy parts. Margaret's eyes were slitted, her lips peeled back in carnal pleasure, foul words tumbling from her as she thrust her hips towards him and knotted her fingers in his hair so that he could not pull back.

There was a roaring in Jane's ears. She went hot, and then cold, and then burningly hot again as she backed, unnoticed, from the door.

Her husband, his mother. Nausea heaved up into her throat without warning and Jane fell back against the passage wall, pressing her palm to her mouth to stop herself vomiting. She had known Margaret and her son doted on each other, but *this*? How could she have known such a thing? A depravity so unnatural had been beyond Jane's imagining.

Unless . . . The dread thought swooped out of the darkness. What if Sybil's spell were to blame? Margaret and Robert had both eaten the capon in its broth. Had that tipped them over into warped desire? Or had there always been this darkness between them? Jane remembered Margaret whispering in her ear all the things Robert liked to do, liked to have done to him. It hadn't occurred to Jane to wonder how his mother had known.

When the worst of the nausea had passed, Jane pushed herself away from the wall and made her way unsteadily back down the passage. The dark hall seemed to mock her. It had known all along. It was only minutes since Jane had come down the stairs so quietly, so carefully in case she woke Robert. So certain that a spell and a little effort on her part would be enough to change her husband.

Now Jane felt as if she were standing on the other side of a deep, dark chasm, looking back at her earlier innocent self with disbelief. Had she really not understood the wrongness at the very heart of the house? How could she have watched Margaret stroking Robert's face and not seen how unnatural they were together? But she, simple fool that she was, had thought that an old woman out on the common could mutter a few words over some herbs and make it all right.

And now what was she to do?

Jane faltered in the middle of the hall. Where did she think she was going? Up to her chamber to pretend that nothing had happened?

The image of Margaret's head tipped back, the lascivious smile that curled her lips as she urged Robert between her thighs was seared into the darkness, but when Jane closed her eyes, it was still there. She pressed her fingers to her mouth, fighting the disgust and the panic. She couldn't go back to bed, but where else could she go? What else could she do?

She thought of her father, of trying to explain to him what she had seen, but she knew what he would say. He wouldn't believe her. Henry Birkby had paid out a dowry and bought his family an entry into gentility. He would not be prepared to throw all that away for a megrim. She must be mistaken, Jane could hear him roaring already. Robert's mother? What a grotesque idea! It must have been another woman, and so what if it was? What was she thinking to spy on her husband in his closet anyway? A man was entitled to do what he wanted without his wife poking her nose in his affairs. Jane was a Holmwood now. She should go back to her husband and be glad of the roof over her head.

No, her father would not welcome her.

Jane stood stock-still in the dark, absorbing the truth. She had nowhere else to go, and there was nothing she could do.

So she walked back up the stairs, back to the great chamber. She climbed into the bed and pulled the coverlet over her. There would be no escape. There would be no child.

She didn't cry. What would be the point? She just turned on her side and curled herself tight like a cat. She refused to let herself think. She just listened to herself breathing and concentrated on lying very, very still.

'So, you'll have alarms on every floor, all controlled by a panel here.' The fire risk assessment officer was a quiet-faced man called Alan Martin. He tapped the floor plan spread on Roz's desk. 'It'll be linked directly through to the station and if there's any suggestion of fire, they'll be alerted. For a historic building like this, they'll respond instantly and send out a minimum of three fire appliances.' He smiled reassuringly at Roz. 'You'll be well covered.'

Roz just hoped he was right. Alan had spent the morning going round Holmwood House with her and together they had drawn up a fire plan. There was something steadying about his calm presence and it made it easier to go into the rooms she remembered so clearly as Jane.

Jane's discovery of the perverted relationship between Margaret and Robert was still disturbingly vivid in her mind, and she had been wary of going back to Holmwood House that morning. The wretchedness and disgust that swirled in her head had lasted all of Sunday and lingered still as she had walked over Ouse Bridge and up Micklegate.

'Come home,' Nick had said when she rang him.

Roz had told him about seeing the shed, and experiencing her first glimmer of memory. She'd told him that she was having strange dreams, too, but not about wandering around the streets without being aware of who she was. Not that she was afraid that Jane was real, that she had a hold on Roz that was tightening inexorably every day. She wanted to tell him – she *would* tell him – but she didn't know how to begin explaining over the phone, how to make him understand the strange mixture of horror and fascination that Jane's life held for her.

She would tell him when she saw him, Roz promised herself. She wasn't a fool. Whatever was happening to her, it was clear that she couldn't deal with it by herself, but she wasn't ready to let Jane derail all her plans. She'd come to York to do a job.

Stubborn, Nick called her, usually with a sigh. Stubborn, wilful, pig-headed.

But she was the one who had compromised, Roz always thought, resentment scraping at her however much she tried to keep it at bay. She had accepted that Nick wasn't ready for a family. She had agreed that they would carry on as they were: no ties, no responsibilities, no broken nights or dirty nappies for them. 'We're free to do whatever we want,' Nick had said persuasively. 'Let's enjoy it while we can. When we do have kids we'll be glad we made the most of having money and time to ourselves.'

So Roz had thrown herself into making a career for herself instead. And now she had a chance to make the leap into a successful freelance business, suddenly Nick wanted her to give it all up and go home, because he had a son now and had realized that he was a family man after all.

Her shoulders were hunched up to her ears, her knuckles white around the phone. Roz made herself relax her grip and lowered her shoulders with an effort. She had enough to worry about without picking away at old scabs.

'Nick, you know I can't come home yet,' she said, unable to prevent the impatience feathering her voice. 'This is my career. I can't just give it up because of a few bad dreams.'

At the other end of the phone, Nick sighed. 'You sound

strung out,' he said bluntly. 'I don't like it. I think going back to York is getting to you. If you're starting to remember, it could be more stressful than you realize, Roz. I think you should consider some therapy.'

'You make it sound like I'm losing my mind!' Roz wriggled her shoulders, which were tensing up again. What if Nick was right? What if she was having some kind of breakdown? Somewhere she had a brother who was a sociopath or schizophrenic, depending on which report Nick had been reading. Who was to say there wasn't a strain of instability in her family?

'I'm just talking about someone to help you deal with the reality of what happened in the past,' said Nick patiently. 'I told you about Rita before. She'll help you recover the memories you lost and come to terms with them. I think it would help you, Roz, I really do.'

Roz rubbed her forehead. She was tired and her head ached. She'd been unable to get back to sleep after waking in the middle of the night, curled in a foetal position, just as Jane had lain in the great chamber.

'All right,' she said, 'I'll try it. But I can't drop everything and come down for that,' she warned before Nick could start making appointments. 'I'll come home this weekend as we agreed, and I could probably come back a bit later on Monday. Find out if there's any chance of me seeing her on Monday morning.'

For the rest of the Sunday, Roz had stayed in the flat in St Andrewgate. She had her laptop, and plenty of work to catch up on, but she kept stopping to lift her head and listen, or look hard around the room, waiting to see if the world would shift, if she would find herself wrenched into another time, another life. Sometimes she could have sworn the air bent strangely, like a voile billowing in a gust of breeze, so that she almost, *almost*, caught a glimpse of a different world. A darker, dirtier, more intense world. Jane's world.

Roz had always thought of the past in linear terms, something that had happened and was over, but now she wasn't so sure. Now it felt as if time was looped, knotted, as if the sixteenth century was just the other side of an invisible veil, as if all it would take was a tiny rip, the smallest tear in time, and the past would be there, waiting, more present than the present Roz had always taken for granted before she came to York.

By the time Monday morning came round, Roz wasn't sure whether to be relieved or disappointed that Jane hadn't reappeared. She was tense with waiting for things to change, just as Jane had been, and she was glad of the distraction of showing Alan Martin around Holmwood House. His was a blessedly sane, solid presence. His calm blue gaze didn't flicker in the great chamber. He didn't mention the dragging, desperate atmosphere in the hall, or the faint, rickety sound of an electric train rattling around a miniature track. He didn't comment on the lingering smell of smoke in the attics.

To Alan, it was just a house. Roz watched him carefully, but it was clear he felt there was nothing amiss. He couldn't feel Jane, accompanying them, pressing close. Roz went to the loo before Alan arrived, and when she washed her hands, for all her bravery and insistence on staying in York, she couldn't bring herself to look in the mirror. Jane was there behind her. Roz could *feel* her, but the thought of raising her eyes and seeing her reflected, or worse, seeing Jane's face in place of her own, made the skin on Roz's skull shrink. She kept her gaze firmly lowered and concentrated fiercely on lathering her hands. On rinsing them under the tap. On trying not to notice the faint tremor.

Now she summoned a smile for Alan. It would take more than a fire plan to reassure her, but she couldn't tell him that. 'There'll be no problem about getting everything set up before the launch?'

'We'll get it all sorted in good time,' he promised as he got to his feet. He held out a hand. 'It was nice to meet you, Roz.'

'And you.' Roz shook his hand and found a better smile this time. 'I'll show you out.'

She led him down the staircases, marvelling that he couldn't see the smoke that hung in the air like a fine gauze, or smell the bitter stink that drifted, faint but unmistakable, after them.

'Strange place,' Alan commented as they walked past the great chamber. He had no idea, Roz thought. 'What's it like working here?'

'It's certainly different,' she said. 'I was working for an art gallery in London before I went freelance.'

'You're not from York then?'

Roz ducked that one. 'I grew up in London.'

'It's just that Acclam's an unusual name. I've only come across it once before, a long time ago now, when I was in the service.'

'The service?'

'The fire service. I was a fireman – fire*fighter*, I should say.' He caught himself with a downward turn of his mouth. 'For twenty-odd years.'

Roz stopped with her hand on the door and looked at him. 'In 1986?'

'Yes, I was – ' He broke off. 'You're the little girl I found in the shed,' he said slowly.

'Yes.' It felt like a confession. The word shuddered out of her on a long, falling breath. 'So you remember that fire?'

'It's hard to forget the bad ones.' His expression sobered, remembering. 'I carried one of your sisters out of the house that night.'

Roz could imagine him in uniform, his face grim and grimy with smoke, the limp body of a little girl in his arms. Had it been Amanda or Emily? Her throat felt tight and she swallowed. She hadn't wanted to know any more about the way her sisters had died, but Alan was a tangible link to a past that seemed to be drawing closer whatever she decided.

'Would you tell me about it?'

They found a coffee shop and sat on stools at the high bar, looking out at the street. Now that she was there, Roz didn't know where to begin. She watched Alan's capable fingers ripping open a packet of sugar and emptying it into his coffee. 'What do you remember?' he asked at last.

'Nothing. I didn't even know about the fire until a few months ago. I was adopted by my aunt, who told me my family had been killed in a car accident.'

His brows rose. 'You don't remember *anything*?'

'No . . .' But she was thinking about looking at the shed, and the sense of confusion and fear that had crashed over her. 'Not really.'

'It must have been a shock when you found out the truth.'

'You could say that.' Roz cradled her hands around her cup. 'Mostly I felt stupid,' she confessed. 'I mean, I should have realized something was odd before. When I look back, there are all sorts of things my aunt did and said that make sense now, but I never queried them at the time. Like, if my entire family had been killed in a car crash, why wasn't I in the car with them? It never occurred to me to wonder why I didn't remember anything from when I was small. I was five, after all. You'd think I'd remember something about the fire. You'd think I'd remember *you.*'

'Not necessarily. Your brain probably dealt with the trauma by wiping out all memories of the night. It's quite a common reaction, I've heard. But the memories are probably still there,' said Alan. 'There are people who could help you recover them if you wanted.'

It was what Nick was suggesting. 'I'm not sure I really want to remember,' said Roz, sipping her coffee. 'I'd like to know what happened without necessarily reliving it.'

'I can understand that,' he said. 'A fire is a terrible thing.'

For a second, terror twisted her stomach as the wild snap and crack of flames filled her head, the foul belch of smoke, and coffee sloshed into her saucer as she put her cup down unsteadily.

'I think it must be.' She drew a breath. 'Tell me what *you* remember.'

'When we arrived at the fireground that night, the fire was already well established on the top floor. Piecing it together afterwards the fire investigation officer thought the fire had been laid in a wastepaper basket or something similar – probably some paper drenched with petrol from a lawnmower – and then a trail laid to outside the bedroom door.'

'So it was definitely deliberate? There's no chance Mikey started the fire by accident and then was too frightened to tell anyone what had happened?'

'I'm afraid not. It must have been carefully planned. He'd have had to get hold of the petrol and take it up to his bedroom. It was a very unsophisticated fire, but then he was only eleven, and there was no Google in those days. But by all accounts he was a smart lad. He'd have worked out how to start the fire and lay a trail.' Alan shook his head. 'He was probably disappointed that it didn't take hold faster.'

Roz was still mopping up the mess in her saucer. She was trying to imagine having a brother, a boy who had calmly laid a trail of petrol and lit a match. Who was disappointed when the fire he'd built so carefully didn't burst into spectacular flames.

'If it was slow to get going, why didn't everyone get out?' It had puzzled her, why her parents hadn't stamped the fire out, carried them all to safety.

'Once the initial fire burned out, the room would have filled with smoke.' Alan picked his words carefully, pedantically, as if he were giving evidence in a court. 'We found your mother at the top of the stairs, where she'd collapsed on her way to the bedrooms. The fire inspector surmised that she'd been woken by the smoke, and run to you first of all. Instead of calling 999, she carried you out and hid you in the shed, and then she seems to have tried to rescue the others, but by then the heat from the fire would have broken the window, creating a backdraught and . . . boom!' His mouth turned down and he shook his head regretfully again. 'There wouldn't have been anything she could have done. The fire exploded and consumed the whole of the top floor.

'I was on the lead appliance, on the BA team – breathing apparatus,' he added when Roz looked puzzled. 'That meant we were first inside. The neighbours who called in the fire said there was a family of six in the house, so we headed up to the bedrooms at the back. We found your mother first, then your father, who had tried to get to his daughters, and last of all we found the little girls. They were huddled in the wardrobe, poor kids.'

Roz flinched at the image of the two terrified children, clinging together in the dark and smoke. 'Why the wardrobe?'

'It doesn't make sense, but who expects kids to be thinking sensibly? It's a natural instinct to hide when you sense danger, so they must have been woken by the smoke and decided that they would be safe if they hid.' Alan looked at Roz's face. 'They wouldn't have known about the fire. They would have been asphyxiated by the smoke long before the flames got to them.'

'And . . . Mikey?' It was an effort to say his name.

'It wasn't until we'd been through the house with another BA team that we realized there were two children unaccounted for. At that point we instituted a search and that's when we found you in the shed. I'll never forget your huge eyes,' said Alan. 'You weren't hiding, you were just standing there. You were just a little thing,' he remembered. 'You were sucking your thumb, and clutching a toy dog. I asked you if you would give him to me so I could pick you up, but you wouldn't let go.'

A memory was struggling to the surface, flailing, dim but unmistakable. A dog, battered and soft, the smell of it on her pillow. The comfort of burying her face in its fur. 'Pook.' The name emerged as if out of nowhere, so clear that she couldn't believe she had forgotten it.

'Is that what you called it? You wouldn't let go of it. In the end I had to pick you up together. I carried you both out of there myself, and you didn't say a thing.'

Roz's smile was crooked. 'Maybe I can say thank you now. I must have been glad to see someone.'

'It's hard to tell. It was a cold night and you were chilled and obviously traumatized. I'm not that surprised you don't remember, to be honest. It must have been a terrifying experience for a small child.'

'But why did my mother hide me?' asked Roz in frustration. 'Why didn't she just call the fire brigade and get everyone out?'

'I don't know.' Alan sighed and stirred his coffee. 'Nobody knows.'

Another image blew through her – a figure slumped despairingly in a doorway – and then it was gone, leaving only a fragmentary echo in Roz's head: *What have you done?* She put a hand uncertainly to her forehead, and Alan looked at her in concern.

'You okay?'

'Yes, I . . . I thought I remembered something, but it's gone. I'm not sure.' She shook her head, trying to dislodge the memory, but it had vanished, except for those four lingering words. *What have you done?* She glanced at Alan. 'Did you see Mikey that night?'

'I did. I didn't know who he was at first,' he said. 'We were looking for him, but we thought he might be hiding. I was carrying you up from the shed when I saw a boy standing in the middle of the garden, watching the house. He was fully dressed, and I thought he'd come to rubberneck.

'You see it quite a lot in boys that age,' Alan told Roz, who was twisting the spoon between her fingers, wanting but not wanting to know at the same time. 'Eleven to fourteen is typical. They're fascinated by fire, and usually they grow out of it, but there was something eerie about Mikey's expression. He wasn't just rapt in the flames, he was . . .' He paused, searching for the right word. 'Gloating, I suppose,' he decided in the end. But it was more than that.

'I'm not sure how to describe it.' Alan scratched his head, puzzling over the memory. 'It sounds a bit melodramatic, but that was the closest I've ever come to seeing evil,' he said, and a quick, uncontrollable shiver jerked down Roz's spine.

Evil. Such a powerful word, and out of place in this ordinary coffee shop, where the two women behind her were discussing a mutual friend's relationship crisis, and a young man was slouched low in an armchair, scrolling through his phone. A mother manoeuvred a pushchair through the door, which was held open by an elderly man with a kindly smile. The baristas were cheerful and efficient, and the hum of conversation was punctuated by the hiss and grind of the coffee machines. It was all so normal, so ordinary. It was no place to be talking about evil.

'I don't mind telling you, it gave me the creeps,' Alan went on. 'I jerked my head at my mate to get him away, and that's when he turned and saw me with you in my arms. His face changed completely. It was weird. One minute he had this inhuman expression, and the next he just seemed confused. He looked at you, and he just said, "Boo". I wasn't sure whether he was trying to be funny or what.'

Roz smiled painfully. 'Boo was my nickname in the family, apparently.'

'Ah.' She saw him digest that information and file it away before carrying on with his story. 'Right then, I could have sworn that he was just a lost little boy, but I remember how you looked back at him and shrank into me, and the next second it was like a hand had wiped all the expression off his face. He turned back to the fire. "It's burning," he said, and he smiled.'

Alan picked up his coffee, but Roz could see the twitch of his shoulders at the memory. 'It still gives me the heebie-jeebies to think about that smile,' he confessed. 'Anyway, my mate took him round the front, and one of the neighbours recognized him. We'd been looking for him, of course, thinking that he would be hiding like you. That's when it became clear that he'd set the fire.'

'There wasn't any doubt that he did it?'

'I'm afraid not. He was fully dressed, and they found traces of liquid petrol on his clothes. I heard later that when they interviewed him all he would say was, "It wasn't me," but all the evidence said that it was him.'

Chapter Ten

Roz was silent for a moment. She turned her bangles round and round on her arm, thinking about the brother she had never known. The brother who had calmly set fire to a house and watched his family die with a smile.

'When I spoke to my aunt's friend, she said they'd diagnosed Mikey with early onset schizophrenia,' she said. 'I don't know much about it, but perhaps he felt that he didn't do it because he had someone else in his head.'

Like Jane was in *her* head. Roz shuddered. What if she were schizophrenic like her brother? The thought of seeing a doctor, of explaining what was happening, having tests and being given drugs was appalling. She caught herself manically turning the bangles on her wrist and made herself stop with a grimace. She didn't *feel* ill, but then, perhaps Mikey hadn't either. She would have to talk to Nick at the weekend and take his suggestion of a hypnotherapist seriously.

'I'm sorry,' said Alan, watching her expression. 'I didn't mean to upset you.'

'No, it's okay.' She mustered a smile. 'I'm glad you told me. My husband did some research and found some accounts of the fire, and Karen – my aunt's friend – told me what she could, but it's not the same as hearing from somebody who was actually there.'

'You haven't been in touch with your brother yourself?'

Nick had said that she ought to try and track down Mikey and find out for herself what had happened and why, but Roz had resisted the idea. What was the point? Knowing why wouldn't bring her parents or her sisters back, and she had managed fine without a brother up to now. Why go out of her way to get in touch with one who was a murderer and an arsonist? Roz didn't think that would be much of a family reunion.

'No. I mean, if Mikey did have schizophrenia, then I'm sorry he was ill, but he must be better now or they wouldn't have released him.'

'That's true. There would have been a risk assessment to decide whether he was a threat to society or not.'

'That's what Jim Hebden said. He was a police officer who worked on the case,' Roz said when Alan lifted his brows. She told him about the letter she had found in her aunt's papers, and his enquiring look turned to a frown.

'It's very unorthodox to write like that,' he said disapprovingly.

'Jim said that, but he was obviously concerned enough to

write. He thought Mikey was manipulative and might still be dangerous, which didn't exactly make me want to rush out and find him. Besides, I gathered they gave him a new identity when he was released.'

Alan nodded. 'They would have done. It was a tragic case, and Acclam is an unusual name. People in York would remember.'

'I worked it out. He was six years older than me, so he'd be coming up for forty now, but I've no idea what he looks like. He's white and brown-haired, but that doesn't exactly narrow things down.'

Roz looked through the window at the shoppers and tourists wandering in the middle of the pedestrianized street. There were plenty of men of about forty passing by. Some of them were clearly tourists, but with others it was harder to tell. Men in T-shirts and jeans, apparently under the impression it was still high summer. Men in suits, walking briskly. Men in hoodies, and shirts, and jackets, and overalls. 'He could be Mikey,' she said, pointing. 'Or him . . . or him . . . or him. There's no way of telling. He might not even be in York any more. That letter was nearly twenty years old. He could have moved on. I can look at every fortyish-looking brown-haired man who passes me in the street and wonder if he's my brother, or I can let it go. So . . .' She lifted her shoulders and let them fall. 'I think I have to accept that somewhere I have a brother and leave it at that.'

*

'Where have you been?' Helen had been watching out for Roz, who didn't even have the grace to look embarrassed at being caught strolling into the office this late in the morning. She even had the nerve to raise her brows at Helen's tone.

'Out for coffee,' she said in that snotty southern voice of hers.

That was typical. The rest of them were happy with a mug of instant, but that wouldn't be smart enough for Roz, would it? She would have to go to some coffee shop and have a *latte* or some pretentious cappuccino with soya milk or some such nonsense.

Today she had on boots and leggings and some kind of weird elegantly asymmetrical top that Helen couldn't put a name to but which she bet cost a fortune. It would look ridiculous if Helen wore it, but on Roz it looked striking and stylish. Her hair fell shining to her shoulders. There were silver bangles chinking at her wrist and Helen caught the wink of silver dangling from her ears. She hated the way Roz always made her feel frumpy and dumpy and out of place. *Roz* was the one who didn't belong, and she ought to feel that way, instead of giving Helen that long, cool stare of hers.

'Sir Adrian's been looking for you,' Helen said accusingly.

'Okay.'

No apology, no awkwardness at the idea that she'd kept her boss waiting. Oh no, Roz just swanned past her to Sir Adrian's office like it was hers. Helen curled her fingers into fists. God, she wanted to slap that smug look off Roz's face. She *hated* her. She even hated the way Roz walked, straight-backed like a model, like the world owed her a living.

Helen could just imagine her growing up a pampered princess, with Mummy and Daddy fawning over her. She'd seen the wedding ring on Roz's finger. There would be some rich husband in the background, a banker probably, and a massive house in London, while Roz played at her little job.

Events director! Helen's lip curled. Anyone could arrange an event. She did it all the time for Sir Adrian, but she didn't feel the need to give herself a fancy title.

When Sir Adrian called out for a cup of coffee for Roz, Helen poured some from the percolator into a cup, added some milk and very deliberately spat in it.

Roz didn't want coffee. She tried explaining that she had already had some that morning, but Adrian was so insistent that she couldn't be bothered to keep refusing. She was still thinking about the fire and her brother and whether schizophrenia was hereditary. She should have thought of that before, but until these episodes with Jane it had never occurred to her that she might be mentally ill. She would need to google it.

She barely listened to Adrian wittering on about his extensive contacts in Yorkshire and when Helen ungraciously set a cup of coffee by her side she glanced up with a brief absent-minded smile of thanks but ignored it.

'So you'll come?'

Belatedly, Roz realized that Adrian was looking expectant, and she gave herself a mental shake. 'I'm so sorry,' she apologized. 'I was miles away there for a moment. Come where?'

A hurt expression flickered over Adrian's face. Clearly she

was supposed to have been hanging on his every word, the way Helen no doubt did. Roz caught herself. She was being bitchy. Buffoon or not, Adrian was her boss and this was her career. She had to concentrate.

'To Holme Hall,' he said. 'As I was saying, I'm having one of my house parties,' he explained, oozing self-satisfaction. 'I know one or two people, who shall be nameless, who have been angling for an invitation for quite a long time. They're really quite sought after.' He folded his hands on his stomach and leant back with a complacent smile. 'I've been thinking about the launch and this time I've invited people with *connections*. I think it would be useful for you to meet them socially.'

'Well, er, that sounds lovely,' said Roz, grimacing inwardly. A house party with Adrian Holmwood and 'people with connections' – she couldn't think of a worse way to spend a weekend. The worst thing was that Adrian was probably right. It *would* be a good opportunity to make some contacts. She was new to York and she couldn't afford to turn down the chance to make any connections. 'When were you thinking of?'

'This weekend.'

'Oh, I'm sorry,' she said, relieved. 'I've arranged to go back to London this weekend. Nick's expecting me,' she added. No harm in reminding Adrian that she was married. In spite of his carefully cultivated air of old-fashioned distinction, Adrian had always struck Roz as asexual. From a distance, he looked like the kind of man who would have a wife who rode and a bevy of children at public school, but close up, Roz had never picked up any signals of interest in women or men. He seemed to be acting a part, the constant touching no more than directions on a script called *How to be a Country Gentleman*.

But she might be wrong, Roz conceded. She had been wrong plenty of times before.

Adrian was extravagantly downcast. 'Oh, but couldn't you rearrange? I really do think you should come if you can. Couldn't Nick come to York? You could bring him to the party. There's plenty of room. Do at least ask him,' Adrian persisted when Roz hesitated. 'It would be *marvellous* if you could come.'

Roz had seen pictures of Holme Hall, a wonderful early Jacobean mansion. It would be interesting to see it. As for Nick . . . well, he always claimed he wanted to be an author. Freelance journalism was a stepping stone to his first novel, he said. A weekend at Holme Hall would be good material for him.

'I'll ask him,' she promised.

She left the coffee untasted.

Jeff was out in the long, narrow yard with Lucy when Roz came out of the Foundation, obviously on her way back to her office. She looked distracted but stopped at the sight of them. 'What are you two doing?'

'I was just asking Jeff whether he remembered any outbuildings out here,' said Lucy.

Roz looked at him in surprise. 'I didn't realize you'd been here from the beginning of the restoration.'

'I used to come here as kid,' he said.

'Someone said there used to be a model shop here.' The clearness of her pale grey eyes was still a shock. He didn't like the way they seemed to look inside him, as if she knew that he had lied when he said he couldn't hear the electric train still rattling round and round and round in the great hall.

'That's right.' His gaze slid away from hers. 'That's why I came here.' There was a knot in his stomach: panic, guilt, resentment. He didn't want to long for her absolution. It was all her fault. She had made him do it. She hadn't understood him, hadn't understood what he needed –

No, that wasn't right. Jeff frowned. How could his little sister have made him do anything? It wasn't her he had both loved and hated. So why did it feel all at once as if she was to blame for everything? He rubbed his temple, trying to clear his head. Pain was banging behind his eyes, and his thoughts were confused, slipping and slithering away out of his grasp.

He'd been glad at first that Roz hadn't recognized him, but now he wasn't so sure. Perhaps he should have told her straight away, but what could he have said? *Oh, by the way, I'm your half-brother, you know, the one who killed our mother?*

He shouldn't have come back to York. He shouldn't have come back *here*, to Holmwood House. But this was where he needed to be, Jeff felt it in his bones. He was different here, stronger, more certain. At least when Roz wasn't there, looking through him with those clear eyes. Sir Adrian could boast all he liked, but the house was Jeff's domain. He liked it when he was there on his own. He would walk across the hall and listen to his footsteps, firm and in command, and he would feel himself unfurl and expand with power, and he'd know that this was the only place he had ever felt truly at home. He belonged here, but he hadn't been able to enjoy it in the same way since Roz had arrived. Jeff wished she would go back to London. She made him feel . . . confused.

'We're thinking of extending the house into the yard next year,' Lucy was saying. 'There must have been a kitchen, and maybe a dairy of some kind or a brewery. I've been doing some research and I was wondering if there might have been a still room. The mistress of a big house like this would probably have made her own remedies.'

'Of course I make my own.' Roz sounded puzzled. She turned and pointed down the yard, and the hairs on the back of Jeff's neck rose in a slow wave as something slid through the air, shifting and bending it, wiping the Roz-ness from her face, flattening her vowels. 'My still room is there,' she said.

'Your sister is here.' Annis found Jane in the still room, making an ointment. Robert had been complaining of an itch, and Jane was carefully measuring out the oil she had made from bay berries earlier in the year. She had steeped quicksilver in vinegar ready to be mixed with camphor and the bay oil.

Jane liked being in the still room. It was quiet and clean, and even on this chill February day the air smelt like summer, fragrant with the bunches of herbs dried and tied and hung from the ceiling: lavender and thyme, sweet marjoram and pennyroyal, wormwood and sage and mint and chamomile and other herbs she gathered in the summer. In pride of place stood a little apothecary's chest, its drawers full of berries, of hawthorn and sweet briars, and seeds and dried rose petals.

The still room was Jane's refuge, the only place in the house that felt like hers, and where she could arrange the bottles, bowls and jars the way she wanted. She looked after the rest of the house, but the other rooms were dark and oppressive, engrained with resentment, and no matter how often she bade the maids clean and polish and lay fresh herbs the air smelt tainted, with a foul undercurrent that struck the back of Jane's throat.

Nothing had ever been said, but Margaret and Robert had somehow known that she had discovered them, and they no longer bothered to conceal their depravity when the three of them were alone. Robert abandoned his futile visits to the great chamber, and Jane lay alone every night, mistress in name only. The servants must know, but what could they do? Like Jane, they must bear the offence of it, or else lose their posts.

Small wonder Jane spent as much time as she could in the still room.

'My sister?' She put down the oil and wiped her hands on her apron. Juliana rarely came to Holmwood House. She liked Jane to visit her. 'Is she well?'

'Can't say.' Annis sniffed. She didn't approve of Juliana, who she considered flighty and spoilt. 'She's in't chamber, anyhows, and in a right old state. Nowt new there.'

'I'd better go to her.' Jane tried not to sigh as she pushed the stopper into the oil jar. She had been enjoying the tranquillity of the still room and whatever mood Juliana was in, it was never tranquil.

'Where have you been?' Juliana pounced as soon as Jane pushed open the door to the chamber. 'Didn't Annis tell you I needed to see you straight away? I told her it was important! She hates me, I know. She dawdled off as if I had all the time in the world to wait. You should keep your servants in better order, Jane.'

Juliana's eyes were feverishly bright, and there were hectic spots of colour in her cheeks. Jane smoothed her apron down. She had learnt to keep her voice very calm when dealing with Juliana in this state.

'Annis doesn't hate you, Juliana. I was in the still room and it took her some time to find me. Now, come, sit by the fire and tell me what is so important.' She steered Juliana over to the turned chair and plumped up the cushions. 'You're cold,' she said. 'Would you like some wine to warm you?'

'Yes . . . no . . . I don't know!' Juliana threw herself wretchedly into the chair. 'I am too unhappy to know what to do!'

'Come now.' Jane sat on the stool beside her sister and took her hand. 'What is wrong? Is it our father?'

'No, he is interested only in his grazing,' said Juliana bitterly. 'You do not know what it is like for me, Jane, in that house on my own. You live in luxury here with your fine husband, and you have no idea how wretched I am.'

Jane thought of the silent meals, of her lonely bed. She thought of Robert on his knees in front of Margaret, and she said nothing.

'I am lonely,' said Juliana, her beautiful mouth downturned in a petulant curve.

'You could visit the neighbours,' Jane suggested, but Juliana dismissed the local gossips with a bitter twist of her hand.

'Butchers' wives!' she said, her beautiful face curdled with contempt.

'You are a butcher's daughter,' Jane reminded her in a mild voice. 'As am I.'

'You have left the Shambles far behind,' said Juliana jealously. 'Why can my father not arrange a great marriage for me too? And why do you not make me a connection, you with all your fine kin now?'

'I have little influence,' Jane said quietly. 'Marriage is not always what we expect, Juliana.' More than that she could not say. 'I am sure our father will find you a good husband. He loves you dearly, you know that. He will want only the best of husbands for you. You must be patient.'

'I cannot be patient!' Juliana leapt up in a whirl of skirts. 'I need a husband now, and not some sweaty butcher!'

Jane watched, a frown in her eyes, as her sister paced furiously. She hoped Juliana wasn't working herself up into a full-blown tantrum. It could take hours to coax her round from one of those, and there was still the meal to be prepared.

'I will talk to our father,' she promised. 'I will tell him you are ready for marriage.'

'It is too late!' Juliana swung round with an anguished cry and threw herself down on the floor to bury her face in Jane's lap. 'Oh Jane, you have to help me! Promise me you'll help me!'

'Juliana, what is it?' Jane stroked the soft golden curls. 'Of course I will help you, dear one, but you must tell me what is the matter.'

Juliana's answer was muffled in Jane's skirts.

'Juliana?' Jane lifted her sister's chin and looked her in the eye. 'Tell me.'

'I am with child,' Juliana whispered.

Jane's first thought was not a thought at all but a feeling: envy, jabbing like a hot poker in her entrails. Then cool reason washed over her and left her chilled with a sense of the disaster that had struck sure at the centre of their lives. Outside in the street, she could hear the clop of hooves, the rumble of a cart on the cobbles. Someone was laughing, two women were quarrelling. Right underneath the chamber window, Francis Bain and Henry Warriner were having a loud conversation about whether or not William Byrnand should be given a hogshead of Gascony wine. What did it matter? Jane thought wildly. How could they be fussing and fretting about council business when Juliana's future was cracking and crumbling into ruin?

'Are you sure?'

'My flowers haven't come down for two months now. I went to that old witch out on the common, but she said there was nothing she could do.'

Jane was still struggling to understand. 'Juliana, how is this possible? When . . . who is the father? You must marry him without delay.'

'I cannot,' Juliana muttered.

'If you have lain with him, you can marry him,' said Jane, unable to keep the tartness from her voice.

'He is already married. Oh, do not look at me like that, Jane!' Juliana flung herself away. 'You do not know how lonely I have been since you left.'

'Juliana, how could you?' Jane couldn't disguise her shock.

'He made me feel . . . excited.' In spite of herself, a smile of reminiscence curved Juliana's mouth and Jane's heart twisted a little. How did that feel? she wondered. 'And he is handsome, and he makes me feel special. Don't pull that sour face,' she added snappishly. 'You have a husband to pleasure you.'

Jane sighed. 'Who is he?'

'John Harper,' said Juliana sulkily.

'The tailor?' Jane was horrified. She remembered him measuring her for her wedding gown, that lascivious smile, that carnal mouth. 'How in the name of sweet reason did you meet him?'

'I wanted a new gown.' Juliana plucked at her skirts. 'He came to the house.'

'But where was Mary? Or Alison?'

'I sent Mary away. I do not like her hanging around me all the time.'

'And now you are with child,' said Jane heavily.

'I've tried to kill it but I can't.' Juliana began to weep. 'Once I grow large, I will be ruined. I will never be married!'

'Our father is wealthy. He will buy you a husband.'

'A gentleman won't take me,' said Juliana between sobs. 'I won't be married off to some clodhopping journeyman or a fat old man. I won't, I won't, I won't! I would rather be dead! You said you would help me, Jane. If you do not, I will throw myself in the river!'

Jane's head was aching. 'Calm yourself, sister,' she said wearily. 'I will think of something.'

'What?'

Jane didn't know. 'I can't think while you are pacing around like that, Juliana. Come and sit down.'

Juliana sat dabbing at her eyes, while Jane tried to think. It was a bitter irony that Juliana, who didn't want a child, should be carrying one, while she, who yearned for one, had no chance of –

Unless.

Unless . . . Jane sat up straighter.

'What?' demanded Juliana, watching her expression.

'We will go to Holme Hall,' said Jane slowly. Very slowly, thinking as she searched for the right words, testing them as they came out of her mouth. 'We'll say you are unwell and in need of country air and quiet. You will give birth there. Nobody need know.'

'Yes!' Juliana clapped her hands. 'And then I can come home. There will be a woman to take the baby,' she added as a careless afterthought.

'*I* will take the baby,' said Jane.

'You?'

Juliana looked astonished, and Jane coloured. 'I have not conceived,' she said with difficulty. 'My husband longs for a son.'

'You are barren?'

'Perhaps,' said Jane, although in truth she had no idea. If Juliana thought so, she might be more willing to keep the secret. The more Jane thought about it, the more certain she became. Surely, *surely*, if she gave Robert a son, things would be better? The Holmwoods wanted it as much as she did.

'Your husband will know the child is not his,' said Juliana.

'Not necessarily.' Jane wouldn't meet her eyes. 'We will say the babe is a seven-month child. I will write and say that I am staying in the country until I give birth.'

'What if he comes?'

'He won't.' Robert had little interest in Holme Hall, and Jane knew he would be only too pleased to get rid of her for a few months. She wouldn't think of what he and Margaret would do while she was away. 'Annis can come with us. She can keep the other servants away in case it be too obvious that I am not increasing. Then you will give birth and I will pretend the babe is mine.' A warmth spread through Jane at the thought.

'Do you think it could work?' Juliana asked hopefully.

'I think so. I will talk to Annis.'

Annis pursed her lips when Jane told her the plan. 'Haven't you forgotten summat?'

'What?'

'Even your husband must know how babes are conceived,' she said bluntly. 'You're going to have to get him back to your bed before you go.'

Jane swallowed and looked away. 'He doesn't love me,' she said, low-voiced.

'You can get a babe without love,' said Annis. 'But you'll still need to get him back to your bed and you'll need to arouse him. Think you can do that?'

Jane's flush deepened. She remembered how crudely Margaret had spoken to her. *Take him in your mouth*, she had said. *Let him bend you over and go at you like a dog. He doesn't*

want to see your nimiy-piminy face, and he doesn't want to
hear you bleating about love. You are just a cunny to him.

Her gorge rose just thinking of the things she would have to
do, but if she wanted a baby, this might be her only chance.

'I know what to do,' she said.

That night, Jane made herself look as good as she could.
'Sure you can do this?' Annis asked doubtfully, as she helped
Jane on with her nightshift.

Nausea rolled in Jane's stomach, but she nodded.

'I must,' she said.

'You could always let Juliana sort out her own problems,'
Annis pointed out.

'I promised our mother I would look after her.'

'You were a bairn. Do you always keep your promises?'

Jane thought about Ellen, swinging at the end of a rope
because she had told after all. 'Not always,' she said. 'But this is
one I will keep. Besides, Annis, what else will happen to the
baby? Juliana talked of giving it to a country couple, but such
folk need money to feed a child. They have little enough of their
own. Where is Juliana to find enough to pay them regularly? I
only have money for housekeeping. Juliana is so desperate to
come back to York and make a good marriage that I fear she
would throw a few coins to a countrywoman and leave the
babe and that will be that as far as she is concerned.'

'I'd not give the babe much of a chance if that happened,'
Annis agreed.

'It will die if I do not save it,' said Jane. Already she had
seen one newborn baby die before it had barely drawn a breath.

She would not see it again. She *would not*. Her soft mouth set in a stubborn line. 'If I must do these things to make sure the babe lives, then I will.'

She let Annis brush out her hair. It was her best feature, a warm brown like sunlight pouring through honey, and it fell long and straight to her waist. There was no point in hoping that Robert would come to her.

She made her way down to his closet, just as she had done once before. This time Robert was there, sprawled in the turned chair, and Margaret was on a cushion in front of the fire. Her hair was loose too and she looked young and beautiful as she laughed up at her son. The smile froze on her face when she saw Jane standing in the doorway.

'I would like to speak to my husband,' said Jane steadily. 'You need a son, and I want a child.'

Robert looked uncertainly at Margaret, who nodded slowly and rose to her feet. She stroked Robert's hair as she went past, and bent to whisper in his ear. 'Think of me,' she said, not caring that Jane could hear.

'Well, madam?' Robert was flustered without his mother's presence.

'We need to make a child, that is all,' said Jane. 'I will go to the country and be with my sister, but first, let us make the baby we both need.'

His eyes slid away from hers. 'You do not please me. How can I be expected to serve you when you just lie and look at me like that?' he asked pettishly.

'Then I must try harder to please you,' said Jane, walking

forward until she stood in front of him and could sink down to her knees.

'God, Roz, you look awful.' Lucy was staring at her, and Jeff's gaze narrowed at the look of revulsion on Roz's face as she stared off into the yard. There was an eerie blankness to her eyes, and he had the uncanny notion that she was watching something horrifying, but when he turned to see what she was looking at, there was nothing there, just an old brick wall, a dilapidated outhouse and a green wheelie bin.

'Roz?' Lucy put a hand on Roz's arm and she jerked as if Lucy had slapped her. Jeff saw her eyes snap into focus before she gagged and clapped a hand to her mouth.

'Sorry,' she muttered after a moment. 'I just felt a bit sick.'

'You don't look well,' said Lucy in concern. 'Do you want to sit down?'

'No . . . no, I'm okay.' Tentatively, Roz lowered her hand from her mouth and swallowed hard. 'The feeling's gone now.' She cleared her throat. 'What were you saying, Lucy?'

'I was talking about whether or not there would have been a still room, and you suddenly pointed at the bin and said of course, you made remedies there.' Lucy's smile was a little uncertain. 'It was weird, wasn't it, Jeff?'

He gave a nod, but he was watching Roz's face. Something was going on. Her eyes were skittering around, searching frantically for an explanation. He could tell that just by looking at her.

'I was just thinking . . . a still room is a great idea,' she managed in the end. 'We could have an actor playing the mistress of the house ... and talking about the remedies she's making. A sort of interactive display.'

It wasn't a bad effort, but Jeff didn't believe her for a moment. Lucy seemed to accept it, though.

'Oh, I see,' she said, her face clearing. 'Yes, that might be fun, mightn't it? Especially if we used herbs and things that are readily available today. I must do some research.'

'I could probably help you with that.' Jeff didn't understand the wry note in Roz's voice. She still looked ghastly, but went inside with Lucy, all the while talking about Tudor remedies, and Jeff was left looking at the bin with a suspicious frown.

'Jesus.' Nick peered up through the windscreen at the imposing gatehouse that straddled the turn-off. 'I didn't realize we were going to be staying in a castle!'

'I don't think it's a castle exactly,' said Roz, but she hadn't been expecting quite such a grand entrance either. The gatehouse was a huge stone arch, with towers on either side. Carved over the arch was the Holmwood coat of arms, and there, in one quarter, was the red boar. Roz shuddered at the sight of it, and averted her eyes.

'I should have brought my valet,' said Nick, putting on an exaggerated upper-class accent that sounded disconcertingly like Adrian's.

A reluctant smile tugged at Roz's mouth as she let off the handbrake and drove carefully under the arch. 'God, I hope it's not going to be too awful.'

In the end, it hadn't been as hard to persuade Nick to come for the weekend as she had imagined it would be. His only objection had been the fact that he had booked an appointment with the hypnotherapist for her.

'Can you change it?' Roz had asked on the phone. 'Please, Nick. This weekend is important to me.'

She'd met him at the station the night before. It was a fortnight since they had seen each other, but it felt like much longer. Roz watched Nick walking down the platform, and it was as if she had never seen him before. He looked like a stranger, a lean man with a bony, quirky face and intelligent eyes. His hair was a little long, his clothes a little scruffy, but he walked like a man easy in his own skin, and he was wonderfully solid, wonderfully real. For some reason she found herself blushing as she greeted him with a hug.

Nick was awkward too. 'It feels like a first date,' he said with a grimace. 'You'd never think we'd been married for eight years.'

'I know. Maybe it's being in a strange place?'

'Or maybe we've changed without realizing it.' He studied her with shrewd brown eyes. 'There's something different about you. I can't quite put my finger on it . . .' Then he pulled her back against him and buried his face in her hair. 'You still smell the same, though. Nice.'

'Same perfume,' said Roz.

'Same you.'

Still, it was strange at first sleeping in the same bed again. All evening, Roz tried to find a way to tell Nick about her experiences as Jane, but there never seemed to be a good moment and conversation was sticky, coming out in great dollops and then drying up abruptly. They talked about their jobs, about their flat, about friends, but they didn't talk about Daniel. They didn't talk about any of the things that had lain between them for too long.

When they went to bed, the darkness vibrated with everything unspoken between them. Nick turned on his side to face her, and after a moment, Roz turned too. It was sad, she thought, that they could only look at each other properly in the dark now.

'I missed you,' he said, and there was an ache at the back of her throat, a stinging behind her eyes.

'I've missed you too.'

Then his hands were on her skin, warm and sure, and she reached for him, welcoming the spike of her pulse, the lovely, liquid pull of desire after so long apart, letting the familiar feel of him blot out Jane's memories of Robert's fumbling attempts to mount her, the way she had had to degrade herself to ensure a child was at least a possibility. Roz gave herself up to the arching pleasure of Nick's hands, Nick's mouth, Nick's body. Every touch, every taste, loosened the tight, tense knot inside her, and as the pleasure built, stroking and skimming, streaking, it unravelled further until she felt it spin wildly free at last with her shout of release.

And afterwards, it had been the most natural thing in the world to press up against his spine and tuck her arm over him, to feel the steady rise and fall of his chest. It had felt like coming home. Easy then to forget the bitter words, the recriminations and the resentment. Perhaps this was all they needed, Roz thought hopefully, and she remembered Jane, poor Jane, who had never known the comfort of lying close to someone she loved, of skin on skin, of breathing quietly together.

But the next morning, watching Nick peering through the window and grumbling about pastiche architecture, Roz realized that sex could only go so far. It might have broken down the barriers, but there was still so much that she and Nick needed to talk about. Daniel hadn't gone away just because Nick was here with her.

And nor had Jane.

She went to join Nick at the window. 'What do you see?' she asked him.

'I see a botched, unimaginative building,' he said, snorting. 'Nostalgia'r'us.'

'What else?'

He glanced at her. 'Is this a game?'

'No.'

'Well . . .' He looked back at the scene. 'I see some cars. Some planting, equally unimaginative. A satellite dish. A few puddles. Is that the kind of thing you mean?'

'The first day I arrived in York, I looked out of that window, and I saw a stable and a long yard with apple trees and a woodstore and a herb garden.'

There was a long silence. Roz could feel Nick's eyes on her face, but she couldn't look at him.

'I know, it sounds mad, doesn't it?' she said, her voice rising, rattling out of control, and her breathing with it. 'It *is* mad.' Now the words were out, she started to shake as the reality hit her. 'I'm losing my mind, Nick. I'm afraid I'm going mad.'

'Hey.' Nick took her hands, held them firmly, gave them a little shake. 'Look at me, Roz. Good,' he said as she lifted her gaze unwillingly. She was breathing in short, panicky gasps, and her eyes skittered wildly around at first, as if terrified of being trapped, but he kept watching her steadily and eventually her breath calmed and her eyes settled on his. 'Good,' he said again. 'Now, we're going to sit down and you're going to tell me all about it, and then we'll decide whether you're mad or not.'

Chapter Eleven

They sat on the beige sofa and she told him everything that had happened since she had first looked out of the window. Right until the moment Jane had sunk to her knees in front of Robert.

'I looked up schizophrenia,' she finished. 'It's a psychotic disorder, when you can't distinguish between your imaginings and reality. Schizophrenics can see and hear and smell things that other people don't – like that yard out of the window there.'

Like the sound of a wet baby being dropped into the straw.

Like the smell of Robert's penis.

She pushed the memories away with an effort. 'Sometimes it can be triggered by stressful events.'

'And you're thinking about Mikey,' said Nick, who had listened carefully. Roz was grateful and amazed at how calmly he had taken it. There had been no interjections, or insistence that she must be making it up. 'You think that because your brother was diagnosed with schizophrenia, you're going to be genetically predisposed to having schizophrenia too.'

'It's not unlikely, is it?'

Nick's mouth turned down as he considered. 'It's not *impossible*,' he allowed, 'but, Roz, I don't think you're mentally ill. You're functioning perfectly normally.'

'It's not normal to think you're living in the sixteenth century!'

'Okay,' he said calmly, 'you're functioning normally most of the time. You're eating, sleeping, working. You're communicating clearly with other people. You're not withdrawn. If it wasn't for these episodes as Jane, you wouldn't think you were ill, would you?'

'But if I'm not hallucinating, what's happening to me?' Roz could hear the precarious control in her voice, and Nick obviously heard it too. He put an arm around her and drew her close.

'I don't know,' he admitted. 'I don't think you're ill, but obviously something's wrong. The mind is a very powerful thing. I just wonder if this is all some bizarre way of dealing with the trauma from when you were a child.'

'Or?' Roz said, challenging him to come up with another suggestion, the one neither of them wanted to face.

'Or you're possessed,' said Nick. 'By the ghost of a decent woman who lived here a few hundred years ago.'

They stared at each other solemnly for a long moment, and then they both broke into shaky laughter. 'I can't believe we're even talking about being possessed!' said Roz. Everything felt so normal, so real, when Nick was there. The walls were solid, the floor fixed. The Ikea furniture looked as if it had never been the setting for anything more remarkable than an evening watching television.

'I know.' Nick pushed a hand through his hair. 'It does seem incredible, and yet . . . it's happening. And the last time you . . . were Jane . . . was Monday?'

Roz nodded, but she wasn't foolish enough to hope that it was over. All week when she had been walking around York, she had been aware of a different world flickering at the edges of her vision. A gowned figure would flit past, only to vanish when she turned her head sharply to look. Or she'd be walking along and it would seem to her that the streets were crowding in behind her, that if she stopped and looked over her shoulder, she would see the stalls built out into the road, the goodwives sitting in the doorways, a pig snouting along a gutter, or a cart laden with cabbages. Sometimes she tried to catch it out, whipping round, but everything was just as it should be. Only her heart was kicking hard and high in her throat.

She felt peeled, as if all her senses were raw and so highly attuned that they were reaching into the world that existed like a shimmer behind her own, so that she could smell the dray horse, smell the timber and the dung and the wood and the wet straw. She could hear the clamour and the clatter of the work-shops, the barking dogs and the laughing women and the quarrelling men. And sometimes it seemed that her comfortable tops would shrink against her, pulled tight by the laces of a bodice, and she had to put up a hand against the scratchiness of a ruff that wasn't there.

Nick could obviously see the hesitation in her face. 'Look,' he said, tightening his arm around her, 'let's take this one step at a time. Why don't you go and see Rita as we agreed next time you're in London? If there isn't a psychological explanation, we can think about going down the medical route or talking to a priest.'

Roz swallowed. 'You mean exorcism?'

'Well, it seems to work in films.'

'I hope I don't start projectile vomiting,' she said in a feeble attempt at a joke.

'Don't worry, the moment your head starts spinning on your shoulders, I'll be straight off to google the nearest exorcist.' Nick's expression sobered. 'It'll be okay, Roz, I promise. I'm glad you told me.'

She smiled waveringly back at him. 'Me too.'

Roz hadn't realized quite how frightened she had been until she had confided in Nick, but now that she had, everything felt more manageable, and her spirits had lifted as they headed out to Holme Hall.

She had hired a car that morning, and in spite of the damp start, it had been a beautiful drive out through the Wolds. She liked to drive, and, thank God, Nick wasn't one of those men who thought their masculinity was in doubt if they were driven by a woman.

It was good to get out of the city. In late September, the hedgerows were still green, but the countryside had a faintly tired and tattered feel after the summer and the leaves were just starting to turn.

She took her eyes off the road to glance at Nick, aware of the pleasant hum in her blood as she remembered the night before, and her mouth curved.

'What?' said Nick, becoming aware of her gaze.

'Nothing. I'm just grateful to you for coming this weekend.'

'Oh, well, I don't want you getting seduced into the landed gentry,' he said and she laughed and patted his thigh.

'Don't worry, I'm not into the huntin'-fishin'-shootin' type.'

'Just as well,' he pretended to growl.

Lime trees lined the avenue, and on either side stretched lush parkland dotted with oaks and spreading chestnuts. Fat cows browsed amongst a herd of fluffy sheep. Horses cropped the green grass.

'It's all very *Pride and Prejudice*, isn't it?' said Nick. 'Do you think we'll meet Mr Darcy bowling along in a carriage?'

Roz didn't answer. She was frowning at the tarmacked avenue. It looked so strange, unlike the rough and jolting track they had been travelling on for what felt like days. Juliana had spent the entire journey complaining of nausea at the lurch and sway of the carriage, in spite of the fact that she had insisted on her father's new coach. Jane would rather have ridden like Annis, who had flatly refused to get inside.

'The back of a cart or the rump of a horse is good enough for me,' she had said firmly. She was having nothing to do with carriages. They were the work of the Devil, newfangled monstrosities that took over the calseys and blocked the streets so that nobody could get by without sucking in their breath and squeezing between carriage and stall if they were lucky. It was bad enough with all the carts in the city, but gentry folk and their fancy coaches were a curse in Annis's view. And who would want to be shut up inside the belly of one for hours on end, anyway?

Not Jane, for certain. Surely they must get there soon? The lurch of the coach over the ruts in the track and the smell of wood and leather mingled with Juliana's pomander, stifling in the enclosed space, was making her feel as sick as her sister, and she had not the excuse of being with child.

It was six weeks since Jane had abased herself before her husband. If anything, Robert was even more uncomfortable with her now, and avoided her eyes. When she had suggested taking her sister to the country for the summer, she could see the relief in his face.

'Send word if you are with child,' he'd said.

Her flowers had come down three weeks later, but Robert didn't know that. He knew nothing of Jane's body. He had finally succeeded in bending Jane over his desk, pushing into her from behind as he called for his mamma, and releasing a trickle of seed after a few ineffectual pumps. Jane just hoped it would be enough to convince him she might have conceived.

It was all going to plan. Jane had kept her eyes lowered to hide her triumph. The thought of leaving the stifling house in Micklegate and spending the summer without her husband or Margaret left her giddy with relief. And, God willing, there would be an heir for the Holmwoods at the end of it. A boy would ensure her position, but even a girl would be a child to love.

All would be well if only they could get out of this cursed coach!

She shifted forward to peer out of the window. More woods. 'I hope we get there soon,' she sighed.

'We're almost there.'

How strange. Juliana's voice had deepened in surprise. She sounded almost like –

Nick.

Roz sucked in a breath and slammed her foot on the brake. The car lurched to a stop in the middle of the avenue and she dropped her head onto the steering wheel.

'Hey.' Nick put a hand on her shoulder in concern. 'Roz, what's the matter?'

Roz couldn't answer immediately. Her mind was ringing with alarm. How could Jane have followed her here, in the car?

Drawing a shuddering breath, she sat up and tipped her head back against the seat. 'Sorry,' she said.

'That was it, wasn't it?' Nick's voice changed and she nodded miserably.

'Roz, this is serious. We should have thought of this. What if you'd been driving on a main road with other traffic? You could have been killed.'

'I *know*. I never thought Jane would be able to follow me here, but of course she came to Holme Hall too.'

'I think we should go back to London right now,' said Nick, but Roz set her mouth stubbornly.

'No. We've come this far, we may as well go on. I'll be prepared now. You can see that when I go back it only lasts seconds in this time, so you can cover for me if necessary.' She unbuckled her seatbelt. 'But you'd better drive from now on.'

They changed places and continued up the drive, crunching to a halt on a circle of immaculately maintained gravel in front of a sprawling Jacobean mansion. Nick whistled. 'Your boss isn't short of a bob or two, is he?'

Adrian came out onto the steps to meet them wearing cords and a checked shirt, very much the country gentleman. Roz glanced at Nick's jeans and faded long-sleeved T-shirt. She had a feeling he wasn't going to fit in.

But Nick wasn't a man to be thrown by finding himself out of place, and they brushed through lunch and an afternoon's walk without any faux pas. Adrian showed them all proudly round the house. 'This is one of the best-preserved examples of an early Jacobean house in the country,' he told them as they trailed politely after him up the magnificent staircase and into an impressively long gallery. A row of bay windows looked out over the knot garden and the estate beyond, while the other wall was covered in portraits.

'And here is Sir Geoffrey himself.' Adrian gestured up at the painting hung in the centre of the gallery. It was a full-length version of the portrait Roz had seen in his office in York. Dressed in a gorgeously embroidered doublet and white stockings and hose, Sir Geoffrey had a dashing scarlet cloak swinging from one shoulder. Above the wide ruff, he looked out from the canvas with the same malevolent black eyes. When Roz's gaze met them, an icy finger seemed to touch the nape of her neck, making her back twitch uncontrollably. She felt sick and a little giddy as she averted her head.

'What's that on the table beside him?' Nick went right up to the painting to peer more closely at the detail and Roz had to bite down on the urge to shout at him to step back, that he was too close. She could have sworn Sir Geoffrey was watching him derisively, a sneer hovering around his thin lips.

'It's a tinderbox,' Adrian was saying, pointing it out to the others, who crowded round, apparently unperturbed by Sir Geoffrey's malign gaze. 'Rather an odd thing for him to be painted with, I agree, but he seems to have been a singular character. A man ahead of his time, I always feel. It was Sir Geoffrey who built the house we see today. Tragically, the older Holme Hall burned to the ground just after he attained his majority. Legend has it that his grandmother was killed in the fire,' Adrian went on, regarding his ancestor admiringly. 'She's even said to haunt the Hall today!' He twinkled at the stir of interest. 'I can't say I've ever seen her, but a ghost in an old house like this is almost *de rigueur*, isn't it?' he said, and his guests all laughed obligingly.

Roz was glad when they moved on, but as Adrian led them out of the gallery, she could feel Sir Geoffrey's gaze following her, and when she glanced over her shoulder, almost unwillingly, she was certain that his cruel almost-smile had deepened. Her heart jerked unpleasantly, but the chief executive of one of York's biggest companies was standing back so that she could go ahead of him, and when Roz glanced again, it was just a portrait in an ornate frame, hanging motionless on the gallery wall.

As promised, the other guests were pretty standard representatives of Yorkshire's wealthy and influential and over lunch the air in the grand dining room positively reeked of pomposity. Roz had to be careful not to catch Nick's eye on several occasions, but she had to admit that everyone was friendly enough.

Everyone except Helen, who had been waiting in the hall with a clipboard when they arrived. 'I'm just here to help Sir Adrian,' she had said coldly when Roz greeted her and pretended to be pleased that she was a fellow guest.

'Who was that stone-faced female who showed us to the room?' Nick shouted through into the en suite bathroom that evening as they got ready for dinner.

Roz groaned. 'That was Adrian's PA, Helen.' She turned on the shower and put a hand underneath to test for temperature.

'She doesn't like you very much, does she?' Nick appeared in the doorway, hooking his T-shirt over his head.

'No,' said Roz with a sigh. 'I think she's afraid I'm going to take advantage of Adrian, who obviously can't see that she's in love with him.'

'He's a strange guy, isn't he? One of those people who can only cope with modern life by pretending that they're still living in a different century.'

'I'd wondered why he wasn't married, but he told me this afternoon that he's been engaged twice and he's called it off both times.'

'Yes, I heard that too. How, when it came down to it, he

couldn't contemplate facing either of them over a breakfast table for the rest of his life. All protesting a little too much if you ask me.'

'Funny, though, that someone so obsessed with his family's history wouldn't be keen to pass on the name,' she commented as she stripped off her clothes. She couldn't help thinking about Robert, and his desperation to have a son. 'I'd have thought it would be worth a bit of a chat over tea and toast to have an heir.'

'Maybe the thought of all that intimacy is too much for him,' said Nick. 'Not everyone wants kids.'

His words fell into an abrupt silence. To Roz it rang with everything he himself had said in the past. *It's too soon. We don't need a baby to complete us. Kids are a lot of work. I'm not sure I'm ready to be a father yet. It wouldn't be the end of the world if we didn't have children.*

'No,' she said without looking at him as she pulled open the shower door. She wished they hadn't picked at that particular scab. 'No, they don't, do they?'

'Hush now.' Jane wiped Juliana's forehead and winced as her sister screamed again. She looked across the birthing stool at the midwife. 'Should it be taking this long?'

'It takes as long as it takes,' snapped the midwife, but Jane thought her eyes were worried. 'Come on, lass,' she said to Juliana. 'One more little push.'

'I can't . . . I can't . . .' Juliana sobbed and screamed. She had been walking very slowly with Jane in the garden when her waters broke. The midwife had advised staying in the chamber and sealing it up tight, but Juliana had been fretful and bored and Jane hadn't thought a little air would do any harm. She couldn't remember the last time it had rained. The earth was cracked and grey, and the crops were shrivelling in the fields. A hazy heat lay over the Wolds like a suffocating blanket. It was too hot to sleep, too hot to move, too hot to *breathe*.

All morning they had been watching clouds boiling on the horizon, where the air grew dark and heavy. Jane longed for the storm to break, for the rain to fall and a breeze to stir the thick air, but it had sulked obstinately in the distance.

Now Jane wished she had made Juliana stay where she was. Perhaps if she had kept her still and safe in this room, her sister might not be in such agony. She had hurried Juliana back to the chamber as quickly as she could and Annis had sent one of the servants off to fetch the midwife. Between them they had coaxed Juliana into the bed and stoked up the fire. The room was stifling now and sweat was trickling between Jane's breasts and on the inside of her thighs.

She couldn't help thinking of Ellen, whose labour had at least been quick. Juliana had been screaming with pain for hours now, and she was getting weaker.

'Is there anything else we can give her?' she asked the midwife in a low voice. They had rubbed almond oil on Juliana's swollen belly and given her buttered eggs to eat. A woman in the village had given birth recently and the midwife sent for four spoonfuls of her milk which Juliana had been cajoled into drinking, but none of it was helping. 'I have some poppy seeds in my still room. I could make a syrup to ease her pain.'

But the midwife shook her head. 'She needs to stay awake to push.' She was feeling Juliana's stomach, her face grave. 'The babe is the wrong way round,' she said to Jane in an undertone. 'I will have to try and turn it.'

Jane exchanged a look with Annis. Everything had gone well so far. Juliana had been bored and petulant these last few months, but she had understood the need for no visitors. For Jane, it had been a peaceful interlude. She organized the house, and tended the garden, and fed Juliana meals to tempt her appetite.

A few servants left at Holme Hall year round were country folk. 'Don't worry about them,' Annis had said when Jane fretted that they might tell the Holmwoods that it had not been Jane who had been growing fat and cumbersome. 'When will they ever have conversation with either of them? They never come here anyways. We'll send word that there is sickness here for a month or two and that will keep the master away, even if he was minded to see his child. He won't be able to tell the difference between a baby that is two months old and one that is four months, even if he cared. 'Sides, the servants here like having you as their mistress. They'll keep your counsel.'

At first the midwife hadn't been happy about Jane and Annis as companions to Juliana. Neither of them had had a child, she'd said, able to tell apparently just by looking at them. They would be no use to her.

'I have seen a child born,' said Jane quietly. 'I will do as you tell me. I will not leave my sister to endure this alone.'

'Help her back to the bed,' the midwife instructed at last, and together they lifted and half-carried Juliana.

'Make it stop, Jane,' she wept piteously. 'It is tearing me apart.'

'It will not be long now,' Jane said, as if she would know.

'You've been saying that since my waters broke.' The pain eased for a moment and Juliana let Jane lift her head and give her a little ale to drink. 'What time is it?' she asked, falling weakly back on the pillow. 'Is it morning yet?'

'Morning? No, you have not been in travail so long,' Jane reassured her in a bright voice, although it felt as if they had been shut in this sweltering chamber for a week at least. She glanced at Annis. 'Is it even night yet, Annis?'

Annis opened the shutters a chink. 'The edge of dark,' she informed them over her shoulder. 'The chickens will be coming home to roost and you'll have your babe before the night,' she told Juliana kindly.

'I do not want it!' A tear rolled down Juliana's cheek. 'It is killing me!'

'Lie still now,' tsked the midwife. She nodded at Jane. 'Hold her down.'

So Jane climbed onto the bed behind her sister, and held on to her tightly as the midwife rolled up her sleeve and groped for the baby, while Juliana screamed and tried to writhe.

'Ahh . . .' The midwife straightened. 'It's coming now. Almost there. One more push.'

'Do you hear that? It will soon be over,' Jane encouraged Juliana.

'I don't want to . . . I don't want to . . .' Juliana thrashed from side to side but they managed to haul her up and back to the birthing chair.

'See, the head!' Jane was filled with emotion and she smiled at her sister through her tears. 'Oh Juliana, here it comes!'

A few moments later, the baby slithered into the midwife's callused hands, just as a loud crack overhead announced that the long-awaited storm had arrived, and foreboding raced across the midwife's face. She looked up, crossing herself surreptitiously. Another crack, a boom of thunder and then the rain came: crashing onto the roof, thundering past the windows, drumming on the ground.

'At last,' said Annis, taking advantage of the midwife's preoccupation with the baby to open the shutters and let a thread of cool air into the room.

Jane barely noticed. Her gaze was fixed on the midwife, who wiped the baby down in practised movements, before turning it over her hand and delivering a brisk slap that had it drawing breath for a wail of outrage.

'A boy,' she said, offering the baby to Juliana, who turned her face away.

Jane was there to take him, though. 'A boy!' she said and her eyes met Annis's. 'Thank God, a boy! Oh, he is beautiful!'

Giddy with elation and emotion, she cradled the baby while the midwife and Annis tidied Juliana and disposed of the afterbirth. Her eyes were stinging with emotion. 'There now,' she cooed to the baby, wiping blood from the creases in his neck and the crooks of his limbs, 'who is my precious?'

But after that first outraged cry, the baby lapsed into silence. His eyes were dark and furious as they stared blindly up at Jane and his tiny face was set in a scowl.

'Try and get your sister to let him suck,' said the midwife in a low voice. 'Else you must send for a nurse.'

'I'll go,' said Annis, edging towards the door. 'There'll be a woman in the village with milk.'

'Shut that window before you go,' advised the midwife tartly, and Annis rolled her eyes and closed the shutter before slipping gratefully out of the chamber into the cooler air.

Jane gave the baby to the midwife to swaddle, and went to smooth the sweaty hair back from Juliana's forehead.

'You did well, little sister,' she said, smiling down at her. 'He is a fine boy. What will you call him?'

'I do not care,' said Juliana listlessly.

'Come now, we must name him.' Jane cast her mind over Robert's ancestors. She couldn't bear to name the babe after her husband. 'What about Geoffrey?'

'If you wish.'

'Well, then, Geoffrey he will be. Do you not wish to see your son?'

Juliana's expression was blank, uncaring. 'I don't want him.'

'He needs milk, Juliana. Look.' She beckoned the midwife over, and took the baby from her. His mouth was opening and closing, although his expression was as empty as his mother's. 'He is hungry.'

If Juliana would just put the baby to her breast, she would love him, Jane was sure. But perhaps then she would want to

keep him after all? Jane was ashamed of herself for even thinking it.

She did her best to cajole Juliana into nursing, but Juliana
would have none of it. She just turned her face away from the
baby and in the end Annis brought in a plump, placid woman
from the village who had a babe strapped to one breast, and
who let Geoffrey suck at the other.

'Don't go.' Juliana's eyes filled with tears when Jane made to
fetch a bag of coins for the midwife. 'Don't leave me, Jane.' She
clutched at Jane's hand and grew so distressed that Jane sent
Annis for the money and settled by her sister, stroking her hair.

'I won't leave you,' she said. 'I promise.'

Juliana ran a tongue over her cracked lips. 'Promise me you
won't tell anyone about my disgrace.'

'Of course I won't,' Jane soothed her. 'No one else need
know. Annis will not tell, and the midwife does not care.'

'I don't want anyone to know.' Juliana tossed her head fretfully. 'If I die . . . tell our father it was a fever. Don't tell him the
truth.'

'You're not going to die, Juliana.'

'Swear you won't tell!'

Jane sighed. 'I won't tell, I swear it.'

'Whatever happens?'

'Of course,' said Jane.

'Swear it!' Juliana's voice rose frantically.

'I will never tell anyone the babe was yours,' Jane reassured
her. 'Never. I promise.'

'Now what?' asked Annis, when Juliana was sleeping at last,

the midwife had gone and Geoffrey lay in the cradle, staring silently up at the ceiling.

Jane took a breath. 'You get some sleep. I will stay with Juliana and the babe, and tomorrow I will write to my husband and tell him that he has a son.'

Be careful what you wish for. Sybil Dent's words seemed to reverberate in Jane's head as she watched her sister. Juliana's pretty face was grey and sunken, and she tossed her head from side to side on the pillow, muttering to herself. She had sunk into a fretful fever two days after the birth, and none of Jane's remedies could bring her fever down. The midwife had come back, but she just shook her head and pulled down the corners of her mouth.

'Prepare yourself and look to the infant,' was all she had said.

Tell me what you really want, Sybil had said, and Jane had told her the truth. *I want a child*, she had said. But she hadn't meant for Juliana to die so that she could have her babe.

Annis laid a hand on Jane's shoulder. 'How is she?'

'She's dying.' Jane's voice was cracked and dry as she acknowledged the truth. She had told Juliana that she wouldn't die, but she had been wrong. 'She's dying and I can't save her.'

Annis didn't try to deny it. 'I'll sit with her for a while,' she offered. 'You need to rest.'

'I can't. I promised I would stay with her.'

'You won't be any good to the babe if you fall sick too,' said Annis bluntly.

Jane bit her lip. 'Is this my punishment? Did I want a child too much?' she asked Annis.

At first she had thought all would be well. She had sent word to Robert that he had a son, but added a warning that there was sickness in the village. She would keep the baby safe before risking the journey back to the city.

The wet nurse was feeding the babe, who suckled with an odd expression of distaste. Annis and the midwife had taken him to the church and told the priest that he was Jane's child, and he had been baptized. He was a silent child. Annis shook her head over him. 'Tisn't natural for a baby not to cry,' she'd said, but Jane refused to accept any criticism.

'He is a good baby, that is all.'

But even Jane noticed how the wet nurse avoided picking Geoffrey up unless she had to. Annis made excuses to bypass his cradle. Jane tried to compensate by cuddling him, but the baby was oddly unresponsive. He had dark, knowing eyes that seemed to look inside her. Jane wouldn't admit that there was a repellent quality to him. How could there be? He was just a baby.

'You can't think like that,' Annis said with rough affection. 'It wasn't you got her with child, was it?'

'I should have taken better care of her. I should have taken her to live with me.'

'Oh yes? And how were you supposed to do that?' Annis wasn't having any of it.

'I could have spoken to my father.'

'Would've, should've, could've . . . you did what you could,' said Annis.

Outside, the trees still drooped forlornly after the storm. The rain had turned the tracks to mud, and left the garden behind the house battered and bedraggled. Water still dropped slowly, drearily, from the eaves.

Jane sighed. 'Why is it never enough?' she said.

Juliana died that night, so quietly that Jane couldn't believe it. Her sister had always been extreme in everything. It seemed all wrong that she should just slip away without making a fuss.

Look after your sister, her mother had said as she died. *Keep her safe. Promise me.* Another promise Jane hadn't been able to keep.

Her throat ached as she lifted Juliana's limp hand to her lips. 'Forgive me, Juliana,' she whispered. Guilt and grief pressed down on her, weighing on her shoulders so heavily that she leant forward and rested her forehead on the bed next to her sister's body. 'I will keep your son safe,' she vowed. 'I will keep him close. I will be a mother to him as if I had borne him myself. I will care for him and love him, and I will never abandon him, not while breath is in my body. This I promise you, sister. I swear it on my life.'

'How will I find the words to tell him?' she asked wretchedly.

'Hmm? What? Tell who?' a sleepy voice mumbled.

'My father.'

There was a pause. 'Your father's been dead for years.'

'Dead? No, he is in York, and his heart will break. Juliana was his pet, and now she is dead.' Her voice caught on a sob.

'Now I must write and tell him the news, and he will never forgive me.'

Firm hands took hold of her. Why did Annis shake her so? 'Wake up,' a voice said. 'Wake up, Roz.'

Ah, if only she could! If only she were asleep, she could open her eyes and this would all be a dream. She would still be walking with Juliana in the garden, feeling the heat damp on her neck, longing for the storm to break. But alas, it was all too real. The weave of the coverlet pressing into her forehead. The rank smell of sweat. The steady drip, drip of raindrops on the windowsill. The flaccid chill of Juliana's hand in hers.

But then the dimness of the chamber exploded with a brilliant light that made her gasp and shrink back in terror, as a figure loomed over her. 'Come on, Roz, wake up now. You're having a nightmare.'

Roz stared up at Nick, her eyes huge and terrified. 'Oh . . . Nick!' she stuttered, unable to catch her breath properly. Struggling up onto the pillow, she dropped her head onto her knees, heaving in air, while Nick rubbed her back and cursed under his breath.

'Shit, I'm sorry. Maybe I shouldn't have woken you, but I was worried. You were crying.'

'Juliana's dead,' Roz managed unevenly, still leaden with sadness for her spoilt sister, only to shake her head on her knees at her own confusion. Of *course* Juliana was dead. Over four hundred years had passed since she had waddled awkwardly through the garden, her belly swollen, complaining about the heat and the boredom. They were all dead: Juliana, Annis, Robert, Margaret.

Jane.

Jane was dead too, remember? Roz shuddered. It was too easy to forget that when Jane's life felt so real, so vivid, so *now*.

Nick's hand circled warm and comforting on her bare back. 'Can you tell me about it?'

So she told him about those long, desperate days and how hard she had fought to save her sister. She told him about the baby, with his flinty, black stare. She told him about the promise she had made to care for Geoffrey always.

'I think he's going to grow up to be Sir Geoffrey, who built this house,' she said to Nick when her breathing had steadied and she could hug her knees to her chest. 'I don't really understand how, but he seems to be at the centre of all this. Do you remember his portrait in the long gallery? Did you notice anything odd about it?'

'It was just a painting,' said Nick, handing her a glass of water. For a moment Roz stared at it dubiously. Water was so often unwholesome. Ale would be better, she thought, and then she remembered who she was, when she was, and she took a sip. It tasted strange, as if she had never drunk water before, but it was cool and clear.

Nick climbed back into bed beside her. They'd been given a guest room in the east wing. It had a low ceiling and a charming lead-paned window overlooking the gardens, but unlike the rooms in the main part of the house, it was decorated in a contemporary style. The walls were papered with a stylish chintz, the carpet was soft, the sleigh bed firm and comfortable. Roz had been relieved to find that the air didn't hum with the past there, unlike the house in Micklegate. She felt safe there – or she had done until she had dreamt of Juliana's death. Now Jane felt very close again.

'What am I going to do, Nick?' she said, and she fumbled the glass onto the bedside table so that she could hug her arms together. 'What in God's name am I going to do?'

Chapter Twelve

'I've been thinking.' Nick stretched out on his side and propped his head on one elbow. 'I know this dream was distressing for you, but the more you tell me about Jane's story, the more convinced I am that this is you working through some issues to do with your past.'

'What do you mean?'

'You woke up crying for a sister who was dead, right? You've only just discovered you had two sisters who died. You haven't had a chance to grieve for them. Jane feels responsible because her mother is dead. Your mother is dead too.'

Roz had thought of that before. Part of her even wanted to believe it. 'What about the baby? And her awful marriage?'

'I've thought about that too.' Faint colour crept along Nick's cheekbones and he sat up. 'Look, we've never really talked about what went wrong, have we?'

Roz stiffened. 'We did.' She remembered too many bitter discussions about Daniel.

'Not properly, and things weren't good before then, before Sue died. You wanted a baby,' said Nick deliberately, and she couldn't help it, she flinched. 'And I didn't.'

'What was there to talk about?' Roz rested her head back on her knees. Her voice was dull. 'You can't compromise on a baby. You can't sort of have one. You've either got a child or you haven't.' She had wanted a baby so badly, but now Sybil's words to Jane still rang in her head: *Be careful what you wish for.*

'I thought we *had* talked about it,' said Nick, 'but we didn't, not really. You asked what I thought about having kids, and I said I wasn't ready, and yes, I was relieved that seemed to be the end of the discussion, but neither of us talked about what we felt. I couldn't tell you that I was terrified at the thought of being a father. That I couldn't cope with the responsibility.'

'Funny how you seem to be coping fine with fatherhood when it comes to Daniel.' Roz couldn't keep the bitterness from her voice and Nick scrubbed a hand wearily over his face.

'I'm not really his father,' he said. 'Ruth's been happily married since he was a baby and Daniel thinks of her husband as his father. He's just an adolescent boy, using me as a way to kick out at his parents. Tony understands that. I'm never going to replace the man who bathed him and put him to bed and taught him how to ride a bike. Tony's Daniel's father. I'm just a biological coincidence. I didn't expect to feel anything for him at all but . . .' Nick's voice petered out. He sounded almost perplexed.

'I don't know how to explain how it feels,' he went on

eventually. 'Daniel's my *son*. It doesn't feel real, and yet there's a kind of connection, I suppose. I like him,' he said simply. 'I like spending time with him and getting to know him.'

'What are you trying to say, Nick?'

'Just that I wish I had listened harder to you,' he said quietly. 'The truth is, when you first brought up the question of kids, I felt rejected, like I wasn't enough for you. I know,' he said as Roz opened her mouth to speak, 'I was being selfish. I wanted things to stay as they were. I thought we were great together and we didn't need anything else. Now . . . well, now I realize that having a child doesn't necessarily mean that you lose something. You can gain something too, something special. But at the time I felt you resented me for not agreeing straight away, but you wouldn't come out and say it. And then – since we're being honest – I resented *you* for making me feel bad about myself.'

She *had* resented him. 'I resented you more for not telling me that you were a father,' she said. Her aunt had lied, her husband had lied and Roz's world had been staggering on its foundations. But Nick was right. She hadn't wanted to acknowledge it, retreating instead into a silence that grew longer and colder. When Adrian had offered her the job in York, she had taken it without even asking Nick what he thought. She had been desperate to get away from London and the tense atmosphere in the flat.

Be careful what you wish for.

'I should have told you as soon as Daniel contacted me, I know, but you were in a worse way than you thought,' Nick said carefully. 'I knew it would be another knock.' He blew out a breath and rubbed his hand over his hair. 'I don't know what I'm trying to say really. Just . . . I'm sorry. I made a mess of things.'

Only when it loosened did Roz realize just how tight a band had been clamped around her chest. Reaching for Nick's hand, she curled her fingers around his. 'I guess we messed them up together,' she said.

They slid down under the covers and were silent for a while. Nick smoothed a hand over Roz's arm. 'I just can't help thinking that these dreams, hallucinations, whatever you want to call them, must be related to you and the stuff going on in your head,' he said. 'I'm not doubting that it seems real to you,' he went on quickly as Roz began to object. 'But what if it really *is* your mind just working things out? Jane lost her sister, you lost your sisters. Jane wanted a baby, you wanted a baby. You've got to admit it kind of makes sense.'

'How do you explain Robert? I don't recall impotence being a problem you've ever suffered from, and your mother's always been lovely to me.'

Nick made a face. 'I don't like to think about it, but maybe Robert represents your dissatisfaction with our marriage.'

'And Geoffrey? Why is everything related to the Holmwoods?'

'You saw the portrait of Sir Geoffrey downstairs. You said it made an impression on you. Perhaps it was the first name your subconscious picked out. And you're working at the Holmwoods' sixteenth-century house, for the Holmwood Foundation.

It's not surprising that they'd be part of whatever your mind is processing.'

He made it all sound so reasonable. Roz chewed the inside of her cheek. 'Maybe,' she said reluctantly.

'I just think it must all be connected somehow,' said Nick. 'I'll make another appointment with Rita and you can talk it all through with her. I'm sure if you can sort out how you feel about the past, Roz, the present will fall into place too.'

Roz wanted to believe that Nick was right, and as the next few days passed and she stayed firmly in the present, she began to think that he might be. Perhaps it *had* just been her subconscious working overtime after all, and now that she and Nick had talked properly, the link between Roz's reality and Jane's imaginary world had been severed. She wasn't naive enough to think that one chat would solve all their problems, but she would go and see the hypnotherapist he had suggested, and they would both work harder to talk openly about how they felt. Everything would be fine, she told herself firmly.

She went back to work with renewed optimism and smiled at Helen as she sailed into the office to see if there was any post. It had been good to see Nick, and Roz was feeling fortunate. She should make more of an effort to be nice to Helen, she had decided. The other woman's unyielding expression was probably a sign of shyness or insecurity.

'Lovely weekend,' she said. 'Everything worked like clockwork. Adrian said it was all down to you, Helen.'

She didn't need Roz to tell her what Sir Adrian thought.

Helen's lips tightened. Sir Adrian had already thanked her himself. 'I don't know what I'd do without you, Helen,' he had said, and she had blushed with pleasure.

'You know I'm always happy to help, Sir Adrian,' she had said, and then – *then!* – he had put his arm around her and given her a quick squeeze.

'You're a *marvel*,' he said.

Helen hugged the memory to her as if she could still feel his fingers pressing into her arm. He was so handsome and kind and clever, and he relied on her. He might flirt with the likes of Roz Acclam and the other women who had been his guests, but when it came down to it, she was the one who knew him best, the one he depended upon to make him comfortable. Did Roz know how he took his coffee? That he couldn't bear untidiness? Helen knew his shirt size – she had checked when taking his clothes to the dry cleaner. She knew his birthday and every year presented him with a tasteful card. 'Helen, how *do* you remember?' he always cried with delight. She knew his favourite biscuits and where he liked to sit on a train. What did Roz know about him in comparison? *Nothing*, thought Helen with satisfaction.

'I was sorry you weren't at the dinner on Saturday,' Roz went on. 'I asked Adrian where you were, and he said you preferred to eat on your own.'

'I was there to work, not to socialize,' said Helen stiffly.

'So was I, in a way.'

She hadn't looked as if she was working. She had made it look easy, swanning in with her husband, fitting right in with her jeans and suede boots and perfectly cut white shirt. Adrian's friends had all liked her. Helen had seen the men leaning in towards her with fatuous smiles when she served drinks before dinner. By then Roz had changed, of course, into an effortlessly simple shift dress that would have made Helen look like a sack of potatoes.

Roz's husband hadn't been what Helen had expected. Not a banker at all, it turned out, but a freelance journalist, one of those thin, intelligent men with a mobile face and a dry voice that meant you could never tell if they were laughing at you or not. He didn't possess a dinner jacket, he'd said coolly, not sounding in the least embarrassed about it. Helen had heard Sir Adrian telling someone that he suspected Nick was 'a bit of a lefty', but even he fit in better than she did, Helen recognized bitterly.

While they were all at dinner, Helen had slipped up to their room. It smelt of Roz's perfume: subtle, expensive. Helen fingered her suede jacket, the silky blouse. She picked up the cashmere cardigan draped over the back of a chair and held its softness enviously against her cheek. That smelt of Roz too, and she dropped it back with a scowl. In the en suite bathroom she unscrewed the top off a pot of moisturizer and sniffed at it before dipping her finger into the pale pink cream. Leaning into the mirror, she rubbed it into her cheek. She looked at her reflection, and for a moment it seemed as if she was looking at someone else entirely, as if she had stepped out of herself and felt appalled at what she was doing. She had been brought up in a decent house, where you didn't go through other people's things like a thief.

But the thought had barely shocked her before it was barrelled aside by a rush of gleeful satisfaction that she could do whatever she liked. It was all Roz's fault, anyway. Helen wouldn't have dreamed of behaving like this before, but something about Roz had flipped a switch, sending an insidious bitterness and loathing slithering through her, intensifying her feelings for Sir Adrian. Ever since Roz had arrived Helen had felt raw, as if all her skin was peeled back, leaving every emotion exposed. She had been looking forward to getting away to the country, but she felt even worse here at Holme Hall. Helen wasn't an imaginative woman, but sometimes it seemed to her that the very air in the house was vibrating with frustration.

And with fear.

She finished creaming her face, and smoothed the top of the moisturizer to disguise the dent of her finger. Roz was so careless with her things, she thought disapprovingly. Look at the cosmetics scattered by the basin, the jewellery she had been wearing earlier left in a gleaming tumble. Helen poked at the pile. Roz had had some kind of Middle Eastern thing going on, obviously. There was a necklace of beaten silver, the bangles she usually wore, the dull gleam of earrings set with red stones and trembling with tiny silver balls.

Helen's fingers hovered over the jewellery. A bangle or an earring? An earring was more easily lost, she decided. Roz might not even notice for a while if one of the bangles was missing. Delicately she picked up one of the earrings and held it to the light. It was quirky, interesting, unlike the plain gold studs she wore in her own ears. Helen's fingers closed around it and she smiled grimly. She would take that.

Now she rebuffed Roz's attempts to chat about the weekend and flipped her notebook open. 'Since you're here, Roz, does the name Charles Denton mean anything to you?'

For once Roz looked discomposed. 'Oh, yes . . . I forgot about that,' she said, making a face.

'He says he's going to do – and I quote – "a psychic reading" in the hall on Thursday.' Helen didn't bother to conceal her distaste. 'Does Sir Adrian know about this? I can't believe he'd give permission for anything quite so silly.'

Roz's expression cooled. 'Adrian understands that we've got to do something different to attract visitors across the river. If nothing else, it would make a good marketing story. I'll call him when I get back.'

'Are you out for coffee again?' Helen got a perverse satisfaction from seeing Roz's jaw tighten.

'I'm interviewing caterers all morning,' she said. 'I'm hoping I might get a demonstration lunch. If Adrian asks, I'll be back this afternoon. Oh, by the way,' she remembered as she turned to go, 'I don't suppose anyone found an earring at the Hall, did they?'

'No.' Helen widened her eyes innocently and thought of the earring tucked away with the button from Roz's coat in her drawer. 'What did it look like?'

'Arabian silver, dangly, with a red garnet, I think.'

'I'll ask the housekeeper, but nobody mentioned finding an earring.'

Roz pulled down the corner of her mouth. 'I can't understand where I would have lost it. It was my favourite pair, too. Nick bought them for me on our honeymoon in Morocco.'

'Oh dear,' said Helen. 'What a shame.'

By the time Roz made it to the fourth caterer on her list of recommended companies she was stuffed with homemade biscuits and sloshing with tea.

Maggie's Catering was based in a unit on an industrial estate. When Roz pushed open the door, a neat woman in her fifties was standing behind the reception desk leafing through invoices. She looked up at the sound of the door, though, and Roz saw shock race across her face.

'Hi. I'm Roz Acclam.' Her professional smile faltered at the other woman's expression. 'I've got a meeting with Maggie Wray.'

'Oh, yes, of course. I'm Maggie.' Obviously flustered, Maggie came round to shake hands with Roz. 'I'm sorry I was staring,' she said, spreading a hand and patting her chest as if to calm palpitations. 'I feel like I've seen a ghost!'

A tingle zipped down Roz's spine. 'A ghost?'

'I wondered when I saw the name Acclam, but I never expected . . .' Maggie shook her head and laughed a little shakily. 'You must be Amy's little girl. You look *so* like her!'

Her aunt had said the same thing, but peering at fuzzy snaps from the seventies and eighties, Roz had never been able to see it herself. Amy Acclam had been dark-haired and pale-eyed like

Roz herself, but Roz hadn't realized that they looked quite that alike. It gave her a strange, light-headed feeling, as if she were as insubstantial as the ghost Maggie had thought her.

'You knew my mother?'

'Oh yes. We were all in Millingham Road together. You know what it's like when your kids are small,' she said, and Roz nodded, although she didn't. 'You end up making friends with other women that are in the same position just to stop yourself going mad! But here, come and sit down.' She ushered Roz over to the functional sofas in the reception area. 'My goodness, I haven't seen you since you were this high,' she said, gesturing vaguely to her knee. 'Roz . . . Rosalind . . . I should have realized, but when you came in, it gave me such a turn! It could have been Amy walking through that door!'

Her expression sobered. 'That was such a terrible thing that happened to your poor parents,' she said, shaking her head. 'What a tragedy. I remember how shocked we all were. You just don't think that kind of thing happens to people you know, do you?'

'No,' said Roz with feeling. She had certainly never thought it would happen to her. She put her briefcase on the floor beside her. It seemed the wrong moment to bring out costings and menu options. 'I've never met anyone who knew my parents before,' she said, smoothing her skirt over her thighs and realizing that she felt oddly nervous. 'Well, my aunt and uncle, of course, but they were different. It's funny meeting someone who knew them in York.' She looked at Maggie. 'What were they like?' she heard herself asking.

'Oh, they were a lovely family. Lovely. Patrick – your father – was such a nice man. Always had a smile and a nice word, and he was devoted to his little girls, you and Emily and . . . oh, what was the other one called?'

'Amanda.'

'Yes, Amanda. A pretty little thing.' Maggie shook her head sadly at the memory.

'And my mother?'

'Well, I always thought there was something rather mysterious about Amy.' Maggie settled herself onto the opposite sofa. 'She was very pretty – like you, with dark hair and your lovely silvery eyes – and she was always very nice, but there was a wariness about her too, like she was braced for a blow. I'm not one for gossip,' Maggie said comfortably, 'but I did hear her first husband was, you know, handy with his fists. I think she had a hard time before she met Patrick.'

She smiled at Roz. 'But she was so happy when she had you. I remember her saying how she felt like she'd stumbled into paradise. Stumbled into paradise,' Maggie repeated, turning the words around in her mouth with pleasure. 'She had such a lovely way of putting things sometimes. And to think what happened . . .' Her eyes filled with tears. 'I still can't believe that boy could have killed them all.'

From the kitchen, Roz could hear the clatter of pans and cheerful voices tossing abuse over the sound of the radio. 'You must have known Mikey. My brother.' She said it deliberately. Her brother, the killer.

'Of course.' Maggie fished out a tissue from behind her bra

strap and dabbed at her eyes. 'People said afterwards that they always knew there was something funny about him, but I didn't. Not at first. He was a quiet little boy, who didn't mix much with the other kids. I think he and Amy had been living in Selby before they came to Millingham Road, and I suppose it was a bit of a shock starting at a new school, moving in with a whole new family. Patrick tried so hard with him, but Mikey was jealous. He didn't want to share his mum. Well, you can understand it, can't you?'

In the kitchen they were singing along to a song on the radio, voices raised raucously. Maggie looked embarrassed. 'Sorry about the noise.'

'It's okay.' Roz mustered a smile. 'It's nice to hear people enjoying themselves at work.' She paused. 'So you never thought Mikey would do anything like set fire to the house?'

'Not then,' said Maggie. 'But after you were born, he got obsessed with making models: planes, cars, boats, everything. He used to spend all his time in that shop in Micklegate . . . oh, what was it called now? Well, it doesn't matter, but he definitely changed. Amy wondered if he'd met another boy there who was influencing him. He'd been shy before, but now he was mean. Sam, my eldest, he said Mikey was bullying Emily and Amanda, and there were stories about things being broken, things going missing . . . nasty stuff . . . but it's hard for adults sometimes to know what's really going on. Children don't always tell you everything.

'All I knew was that Amy was worried about the girls,' Maggie said. 'I remember saying to her, it's just a phase. He'll settle down.' Sighing, she tucked the tissue back inside her bra strap. 'But he never did, did he?'

'No,' said Roz slowly, thinking about the model shop that had been built over the original hall in Holmwood House. Thinking about the whirring, rattling echo of an electric train circling endlessly along its track. About the way the past and present seemed to overlap in the house and what that might have done to a small boy. 'No, he didn't.'

'Anyway, it's good to see you back in York,' said Maggie with a smile. 'It's quite brought it all back! But you're here to talk about our catering service, aren't you?'

'I am.' Glad of the shift to professionalism, Roz bent and pulled out a brochure and plan of Holmwood House. 'Let me show you the kind of events we have in mind.'

'Can you all make sure your mobiles are turned off?' Charles Denton looked around the great hall with an assessing eye. He was not what Roz had expected. Not that she had had a clear idea of what a psychic might look like, but Charles certainly wasn't it. He might have been an accountant with his sober face and faintly shiny suit and tie.

On his instructions they had laid a white cloth over a circular oak table that Lucy had sourced the week before. A bowl of water and some salt were set in the centre of the table with a feather, seven candles burning around them. There had been some discussion about whether or not they should have real candles.

'It's a fire risk,' Roz had said dubiously, but Adrian, who

had proved surprisingly enthusiastic about the idea and insisted on taking part, overruled her.

'We can't have a séance without candles,' he said, and Charles had agreed.

'The séance will work better with the four magic elements in place,' he said, and touched the salt, the feather and the dish of water in turn. 'Earth, air, water . . .' He passed a hand through a candle flame, making it duck and weave. 'And fire.'

Now they took their places around the table. Adrian and Helen, Lucy and Mark, Jeff and Roz. 'Three men, three women – that is good.' Charles nodded approvingly. 'That will create energy for the spirits. I sense that some of you are sceptical,' he went on, 'but I would ask that you be respectful of the spirits we invite here tonight. A séance should be taken very seriously, whether you are a believer or not. I sense that there are strong spirits here, and some psychically gifted people around this table.' His gaze travelled round them, and Roz kept her face as blank and puzzled as everyone else's. He nodded as if satisfied. 'Now, join hands and we will make a sacred circle.'

Roz was sitting between Jeff and Mark. Her heart was thudding uncomfortably. Charles had set out bowls of cinnamon and sandalwood which he had claimed would help create a relaxed atmosphere but to Roz the smell of them was having the opposite effect. The air seemed charged with expectancy and in spite of the inevitable jokes when they had all gathered that evening, their faces in the candlelight were solemn.

It's a marketing exercise, Roz told herself again as she linked hands with Mark. She hadn't slipped back to Jane's life since the night at Holme Hall, and she was beginning to think that Nick might be right after all and that her experiences as Jane were just some bizarre psychological episode. She might even have been tempted to cancel the séance if Helen hadn't been so sniffy about it, but it wasn't a bad idea and she noticed that Helen had tagged along with Adrian anyway and was sitting across the table looking deeply uncomfortable.

On her other side, Jeff seemed reluctant to take her hand, and thinking that he might be shy, she reached out and took his instead, but the moment his fingers closed around hers, a warning shrieked through her, a shock that made her flinch but was gone so quickly that afterwards she thought she must have imagined it.

Charles was mixing a little of the salt with the water, and drawing circles in the air with his wet finger. 'Spirits of this place, we summon you,' he said, his voice sonorous in the hall. 'Please, come, move among us and communicate with us.'

Silence. But a silence that hummed and twanged with warning. Roz glanced around the table. She wanted to get up, to break the circle and leave, but how could she? Nobody else seemed to notice anything amiss.

'Is there anybody there?' Charles asked.

A muffled thump. There was a stir around the table, quickly shushed. Helen's face was tightly set, her eyes screwed shut as she clung to Adrian's hands. She looked terrified, thought Roz, who had suspected her at first of making the noise.

'Do you wish to speak to someone here?'

This time, there was no noise, just a puff of air, a breath on the back of Roz's neck that had her jerking her head around. When she looked back at Charles, he was watching her steadily.

'Where are you, Jane?' he asked, and Roz felt her lips part as the words were pulled out of her throat.

'I am here,' she said.

At the sound of Margaret's voice, Jane straightened from the cradle with a puzzled frown. It wasn't like Margaret to come in search of her. She normally sent a maid with a summons to her chamber, and she had little interest in Geoffrey.

Robert had accepted Jane's excuse of sickness in the village without demur. It was enough for him to know that he had a son, and he was glad for her to stay away, but when the chill seeped into the air and the wind lifted the dead leaves in the courtyard in little eddies, she had returned reluctantly to the city with Geoffrey and Annis before the roads became impassable. They left Juliana behind in the village churchyard, where she had been buried with only Jane, Annis and the midwife as witnesses to her passing. Poor Juliana, Jane had thought sadly, who had longed so for the excitement and bustle of London, laid to rest for eternity in an obscure hamlet.

Robert came with his mother to inspect Geoffrey in his cradle when they returned to Micklegate. Margaret insisted that Jane unswaddle him so that she could check that he was indeed a male child. 'Good,' she said, covering the baby indifferently. 'He is healthy?'

'Yes, he—'

'Then we have what we need.' She and Robert smiled triumphantly at each other.

A son gave Robert access to his fortune at last, and he was well pleased. Had his father known of the warped relationship between his wife and his son? Jane often wondered. Was that why he had arranged matters so? Perhaps he had hoped that a wife and a child would lessen Margaret's malign influence.

If so, he would have been disappointed. Geoffrey's existence changed little in Micklegate for Robert and Margaret. At least Jane now had a child to care for, and she lavished attention on him as if to make up for the fact that she did not, could not, love him as she had promised to do.

Geoffrey was a good baby, she told herself again and again. He ate, he slept, he soiled his swaddling. He grew. He rarely cried. But there was something furious she sensed in him, as if he resented his baby form, and was contemptuous of her endearments. When she tried to cuddle him, he lolled his head away in distaste and his black eyes stared flintily back at her, and she would find her voice trailing off, feeling foolish and uneasy. The only time his face brightened was when she held a candle over the cradle to check on him at night. She had noticed that he was captivated by the flickering flame. It was the only time Jane ever saw him smile.

She had longed so for a child, but she had never imagined it would feel like this.

Now Juliana was dead, and her child looked back at Jane with a black, blank stare.

Be careful what you wish for.

I will be a mother to him as if I had borne him myself, she had promised Juliana. *I will care for him and love him, and I will never abandon him, not while breath is in my body.*

Perhaps she might not be able to love Geoffrey as much as she wanted, but she would keep the rest of her promise to her sister, Jane vowed. So she continued to sing as she sewed, pushing the cradle with one foot, and she was trying to coax a smile from him with a rattle when she heard Margaret calling for her.

'I am here,' she said.

Margaret didn't even glance at the cradle as she swept in, her skirts so wide and stiff that she grazed the doorway.

'We will have a feast to celebrate the birth of Robert's son,' she announced. 'It will be Christmas soon. Robert will invite his friends to a Yuletide feast, let us say on the feast of St Nicholas. See to it that the best dishes are prepared. Let no expense be spared.'

Jane inclined her head. The Holmwoods, it seemed, were determined to flaunt their change in fortune. Her dowry had been welcome, but it was Geoffrey's existence that unlocked the coffers of the estate. 'I will make sure that all is arranged, but I must beg to be excused the feast itself. I am still in mourning for my sister.'

She did not expect Margaret to care, but to her surprise Robert's mother looked concerned. 'But you must come!' she said, frowning. 'You are Geoffrey's mother. To be sure, it is sad about your sister, but is your son's birth not something to make you rejoice?'

Jane was torn. She grieved most sincerely for Juliana, and it did not seem fitting to carouse at a feast, but was Margaret's insistence that she attend not an olive branch? Perhaps she and Robert had been moved by Geoffrey's existence after all, and were trying in their own way to include Jane and the babe in the household.

'You may ask your father too, if you wish,' said Margaret as Jane continued to hesitate.

He would not come. Henry Birkby was a broken man since learning of Juliana's death. Jane had hoped that news of a grandson would console him in some way, but her father refused to see Geoffrey or Jane, whom he blamed for taking Juliana to the country. They had told him Juliana would keep Jane company in her confinement. Jane would not distress him further by telling him the truth, and besides, she had promised Juliana she would keep her secret.

But Margaret's invitation, careless as it was, seemed to suggest that they were prepared to include Jane more. It would be churlish to refuse such a gesture.

'Very well,' she said. 'I will be there.'

'Good.' Margaret's smile warmed only for Robert, and when she summoned one now it struck Jane as more like a baring of teeth. 'Buy yourself a new gown too,' she said. 'The black does not suit you.'

Juliana would have said the same. Jane did her best to shake off her sadness. Here, at last, was a chance to make things better. She should not waste it. So she set the maids to work in the kitchen and took Annis to Coney Street to buy cloth for a new gown.

The draper, Christopher Harrison, had already sniffed out the change in the Holmwoods' fortunes and served Jane himself, pulling out roll after roll of costly fabrics with his stubby fingers and spilling them across his counter in a jumble of blues and reds and greens so rich they hurt Jane's eyes. She and Annis fingered velvets and broadcloth, taffetas and scarlets, damasks and satins.

'It is too hard to choose,' sighed Jane, remembering Juliana with a pang. Her sister had ever had an eye for colour. *This one*, she would have said instantly. *This one, not that one, and this for the sleeves. Not black or white for you, Jane. You must have colour.*

In the end Jane chose a shot taffeta in a dazzling blue for the gown, with a creamy damask to embroider for the stomacher, and slashed satin for the sleeves. In a giddying moment of extravagance she ordered velvet for trimming and coloured threads and the finest lawn for a new ruff too.

'Oh mistress, it will be beautiful,' said Annis, stroking the satin enviously under Mr Harrison's hard gaze. '*You* will be beautiful.'

Jane laughed and gave Annis's arm an affectionate squeeze. 'I fear it would take more than a gown to make me beautiful, Annis. I know well I am plain, but I will feel fine indeed in this lovely blue.'

'Where will you take it to be made up?' asked Annis as they left the shop, their breath puffing in white clouds on the frosty air. 'They say John Harper in Stonegate knows how to ply a needle,' she smirked, only to look puzzled when Jane's face clouded. She did not know Jane was thinking of Juliana, and of John Harper's hairy hands and lascivious red mouth making merry with her sister, ruining her reputation without a thought.

'No,' she said sharply. 'Not there.'

The servants would have their own feast after the main meal had been served and would be dancing in the yard. Jane couldn't help thinking wistfully that she would rather spend the evening with them than with her own husband and his gentlemanly friends. Annis was looking forward to it. She had renewed her flirtation with Jack, whose master lived next door and who would be one of Robert's guests. 'Jack says he's a clodhopper but I will wear my best kirtle.' Annis mimed tugging down her bodice to reveal more of her breasts with a mock lascivious roll of her eyes. 'I'm hoping he'll dance "John, Come Kiss Me Now" with me!'

Jane smiled at her maid's antics. 'Annis,' she said impulsively. 'I am to have a new gown, and you should too. The red kirtle I wore for my betrothal is barely worn. You have it,' she said. 'You can furbish it with new sleeves and buttons and Jack will not be able to resist you!'

'Oh mistress!' Annis came to a complete stop in the middle of Ousegate, her eyes round like an owl's. 'Oh Mistress, do you mean it? But it is too good for me!'

'Nonsense,' said Jane briskly. 'It is just sitting in a chest.' She hadn't been able to bear to wear it since Juliana had told her she was with child. It made her think of John Harper sewing it, his fingers stroking the fabric, the lewd gleam in his eye. 'I will not wear it again, Annis,' she said. It was too cold to stand still, and they set off walking again, their clogs skidding on the icy cobbles. 'I would like you to have it.'

Margaret had said that no expense was to be spared, and Jane took her at her word. Outside the city glittered with frost, and the cold made Jane's teeth ache whenever she stepped outside, but in the house on Micklegate the kitchen was so hot the door into the yard had to be kept open all day. Jane laboured with the maids to make the great feast she had planned.

For the first course, a pig roasted on the spit, roasted veal and roasted beef. Geese and chickens. Pies and stewed meats and custards. Then there were to be capons and coneys, peahens and larks and pigeons, all roasted. A baked venison and tarts, and at last, sugar dainties in the shape of goblets. Jane made those herself, shaving the sugarloaf and shaping the goblets carefully.

In spite of the heat she was sorry to leave the kitchen where the maids were chattering excitedly about the dancing to come, and blushing and giggling and nudging each other whenever any lad came with a message or a delivery. But Annis came with her to help her dress and together they checked that the hall was ready for their guests.

Two long trestle tables lined the hall, adjoining the top table, and all were laid with damask cloths and linen napkins. Robert had insisted on glass goblets for everyone, and Jane straightened one nervously. 'Finger bowls . . . salt . . . pepper boxes . . .' She put a hand to her head. 'The chafing dishes! Annis, are there coals ready?'

'Everything is ready,' said Annis firmly. 'Everything except you! Now come, mistress, and let me dress you or you will be late for your own feast.'

The tailor had wrought a small miracle with her gown, Jane thought, swaying her hips this way and that to feel the fabric rustle luxuriously over the French farthingale. She had embroidered the stomacher herself with scabious and pinks and wild strawberries, and Annis helped her pin it into place before fixing pearls around her waist.

'I'm not sure I can breathe,' said Jane, putting a hand over the bodice. 'You have laced me so tight!'

'Nonsense,' Annis tsked. She tweaked the pearls into place and stepped back, eyeing Jane critically. 'Oh mistress, you look a perfect pippin! Tonight, you'll see, your husband will realize what a treasure he has in you.'

Chapter Thirteen

At first it seemed as if it might indeed be so. 'You are in good looks tonight, wife,' Robert said, loudly enough for others to hear. He took her hand and kissed the tips of her fingers. 'Friends, you must let me present my wife to you,' he said, turning to show her off to four young gentlemen about his own age. He gabbled off their names, so that Jane couldn't catch them properly. 'Sir Francis . . .' he said, waving vaguely, '. . . Charles . . . Mortimer . . . Sir Thomas Parker. Gentlemen, my wife,' he said, an undercurrent in his voice that Jane couldn't quite identify.

Jane sketched a curtsey, uncomfortable beneath their avid gazes. For once she was pleased when Margaret appeared beside her. 'That colour becomes you,' she said to Jane, looking her up and down, and even producing a thin smile. 'Something has put a glow in your cheeks!'

If she was glowing, it was from being in the kitchen all day, but Jane bit back a tart response. Margaret and Robert were making an effort to be pleasant. She should do the same.

'Come, sit.' Robert waved his friends to a place at the table, but insisted that Jane sit beside him. This was how she had once imagined marriage to Robert, thought Jane, puzzled but pleased. Sitting next to him, feeling welcomed, and valued.

It didn't feel quite real.

The great hall was soon ringing with noise and laughter. Jane nodded to Annis, who supervised the bringing out of the first course, and there were murmurs of appreciation as dish after dish was laid on the tables. Other servants moved up and down the room refilling goblets with wine, replenishing finger bowls or replacing crumpled napkins. In the fireplace at the other end of the hall, the Yule log spat and crackled.

The feast was a triumph. Everyone said so. Jane could tell it for herself as the volume rose and the faces along the tables shone with grease and gluttony, and she felt bad for longing for it to be over. She had worked so hard to prepare everything that she was weary now, and self-conscious in her fine new clothes. The ruff around her collar was growing limp in the heat, and the farthingale bunched behind her. Her laces were so tight she hardly dared eat anything.

Catching Annis's eye, she gestured for the second course to be removed. Soon the sugar surprises would be brought in, and then the tables would be cleared and pushed back; she would just have to get through the dancing and *then* she would be able to go to bed.

The sugar comfits caused more murmurs of delight. 'You have done well, wife,' said Robert to Jane's surprise, and she turned to see him pouring more wine into her goblet. 'Come, have some wine and let us drink to our son.'

Another unexpected compliment! Was it possible that this might be the start of a new relationship between them? Jane couldn't help the flicker of guilt as she accepted the goblet. He would not be so pleasant if he knew that she had lied to him, that Geoffrey was not his son, nor hers, but a cuckoo in the nest.

But it was too late to confess now. She was bound to keep Geoffrey safe. And Robert was pleased to have a son. All was for the best.

So she smiled a little stiffly and raised her goblet to Robert. 'To our son,' she agreed, and drank.

The hall grew hotter and hotter. Heat piled upon heat, noise upon noise. When the guests had eaten their fill, Jane signalled to the servants to clear away the dishes and dismantle the tables, and the waits began tuning up for the dancing. She was starting to feel dizzy and a bit sick, but she couldn't leave her husband's feast, not yet. She plastered a smile to her face and prayed that she would not faint.

She was just wondering if she could slip outside to cool down when Margaret appeared by her side. 'The babe is crying in your chamber,' she said. 'You'd better go and see to him.'

Jane was too relieved at the chance to leave the overheated room to wonder why Margaret was concerning herself with Geoffrey, or why she hadn't sent a servant. She'd hoped that the dizziness would clear away from the heat, but it seemed to be getting worse, and she had to hold on to the wall as she climbed the stairs. Every step was an effort and she was breathing heavily by the time she got to the top. Swaying slightly, she stood holding on to the newel post. If she could just get to the chamber, she could lie down for a minute. Perhaps that would help.

Geoffrey was sleeping, his face screwed up in furious concentration, but with no sign of distress. Jane frowned, but her head was fuzzy and she groped her way over to the bed, practically falling onto it when she got there.

'Aha, at last, my partridge!'

There was someone in her bed. 'Wha . . .?' Her farthingale was tipping her off balance and she struggled to right herself, but the chamber was spinning around her; her eyelids were weighted with lead, and she couldn't make sense of anything.

She was dreaming. There couldn't be anybody in her chamber, in her bed. But if it was a dream, it was a nightmare. Greasy fingers were fumbling at the neck of her smock, ripping her lovingly embroidered stomacher from its pins and scrabbling determinedly into her bodice to expose her breasts.

'No . . .' From somewhere Jane summoned the strength to open her eyes. Thomas Parker, gentleman, was kneeling over her, fumbling at the ties of his breeches. He stank of stale wine and unwashed linen. His face glistened with sweat and grease from the meal and his eyes were glassy.

'You're not as bad as Robert says,' he informed her, slurring his words. 'You've got a nice pair of titties on you.' To prove his point, he kneaded them roughly with one hand, digging into his breeches with the other. 'I've had worse.'

To Jane, everything seemed to be happening at a distance.

Her mind was sluggish, and when she tried to lift her hands to push him away they flailed limply. Now his yard sprang free of his breeches and he was burrowing beneath her skirts, pushing them up. She tried to scream, but her body wouldn't obey her mind, and her eyes rolled back in horror. She was not dreaming, no. This was horribly real. It was as if she were floating above the bed looking down at her slack form and Thomas Parker, her husband's friend, fondling himself as he grunted over her.

Poison. The word swam through the blur in her head, the only thing that made terrifying sense. She had been poisoned. Desperately, Jane willed her hands to move, but they flopped uselessly, as if they belonged to someone else entirely.

Below, the revelry was continuing in the hall as if nothing was happening, the babble of conversation barely drowned by the fiddling and drumming from the waits, the stamp of feet and the clapping of hands as the dancers circled. They were dancing while she was being violated in her own home, and there was nothing she could do. A tear trickled down Jane's numb cheek and she struggled again to wrest control back over her limbs.

'What is the meaning of this?' Margaret's voice cut sharply through her befuddlement, and Jane closed her eyes in relief. She had never been so glad to hear Robert's mother. With an enormous effort, she rolled her head to one side to see Margaret looming by the bed. She looked strange from this angle, her head swollen, her mouth a red slash that opened and closed, her dark eyes glittering. 'You, sir,' she said to Thomas, 'what do you do there with my son's wife?'

'It's too soon,' Thomas grumbled in an undertone. 'I haven't fucked her yet.'

'Wha . . .? Whaa . . .?' Jane's tongue was thick and unwieldy, and her voice came out as slurred as Thomas's, but her mind was clearing.

This was planned. Margaret knew Thomas would be here. That was why she had sent Jane to the chamber to care for Geoffrey.

And that meant Robert knew too. *Let us drink to our son.* Jane pictured him slipping the poison into her goblet, pouring more wine, lifting his own glass. *Smiling.* And *she*, thought Jane in disgust and despair, she had hoped that he was having a change of heart, that things might be different between them, simpleton that she was.

On cue, boots stamped along the passage. 'Ho, there!' came Robert's voice, and Margaret went to the door with a fine display of distress.

'Oh my son, I cannot bear to let you see what is happening within!'

'Stand aside, madam.' Robert shouldered his way into the room.

He had brought witnesses, of course. The three fine gentlemen he had introduced to Jane earlier, when he was playing the part of an attentive husband. Did they not wonder why they were being taken up to his wife's chamber? Jane wondered in her strange detached state. Surely they must ask why they had been taken from the drinking and the dancing to surprise Robert's wife?

But when Robert gasped, 'Thomas!' and reeled back, they didn't even blink at his blatantly false show of shock.

They were part of the plan to shame her too.

Thomas scrambled sulkily off Jane, tucking his yard away. 'Indeed, I am sorry,' he said, parroting the words from his script. 'But your wife did entice me.' They were poor players, Jane thought bitterly. They would have been booed off the stage by any other audience.

There was a tiny pause, and then Thomas resumed at a nod of encouragement from Margaret. 'She said you would not notice if we slipped away from the feast,' he remembered.

'No,' Jane managed, desperation and outrage giving her the strength to speak, but her voice was still thick and blurry. It was like trying to talk with a blanket stuffed in her mouth.

'Drunk,' said Margaret in disgust. 'Bah, what can you expect from a butcher's brat? I thought she was in unexpected good looks, Robert, but never did I imagine your friend Sir Thomas had put the sparkle in her eyes or the roses in her cheeks.'

Robert wore a heavy scowl. 'You have made a cuckold out of me,' he said to Thomas. 'Now I am shamed before my friends.' He turned to his companions. 'You see how I am served? A wife who plays the strumpet, and with my dearest friend . . . oh, how shall I bear the pain of it?'

'Come, sirs.' Margaret moved smoothly forward to usher them towards the door, Thomas shuffling along with them, his part played. 'I beg of you, do not blame my son. He will deal with his wife, I do assure you.'

Closing the door behind them, she exchanged a look of smug complicity with Robert. 'So it is done,' she said with satisfaction.

With a huge effort, Jane leant across so that she could be sick over the edge of the bed. Her vomit splattered sourly on the floorboards and Margaret grimaced with disgust and twitched her skirts clear of the mess. 'Send for a servant to clear this up,' she said to Robert. 'I knew this rush matting was a mistake. Plain rushes are so much easier to deal with.'

'You have poisoned me,' Jane whispered, her head still spinning.

'A little potion to make you sleepy, that is all,' said Margaret dismissively. 'We cannot poison you and keep your dowry.' She put her face down to Jane's and smiled a vicious smile. 'Do not think we have not considered it, but your father, it seems, made provision. Perhaps he realized that no one else would want you. To hide our shame, we will send you back to the country, where you may stay out of our sight and grow old with our good wishes.'

'Mistress?' Annis appeared in the doorway, looking wary, holding a basin and some rags.

'Clear that mess up!' snapped Margaret, jerking her head towards Jane, who was retching again, and she swept out, her skirts swishing contemptuously.

'What did they do to you?' Annis asked in a low voice. She held the basin for Jane, who couldn't stop vomiting and was shaking and sweating.

'Something in the wine,' Jane gasped.

Annis cursed under her breath. 'Here, keep that,' she said, thrusting the basin into Jane's hands. 'I'll go and get another.'

It took more than an hour for Jane to stop retching. When she had finished, she lay exhausted in the bed and Annis wiped her forehead with a damp cloth. 'Better out than in,' she said. 'Any idea what it was?'

Jane shook her head. 'Margaret said they didn't want to kill me.' Her throat was raw, her voice little more than a thread.

'Kind of them,' said Annis grimly.

She was wearing the dress Jane had given her, the one Jane had worn to her betrothal. It made Jane ache for the innocent she had been then. Before she knew the depths to which her husband would sink to be rid of her.

'I am sorry you had to leave the feast,' she whispered. 'Did you get a dance with Jack?'

Annis's expression softened. 'Aye, one, before the message came that you needed me. But it were worth it.' She smiled in a way Jane envied.

Jane's fingers crept around her maid's. 'Annis, what am I going to do? Margaret talks of banishing me to the country. How will I manage without you?'

'I'll come with you,' said Annis. 'I'm not staying to serve these scoundrel Holmwoods,' she said stoutly.

'But what about Jack?'

Annis hesitated, but only for a moment. 'He can come find me if he cares for me.'

Jane tried to smile, but she was too weak, and to her shame her lips trembled and a tear slipped out of the corner of her eyes. 'Come now,' said Annis, patting her hand. 'It will not be so bad. At least you won't have to put up with their meannesses any more.'

'If I could be sure they would let me take the babe, I would be content enough,' said Jane, swallowing painfully. 'I don't care what tales they spread about me being of dishonest conversation with Thomas, but what if they deny me Geoffrey? What will I do then?'

'Perhaps they will not want to care for him?' said Annis hopefully.

But Margaret was triumphant, and in no mood to compromise. 'The child stays here,' she said when Jane was well enough to get out of bed. 'We have been lenient with you. Already the whole city knows how you dishonoured my son, and they consider banishment an unseemly kindness.'

Fury, cold and clear, flooded Jane. 'When it is just the two of us, let us not pretend that we do not both know the truth,' she said tightly. 'Let us not pretend that I am the one whose honour has been called into question. It was not I who slipped a potion in my wine or staged a wooden play to shame me!'

But Margaret was indifferent. 'The ground is hard with frost. You should have no trouble travelling on the roads, and you cannot stay under this roof another day. You may take some servants for your household, but the babe you cannot take.'

'Then I will not go,' said Jane evenly. 'Geoffrey is my son. I will not leave him to you.'

Abruptly Margaret's face flared with anger. 'It is not your

decision to make. It is *you* who are in disgrace. Go, and be grateful banishment is the only punishment we seek.'

'Please.' Jane was getting desperate. She knelt at Margaret's feet. 'I beg of you. You know what it is to care for a son. Geoffrey is mine. How would you feel if someone wanted to take Robert from you?'

Margaret's eyes blazed. 'They never will!'

'Then you will understand when I beg you to let me take my son with me.'

'No. We need the boy here.' A smile that chilled Jane's blood swept over Margaret's face. 'I will look after him.'

As she had looked after Robert? 'No!' said Jane, surging to her feet. 'No, you will not have him to serve your depraved tastes!'

'You forget yourself,' said Margaret, her tone sharp as a slap. 'Who are you, a butcher's daughter, to talk so to me? Be glad we do not send you for trial. Now take your servants and begone.'

'Begone . . .' The sonorous voice was ringing in her ears, deeper than Margaret's and more urgent. 'Go now in peace, Jane.'

Peace? What peace was there to be found knowing that she had broken yet another promise? 'No,' she mumbled, moving her head restlessly from side to side. 'No, I will not go.'

'We ask you to depart in peace,' said the voice more firmly. 'Now you must go.'

She covered her face with her hands. What choice did she have? In the eyes of the law, Geoffrey was Robert's son, and she was just his wife. She had no power, no possessions of her own. Nobody would believe her if she told them that Robert had deliberately arranged for his own cuckolding to be rid of her. No man would shame himself so, they would say.

Her father would not stand by her. Her friends from St Andrewgate had been lost to her since her marriage. There was only Annis who believed her, and she was just a servant, even more powerless than Jane.

For now she had little choice but to go. But somehow, Jane vowed, lowering her hands, *somehow* she would keep her promise.

Drawing a deep breath, straightening her shoulders, she looked up, and blinked in confusion. Why was it so dark suddenly? A moment ago Margaret's chamber had been ablaze with candles; now they were all snuffed except for seven flames in the middle of the table, leaping and guttering in the draught.

She turned to look for Annis, but Annis had gone and in her place was a man who looked vaguely familiar and who was staring at her in fury. Uneasy, she glanced back at Margaret and found herself meeting the implacable gaze of a woman sitting across the table.

'Roz, are you awake?'

Another man was looking directly at her. He was speaking to her. Like a key turning in a well-oiled lock, understanding clicked into place. Roz. She was Roz.

Her mouth was suddenly dry. She ran her tongue around her lips.

'I see you're back with us.' Roz remembered his name now:

Charles Denton, the psychic investigator she had booked so casually.

'Yes.' Her eyes flicked around the table. In the candlelight, everyone was watching her with a range of expressions from open curiosity (Lucy and Mark) to concern (Adrian) and ill-disguised impatience (Helen). Why did she think that Jeff was furious with her? Now his face was carefully blank. How much had she given away? Roz smiled nervously. 'What did I miss?'

'You were under the influence of a very powerful spirit,' Charles told her.

'It was really creepy,' Lucy added. She rubbed her arms. 'God, I can't believe it happened. I never thought there would really be anything here!'

'You were in a trance,' Mark told Roz. 'We couldn't work out what was happening. You were trying to speak, and I think you were saying no but it was hard to tell. Your voice was all slurred.'

'You were obviously in distress,' said Adrian.

Obviously putting it on, thought Helen, unimpressed. *God, what a fuss!*

'I wanted to wake you up,' Adrian was saying, 'but Charles said it could be dangerous.'

'It's normally better to let someone come round naturally but Jane had such a strong hold on you that I had to intervene in the end and tell her to go, but she was very resistant.'

'Jane?' said Roz hesitantly.

'I sensed her too,' said Charles. 'She is driven by the need to tell her story.' Helen rolled her eyes but Charles ignored her.

'You should be careful, Roz. Did you know that you were psychically sensitive?'

Oh yes, of course Roz would be 'psychically sensitive'! She couldn't be like everyone else, could she? Tight-lipped, Helen drummed her fingers on the table until a worried look from Adrian made her stop. But honestly, couldn't they all see that Roz was just a massive attention seeker? Look at her now, hugging her arms together as if she was scared and nervous!

'I never used to believe in ghosts,' Roz said.

'And now?'

She shivered and her eyes slid away from Charles's without answering.

Lucy leant forward eagerly. 'Do you remember what happened?'

'Not really,' said Roz, but so carefully that even Helen could see that she was lying. There was something Roz wanted to have coaxed from her. Being Roz, she couldn't just tell them. Oh no, everyone would have to keep looking at her and asking her questions and cajoling her into answers.

Helen looked round the table. Sure enough, they were all hanging on Roz's every word.

All except Jeff, who was looking at Roz with a hard expression that Helen couldn't identify but that brought her up short.

She didn't like Jeff. There was something downright creepy about him, although Sir Adrian couldn't see it, of course. He thought Jeff was a 'good chap'. Sir Adrian saw the good in everyone, Helen thought with fond exasperation. She was less trusting. She'd seen the way Jeff looked at Sir Adrian sometimes. Once or twice, Sir Adrian had spoken to him and then turned to go, and Helen had caught the naked contempt on Jeff's face. What right had *he* to be contemptuous? Helen bridled at the very thought. She knew Jeff had been in a secure unit for youths before his release, but not why. It had to be something bad for a boy to be put away, though, didn't it?

Now Helen's eyes sharpened with interest. It hadn't occurred to her that Jeff might dislike Roz too. Well, well, well.

The psychic was looking disappointed. 'You don't have a message for anyone here?'

'A message?' Roz echoed blankly.

'There must be a reason this spirit cannot rest.'

'But why would she have a message for someone here?' asked Lucy.

'Jane is not the only spirit here,' said Charles. 'This house is a vortex of hostile energy.'

Only since Roz had arrived, Helen wanted to tell them. It wasn't ghosts disrupting the atmosphere. It was Roz, coming here, distracting Adrian, *spoiling* everything.

Adrian was looking delighted. 'So Holmwood House really is haunted?'

'Oh yes.'

'How splendid!'

Helen thought it was time to inject a note of practicality into the discussion. 'How come nobody has seen these ghosts if the house is haunted?'

'You don't have to see a ghost to be aware of its presence.' Charles was unfazed. 'You tell me this house was only recently reconstructed. The spirits may have been waiting for just such an opportunity to return. Has anyone noticed themselves feeling different lately? Perhaps angrier or more hostile than they usually are without understanding why?'

Helen's mind flickered to the earring she had taken from Roz, to the button she had snipped from her coat. To the suffocating loathing that swept over her sometimes when she looked at Roz. But that wasn't because of any ghost, and she certainly wasn't going to encourage this so-called psychic by saying anything. There was no puzzle about why she hated Roz.

Charles looked around the table and it seemed to Helen that his gaze stopped on her for an uncomfortably long while, but she lifted her chin and outstared him, and after another moment, he moved on.

'Even so, I think it would be a good idea to set a healing process in motion,' he said. 'I can come back when I'm prepared and conduct another séance to ask these troubled spirits to depart.'

'I don't think that's necessary,' said Adrian, leaning forward. 'The whole purpose of this exercise was to find evidence of some ghostly activity, and now we have, we have to admit it would be good for business to have a resident ghost or two.'

Mark nodded eagerly. 'It would be a big draw. It could make quite a difference to the number of visitors we get.'

'I say we use this ghost.' Adrian looked around for agreement. 'Roz, can you really not remember anything about her? Charles says her name is Jane, but that doesn't tell us much.'

Roz was looking a bit sick. Helen was sure she could see

sweat breaking out on her forehead. 'I . . . don't remember,' she said.

'I was sitting next to you. I thought I heard you say Geoffrey a couple of times,' Jeff volunteered. It was his first contribution to the conversation. Helen's eyes narrowed. She hadn't heard Roz say anything of the kind, but of course Sir Adrian's face lit up straight away.

'I wonder if there's a possible link with our Sir Geoffrey? She could be his wife perhaps?'

'Or his mother? Or sister?'

Charles cut through the speculation. 'Whoever she was, using her spirit as a business asset is disrespectful,' he said disapprovingly. 'I advise you to be very careful. You don't know what you're dealing with here. Roz, you in particular must find a way to protect yourself until we can persuade this unquiet spirit to move on.'

Roz in particular. As always.

Helen glanced at Jeff again. The candle flames threw flickering shadows over his face and his expression as he watched Roz sent a sharp shudder down Helen's spine.

Adrian was fulsome in apologies to Roz. 'I should have thought about you. It must have been a very strange experience. If you don't want to be involved in anything related to promoting the haunted house side of things, then of course we'd understand.'

'I'm the events director,' Roz reminded him. She seemed to have recovered some of her control. 'Of course I need to be involved in any promotions.'

'You won't find it too upsetting?'

Helen noticed that Roz avoided answering that one directly. 'Mark is right. It would be a fantastic opportunity to get more visitors to Holmwood House. We don't need to turn it into a tacky house of horrors, but I don't see any harm in mentioning that we've had a séance here, and that in spite of some scepticism there were indications of a ghostly presence.' She hesitated. 'Perhaps we could do some research and see if we can find out who Jane really is – or was.'

'That's a great idea,' said Mark.

'Or,' said Sir Adrian, 'we could ask Charles to do another séance. We could see if he could reach Jane again through you and ask her.'

But Charles was shaking his head. 'It's too dangerous. I've encountered a lot of spirits in my time, but there is something very wrong here. I won't be involved in anything other than a cleansing séance. Spirits are not something to be played with or exploited for marketing purposes.'

'We're planning to be respectful. You heard what Roz said.' Helen could see that Sir Adrian had made up his mind. If *Roz* had said something, that was what they were all going to do. For a moment she felt a spurt of contempt so vicious that she flinched, but the next moment it had gone, leaving her confused and distressed. Her admiration and longing for Sir Adrian structured her entire world and even a flash of contempt for him shook her foundations. It was almost as if somebody else had been in her head, looking at him with different eyes.

Has anyone noticed themselves feeling different lately?

Charles Denton had asked. *Angrier or more hostile than they usually are?* Helen brushed the memory away as if it were an irritating fly buzzing in her head. There had been enough nonsense here tonight. Sir Adrian relied on her to be practical and sensible. *She* was not going to join in all the hysteria about ghosts.

She glanced up to find Charles Denton watching her. 'None of you know what you're dealing with. I think you should all be very, very careful.'

'I was hoping for rain.' Jane and Annis were lurking in the churchyard of the old priory, trying to look inconspicuous. Over Annis's shoulder, she could see the sign of the red boar swinging gently in the spring breeze. Micklegate was thronged with folk, all glad to see the sunshine after months, it seemed, of a dreary mizzle that cast a damp dew over everything. For weeks the sodden guards on Jane's kirtle had dragged at the roll on her waist, and inside every house the smell of wet wool from doublets, gowns, kirtles and breeches steaming in the heat of the fire had been overpowering.

But today the lowering carpet of cloud had vanished as if it had never been. The sun was shining and the promise of spring at last drew people out into the street. It was as if they had woken to a different world. Instead of huddling into their gowns and hurrying home, heads down against the rain, they dawdled and smiled at each other. They stopped to talk and exclaim at the softness of the air, the brightness of the sky. The cobbles might be slippery still, the gardens still clogged with mud, but the sunlight glittered on the Ouse and the whole city seemed to be out and about and in a sociable mood.

Which was the last thing Jane wanted. She was in disguise and she couldn't afford to be recognized today. She and Annis were dressed as countrywomen in short skirts and coarse aprons, their neckerchiefs pulled up over their noses the way peasant women did on dusty tracks. There was little enough chance of dust after the last few weeks, and the real country-women in the market that morning were all bare-faced, breathing in the sparkling spring air, but Jane didn't want to risk anyone seeing her face. Because this was the day she was going to steal Geoffrey back.

For months she had wracked her brains about how to keep her promise to Juliana. She had been bundled off to Holme Hall with Annis, a groom and two male serving men the day after the feast, before she had an opportunity to appeal to her father or her friends. Not that her father would have taken her part anyway, Jane knew. He would not forgive her for Juliana, and her friends would soon hear the rumours that she had been found making merry with Sir Thomas Parker. They might shake their heads at her banishment, but they wouldn't question Robert's right to keep his son. No smoke without fire, they would say.

Jane was on her own.

She fretted constantly about Geoffrey, and would not be consoled. 'They need him for his inheritance,' Annis had tried pointing out. 'They will have to take good care of him.'

'Oh, they will feed him, I dare say,' said Jane, wringing her hands, 'but they will not be tender with him. They will not sing to him or rock him to sleep.' She imagined Geoffrey left to cry in his cradle, or worse, Margaret lifting him up, as she must once have lifted Robert, playing with him in ways that made Jane's skin crawl to think of. 'I *must* find a way to get back to him!'

Swallowing her pride, she wrote begging for forgiveness for the things she had not done. She asked if she could go back to York. She would live as a servant, she said, as long as she could care for the child.

Robert's answer was gleefully cruel. She must stay in the country. She had shamed him too much. She was lucky he had not sent her for trial for adultery and fornication. He would not have her tainting his son.

Jane tore up the letter, her lips compressed in fury. If Robert would not let her care for the child, she would take Geoffrey, she vowed.

Annis was doubtful. 'Where would we go? This is the first place the Holmwoods would look for him.'

'We will go to London.' The idea appeared fully formed in Jane's head, and the words were out of her mouth before she had a chance to think about them. 'York is too small to hide. They would find us in no time.' She turned the idea over in her mind, testing it, liking it. 'No, it must be London, or I will never be free of them. They say there are so many folk there, you can walk a mile and never see a face you know. How would Robert find us in London?'

'But how would we get there?' Annis's eyes were wide. 'What would we do? We know no one in London.'

'We know Jack.'

For Jack had come a-wooing of Annis at the first break in the weather. He was quiet but sturdy, like Annis, with a calm face and steady blue eyes, and Jane had rejoiced to see how Annis glowed when he arrived.

Jack brought news of the city, and of Geoffrey. A girl had been brought in to care for the baby, he reported, but she was reputedly a slattern, and although Jack was only next door he hadn't seen her for himself. He had heard the babe crying occasionally, so he knew Geoffrey was alive, but more than that he could not say.

Geoffrey, cared for by a doxy. Jane could not bear the thought. She had to get him away.

Jack, when applied to, was definite. Jane and Annis could not go to London on their own, babe or no babe.

'Annis, let us be wed,' he said. 'I will tell my master I need to go home to London. My family have an inn near Aldgate. We can go there. There are so many people coming and going, there will be none to notice you amongst so many. Annis and I can work in the inn but you, my lady . . .' He looked doubtfully at Jane. 'You are a gentlewoman. What can you do?'

'You forget I am a butcher's daughter,' said Jane. 'I will do what I must.' She turned over her hands to show Jack her palms. 'These are not a gentlewoman's hands, Jack. I can cook and I can read and cast accounts. I can sew and make remedies. I do not sit in my chamber sighing for company.'

She glanced at Annis for confirmation and saw that her maid was poppy red. Jane bit down a smile. 'Well, anyway, we will make our plans, but first I have things to do. Do you stay with Jack, Annis, and perhaps he can find better words to ask you to marry him!'

Jack looked sheepish. 'I'll try, my lady, but I'm not handy with words.' His eyes rested on Annis and what she saw in his expression made Jane's heart twist with envy. 'And I might need you as a witness in case she changes her mind.'

'Will you marry Jack, Annis?'

Annis tossed her head. 'I'll have to think about it,' she said, and Jane laughed.

'Jack, if anyone asks, I will swear that I heard her say yes!'

Annis's betrothal and marriage were the only bright spots in the dark of those few months. Jane worried away at a plan to rescue Geoffrey but in the end could think only of the simplest: to walk in and take him for herself.

Today was the appointed day. Jack had struck up a flirtation with Geoffrey's nurse, and had arranged an assignation with her when he knew that Robert would be out of the house. Margaret's movements were less predictable, but Jane had waited long enough. Robert's mother didn't concern herself with the running of the house. She stayed in her parlour, a spider at the centre of her web, and rarely ventured out. Jane would have to risk walking past her door.

Annis didn't like it. 'What if someone sees you? Do you know what they would do to you if they caught you stealing the child? Let me go.'

'Do you know what they would do to you if they caught you stealing the child?' Jane quoted her words back to her. 'I could not have that on my conscience, Annis. No, Geoffrey is my responsibility. I will go myself.'

Across the street, Jack had emerged from the passage leading down to the yard with his arm around a buxom maid whose bodice was laced tight over a scandalously low-cut smock. She was tittering and tossing her head, and she didn't even try to resist when Jack drew her into a doorway and let his hand dabble at the edge of her smock.

Annis's eyes narrowed above her neckerchief. 'I hope he's not enjoying that too much!'

'Quick, I must go now,' said Jane. She picked up her basket. If anyone asked, she was delivering cheese to the kitchen. She had bought some in the market that morning and covered it with a cloth.

Annis touched her arm. 'Be careful.'

Chapter Fourteen

Making herself saunter casually like everyone else that fine day, Jane walked under the lychgate and was heading directly for the arched passageway leading to the back of the house when the front door opened and Margaret swept out, accompanied by her slack-jawed maid. She would have walked right across Jane's path if Jane had not veered away through the crowd, her heart beating like a wait's drum.

Her knuckles were white on the handle of her basket. If Margaret spotted her, she would drop the basket and run, she decided wildly – but run where? The slightest suspicion that she was in York would make the Holmwoods guard Geoffrey carefully. She would not get another chance, Jane knew. She stopped and put her basket down, stooping as if to adjust her garter, and watched under her lashes as Margaret swished past, her maid trailing behind her.

Straightening in relief, Jane met Jack's eyes over the nurse's shoulder. He jerked his head towards the passage, and Jane nodded briefly back, telling him that she understood that she had to hurry.

It was strange to be back in the house of which she had once been mistress, but Jane had no time to linger over memories. The fine weather worked in her favour now. Most of the servants, it seemed, had found an excuse to be outside and only a sulky crashing of pots in the kitchen indicated that one of the younger maids had been left to clear up. Meg, probably. Jane tiptoed past the door and along the passage to the buttery and then into the hall. It was very quiet, so quiet that Jane could hear a fly, warmed from its cold-induced stupor, beating itself against one of the expensive glass windows.

It was hard to keep her sturdy shoes from ringing on the wooden stairs, but Jane went up as quietly as she could. She had put Geoffrey's cradle in her chamber, but when she peeped inside, the room was empty. So was the parlour and Margaret's chamber.

Cautiously, she stepped over to the doorway and listened. The house felt empty. Where else might a child be? Moving as silently as she could over the creaking floorboards, she climbed the next flight of stairs and was almost at the top when a latch clattered and Nan, one of the servants Jane had employed, came whistling to the top of the steps.

There was nowhere for Jane to hide. Nan saw her the moment she swung down the stairs and she opened her mouth to cry out in shock. Quickly, Jane tugged down the kerchief to show her face. 'It is I, Nan,' she said as calmly as she could. 'Where is my child?'

Nan swallowed. 'In the chamber above, mistress.'

They had put Geoffrey up with the servants. 'I wish to see him.' Jane was amazed at her own calmness, the authority in her voice that had Nan turning obediently and leading the way up to a sordid room under the eaves. There stood the cradle, unrocked, and within it Geoffrey, black eyes blank and unresponsive.

When Jane lifted him up, she smelt that he had soiled himself and she was so angry she felt dizzy. 'What have they done to you?' she whispered. She swung round to Nan. 'I am taking him with me, Nan, but I don't want you to suffer for it.'

'I will say I saw nothing.' Nan looked at the baby. 'That slattern should be caring for the babe, but she don't like him. Says he looks at her funny.'

'He is a *child*.' Jane had been worrying about how the Holmwoods would react to losing Geoffrey, and whether they would take it out on the maid, but now she had seen how little the nurse did for him, she didn't care any more.

'She holds the candle right up to his face. Like a game.' Nan shivered. 'She *says* he likes it but it don't seem right to me.'

'No,' said Jane, grim-faced.

'Here.' Nan snatched up some clean swaddling cloths, tipped the cheese out onto the floor, and pushed the cloths into Jane's basket. 'I'll carry this if you bring the bairn.'

She led the way softly down the stairs, but as they turned for the next flight, they heard someone coming up. Frantically Nan shoved the basket into Jane's free hand and gestured her into the nearest chamber.

'Is that you, Meg?' she called.

'Where have you been?' Meg grumbled, stumping up the stairs. 'I've been calling and calling you.'

'I've been in't parlour. You'll never guess what I saw from the window.'

'What?'

'Come and see.' Nan drew Meg into the parlour, and Jane slipped down the stairs, tucking Geoffrey into the basket on top of the swaddling and covering him with the cloth. It wasn't right for a baby to lie so still and unprotesting, but right then she was glad of his quietness. In the doorway, she pulled up her kerchief once more, took a deep breath and stepped out into the street. No one shouted, 'Stop, thief!' No one stared.

Her heart was in her mouth as she walked, not too quickly, across to the churchyard, and her hands shook as she handed the basket to Annis while she got her breath back.

'You got him?' Annis said, feeling the weight of the basket, and Jane let herself smile at last as she nodded.

'I did it!'

'When you came out with just the basket, I felt sure you hadn't been able to find him. I wondered what we were going to do.'

'Now we can go.' Jane took the basket back. 'You give Jack the signal all's well.'

Annis sauntered across to where Jack was still dawdling with the maid and offered him a posy of flowers from her basket. 'A posy for the pretty lady?' she begged him.

The maid looked hopeful, but her face fell when Jack made

an irritable gesture. 'Begone!' he said to Annis, then he turned with a flourish to lift the maid's hand to his lips. 'I have tarried too long. I must go, my dove.'

'My dove?' Annis echoed caustically when they met down on the staith as they had planned and Jack grinned.

'It worked, didn't it? Now, come, we'll miss the tide if we're not quick.' The captain of one of the keelboats plying between York and Hull owed him a favour, he'd told Jane. He would take them to Hull and there they would find another boat to take them to London.

Jane sat stiffly on an upturned barrel and kept her head bent and her face covered in case anyone noticed them. It was the kind of day when people dawdling over Ouse Bridge might stop and watch what was going on at King's Staith. She didn't dare take Geoffrey out of his basket, but turned back the cloth so that he could feel the sun on his face. She had tried cooing comfortingly to him but there was something so sly in the way the black eyes glittered back up at her that the baby words had died on her lips. It was as if he knew that she had slunk in like a thief and snatched him, as if he were reserving judgement on whether he approved the change or not. It made Jane uncomfortable. But better that he had some expression, however disquieting, than none, she argued to herself.

She was wild to be gone. The tide would be right, Jack had said, but they needed the wind too and now even the soft breeze had dropped, leaving the city basking in a summery warmth. The sun flashed and glittered on the water, but the sails hung listlessly on all the keelboats drawn up at the staith.

Any moment now the nurse would discover that Geoffrey had gone. Nan, Jane hoped, would keep her counsel, but when Margaret or Robert discovered what she had done, their fury would know no bounds. Jane feared for Annis and Jack if the Holmwoods ever knew their part in this.

Jane didn't dare look round. She kept her eyes fixed on Geoffrey, who looked back as if disappointed by her impatience. Annis perched on the meagre roll of possessions they had brought with them while Jack bantered with the mariners preparing the keelboat. He had an apparently inexhaustible supply of jokes, but when she risked a glance Jane saw that his eyes were scanning the staith for any sign of suspicion or pursuit.

'Make haste, make haste,' Jane muttered under her breath.

'Easy now,' Annis murmured in return. 'People will notice if we seem in a hurry. We don't want them Holmwoods knowing which way we've gone.'

They were so nearly there. Jane couldn't bear to look now, but at last Jack was turning, gesturing them forward. The boat rocked alarmingly beneath her as she clambered forward with the basket to sit in the prow with Annis.

'Keep them women out of the way,' the mariner ordered, and Jack winked.

'Always,' he shouted back and Annis rolled her eyes.

One of the mariners pushed them away from the quayside, and there was some jumping and shoving as the others hauled up the sail. It flapped and snapped in the wayward breeze, only to collapse a moment later.

The captain cursed and spat. 'Wind's teasing like a whore today.'

Jane clutched Geoffrey closer. 'What happens if the wind drops?'

Annis didn't answer. She was watching the sail as it sagged against the mast and her expression was worried.

Then out of nowhere, the breeze lifted again. Jane felt it brush her cheek, and the sail stirred. She sat up straighter, seeing the expectation in the mariners' faces. Another sigh of breeze, and then a gust came down the river, puffing out the sail and sending the boat scudding out into the middle of the water.

'There she blows,' said Jack, standing by the mast. He grinned back at Jane and Annis. 'We're on our way.'

The boat felt small and unsteady, but Jane's heart lifted in relief. The river was deep and powerful around them, a brown serpent gleaming in the light. She could hear the rush of water against the hull, the creak of the ropes and the snap of the sail. Perched in the prow, holding Geoffrey close, she watched Ouse Bridge recede into the distance. *It is the last time I shall see it*, she thought, hardly able to believe that she had escaped after all. The Minster slid away, the houses clustered down to the river. Away went the Skeldergate ferry and St George's Field, where the laundresses were spreading the linen out to dry. Away went the last signs of the city, and then they rounded a bend in the river and there was only the tangle of trees and weeds and the sky and the water. York was gone.

*

'Ladies and gentlemen, we will shortly be arriving at King's Cross. Please ensure you take all your belongings with you when you leave the train . . .'

Roz came to with a jolt. One minute she had been gazing out of the window as the train sped through the countryside, the next she was in the churchyard with Annis, the sunshine warm on her back, her jaw set with determination, watching the sign of the red boar. Roz could still smell the neckerchief they had bought from a bemused countrywoman on the road to York, and the coarseness of the woven hemp was so vivid a memory that she lifted a hand to her face to pull it from her nose.

Disorientated, she blinked and her surroundings came into focus. She was on a train. She held on to the arm rest, fingering the plastic, the metal button you could use to push the seat back. Around her people were standing up, putting on coats, pulling down bags from the overhead. Taking it for granted that they could be whisked from York to London in two hours.

Roz drew a careful breath. Wrenched from the slow drift of the keelboat down the river to the train shooting down the tracks at a speed beyond her comprehension, she felt sick and a little dizzy. Across the table, her eyes met those of the passenger opposite, an elderly woman who was just folding her magazine. She smiled at Roz and nodded her head at the other passengers, already queuing to get off the train.

'Everybody's in such a rush nowadays,' she said.

'Yes.' Roz's voice was husky and she cleared her throat.

'I mean, the train's not going to get there any quicker, is it? They're still going to have to wait for the doors to open.'

Roz used to be the first to leap up. She liked to be ready to get out the moment the doors opened. Impatient, Nick called her, but she had preferred to think of it as being eager to get on to the next thing. Now she sat as if pinned to her seat, watching the queuing passengers as if they were an alien species, acting in a way she couldn't understand.

'I like to wait comfortably and get off in my own good time,' the elderly woman said. She looked at Roz with open curiosity. 'You've been miles away,' she said.

Roz smiled feebly back at her. *You have no idea*, she thought.

It was only three weeks since she had left, but it felt more like three years. Three hundred years. Roz wandered around the flat touching things, trying to reconnect with her old life, but part of her marvelled that she had ever lived there. She could remember, but it was like remembering a film she had once watched, with an actor playing her part, saying her lines. They didn't feel like her own memories. Not like the flashing sunlight on the river, or the shouts of the mariners. Not like the hard wooden seat in the prow or the weight of Geoffrey on her lap.

She told Nick about the séance while he made her a gin and tonic. He frowned as he twisted ice cubes into a glass. 'I think your psychic guy is right. It sounds dangerous to me.'

'I thought that at first, but now . . . it seems to me that Jane wants her story to be told. It might turn out to be a good thing. I was thinking I could do some research and see what I could find out about her, but that was when she was in Yorkshire.

Now she's on her way to London I don't suppose I'll ever be able to trace her here.'

Nick quartered a lime, ran one piece around the rim of the glass and squeezed the juice in before dropping the quarter onto the ice cubes and topping up with tonic water.

'You sound disappointed.'

It was only a mild comment, but it brought Roz up short. The truth was that she *was* disappointed. It had been such a relief to sail away from York. She wanted to go back, to drift on down the river in the spring sunshine and feel free.

'I just want to know what happened to Jane,' she said. 'It's not that I want to be haunted. It's just . . . well, I want to know that she was okay.'

Nick handed her the glass. 'I think she'll be okay if you want her to be okay.'

'What do you mean?'

'Roz, hasn't it occurred to you that *you* have just escaped to London?' Nick pulled a beer from the fridge and eased off the top. 'It's just another example of the parallel between your experience as Jane and what's going on in your own head.'

Roz was silent, swirling the ice cubes round in her glass so they clunked together in the fizzing tonic. It was true that she had been glad to get away after the séance, but that was mostly to escape the curious glances of the others. She hadn't liked the idea of them witnessing Jane's shame, even at second hand. Charles Denton had contacted her the next day to urge her to let him do a cleansing ritual and allow Jane to depart and Roz had been shocked at the instant, visceral jolt of resistance.

Jane didn't want to be moved on, and Roz didn't want her to go.

She didn't tell Nick that, though. She didn't really want to admit it to herself.

'You still think this is all to do with psychological issues?'

'It makes more sense to me than ghosts,' said Nick. 'I think your subconscious is playing silly buggers, and the sooner you see the hypnotherapist the better. I've made an appointment for you on Monday.'

Roz wasn't sure why she was so reluctant. Surely she didn't *want* Jane to be real? Nobody in their right mind would want to be possessed by a ghost. But when she thought about never experiencing Jane's life again, about never knowing what had happened to her, she couldn't deny how she felt. It was more than disappointed. It was bereft.

Nick could see her hesitating. 'I really think you should go, Roz,' he said, and Roz chewed her lip.

He was right. She was crazier than she thought if she would really rather keep plunging back into someone else's life than face up to some thorny psychological issues. It was time to pull herself together.

To put her marriage back together.

'All right,' she said to Nick. 'I'll go.'

'Do you want me to come with you?' Nick asked that Monday morning.

'Why, are you afraid I won't go?' Roz was in a snappish mood, banging the fridge door closed, clattering cutlery, shoving the press of the cafetière down so forcefully that coffee splurted out onto the counter.

Nick held his hands up in a peaceable gesture. 'I know you don't want to go. I just thought you might like some support.'

He was right. She didn't want to go. It was all very well deciding that you were going to talk to a shrink, but the prospect of it was more threatening than Roz had expected. Her mind was twitching, and unease prowled through her, like a wild cat penned in a stable.

Jane didn't want her to go.

The certainty of it left Roz on edge. She was having trouble concentrating, and she was glad in the end to let Nick accompany her. It meant she didn't have to think about where she was going or negotiate buses and tubes by herself. Once she had dashed around London without a second thought. She had spent most of her life in the city, and she had an encyclopaedic knowledge of the tube map, of bus routes, and of overground rail and tram connections. But three weeks away had turned her into a provincial mouse, gawping at the size of buses, overwhelmed by the roar of traffic, petrified by the rush and rattle of the tube.

Like Charles Denton, Rita Panjani was not what Roz had expected. She was tiny and graceful, with beautiful dark, deep eyes and hair as black and shiny as a crow's wing. Roz was fascinated by the tiny diamond glinting in Rita's nostril. It seemed to be winking a message at her. Anyone would think she had never seen a nose stud before.

Rita was unruffled by Roz's distraction and disjointed

answers to her preliminary questions. 'Your husband mentioned that you were having some difficulty coming to terms with a trauma in your early childhood,' she said at last.

Roz had been so preoccupied with Jane that she had almost forgotten about her own history. 'Well, yes . . . although I don't remember it as a trauma. I don't remember it at all.'

'That's quite common,' said Rita. 'A child will often block out memories that are too difficult to deal with. That's a process that can often lead to phobias or apparently inexplicable fears in later life, however. By recovering that memory and facing it, the fear becomes manageable. It's a process that may involve some pain, but should in the end help you to move on with your life.'

The room was bright and airy, painted in neutral colours, deliberately restful, but Roz didn't feel relaxed. She was sitting in a comfortable chair by the window, her hands like claws on the arms. Seeing Rita glance at them, she forced herself to release them and linked her fingers awkwardly in her lap instead.

'Have you ever had a patient who dealt with trauma by living another life entirely?' she asked, and Rita's brows lifted.

'Why do you ask?'

Haltingly at first, Roz explained what had been happening since she went to York. Rita listened carefully and didn't interrupt.

'Nick thinks it's all a way of working out issues in my subconscious,' Roz finished.

'And what do you think?'

'I . . . don't know,' said Roz miserably. 'I used to be so sure of myself, but now I'm confused. I don't know who I am or what I think any more.'

Rita closed her notebook. 'Few of us are certain about anything, Roz. The more we know, the more we understand we can never know everything. There has clearly been a trauma in your past. Why don't we try and regress you to your childhood and confront those memories before we tackle the way you seem to be projecting your concerns onto another life entirely?'

'I suppose so. If you think it will work.' Roz shifted uneasily in the chair. 'How will you do that?'

'Have you been hypnotized before?'

'No, never.'

'It's nothing to be alarmed about,' said Rita as Roz's voice wavered. 'I'm just going to ask you to relax.'

'What if I can't?'

'Then we will try something else.'

There was something relentless about Rita's calm smile. Roz was beginning to feel hunted. 'I just don't feel I'm going to respond very well to hypnosis.'

'Well, let's try, shall we?' said Rita tranquilly. 'I want you to sit back in the chair, Roz, and make yourself comfortable.' She watched as Roz shuffled deeper into the armchair and rested her head against the back. 'Good,' she said. 'Now close your eyes.'

Roz let out a long breath and closed her eyes. Dazzling patterns shimmered and swirled behind her eyelids.

'Good,' said Rita again. 'Now I want you to think back, to the first time you can remember being really happy. Can you do that?'

The patterns behind her eyes were blinding now, the blobs and circles fading to pulsating waves of light. Roz felt as if she were teetering on the edge of a great black hole, but she kept her eyes squeezed shut and forced herself to concentrate. So many happy memories. Her wedding, the honeymoon in Morocco. Nick presenting her with the earrings. Further back, their first kiss. A party with friends, helpless with laughter. Watching the sun rise on a beach in Greece. And before that, university, and school, growing up with her aunt and uncle. She'd always wanted brothers and sisters, but it hadn't been an unhappy childhood. She remembered a holiday in the south of France when she was ten, being sent to buy croissants and French bread from a van every morning. Dusty roads and cicadas whirring.

'Do you remember anything before that?'

'I remember my uncle reading me stories.' Roz's eyes were still closed, but her lips curved reminiscently. 'He used to be brilliant at doing different voices for every character. He was a wonderful mimic, and he used to make me laugh.'

'How did that make you feel?'

'Safe. Happy.'

'Is that the first time you were happy?'

Roz frowned with effort as she strained her memory. 'I was happy in Minchen Lane,' she said.

'Minchen Lane? Is that where your parents lived?'

'My parents?' She was puzzled. 'No, Minchen Lane is in London, hard by Aldgate.'

A pause. 'I don't think I know it.'

'I didn't at first, either,' she admitted. How odd to remember now that somewhere so familiar had once been strange.

'It is not far,' Annis had said. 'Turn before you reach the church in the middle of Fenchurch Street. Go past the Cloth-workers' Hall and look for the sign of the golden lily.'

Annis had offered to look after Geoffrey, even though she freely admitted that the child gave her the fidgets. Geoffrey was three now, walking, and talking, if just a little, and only when he felt like it. He had no interest in baby chatter or songs, but regarded the world out of glittering black eyes that seemed older by far than his years. Jane would never admit it, but sometimes Geoffrey made her uneasy too. He was not an ill-favoured child, but he rarely smiled, and he never looked to her for comfort. From babyhood, only the leap and flicker of flames had the power to soothe him, and he was fascinated still, sitting for hours by a fire while his face glowed with a fervour that Jane was at a loss to understand. She worried that he might burn himself, but he never got too close to the fire, and in truth there had been many times over the last year and a half when she had been glad to leave him in a kitchen, out of the servants' way, while she earned a few more pennies to pay their way.

London had been bewildering at first. Jack's family inn was a busy, bustling place, and there seemed to be people coming and going at all times of the day and night. Jane had clutched Geoffrey tight and shrunk against the wall as serving maids pushed past with trenchers of food and great tankards of ale.

Jack's family was large and cheerful and casually welcoming. Jane was grateful to them for giving her a place to stay, but the truth was she found it all overwhelming. In spite of Annis's objections, Jane had insisted on paying her own way. She had brought little enough with her, after selling her mother's rings to pay for their journey, but she had a fair hand with a needle, and took all the torn linen and clothes at the inn to mend. Before long she had built up a reputation as a reliable seamstress, but she and Geoffrey had been sharing a chamber with Annis and Jack for long enough. Jane closed her ears to their coupling at night, but they had a child of their own now, a bonny baby they called Eliza, and Annis was increasing already with another. Jane had been glad to help and to stand godmother when Eliza was born but she wanted to move Geoffrey away from the inn.

Jack had a network of contacts who kept them in touch with news from York. Carriers and carters, chapmen and peddlers, merchants, servants and other travellers passed through Aldgate, and mariners and sailors made their way up from the Thames, allowing snippets of news to find their way up and down the country. Jack had a good line in guileless looks and artless conversation. From him, Jane heard that the Holmwoods were still searching for Geoffrey, that such a hue and cry had been raised that she would not escape with her life if she were ever to return to York.

Jane kept out of sight as much as she could. The Holmwoods' vengeance would be terrible, she knew, and they were likely to have word of London just as she had of York. Ever since she arrived she had been looking to move deeper into the city. If the Holmwoods did trace her and Geoffrey to London, an inn by one of the great gates in London's wall would be the obvious place for them to start their search.

'If only I still had my still room,' she had sighed to Annis. 'I could sell my remedies and earn enough perhaps for a room for myself and Geoffrey.'

'Then it's as well you don't,' Annis said roundly. 'Have you not heard how folk are turning against wise women? They are hanging witches every week, it seems. I heard Old Mother Dent was hanged in York only t'other day.'

'Sybil Dent? Oh no.' Jane put a hand to her mouth in distress. She remembered the cottage out on the common, Sybil's rough hands on her chin, and she glanced at Geoffrey, who was watching the candle flame through narrowed eyes.

Be careful what you wish for.

'Leave remedies to the apothecaries,' Annis advised. 'Else sooner or later someone will accuse you of casting a spell, and then where would we be?'

'Then I must use my other skills,' said Jane. 'I can manage a household. There must be someone in London who needs a housekeeper.'

It was Annis who heard of the job in Minchen Lane. 'Mr Harrison is a widower and in sore need of a housekeeper,' she told Jane. 'He has three young daughters and his sister is at her wits' end, she said. She has children aplenty of her own, and cannot care for any more. I told her of you, and she said for you to go and see her brother. He is a lawyer, with a fine house, she said,' Annis added. 'Tell him Mistress Blake sent you.'

Minchin Lane was not as far from Aldgate as Jane would

have liked, but she could not afford to turn down the chance of a post.

Four great horses plodded up the centre of Minchen Lane, their shoulders straining with the effort of hauling a cart laden with timber. The carter followed, whistling through his teeth and sending his long whip snaking and cracking through the air. Jane squeezed herself into a doorway to let them past.

'You can tell you're not a Londoner,' Jack teased her whenever she hesitated, momentarily overwhelmed by the press of people. 'You must plunge in, my lady, and battle with the rest of the world, else you will be flattened by the rush!'

Jane was getting more used to London now. The city was rough and vigorous, and it seethed with an energy that sometimes took her breath away. Jack, she soon discovered, was right. There was no point in waiting for folk to slow down to give her a chance to cross the street on her way to the inn or to church or to market. She just had to join the throng.

It was like jumping into a river. Jane felt like a piece of jetsam, tossed overboard, carried along by the current of London life, jostled between rowdy apprentices and goodwives with their baskets, between peddlers and water carriers and beggars and pie sellers, between boys pushing and shoving on their way to school and retinues of servants clearing a passage for their noble masters on horse, and all manner of men in between, all talking, shouting, laughing, bargaining and cursing at the tops of their voices in a babble of different languages. The streets were clogged with carts and wagons and coaches and litters, with pack horses and errant pigs and scavenging dogs and stray

hens. Jane had seen a flock of bleating, baffled sheep being fun-
nelled down a narrow street only to come face to face with a
gaggle of geese being driven in the opposite direction, and the
noise and confusion was so great that she had turned round and
gone a different way.

A true Londoner would never have been so poor-spirited,
Jane knew. Londoners would have forged through the animals
regardless, pushing on their way, with no time for diversions.
Sometimes Jane remembered York and how she and her neighbours would shake their heads at the press of people on the
Pavement or in Thursday Market, and she would smile to think
of how quiet life there had been. In London, just crossing the
street could be a challenge. You had to dash and struggle
through the throng, your ears battered by a cacophony of shouts
and curses, of barking and bleating and squawking and squab-
bling, woven with the cries of the street sellers, the creaking of
cartwheels and the sonorous clang of the church bells marking
the hour or tolling a death.

Everybody in London seemed to be in a hurry. They walked
quickly, talked quickly. Vicious arguments flared up without
warning, only to dissolve the next instant into shouts of laughter. How Juliana would have enjoyed London, Jane often
thought. The city was as tempestuous as her sister, and just as
with Juliana, Jane loved it and was overwhelmed by it in equal
measure. London was a tumbling, jumbling, hustling, bustling
place, its houses so tightly packed that sometimes Jane despaired
of seeing the sky, and the air rank and rich with the smell of the

Thames, with the smell of opportunity, of life. It was a place you could hide, and a place you could find yourself.

When the cart had laboured past, Jane stepped out of the doorway, narrowly avoiding a bolting urchin and a servant carrying a tray of vegetables on her head. Through the crowd she had glimpsed a painted sign. The flower was yellow and peeling slightly but it was unmistakably a lily. *The sign of the golden lily*, Annis had said. It was a fine house, with a double front and glass windows in the upper stories. The beams were intricately carved with leaves and flowers, and she could see rolls of fabric, glowing like jewels, in the draper's shop through the open shutters.

She went into the shop to ask for Mr Harrison, but she had to raise her voice above the sound of children crying and dogs barking and the shouting that came from the house behind. Although the London streets might be noisy, the houses were usually quiet. But not the house at the sign of the golden lily, it appeared.

'Down the passage,' the man said, jerking his head to one side. 'And tell them to be quiet or I'm calling the constable, lawyer or no lawyer! I cannot hear myself think today.'

Jane thanked him and made her way down the passage at the side of the house. She found herself in a courtyard, with an imposing doorway. The heavy wooden door stood ajar, and the sounds of tears and quarrelling spilled out onto the cobbles.

'God's bones!' A man's voice rose furiously above the racket. 'What is happening here?'

Immediately, there was a clamour of hysterical explanations, interspersed with the frantic yapping of a little dog. 'Be quiet!'

the man bellowed, which had no effect at all unless to redouble the volume of the barking. They might have been standing in the street instead of inside a fine house. No wonder the draper had grumbled.

It was a raw December day, and Jane rubbed her hands against the cold as she hesitated, stamping her boots a little. She could freeze if she waited for them to finish their argument. Briskly, she knocked on the door, but nobody heard her above the cacophony, and she took a deep breath before stepping inside.

From the noise she had expected a crowd, but in fact there were only three small girls in the hall, a harassed maid, a tiny spaniel with feathery paws and a tail that seemed too big for it dancing up and down on all fours, and the man. He was clutching at his head and glowering at the girls, making them cry harder.

'Somebody shut that cursed dog up!' he bellowed, and without thinking Jane stepped forward and picked up the little dog. It was so surprised that it stopped barking, and the reduction in the noise level was instant. Jane closed her fingers gently but firmly around its velvety muzzle just in case.

'If you will all be quiet, the dog will be quiet too,' she said as the man swung round and noticed her for the first time.

Ignoring him, Jane identified the smallest girl, who was sobbing hysterically. She knelt by her side. She had had many years of dealing with Juliana's tantrums, and she kept her voice bright and clear. 'Your little dog is frightened of your crying,' she said. 'Can you stroke him and show him not to be afraid?'

Still shuddering with sobs, the child nodded and stroked the dog's head until it licked her hand and she gave a watery smile. 'There, that is much better,' said Jane, giving no sign that she was aware of the man's hard stare boring into her back. 'What is his name?'

'P-Poppet,' she stuttered.

'That is a sweet name,' said Jane, smiling. 'And what is *your* name?'

'C-Cecily.'

The others were just standing and watching as if stunned by the sudden cessation of noise.

'I am pleased to meet you, C-Cecily,' said Jane gravely. 'My name is Jane.' She straightened, Poppet still tucked under her arm, and held down her free hand to the child before turning to the other two. 'I don't know about you, but I always get hungry when I'm fractious. Shall we go into the kitchen and see if we can find something to eat? I feel sure Poppet is hungry too, are you not?' She held up the dog as if waiting for his answer, and he licked her chin, his feathery tail wagging.

The little girls giggled, their black looks evaporating. 'I am Mary,' said the elder, stepping forward importantly, 'and this is Catherine.'

'Mary. Catherine.' Jane inclined her head gracefully. 'I am delighted to make your acquaintance. Will you show me where the kitchen is? And you,' she added to the servant, who was looking harried beyond belief, 'do you clear up the broken pot.'

'Yes, mistress.' She even bobbed a curtsey, clearly grateful that somebody had taken charge.

Chapter Fifteen

'This way.' Mary tugged at Jane's skirt and started pulling her towards the door that Jane guessed led to the buttery and pantry, and the kitchen beyond.

'Just a minute.' The man found his voice at last and Jane stopped and looked at him politely.

'Who in God's name are you?' he demanded, scowling.

'Why, I am your new housekeeper, sir,' she said, a tiny smile tugging at the corner of her mouth.

'Is that so? I did not ask for a housekeeper! The last one wore me out with her bleating. We can manage without. The servants do well enough.'

'You did not seem to me to be managing just now,' Jane pointed out demurely. 'If you do not mind me saying so.'

'You are very impertinent for a housekeeper,' he said with another ferocious scowl. 'What did you say your name was again?'

'Jane. Jane Birkby.' She was used now to using her father's

name again. If anybody asked, she said she was a widow, and
Geoffrey her son. It was a sin to lie, but not so great a sin as
breaking her promise to Juliana. 'And you, I suppose, are Mr
Harrison.'

'Gilbert Harrison, yes. And I remind you, madam, that I did
not ask for a housekeeper.'

'Mistress Blake sent for me,' said Jane and he cursed without apology.

'My damned sister! Will she never cease interfering?'

'Come *on*,' said Mary, and then shrank back as he glowered
at her.

Jane stepped quickly between them before the little girls all
started crying again. 'Why do I not take the children and give
them something to eat? They will settle when they are less
hungry. And then we will talk.'

'Oh, we will, will we? You are a managing woman, Jane
Birkby!' But he didn't say no, and Jane let the girls lead her to
the kitchen, where she found another maid wide-eyed and
trembling.

'I heard the master shouting,' she said, twisting her hands in
her apron.

'I dare say he is hungry too,' said Jane. 'Take him some ale
and a piece of bread and cheese.'

'I dare not!'

'He will not eat you!' Jane said, but the girl, who said her
name was Petronilla, shook her head with a mulish look.

'Master don't like to be disturbed if he don't call for you.'

'Very well. I will go.'

Jane sniffed at the ale and thought she could brew better. She poured some into a tankard and cut some cheese and some bread. The girls were happily playing, their recent quarrel forgotten, so she left them in the kitchen with Petronilla and carried the simple meal through on a tray to the hall, Poppet scampering at her heels.

The hall was empty, but there was a door on the far wall which she guessed would be Mr Harrison's closet. Balancing the tray on one arm, she scratched on the door.

'Go away!' he shouted.

Jane opened the door and went in. Gilbert Harrison was sitting at his desk. He flung down his quill pen when she appeared and set the tray down on the desk.

'I don't wish to be disturbed!'

'I have questioned the maids and nobody appears to have had a decent meal since you chased off your last housekeeper,' she said composedly. 'No wonder you are all so cross. I thought something to eat might improve your temper.'

For a moment he glared at her, but suddenly he laughed, and the change of expression transformed him so completely that Jane blinked. He was tall and solid, a dark-visaged man with a stern mouth, shrewd eyes and ferocious brows. At first glance he was intimidatingly fierce, but a second look showed the hint of humour around his eyes, the telltale crease in his cheeks, the strength in his jaw. He wasn't handsome like Robert, no, but there was something reassuringly uncompromising about him.

'You are mighty cool for someone who has just wandered in off the street,' he said.

'I have not wandered,' Jane replied calmly. 'I came in response to a summons from your sister.'

'My sister is not mistress in this house.' The scowl was back.

Jane looked around the closet. There was dust on the table by the window, and balls of fluff in the corner of the room. The air was musty and the rush mat smelt rotten. The hangings were dull, the carpets unbeaten, the wood unpolished.

'It is clear to me that there is no mistress here,' she said.

'And that is the way I want it to stay,' said Gilbert flatly. 'I want no new wife.'

'I am not applying for the position of wife,' Jane pointed out. 'Your house needs someone to manage it, and you may employ me to do that without taking the trouble of marriage.'

Poppet had snuffled in behind Jane and now stood up on his hind legs to put his front paws on Gilbert Harrison's thigh and yip a greeting. 'What is that creature doing in here?' he said with distaste. 'Get out!' he growled, pushing away the dog, which retreated back to Jane with a wounded expression.

Jane stooped to gather him up. 'Why do you have a dog if you do not like him?' she asked. Poppet was soft and light, and she could feel his little heart beating in her hand. The absurd tail brushed backwards and forwards under her sleeve as he quivered with excitement, his nose sniffing the air.

'It was one of my wife's enthusiasms, and he lasted as long as any of them did, which is to say about a week, after which she got bored with him.' Gilbert eyed Poppet in disgust. 'Now I am left to feed it with the rest of her cast-offs. I would not mind so much if it were a real dog – a greyhound or a mastiff – but that is just ridiculous. Do I look to you like a man who owns a dog called *Poppet*?'

Jane tucked in the corners of her mouth to stop herself smiling. 'He lives in your house and he seems fond of *you*.'

Gilbert glowered over his desk at the dog in her arms. 'It is always in here, getting under my feet, and squealing when I tread on it.'

'It would not hurt you to give him a pat, and then he would settle down.'

'One pat is never enough. It is like a woman. It must be petted constantly or it makes my life a misery.'

'I assure you, I do not require petting,' said Jane, who could not imagine what it must be like to be courted and cajoled into good humour.

Gilbert eyed her across the desk. She stood holding the spaniel, straight-backed and slender, and looked back at him with clear eyes. Abruptly, he pointed at the chair on the other side of the desk. 'Sit,' he barked.

Jane raised her brows at the graceless order, and he sighed as he reached absently for a piece of the bread she had brought in. 'Dear madam, please be seated. Is that better?'

For answer, Jane inclined her head and sat in the chair, stroking Poppet on her lap when he curled up contentedly. The poor creature just wanted attention, she thought.

Still chewing the bread, Gilbert sat back in his chair and steepled his fingers under his mouth while he studied her with a penetrating look. 'Since you are here, you may as well tell me about yourself,' he said grudgingly. 'You are not from London, that is plain from your voice.'

'No, I am from Yorkshire, sir.' Jane had practised this. 'I am a butcher's widow. I know how to manage a household. I can cook and brew. I can sew and dress meat and cast accounts, and I can read, and write a little. I have some skill with remedies too.'

'You are not ill-looking,' he said, eyeing her critically until her cheeks burned. 'Why have your kin not found you another husband? You sound like you would make a most useful wife.'

'I do not wish to marry again,' said Jane.

'In my experience wishing has little to do with it once your family and friends decide you should be wed,' said Gilbert with feeling. 'But for a woman like you, it is better than poverty, is it not?'

'I will not be poor if you employ me,' she pointed out, fondling the spaniel's silky ears.

'I may not pay you a great wage.'

'I will have somewhere to live, and my meals, would I not?'

'Of course. *If* I employ you.'

'Then that is all I need,' she said as if he had not spoken. 'I have been working as a seamstress, but I would like a more certain position for my child's sake.'

'Oho! And now there is a child! You did not mention that before,' he said, glowering. 'This house has enough children.'

'One more will not make any difference,' said Jane composedly. 'Geoffrey is a quiet boy.'

Gilbert grunted. 'I suppose he is a boy at least. I am going mad here with all these girls, and female servants, and my sister yapping in my ear like that wretched spaniel about marrying again. I had thought a housekeeper would do, but the last one wept and shivered and shook if I so much as looked at her, and my daughters have been running wild. My wife had no time for them either, and I do not know how to manage them. I cannot abide crying, and it is all they seem to do.'

'They need some discipline, and some kindness,' said Jane. 'And I think I can promise you that I will not cry when you shout at me. Let me try,' she said, attempting to keep the eagerness from her voice. She hadn't realized how much she longed to be away from the cramped chamber she shared with Jack and Annis, dear as they were to her. There was something about the house of the golden lily that pulled at her. She and Geoffrey could be safe here, with this gruff man and his daughters and the ridiculous dog. 'If I do not please you, you may send me away.'

'Very well,' said Gilbert after a moment. 'A trial. If you are still here after a month, we will see.' He picked up his pen and nodded dismissal. 'But make sure you keep that dog away from me. I don't want to see it in here again.'

Jane rose, Poppet in her arms. 'Thank you, sir,' she said with a smile. 'You will not regret it.'

'See that I do not,' he said grouchily, but Jane thought there was a trace of a smile around his mouth.

Closing the door carefully behind her with one hand, Jane lifted Poppet up to kiss his wet black nose in triumph. Mr

Harrison was cross, his daughters were spoilt. The house was neglected and the servants poorly trained. But she would make them all comfortable, Jane vowed. This she could do.

Still smiling, she looked around the dusty hall. She would set a servant to beating the hangings straight away. Already she could see how the room would look when it was cleaned and the silver was polished and a fire was burning in the grate. She had set out that afternoon in search of a job, but she had found a home, she could feel it in her bones. Already the house at the sign of the golden lily felt like a place she belonged.

'I will be happy here,' she told Poppet. She set him down so that he could scamper ahead of her across the hall towards the buttery and the kitchen beyond. She would bring Geoffrey the very next day. He would be safe tucked away here behind the bustle of Minchen Lane. 'We both will.'

'It's good that you are happy, but it's time to come back now, Roz.'

'No! No, I don't want to go back,' she said, alarmed by the certainty of the voice with its strange intonation. 'I want to stay here. This is where I belong. Don't make me leave,' she begged. 'I am happy at last.'

The voice firmed. 'Roz is happy too, Jane. You must let her go.'

'*No.*' Always she had put others' desires before her own. Now that she understood what happiness was, she could not let it go. She *would* not.

'Roz, I want you to wake up now.'

But the words made no sense and now they were fading, evaporating like the mist over the river until they were gone, leaving only a sense of danger and loss.

Jane put a hand to her throat. She didn't understand the panic suddenly fluttering like a trapped bird in her chest. There had been something – a thought, a memory – tugging at her mind, but it had vanished and now she couldn't remember what it was or why she was frightened. Something she had to do? Something she had to remember?

'Jane? Are you unwell?'

She started and stared at Gilbert as if she had never seen him before. 'No . . . it was just . . . I don't know.'

'A goose walking over your grave?' he suggested, and she shuddered.

'Something like that.'

'It's not like you to be discomposed, Jane.' Gilbert frowned. 'I hope you are not sickening for something?'

She shook herself and smoothed her palms over her apron. 'I cannot afford to be sick,' she told him briskly. 'There is too much to do to keep this household afloat.' She slapped at Gilbert's hand as he reached for an apple. 'Those are for my pie,' she told him.

'This is my house, is it not, Jane? That makes this my kitchen, and my pie and therefore my apple,' said Gilbert, but he put the apple back.

'What are you doing in here, anyway? The kitchen is a place for women,' she said severely. 'It is not for men.'

'I am . . . restless,' he admitted.

'Why do you not play with your daughters?'

'They are running in and out of the yard like hoydens,' he said. 'You should control them better.'

'They are happy,' said Jane, who was used to his scowls by now and set no store by them. 'You should be glad of it.'

'You are always pert, Jane.' Gilbert sat on the table and tossed onions from one hand to the other. 'You never say, yes sir, no sir. Why is that?'

'I am sure I say it all the time,' she said serenely.

'You see? You are disagreeing again!'

Jane gave in and laughed. 'You are determined to find me in the wrong today.'

Broodingly, he watched her as she moved around the kitchen. The kitchen door stood open onto the yard and he could hear the shouts and chatter of the children running in and out from the street. The spaniel lay in a pool of sunlight, his paws twitching as he slept. The kitchen smelt of herbs, of the bacon that hung from the rafters and the spices Jane had set carefully on the table. Up on the roof, a pigeon cooed throatily.

'Are you content, Jane?' he asked abruptly, and she looked up from breaking eggs into a bowl.

'Of course,' she said. 'How could I not be? I work all day for a master who glares at me,' she said, but she was smiling.

The truth was that Jane had never been happier. Nearly two years she had been at the sign of the golden lily, and her trial period had come and gone without comment. Slowly but surely, she had taken charge of the house. She was mistress in all but name, and there was no one to tell her that she should be a lady and sit in the parlour. She dealt with the maids with a firm hand, and every chamber glowed with care. The silver was polished, the wood gleamed, the carpets were beaten, rushes freshly strewn on the floor. Every day, Jane swept London's fine black soot out of the house, knowing that by the next morning it would have settled back. She made sure the girls were clean and dressed. She combed the tangles out of their hair, held them on her lap when they fell and kissed the scrapes on their palms. She taught them to read, and began to teach Mary, the eldest, about running a house.

The meals she set on the table improved Gilbert's credit. Gilbert himself might grumble at the expense of entertaining, but his guests commented on how delicious the food was, and his sister was pleased. Bess was a forthright woman with eight children who lived in Tower Street. She had looked Jane up and down when she first met her and then nodded as if satisfied. 'You'll do,' she said. She often came to visit, and liked to sit in the kitchen and tell Jane who had heard what in the street. They talked about children and their neighbours, shared recipes and remedies.

It was Bess who told her about Gilbert's wife. 'Barbara was a jade,' she said frankly. 'The face of an angel, but a black heart. She would look my brother in the eye and lie to his face, just because she felt like it. He cannot abide an untruth, Gilbert. He is a straightforward man and she was the worst of wives for him. She ran him ragged, twisting the truth until he did not know which way was up. She would run away and wait for him to chase after her and coax her back, all for the pleasure of making him jump. She made him sour and cross. He is like a sulky bear now, which does not dare look less than fierce in case the dogs should set on him again. He was not always so fierce as he is now.'

'How did she die?' Jane was picking the meat from boiled calves' feet for a pie and trying not to sound too interested in Gilbert's wife.

'In childbed,' said Bess, shaking her head at the memory. She reached out and popped one of the currants Jane had ready for the pie into her mouth. 'The babe was born dead, and they could not stop her bleeding.'

'Poor soul,' said Jane and Bess made a face.

'I wonder if the child was even Gilbert's. I know my brother mourned the babe, and he would have liked a son, I'm sure, but I doubt he misses Barbara overmuch.' Sighing, she helped herself to another currant. 'My poor brother. He should marry again. A man should have a wife.'

'He told me he did not wish for marriage,' said Jane carefully.

'I think he may have changed his mind.'

The thought that Gilbert might marry was like a slice through Jane's heart and her eyes flew up from the calves' feet in shock.

'He is to marry again?' She told herself the sinking feeling was because the new mistress of the house would not need a housekeeper to do her job for her. She and Geoffrey would have to leave, and where would they go? The thought of going back to the inn after this comfortable house was more than she could bear.

'I'd say that probably depends on you,' said Bess with a knowing smile.

'Me? But ... Oh no,' she said, understanding. 'There is nothing like that.'

'I know that,' said Bess comfortably. 'I'm just saying that he watches you when you're not looking at him, and I've seen you look at him too. I think there's something between you, and my brother is happier than I have seen him for a very long time. You are good for him.'

Jane swallowed. 'I am his servant.'

'He married to please his kin first time, he can do what he likes now. He wouldn't be the first man to find comfort with a servant. There would be no shame in it.'

'It cannot be,' said Jane, distressed. How could she explain that she was already married? She liked Gilbert, yes, and more than she should, but he was still a lawyer, still a man. He would think she belonged with her husband. She couldn't bear to see the look of disgust on his face when he realized that she had lied to him. Hadn't Bess said that he could not abide an untruth?

'Well, we shall see,' Bess had said, slapping her hands on her lap and hauling herself to her feet.

That had been nearly a year ago. Now Jane studied Gilbert under her lashes. He was absorbed in juggling the onions, his boot swinging rhythmically. Then without warning he looked up and found her watching him, and the breath evaporated from her lungs. Her heart began to thump in her breast, leaving her dry-mouthed and feverish. She wanted to look away, but she couldn't.

'Jane,' Gilbert began, and the urgency in his voice made something twist sharp and pure inside her.

She couldn't have spoken if she had tried. She stood holding the bowl like a simpleton as Gilbert put down the onions and got off the table to move towards her.

He reached for the bowl and set it on the table without taking his eyes off Jane.

'Mamma.' The small, clear voice from the doorway made Jane jerk round, and Gilbert cursed under his breath and swung away, his face dark with irritation.

'Geoffrey!' Jane's heart was battering with a mixture of frustration and relief.

At five, Geoffrey was a slight child with dark hair and black, furtive eyes. Jane was fiercely protective of him, but even she had to admit that he was hard to love. As a baby, he had arched away from her when she cuddled him, and as soon as he was able, he would endure her attempts to kiss him only to ostentatiously wipe his cheek.

Mary, Catherine and Cecily avoided him. Even Poppet, the most foolish and affectionate of dogs, gave him a wide berth. Geoffrey's isolation was the only thing that marred Jane's contentment. She longed for him to be as happy as she was, and she overcompensated, showering him with affection that she suspected Geoffrey knew she didn't really feel. But she had sacrificed her sister for him, or so it had come to seem to Jane, and she had promised to look after him. She did love him. How could she not love him?

'What is it, sweeting?' she asked, her voice high, and her colour rising as the black eyes rested coldly on her. It was as if Geoffrey knew that she had been about to kiss Gilbert.

Geoffrey pinched the servants and pulled the girls' hair. He kicked at Poppet and made the neighbours' children cry. Jane didn't understand why he seemed to hate everyone so much. Most of all, he disliked Gilbert.

'Jealous,' Annis said succinctly when Jane had confessed her worry one day.

'How can he be jealous? It is not even as if he loves me overmuch,' said Jane sadly. 'And besides, Geoffrey has no reason to be jealous of Mr Harrison. I am not . . . we are not . . .' She lost herself in a morass of words trying to explain what she and Gilbert were not. 'Mr Harrison is my master,' she finished, blushing furiously.

'That's as may be,' Annis had said, taking pity on her. 'But that lad don't want you paying no attention to anyone but him.'

Now Jane looked into Geoffrey's face and wondered if Annis might be right. He had a habit of appearing noiselessly when you least expected him, almost as if he were trying to catch you out.

He had caught her looking longingly at Gilbert, and Jane couldn't shake the conviction that he had decided to put a stop to it.

His hands were cupped together. 'Look what I've got,' he

piped in his childish voice, and Jane immediately felt ashamed of her suspicions. He was just a little boy. How could she suspect him of deliberately doing anything?

Relieved at the excuse to move away from Gilbert without looking too obvious, Jane went over to the doorway.

'What is it?' she asked brightly. Too brightly.

'A butterfly.' He parted his hands just enough to show her the butterfly fluttering between his palms. 'I caught it.'

'It's beautiful,' said Jane, pitying the poor, trapped creature. She remembered feeling like that in Holmwood House. 'Why don't you let it fly away now?'

'No,' said Geoffrey, and he closed his small fist tightly around the butterfly, crushing it in one quick, vicious movement.

Jane recoiled, her hand going to her mouth in an instinctive gesture of horror, while Geoffrey smiled up at her, the dark eyes sparkling with malice.

'What is it?' asked Gilbert, seeing Jane tense.

'Nothing,' said Jane quickly, her voice high and tight. If she told Gilbert, he would beat Geoffrey. The only time they had ever argued was when Gilbert had suggested that there was something wrong with Geoffrey. Jane was afraid he would send him away, and if Geoffrey went, she would have to go too.

Now Geoffrey sent her a glance of sparkling complicity, as if pleased to have caught her in a lie. *He is only five*, Jane insisted to herself. He couldn't know how much she dreaded having to leave the house at the sign of the golden lily. He was too young to understand the tension that had been simmering between her and Gilbert ever since they had arrived. *He is an innocent child*, Jane repeated to herself with a kind of desperation. He didn't know what he had done.

But she couldn't forget the look on his face as he killed the butterfly and the thought of it sent disquiet uncoiling inside her, a serpent stirring and twitching its tail in warning.

Be careful what you wish for.

'It's clear that Jane has a very strong hold on your psyche.' Rita was shaken when Roz finally came round that day. She had never lost control of someone under hypnosis before, she confessed to Roz.

'So you believe Jane's real?' Roz sipped the tea Rita had made. Strangely, she was less upset by the power of Jane's hold on her than Rita was. She could still feel the pull of the past, and part of her longed to go back.

'She could be a manifestation of a part of you that you don't want to acknowledge,' said Rita carefully. 'She's certainly real in the sense that she exists as a mental block in your subconscious. It's almost as if you've invented her so that you don't have to face the reality of your parents' death.'

Roz frowned. 'But I don't think I have a problem with the way they died! I mean, I was shocked when I found out, but I don't feel emotionally involved in what happened.'

'You don't remember it,' Rita pointed out.

Roz couldn't argue with that.

Nick was dismayed when Roz told him that the attempt to regress to her own early years had simply tipped her back into

Jane's life again. She didn't mention that Rita had lost control, but did her best to reassure him.

'Rita agrees with you,' she said when she rang him from York that night. 'She thinks it's all connected to what's happening in my head.'

Nick didn't sound noticeably reassured. 'Maybe we should try another therapist?'

No. Roz had to bite back her instinctive reaction. She wanted to see Gilbert again.

'Maybe,' she said neutrally. There was no point in getting into an argument over the phone. 'Why don't I come home next weekend?' she suggested. 'We can talk about it then.'

'Are you sure you're going to be okay up there on your own?'

'Of course.' Roz didn't tell him she was hoping that Jane would come back again, but Nick was obviously suspicious. 'Look, isn't it time that I met Daniel?' she said in an effort to distract him. She was so taken up with Jane's life that her own resentment over the way Nick had kept Daniel's existence a secret seemed unimportant now. 'Why don't you invite him over and we'll do something together?'

'All right.' Nick's tone lightened. 'That's a good idea. Thanks, Roz.'

Roz couldn't help feeling guilty as she switched off her phone. Nick might not have told her about Daniel straight away, but she wasn't telling him everything either, was she? She *would* tell him, she assured herself, but first she just wanted to know if Jane was still happy at the sign of the golden lily. What harm could it do? After all, everyone kept telling her that Jane was no more than a creation of her psyche. If she'd made Jane up, however unwittingly, she could unmake her whenever she wanted, right? She just didn't want to yet.

So she opened her mind and invited Jane to come back. She closed her eyes and sat as still as she had done in Rita's chair. She walked the streets Jane had walked and stood in the empty chamber at Holmwood House, but to her intense disappointment Roz stayed firmly in the present. There was no sign of Jane, just the same sour, elusive stink of old smoke drifting through her office, occasionally making her eyes sting. Roz was almost used to it now.

Preoccupied, she threw herself into her work. It wasn't that long until Halloween and the official opening of Holmwood House, and there was lots to do. She was too busy to notice Helen's small meannesses, or Jeff, watching her from the shadows. Adrian was constantly on the phone, wanting to make changes to the plans for the launch, or suggesting someone else they could invite. Roz set her teeth and forced herself to smile. Adrian was her employer, she reminded herself, unable to prevent a gust of longing for a very different, scowling master.

All in all, it was a frustrating week and Roz was glad to catch the train back to London that Friday.

'You seem a bit down,' said Nick. 'Are you still okay about meeting Daniel? He's coming for lunch on Sunday, but I could put him off if you wanted.'

'No, I'm fine, honestly.' She could tell him that she was missing Jane and Gilbert, but she didn't want to get the weekend off to a bad start. 'I'm just a bit preoccupied with work at the moment.' And desperate to find Minchen Lane if she could. It felt like her last chance to reconnect with Jane, who seemed to have abandoned her. 'Let's go to Borough Market tomorrow and I'll get something to cook for lunch on Sunday,' said Roz, forcing enthusiasm into her voice. 'Then maybe we could have a walk around the City or something,' she added artlessly.

'The City?' Nick echoed in surprise. 'I don't think there's much to see there on a weekend.'

'There's St Paul's. And the Tower.'

He shrugged. 'All right. If that's what you want.'

In spite of growing up on the outskirts of London, Roz had rarely been to the City. She thought of it as a mass of high-rise buildings, a busy financial centre, and she was surprised at how down-at-heel the area outside Aldgate station seemed at first. There were boarded-up windows and lots of 'To Let' signs, and it was eerily empty.

'It's Saturday,' Nick pointed out. 'All the offices are closed. I told you there wouldn't be anything to see.'

Roz ignored him. She was looking around her, trying to get her bearings, but there was nothing familiar about the broad streets with their looming grey buildings or the rumble of the Underground beneath her feet, and she battled her disappointment. She had been so sure that she would find Jane again here.

Nick was watching her with an expression that slipped from puzzlement to exasperation. 'What's all this about, Roz? You've been acting funny all morning.'

Roz shifted the strap of her bag on her shoulder and avoided her husband's eyes. She had thought she had been doing so well at pretending everything was normal too. A trip to Borough Market was one of their weekend traditions. Nick had sat patiently in a cafe with a coffee and read the paper while she poked around the stalls, sampling cheeses and salamis. It was so much more satisfying than shopping in a supermarket, and today it had been impossible not to think of Jane and how carefully she had shopped, digging her hand down into the sack of grain to check that none was rotten below the surface and narrowing her eyes as she inspected every vegetable. For one dizzying moment Roz had even felt herself being drawn back, as if the ground beneath her feet was dissolving like sand on an ebbing wave, and her heart had leapt in anticipation of seeing Gilbert again, but then a man with a backpack had bumped into her. By the time he had finished apologizing and Roz had finished assuring him that it didn't matter, she had been wrenched firmly back to the present.

She could have wept with frustration.

The need to go back was so strong that she had dragged Nick away from his coffee and insisted on taking the tube to Aldgate. She had looked up Minchen Lane on Google and found no mention of it in the City, but Jack's family's inn had been close to Aldgate itself, and Roz thought she could find her way from there. She remembered arriving at the inn, weary to the bone after the journey from York. They had taken a boat the whole way, changing from the keelboat when they got to Hull to a sturdier cog that took them right to the heart of

London. When Jane got off the ship, the ground had seemed to rock like the deck, and she and Annis had clutched at each other to steady themselves.

London was so huge and so crowded it had taken Jane's breath away at first. She was terrified of falling behind as Jack led them through the streets to his family's inn, and she kept so close that every time Jack stopped, she would walk on his heels.

Roz remembered the inn too. She could see the busy cobbled courtyard, and smell the horses and the straw; she could picture the low-ceilinged room with its guttering tallow candles and the way the benches and tables were partitioned off for privacy. She remembered the stickiness of the floor and the taste of the ale, the times she had laboured up and down the stairs to the chambers, sweeping and cleaning, evading the groping hands.

Roz had been staring around her, willing herself back to the city Jane had known, but it was like trying to fall asleep. Just when you thought you might be about to drop off, you would jerk back from tumbling over the brink into unconsciousness.

But now Nick's eyes were fixed on her face, and her shoulders slumped in defeat. 'Jane lived around here. I just wanted to see what the area looked like now.'

Nick sighed. 'Oh God, this isn't still about Jane, is it?' He dragged a hand over his face in despair. 'I thought Rita explained the Jane thing was just in your subconscious? You said you accepted that.'

'I did . . . I do,' said Roz, switching her shopping bag to the other shoulder. 'But I just need to check.'

Standing in the middle of the pavement, she told Nick how Jane had found a home at the sign of the golden lily in Minchen Lane. 'Gilbert Harrison looks fierce but he isn't really,' she said, and her lips curved reminiscently. 'He is all bluster but beneath he is a good man. He makes me smile,' she said, oblivious to Nick's darkening expression. 'When he's there, I feel so . . . I *feel* in a way I never did before.' She laid a hand flat on her ribcage as if trying to stop her heart bursting out of her chest. 'It's like I'm tingling all the time – ' She broke off as she registered Nick's expression at last. 'What?'

'*Jane* is tingling, not you.'

'What? Oh . . . yes, Jane.' But the lovely flutter in her blood was still there, the trip of her heart, the throb between her legs.

'Unless you're saying you're in love with a man who may or may not have died over four hundred years ago?' Nick's voice was hard, flat, his eyes cold. 'I didn't realize you were into necrophilia, Roz.'

Dull colour crept along Roz's cheekbones. 'No, of course not,' she said, struggling to explain. 'You're right: it's Jane, not me. I suppose it's like reading a novel when you're really involved with the characters and you can't wait to read on. I can't leave Jane in the middle of her story. I can't settle until I know what happened next.'

Chapter Sixteen

Why couldn't Nick understand? 'Jane's had such a terrible time,' Roz said. 'I want her to have been happy.'

'It hasn't occurred to you that if Jane ended up living happily there would be no need for her to be haunting you?' said Nick harshly.

'If Jane's just a creation of my subconscious, she's not haunting me, is she?' Roz watched him push a hand through his hair in frustration. 'Look, I know I'm a bit obsessed at the moment, and the truth is that I don't really know what's going on. But you're the one who keeps saying that Jane's story is somehow connected with my own – the one I don't remember. I can't explain it, Nick, but I *have* to know what happens to her next. I can't concentrate on my own issues or anything else until I do.'

'Anything else including our marriage?'

It was Roz's turn to sigh. 'I know how it sounds, Nick, but it's like this relentless tugging in my head. Please, let me see if I

can find Minchen Lane. If I can just see what happens next, I'll
go back to Rita or see a psychiatrist or a priest or whoever you
like.'

'All right,' he said reluctantly. 'But I'm staying with you. Is
this Minchen Lane in the A to Z?'

'No. I've googled it, but there's no street with that name
now.'

They were standing at a crossroads where a modern structure made of a skeleton of timbers marked the spot of the
original Aldgate. 'Do you recognize anything of this?' asked
Nick, reluctantly fascinated.

Roz squinted up at the sky through the timbers. 'Nothing. I
remember Aldgate, of course, but it was nothing like this. It was
a big stone gateway, a bit tumbledown, but it did the job of
funnelling people in and out of the city, I suppose.' She remembered how cold and dank it had smelt under the archway and
how glad she had always been to reach the sunlight on the
other side.

She turned slowly. 'If Aldgate was here, then down there,
where the road divides, that must be Fenchurch Street. There
was a tollbooth there, and the inn was just down there on the
right.' She paused, hoping that Jane might come then, but there
was just a low hum of anticipation in her head.

'Where do you think this Minchen Lane was?'

'Off Fenchurch Street, down there.' Roz set off, eager to find
it. Perhaps Jane was waiting for her to find the right place? But
her disappointment grew as they walked down Fenchurch
Street. Gone were the jettied houses, the workshops with their

stalls jutting into the street. Gone were the barrels and the piles of timber and the occasional dung heap. Gone were the goodwives gossiping in the doorways and the street sellers and the boisterous apprentices. The clamour and cacophony of the Elizabethan street had vanished, and in its place were austere office buildings, looming grey and intimidating on either side of the road and cutting out the sunlight. There were hardly any shops. It was all very dull and Roz couldn't find a single thing to remind her of the past and pull her back to where she wanted to go.

'This is hopeless,' she said after a while, near tears. 'I don't recognize any of this. There's no Minchen Lane here.'

'The City was bombed,' Nick reminded her gently. 'And before that there was the Great Fire of London . . . You can't expect it to be the same.'

'I know,' sighed Roz. 'I just thought there would be something – ' She stopped outside a jeweller and looked up at a street sign.

Mincing Lane.

'Oh,' she said.

Nick followed her gaze. 'Minchen, Mincing . . .' he said. 'Say Minchen quickly enough and you can see how it might have changed.'

Roz let out a long breath. 'This is it,' she said, feeling a warmth brush past her, a subtle shift in the air, a settling as if to say, yes, *yes*, this is home.

Mincing Lane. There was a jeweller on one side, a local supermarket on the other, both deserted.

Roz's heart was beating hard as she looked down the lane. It was just a road, nothing unusual or interesting about it at all, but just for a moment it shimmered like a mirage, and overlaid on it she could see Minchen Lane, bustling with life. The houses jostling together, big and small, broad and narrow, their jettied upper floors leaning over the street, glass windows winking in the sunlight. The gutter in the middle of the street where a cat crouched over a scrap of something it had found, uncaring of the bustle around it until it looked up with great yellow eyes as if sensing Roz's gaze. Its fur puffed up and it spat and fled, leaving its morsel for a pigeon.

It was all so familiar. John Morrison, purse-mouthed, short-sighted, peering over his stall. A cart, pulled up outside the Clothworkers' Hall, two apprentices leaning against it, a glimpse of dice in their hands before a shout from their masters made them straighten hurriedly. Janet Moore and Agnes Phillips arguing again. The high brick tower built by an alderman, punished for his pride, they said, with blindness.

And on the other side of the road, a little further down, beckoning her, was the sign of the golden lily, where a little dog scampered out of sight with a joyful bark and she just caught the whisk of a skirt turning into the passage.

Roz took an eager step forward, and the lane was gone. Tears of disappointment crowded her throat and she swallowed hard.

'It's not going to work,' she said miserably. 'Perhaps it's because you're here?'

'Well, I'm not leaving you,' said Nick. 'I was watching you

just now, and for a moment you just weren't here. You could wander out into a road if you were on your own. I know there isn't much traffic around, but it's too dangerous. Come on, let's go and find somewhere to have lunch. It might still happen.'

They walked all the way down Mincing Lane, but the road stayed stubbornly tarmacked, the buildings bland and flat. They kept turning at random, right, left, right, until they came across a cafe with a row of little tables lined against the wall opposite the sandwich bar. Two young women sat at the table in the window, a pushchair beside them. Their table was littered with coffee cups and plates and baby paraphernalia. Roz chose the table behind them and sat looking listlessly out of the window while Nick went up to order.

She had to snap out of it, she knew, but the absence of her life in Mincing Lane was a leaden weight crushing her heart. She was desolate. She had been so certain that it was Poppet she heard, that a moment more and she could have followed him as he scampered down the passage and into the yard. She could have stepped into the hall and seen the wainscot criss-crossed with sunlight through the windows, the dust glinting golden in the beams of light. She could have walked across to Gilbert's closet and scratched on the door. She just wanted to hear his voice again. Was that too much to ask?

The baby in the pushchair in front of her woke with a wail, and its mother bent down to pick it up. She bounced it on her knee, trying to cajole it into a better humour and give herself a little more time to talk.

'Here.' Nick set down a tray with two coffees on it. 'They're bringing the sandwiches over.' He stopped. 'Roz?'

But Roz didn't answer. Her eyes were fixed on the baby on its mother's lap.

'Good morrow, my sweeting!' Jane took Isabel from Annis and held her up, making faces until the baby giggled and squealed. 'Who's a bonny baby?'

Annis smiled. 'She loves her godmother.'

'And her godmother loves her.' Jane sat down, cuddling Isabel on her lap, distracting her with the rattle of a spoon on a pewter plate. She loved the warm weight of the baby, the sweet milky smell of her. Isabel was a happy baby, happy to be handed from person to person, always giggling and flirting with her lashes. She squealed with laughter when Jane played peekaboo behind a cushion or blew raspberries on her fat tummy. Jane had only tried that once with Geoffrey when he was a baby. The resulting tantrum had left him puce-faced and Jane convinced that he loathed being played with in such a way.

Annis had settled into comfortable motherhood. She was plump and content, but she still kept a proprietorial eye on Jane. Now she leant forward confidentially. 'There is news from York.'

After four years, Jane had stopped looking for the Holmwoods around every corner, but the thought of York still made her heart lurch. 'News? How?' she asked with difficulty as Isabel was standing on her lap now and pushing her little hand into Jane's mouth.

'Isabel!' Annis tsked. 'Here, give her to me,' she said, but Jane shook her head. 'Leave her. I like it that she's so lively.'

'Well then, on your own head be it!' said Annis, settling back onto the stool.

'So, what is this news?' Jane reminded her.

'You know Jack's old master came back to London last year? A friend of his from York is in the city to buy a licence from the court, and told him all the news from up there. Andrew Trewe is Lord Mayor this year, it seems, and there was a big quarrel between Mr Fawcett and Mr Gibson as to which of them should be set down as sheriff first. What else?' Annis rubbed her chin, pretending to think although it was obvious that she was building up to something important. 'Oh yes, Mistress Weatherby has married her husband's journeyman, who must be at least thirty years her junior. Can you imagine? And Barbara Simpson has been whipped around the city at the cart's arse again.'

'And?' Jane prompted dutifully, recognizing her cue.

'And it seems that Sir Robert Holmwood is married again,' said Annis with assumed casualness.

'Married!' Jane stared at her. 'But he cannot!'

'He does not know that, does he?' Annis pointed out. 'You have hidden well. He has taken you for dead, and the boy, and is trying again for the inheritance.'

Jane drew a breath. Relief was dazzling at the edge of her mind, beckoning so brightly that she hardly dared look at it straight. 'Who has he married?'

'Anne Sanderson. That family would not care that Robert's

wife ran off and might not be dead at all. They have daughters to spare, and though there won't be much of a dowry, perhaps the Holmwoods only care about having a son now.'

Jane remembered Anne, a pale, thin girl with milky eyes that blinked nervously.

'Poor lass,' she said with feeling. How would Anne cope with Robert's impotence and Margaret's jealousy?

'You know what this means, don't you?' said Annis.

'That they have stopped looking for Geoffrey and me.' Jane let out a long breath. 'I am sorry for Anne, but so happy to know that we can relax now.' She laughed a little unsteadily. 'Who would have believed that we could get away with it, Annis? Thanks to you and Jack, I am free.'

'And free to marry again,' Annis pointed out.

'I am still married in the eyes of God,' said Jane.

Annis waved that aside. 'You know that, but the rest of the world does not. And more importantly, Gilbert Harrison does not.'

Colour stole along Jane's cheekbones. 'Annis!'

'Come, Jane, I have seen how he looks at you. And he is a fine-looking man, is he not?'

'It would not be right.' Jane's eyes slid away.

Annis leant over and put a hand on her knee. 'There was a time when I called you mistress, and now I am happy to call you my friend. Why should you not call Mr Harrison husband?'

'There is no question of it,' said Jane, flustered.

'You do not have to marry him,' said Annis. 'I'll warrant he could show you some pleasure even so. Tell me you have not considered it.'

Jane's colour deepened. She was all too aware of Gilbert, and she despised herself for a lewd woman, but there were times when she could not wrench her eyes away from his hands or his jaw, and when he smiled at her, her belly would knot with an urgency that took her breath away. She found herself waiting for the sound of his step, and when he came into the room, all at once her senses would leap. It didn't matter if she looked at him or not, she would be excruciatingly aware of her skin, of the brush and slide of the linen smock against her nakedness, the press of her bodice against her breasts, and her blood would roll and thump and there would be a warmth and a tingling pulse in her privy place that left her edgy and disturbed.

Gilbert was an honourable man. He did not touch her, except by accident, when their fingers brushed on a goblet, or when he bent to kiss one of his daughters on her lap, and whenever he did Jane's flesh would flinch as if from a burn. Sometimes their eyes would meet and then it was as if all the air was sucked out of the room, so there was not enough to breathe.

Oh yes, she had considered it.

And why not? Jane asked herself after Annis had gone. She had told Gilbert that she had made her husband a vow to stay faithful to his memory, but why should she not change her mind?

The idea fretted away at her, making it hard to concentrate

on anything else, and she was clumsy and distracted all that day and the next. The maids stared at her when she forgot to add spices to the stew, and the girls giggled when she poured wine into a bowl instead of a goblet and dropped a trencher, spilling bread all over the floor.

Her fingers felt just as thick and unwieldy the next day, and she fumbled as she measured out fine liquorice powder and gum arabic. 'What is the matter with you today?' said Bess, who had come to beg one of Jane's remedies for her daughter's dry cough. Normally crisp, Jane's conversation had been disjointed, and she kept stopping to refer to her book of remedies even though she had made the remedy many times before.

'Nothing.'

Bess lowered her voice. 'Is it that time of the month? I know I'm all over the place when I get the curse.'

'No, it's nothing like that. I don't like the wind,' she improvised, and indeed, it had been blustering around the house all morning, hurling itself at the windows to rattle the shutters and bang furiously against the glass before falling away in frustration. The constant noise had frayed Jane's already tattered nerves. 'I've been on edge all day.'

'It is often windy,' Bess pointed out. 'I've never known you react like this before.' She settled herself more comfortably on her stool. 'You've got something on your mind, Jane. I can tell.'

Jane pressed her lips together. She could hardly tell Bess that she was having lascivious thoughts about her brother. Carefully she stirred the liquorice and gum arabic into the water strained of wheat and barley she had boiled earlier and set it on the fire once more while she tried to think of a suitable excuse.

'It's Geoffrey,' she said at last. She was never quite easy about him so it wasn't a complete lie. 'He's so quiet. He doesn't play with the other children. I'm worried that he's unhappy.'

'He's not like other boys,' said Bess bluntly. 'You've spoilt him, Jane. I've told you that before. You know what they say: spare the rod and spoil the child.' Bess was always ready with a cliché, and it normally amused Jane, but between the wind and this unwelcome obsession with Gilbert, her temper was short.

'I can't beat him when he hasn't done anything wrong,' she snapped. 'He's a good boy.'

'He's sneaky,' said Bess. 'That's why the other children don't like him. Always creeping around.'

'He doesn't *creep*!'

'You're his mother so you don't see it. I'm only telling you for your own good. You're blind to the fact that he's not like other children. Try to smother him less is my advice.'

'He's only six,' Jane objected.

'Time for him to start making himself useful. You molly-coddle him.'

Was it true? Jane felt chilled when she thought about Margaret and her obsessive pampering of Robert. She didn't want to be that kind of mother, but nobody else liked Geoffrey and if she did not look after him, who would? Outside, the petulant wind threw handfuls of rain like pebbles against the windows.

'The liquor is not ready yet. It must boil awhile and then I will strain it and seal it in a clean vessel,' she told Bess. 'I will send it round when it is done. Give Joan some to drink morning and evening until her cough is better.'

When Bess had gone, huddling into her cloak, Jane came back from saying goodbye at the door to find Geoffrey standing silently in the shadows and she jumped. 'Geoffrey, I didn't see you there!' *Always creeping around.* Bess's words echoed in her head. 'What have you been doing?'

'Nothing,' he said, those cold black eyes fixed on her in a way that made her nerves twitch.

'Why do you not go and play with Cecily?'

'I don't want to,' he said flatly. He turned to watch the fire. 'She's a girl.'

'Girls can play too.'

'She doesn't like my games.'

It was true. The few occasions when Geoffrey had played with Gilbert's daughters had always ended in tears. Catherine had been shut in a chest and screamed and screamed until Jane came running to let her out. Cecily had been tied up and left alone in an attic room all afternoon, a scarf tied round her mouth so that she could not call for help. Mary's best lace had been snipped to pieces with shears. Each time Geoffrey had been soundly beaten, but the beatings had little effect other than to distress Jane and leave Geoffrey oddly triumphant.

'Why was she here?' Geoffrey asked abruptly as Jane went to stir the liquorice liquor.

'Who?'

'Mistress Simpson.' The words were innocuous but the malevolence in his tone was not, and Jane felt her colour rise.

Was it possible Geoffrey had heard what Bess had said? *Always creeping around*. Ridiculously, she felt nervous.

'She just came to talk. You know what she is like.'

'She said you should beat me.'

So he *had* heard. 'You shouldn't listen to other people's conversations, Geoffrey,' Jane remonstrated. Reaching for a spoon, she tasted the cough remedy cautiously. 'Eavesdroppers never hear good of themselves.' See, she could pull out a cliché just as readily as Bess.

Geoffrey only hunched his shoulders. 'She'll be sorry,' he said spitefully.

'Geoffrey!' Jane put down the spoon and turned to frown sharply at him. 'You must not speak so of Mistress Simpson! You are in need of occupation, I see. You may take this remedy round to her later when it is cooled. Perhaps that will give your thoughts a better direction.'

'Fire!' Gilbert's servant, Tom, ran into the hall just as they were sitting down to supper. He stumbled to a halt, dropping his hands to his knees and heaving air into his lungs. 'Fire at your sister's house in Tower Street!'

Gilbert's chair scraped over the stone floor as he threw down his napkin and stood up. 'Is Bess safe?' he asked urgently. 'Her husband and children?'

'I don't know.' Tom shook his head, still gasping for breath. 'I came without staying to hear more. I thought you would want to know.'

Gilbert nodded. 'I'd better go.'

Outside the wind was still snatching and grabbing, and tussling with the tiles on the rooftops. Three had already smashed into the yard, and Jane heard another crash to the ground as she hurried to get Gilbert his cloak. 'Take care,' she said anxiously. They all dreaded fire, and the wind could throw it from one house to the next in the blink of an eye.

Gilbert touched her cheek. 'It has been wet all day. Things may not be too bad but I must see how my sister does.'

'Can I go with you?' Geoffrey had scrambled from his stool, his usually sullen face alight and eager, the black eyes gleeful. A feeling like a cold breath on her neck made Jane shiver suddenly. She had sent him round to Bess's house with the cough remedy only an hour or so ago.

Just enough time for a fire to take hold.

She'll be sorry.

But what was she thinking? That a six-year-old, a child, had deliberately set fire to a house? She must have windmills in her head. Jane shook the thought aside.

'No, Geoffrey.' She put her hands on his thin shoulders and he tensed as always at her touch. 'It may be dangerous. You are too young to go.'

'I am not! I want to see the fire!'

'Your mother said no,' snapped Gilbert, swinging on his cloak, and although Geoffrey fell silent, Jane could feel his small body stiffen with hostility beneath her hands.

'Bring your sister and her family back here if need be,' she said to Gilbert. 'We will find somewhere for them all to sleep.'

But when Gilbert did come back, he was alone. Jane had

sent the children and the servants to bed, but she couldn't settle until Gilbert returned. She sat up by the fire, listening to the wind *tap-tap-tapping* at the windows to find a way in, and throwing a sharp rattle of rain against the glass every now and then in frustration. The trees tossed and swayed in a great rush and rustle of leaves. They would be bare the next day, Jane thought, stoking the fire and wishing Gilbert would come back.

She hoped Bess and her family were safe.

She hoped she was wrong about Geoffrey, but she couldn't rid herself of the memory of his gleeful expression when Tom panted out news of the fire.

She'll be sorry.

'What are you still doing up?'

Jane spun round from the fire. She had been so absorbed in her thoughts that she hadn't heard Gilbert's steps on the stairs, and now the breath leaked out of her lungs at the sight of him in the doorway. He was windblown, his face grimy with soot, his mouth stern. He looked wonderful.

A smile of sheer relief blossomed in her face. 'You're back!' She even took a step towards him before recollecting herself and folding her hands firmly in her apron to stop herself reaching for him. 'What news of your sister?'

'They are all safe, God be praised.' Gilbert lowered himself stiffly into the chair where Jane had been sitting. 'It could have been worse. It seems the fire started in the stable and spread to the woodstore, and then the kitchen, but that was when the alarm was raised and between us we managed to stop it going any further. But my sister will not be cooking for a while, that is for sure.'

She had sent Geoffrey round with the remedy. He would have gone to the kitchen. He would have seen the stable. He could have . . . But no, she couldn't think like that, Jane told herself desperately.

'The rain helped,' Gilbert was saying. 'Bess and her husband decided in the end to stay where they were, but I said you would send round food in the morning.'

'Of course.' Jane snapped out of her reverie. 'You must be hungry. I'll get you something to eat now.'

'I don't want anything.' He shifted uncomfortably in the chair and grimaced.

'But you—'

'I said I didn't want anything,' he snarled and Jane's eyes narrowed suspiciously. She looked at him more closely, and saw that he was holding his arm carefully.

'You're hurt!'

'It's nothing. Don't fuss.'

Jane ignored him. 'Let me see.'

'It was just an ember,' Gilbert grumbled, but eventually he let her see the scorch mark on his sleeve where something had burned right through. Jane clicked her tongue.

'That was no ember, was it?'

'Scarce more than that,' he grunted, but now that she was close, she could see that beneath the grime there was a drawn look around his mouth.

'Take off your jerkin,' Jane ordered.

'Jane, there is no need—'

'Take it off.'

Muttering, he started to unbutton the short-sleeved jerkin where it fastened at his waist, but it was awkward with his left hand, and after a moment, Jane pushed his hand away and did it herself, easing the jerkin over his shoulders as gently as she could. Even so, Gilbert couldn't prevent a wince.

'God's blood, woman, be careful!'

'I thought you said it was nothing?' Jane laid the jerkin aside. Its velvet was stained and sooty. She would have to brush it tomorrow and see what she could do about restoring the embroidered trim. 'Come, now the doublet.'

'You are very crisp tonight,' grumbled Gilbert, but he let her start unfastening the covered buttons.

She didn't feel very crisp. Her mouth was dry and her fingers clumsy as she bent over him and fumbled with the buttons. They were very close. She could smell the smoke and the sweat of the evening. She tried to focus on the buttons but the corner of his mouth kept catching at the edge of her vision, the line of his jaw above his ruff, and her breath kept tangling in her throat.

At last it was done, and Gilbert gritted his teeth, cursing under his breath, as Jane pulled the ruined sleeve off. Now there was only his shirt to go.

It was excruciatingly intimate to slide the linen off his shoulders. He was strong and solidly muscled, and when her fingers brushed against the smooth flesh of his upper arm his skin was warm and Jane jerked her hand away as if she was the one who had been burnt.

The sight of the ugly burn drove such thoughts from her mind, though. It was red and raw, the flesh already puffing up angrily.

'Nothing, is it?'

'Did you know you sound very northern when you're cross, Jane?'

Gently, she touched her fingers around the burn. 'I will get you a salve. Do you stay right where you are. I will not be long.' She poked up the fire, took a candle and hurried down to the little room off the kitchen she used as her larder. She had a sealed jar of ointment she had made that summer with cream and boiled-up lichen from a stone wall, and stirred with yarrow and the green of elder bark and fine grass.

In the kitchen, she cut a slice of eel pie and poured some ale into a tankard, not sorry to have some time to steady her thumping heart and remember how to breathe slowly. When she thought she had herself under control she added a clean strip of linen for a bandage, and the salve, and took it all up to the great chamber on a tray. Gilbert was sprawled in the chair, watching the fire, his body lean and strong in the firelight, and Jane made herself take a breath before she walked briskly across the room and set the tray down on the table by his side.

'I have brought you something to eat,' she said. 'You will sleep better.'

Gilbert sniffed at the tankard dubiously. 'Is the ale doctored?'

'Upon my word, no. I hope that the ointment will suffice to help the pain.'

'I didn't say it was painful,' he said quickly.

Jane smiled a little as she pulled up a stool and opened the jar of ointment. 'I have been burned myself,' she said, showing him the scars on her hands. 'Do not pretend to me that it does not hurt, for I will not believe you.'

'These are old scars,' said Gilbert, touching them with his good hand. 'How did you come by them?'

Jane smoothed ointment very gently over the burn on his arm and thought about the moment Ellen had thrown her dead baby on the fire. 'I acted without thinking,' she said.

'That doesn't sound like you, Jane.' A smile hovered around Gilbert's mouth but Jane wouldn't let herself look at it.

'I have learned to be more sensible,' she agreed, tying the bandage firmly in place over the wound.

'My sensible Jane.' Gilbert's voice had deepened so that it seemed to be reverberating over her skin. Jane knew that she should get up from the stool, but she couldn't move. She was pinioned into place, lashed by a beating desire that thudded through her veins. She could hear the crack of a log falling into the fire, the moan of the wind, but the sounds seemed to come from another world, one outside the tiny space around the chair and the stool where she and Gilbert sat, the silence between them shouting with the thumping of her heart.

'Jane,' he said softly.

'Yes?' To her shame her voice came out as a croak, and she blushed in the firelight. She couldn't take her eyes off the bandage.

'Look at me.'

'I cannot,' she whispered.

'Cannot or will not?'

'Dare not.'

'I never took you for a coward, Jane.'

'I . . . I should go,' she said, but she didn't move.

'Don't.' Gilbert lifted his good hand and ran a finger down Jane's cheek. 'I need you.'

'I have done all I can for your burn,' she managed.

'It is not my arm that pains me,' said Gilbert, and the smile in his voice caught at her breath. 'You know that I want you, Jane.'

Very slowly, she raised her eyes to his and what she saw there set such a wild sensation pumping inside her that she could barely speak.

'I am your servant,' she said hoarsely.

'And because of that, I have resisted my desire for you. I told myself it was wrong and would not show you the respect you deserve, but I cannot resist any longer. What is between us burns too strong. I am consumed by my need for you, Jane. Can you tell me that you do not want me too?'

'No, I can't tell you that,' Jane said, but when he would have reached for her, she scrambled to her feet, desperate to put a safe distance between them. She concentrated fiercely on winding up the spare bandage, and putting the stopper back on the salve.

'That is what I love about you, Jane. You are so honest,' Gilbert said from behind her. 'So clear-eyed and so true.'

'Don't,' she muttered, keeping her back firmly turned on

him. If he knew that she had stolen Geoffrey and run away from her lawful husband, that she had lied to him from the first, he would never forgive her.

'I must,' said Gilbert. 'We cannot go on like this, my bird. Let us be married and be done with it.'

'Married?' She almost dropped the jar of ointment as she spun round to stare at him.

'I know, I said I would not contemplate it again, but that was before I knew you. Before I realized how much I had come to rely on you. Before I had started to look for you and want to talk to you when I came in, before my days seemed incomplete if I did not see you press your lips together and try not to smile.'

Jane was shaking her head, but Gilbert pressed on. 'I married to please my kin before, and look how well that turned out,' said Gilbert. 'I am a widower and of independent means. I may marry to please myself this time, as may you.'

'Gilbert, I cannot marry.' She put down the jar with unsteady hands.

His brows drew together. 'You are a widow. Was your passion for your husband so great that you cannot replace him?'

Jane thought of Robert and suppressed a shudder. That, she could not pretend. 'No, it was not that.'

'Then what?'

What could she tell him? Jane twisted her hands together in her apron. That was the terrible thing about lying. One lie begot another and before you knew it, you were lost in a thicket of them.

'I made a vow,' she said after a moment. That at least was true. She had promised Juliana that she would care for Geoffrey, and this was the only way she had known how to do that. 'I promised I would not marry again for my son's sake.'

The thought of Geoffrey made Gilbert pause. She could see it in his eyes, but he recovered quickly. 'I will take the boy and raise him, for you, Jane.'

He didn't like Geoffrey, Jane knew, and in spite of herself, her heart swelled at the thought that he would do so much to wed her, plain Jane, a butcher's brat.

If only she could say yes! To have found a love so strong, and a good man who wanted her for his wife was bitter indeed when she could not seize the chance of such happiness with both hands. If only . . .

Ah, but what was the use in if onlys? Jane asked herself. There was no end to them. If only Juliana had not succumbed to John Harper, if only she had not died, if only the Holmwoods had had some care for Geoffrey, Jane would never have come to London. She would never have come to the house at the sign of the golden lily or found Gilbert. She might never have known what happiness could be.

Now the thought of losing that happiness clutched at her entrails. The temptation to say that she would marry Gilbert was great indeed, but Jane couldn't do it. Robert might have married again, but he at least did not know whether she was dead or alive. Jane had no such excuse. She knew. Her conscience would not let her betray her vow before God, no matter how much she longed for it.

'I promised,' she said again, miserably.

'Some promises are made to be broken.' Gilbert's voice was gentle.

Jane thought about Ellen, swinging from the end of a rope. 'I broke a promise once,' she said. 'I will not do it again.'

'Then there is no hope for me,' said Gilbert heavily.

'I did not say that,' said Jane, suddenly sure. There were so few chances at happiness. Wrong or not, she would not let this one go.

Crossing to the chair, she laid her hand in Gilbert's and felt his fingers close around hers, warm, strong, certain. 'I will not marry you,' she told him, 'but I will share your bed.'

His brows knit and he studied her with a perplexed smile. 'Most women would be eager for marriage.'

'Well,' said Jane serenely, 'I am not most women.'

'No, indeed you are not.' His smile warmed. 'You are unique, my Jane.'

She drew a breath, giddy with exhilaration at the prospect. 'Then are we agreed? I will be your housekeeper by day and your lover by night?'

'If that is the only way I can have you.' He drew her down onto his lap and she spread her hand over his bare chest, marvelling at the smooth warmth of his skin, thrilling at the knowledge that she could touch him at last. She ached with a need she couldn't name, and when Gilbert drew her closer and pressed a smile to her throat she arched with an inarticulate cry and her mind went dark with desire.

'What about your arm?' she said with difficulty as his

mouth drifted down to her shoulder and he tugged at the laces of her bodice.

'What arm?' said Gilbert, his voice thick, and she laughed unsteadily as she wound her arms around his neck. 'How I have longed for you, Jane,' he whispered against her skin.

'And I for you,' she sighed, blizzarding kisses along his jaw, over his face, wherever she could reach. The fire spat sparks, the wind knocked impatiently at the window, the candles guttered, but when Gilbert laid Jane down on the cushions there was only the ragged sound of their breathing, only touch and taste and a gathering of feeling, of senses, of sheer pleasure, rising higher and higher with every caress, every kiss, until Jane felt as if she were standing atop a world spinning too fast to think, to breathe, and she clung to Gilbert as she flew off at last with a shout that was part triumph, part terror.

She was an adulteress. She was lewd. She was a liar. Perhaps it was wrong, but for Jane nothing had ever felt as right.

Chapter Seventeen

'What's got into you?' Nick held Roz away from him, a question in his eyes.

Roz let out a puff of frustration. 'God, Nick, you don't have to make it sound as if we only ever have sex on every third Sunday in the month!'

'We don't do it like this either,' he said, his face set in grim lines, and she pulled sulkily out of his grasp.

'Like what?'

'Like you're . . . desperate.'

'Oh, so I'm not allowed to initiate sex now, is that right?' Churning with frustrated desire, Roz flounced to the other end of the sofa. 'I'm supposed to be a good little wifey, lying back and waiting for my hubby to feel like it? Someone should have told me that we'd changed the rules!'

'You know that's not what I mean,' said Nick with a sigh. 'It's just . . . you're not usually so frenzied. It was like we hadn't had sex for years.'

'Perhaps I've been missing you in York,' she said, but he shook his head.

'I don't think it's me you've been missing.'

She went very still. 'What do you mean?'

'I think it's Gilbert you really want,' he said deliberately. Shifting down the sofa so that he could reach her, he took her chin in one hand and turned her to face him. 'When we were kissing just now . . . I can't explain it, but it didn't feel like *you*,' he said, ignoring the way her eyes were skittering around in an attempt to avoid his gaze. 'It looked like you and it tasted like you, but there was something not quite right . . . like I was kissing someone else. Was I kissing Jane, Roz?'

She flinched as if he had slapped her, but the jolt unclicked something in her head and her vision cleared. One moment she had been wild with frustration and fear, and the next she was looking at her hard-eyed husband, feeling queasy and disorientated.

'Nick?' she recognized him shakily, and he dropped her chin to gather both her hands in his.

'Shit, I don't like this, Roz. Whatever's going on, it's getting out of hand. You've got to get some help.'

'I know.' Roz swallowed and looked down at her hands encased in Nick's warm clasp. All the time she thought she had been acting as herself, had Jane been stealing further and further into her mind, taking over her thoughts without her realizing? Roz's expression was stark as she lifted her eyes to Nick's. 'What am I going to do?'

'I can't believe I'm saying this, but perhaps it's time for a priest. It sounds crazy, I know,' he admitted when she laughed a little wildly. 'But you haven't been yourself ever since you went to York, Roz. I thought it was, you know, the whole business with Daniel, and then all the stuff about your family and being in York . . . I was so sure it had to be some kind of psychological issue,' he said, 'but now . . . I don't know.'

Roz didn't know either. All she knew was that for the first time she was frightened of Jane's hold on her. 'Where do I find a priest?'

'Go to church, I suppose,' Nick guessed, mouth turned down. 'Tomorrow's Sunday. There ought to be some vicars around.'

'Daniel's coming for lunch tomorrow,' she reminded him and he swore and released her hands to rub his hair in frustration.

'I'll ring Ruth. We can fix another weekend.'

He was patting his pockets for his phone when Roz laid a hand on his arm. 'Wait. Don't do that, Nick. You can't start your relationship with Daniel by chopping and changing arrangements when they're inconvenient. That'll only make him feel like he's a nuisance. We said we'd have him to lunch so let's do that,' she said. 'We're both aware of Jane now, and it's not like she's hurting me or anything. You can bring me round if I slip back.' She told him about Charles Denton. 'He's not a priest, but he seemed to understand what was happening, and he talked about a cleansing ritual. I'll contact him when I'm back in York. He'll know what to do.'

*

354

Charles Denton didn't sound surprised to hear from Roz when she rang. 'I was afraid Jane wouldn't let go that easily.'

Roz drew a breath. 'You talked before about some kind of cleansing ritual to get any spirits to depart. Can you come and do that?'

'What does your director say? He seemed pretty adamant that he didn't want me back before.'

'I haven't said anything to him,' she confessed. 'I don't want to tell him that I'm . . .'

'Possessed?'

'Yes.' Roz moistened her lips. 'Yes, possessed.' Charles made it sound as if possession was something that came up in everyday conversation. She didn't know if that was reassuring or not. 'But I'm afraid Jane may be growing stronger. I'm starting to wonder how much of what I'm saying is what I really think or what she wants me to do.'

'Do you sense that she wants you to lay her to rest?'

'No. She doesn't want me to do that. It's like an insistent *no, no, no* at the back of my mind. It was hard for me to pick up the phone and call you,' she told Charles. 'I had to force myself, like picking up a slug.' She grimaced at the memory.

'You're a strong person, Roz.'

'I don't feel very strong,' she admitted. 'And I don't know how much longer I can hold out against her. That's why I think you should come anyway, even if I don't have Adrian's permission. He won't know, will he?'

'Very well,' said Charles. 'Find a time when you can have the house to yourself, but I think you should ask at least one other person to be there to get help if necessary. Jane's is not the only spirit associated with that house. I sensed much violence and hatred there. You must be careful.'

Roz put down the phone slowly. Charles hadn't sounded as confident as she had expected. She had better not tell Nick that. It had taken some time to persuade him that she would be better off back in York. The truth was that Roz was shocked by how easily Jane had taken her over. She still felt a bit sick when she remembered Nick's expression on the sofa.

It didn't feel like you.

She could so easily have lost him. Only now did Roz realize how close their marriage had come to breaking down. How much she wanted to save it.

'Who am I?' he had said that night, braced above her, inside her, he had looked into her eyes. 'Who am I, Roz?'

'You're Nick.' She breathed in the familiar smell of his skin and ran her hands over his back, feeling the familiar flex of his muscles, the lovely lean length of him. Her memories of Gilbert fluttered and faded until he was no more than a long-lost obsession. Nick was here, now. He was real and solid and she held on to him tightly. 'You're Nick.'

It had been strange going back to York. Roz had only been away for the weekend, but after living through the changes in Jane's life it felt like forever. At least four and a half centuries, she thought with grim humour.

Fortunately there was plenty to do in the run-up to the launch. The furniture and fittings Lucy had sourced were arriving even as the workmen frantically tried to finish the snagging.

Mark was organizing a team of volunteer guides, and as they familiarized themselves with the rooms, the house rang with voices and footsteps. Roz listened to everyone moving around and felt less isolated in her attic office. The atmosphere was so different that week that she nearly rang Charles Denton to cancel, but the lingering smell of smoke in her office stayed her hand even as she reached for the phone.

There were other signs, too, that reminded her that it would be foolish to think Jane had gone. If Lucy called her to admire a tapestry they had hung in the great chamber, it was all Roz could do not to say that it was all wrong, and that there hadn't been a hanging there at all. She had to stop herself from moving the furniture around and several times turned to go into a room that she remembered being there only to find herself about to bump into a wall. No, it would be a mistake to think that Jane had gone for good, however normal the house felt.

With so many people around, it was hard to find a time when Charles could come without Adrian finding out about it. Helen always seemed to be around, officiously checking things off some list on her clipboard, while Adrian himself bustled happily from room to room, delighted to see his pet project coming together at last. He was full of last-minute ideas for the launch and kept popping up to see Roz in her office, wanting her approval for his plans.

At first Roz thought about asking Lucy if she would come to another séance, but the curator was so busy with finalizing the displays that they barely had a chance to talk. Besides, she wasn't sure how Lucy would feel about a cleansing ritual. Mark was busy promoting the 'haunted house' side of things, and she certainly couldn't ask Helen, who still regarded her with a dislike that reminded Roz uneasily of Geoffrey. Helen would go straight to Adrian, anyway.

The more Roz thought about it, the more obvious it seemed that Jeff would be the person to approach. He had said little at the original séance but he would be a steadying presence, she couldn't help feeling. And as caretaker, he knew all about the newly installed burglar and fire alarms.

Her chance came when she found Jeff in the parlour one day. He was sweeping up the debris left behind by the workmen, mostly curls of wood shavings and plaster dust.

'Jeff, have you got a minute?' she asked awkwardly and he looked up from the floor. Roz always forgot how disconcerting his gaze was.

'Aye.'

She always forgot how taciturn he was too.

Roz cleared her throat. 'I was wondering if we could have a word?' She looked around the parlour. Anyone passing would be able to overhear their conversation. 'Maybe outside?'

Jeff's brows rose slightly. 'If you like.' He rested his broom against the wall and nodded towards a line of black sacks full of rubbish. 'I've got to take them down t'bin anyway.'

'I'll give you a hand.'

The sacks were light, and Roz carried two as she followed Jeff down the stairs and across the great hall. The sound of their footsteps nearly drowned out the faint whispery whirr and rattle of the toy train. Almost, but not quite.

'It's good to get out,' she said as Jeff shouldered open the door and let her past into the yard.

Swirling leaves chased each other around the yard, rising and falling in eddies as the wind gusted and banged at the windows. It reminded Roz of the time Jane and Gilbert had first made love. The brightness was welcome after the dark hall, and it felt good to be outside, even if only in the dingy yard.

'The air smells good, doesn't it?' she said.

Jeff had hoisted up the lid of the commercial waste bin and was chucking in the black sacks two at a time but he paused at her question, looking from her to the bin and back again. 'What?' he said.

'Can't you smell the grass growing?' she said.

'*Grass*?'

'I love this time of year.' Her lips curved as she closed her eyes and tilted her face up to the sun.

'October?'

'Spring,' she said lazily without opening her eyes as she leant back, propped on her hands in the grass. 'Every year I think, *this is the most beautiful spring I have ever seen*, and then the next year I say exactly the same thing; but this year, I am sure of it: there will never be a spring more fair than this one. The birds will never sing as sweetly, the air will never be as soft, the blossom will never be as . . . as *blossomy*.'

Gilbert chuckled. 'That means you are happy, Jane.'

'I am.' She opened her eyes to look down at him with a smile. He was stretched out on the grass beside her, careless of the stains on his doublet. The dog, Poppet, rested against his side. Gilbert still pretended to despise him, but Jane knew the little spaniel had waged a subtle and successful campaign to win him round. Sometimes when he thought no one was looking, Gilbert would feed him titbits from the table, and once or twice Jane had found him in his closet looking sheepish with Poppet on his lap.

It was May Day, and the sun was shining. It felt as if all of London had poured out of the city gates and onto the open land to enjoy the sweet and wholesome air. Gilbert had a garden with a little house out past the Spittle Field, and like everyone else they had all come to enjoy the sunshine, the girls and Geoffrey on their ponies, and Jane perched up behind Gilbert on the rump of his horse.

'I am happy,' she said again, plucking a blade of grass and tickling Gilbert's nose with it.

Mary, Catherine and Cecily were making daisy chains to crown each other, but of Geoffrey there was no sign. He had an extraordinary ability to vanish into the shadows, only to reappear suddenly and silently when you least expected him. He was eight now, and Gilbert talked of sending him into service, but Jane resisted. Geoffrey was too secretive, too sullen. She feared a master would dislike him and beat him, and that Geoffrey would exact his own revenge. She had never forgotten how he had spat out Bess's name. *She'll be sorry*, he had said, and that night Bess's house had burned. Jane had no proof, but whenever the alarm for fire was raised there would she find

Geoffrey at the front of the crowd of onlookers, his face alight as if the flames had lit a fire inside him too.

She could speak of her fears to no one, for how could she believe such a thing of her own son without proof? And if she did speak, there might be an inquest, and Geoffrey might be taken away on suspicion, whether he was innocent or not. Jane could not do it; she had promised.

'Then let us send him to school instead,' Gilbert had said. 'He can learn to read and figure, and I will find him a place when he is older. He is a clever boy. He will do better at school than tied to your apron strings.'

But Geoffrey hated school. He hated the beatings and the other boys, and he held Gilbert responsible. His sullenness deepened into a cold resentment that cast a chill over the room whenever the two of them were in it, so that sometimes Jane despaired of what would come of him.

On that May afternoon, though, despair was far from Jane's mind. Even so, she lowered her voice and wriggled down next to Gilbert.

'I am happy but I think I may soon be happier still,' she whispered and he raised an eyebrow.

'How so?'

'I think . . . I think I may be with child.'

Gilbert sat bolt upright. 'What?'

'I'm not sure yet,' she said quickly, 'but it has been a couple of months since . . . well, you know.' She had been nauseous too, and her breasts felt tender. When she had whispered it to Annis, Annis had nodded sagely.

'So it was with me with all my babes,' she said.

'But I have been so careful,' Jane had protested. She made her own pessaries with the juice of mugwort and applied them diligently against conception. There were drinks she could try to loosen the child in her womb, she knew, but Jane couldn't bring herself to do that.

A child. A child of her own. Jane was bursting at the thought of it, but she had wondered how Gilbert would take the news. He had three daughters already.

But she need not have worried. Gilbert snatched off his hat with a shout of laughter that made the girls look up from their daisy chains.

'Sshh,' said Jane. 'I do not want anyone else to know.'

'You will not be able to hide it forever, my love.'

'I know, but I want to wait until I'm sure.'

Gilbert laid a tender hand on her belly. 'Another child,' he said wonderingly. 'You will have to marry me now, Jane. The future of my son or daughter matters more than a promise, does it not?'

Jane hesitated, torn. It felt like a risk, like testing her good fortune too far, but Gilbert was right. She and Geoffrey were settled in London now. Robert had married again; the Holmwoods had given up the chase. Surely they were safe?

'Yes,' she said, and before she could stop him, Gilbert was on his feet with a triumphant shout.

'What is it, Pappa?' Sensing excitement, the girls ran up to him.

'I am to marry again,' he said. 'What do you say to Jane as your new mamma?'

'Yes! Yes!' The girls squealed with delight and Jane laughed as they hugged her, but over Catherine's shoulder she caught sight of Geoffrey, who had appeared silently as was his wont. He was staring back at her, white-faced, eyes blazing with rage.

Later, she tried to talk to him. 'Mr Harrison will provide for you, Geoffrey,' she said. 'It is a great security for us.'

'I don't want him to provide for me,' said Geoffrey tightly. 'He doesn't like me.'

'That's not true,' said Jane weakly, knowing that it was. 'And anyway, even if it was, what would that matter? You will be his son.'

'But you are to have his child,' said Geoffrey. 'If it is a boy, he will have no use for me. I will still just be a butcher's brat with a servant for a mother.'

Jane sucked in her breath, dismayed as always by the vitriol in his voice. What had she done for him to hate her so? She had tried so hard to care for him and provide for him, but nothing she did was ever good enough for Geoffrey. She could see Juliana in him often, in that restless discontent with his lot, the conviction that he was meant for grander things, that he was better than everyone around him.

Jane was glad she had never told him the truth about his parentage. As far as Geoffrey knew, his father had been a butcher in York and Jane his widow. She had hoped it would keep his expectations low, but Geoffrey took his lowly background as an affront. Jane dared not think how he would react if he learnt the truth, that he was base begotten by a lascivious tailor. Even more she feared his reaction if he discovered that she had taken him from his inheritance of Holme Hall and the house in Micklegate. She would never be able to explain Margaret and Robert's depravity. She knew she had done the right thing, but Geoffrey would not see it that way.

She kept her voice steady as she faced Geoffrey. 'I will not be a servant when I am married to Mr Harrison. He is a gentleman, and I will be his lady.'

'Lady?' Geoffrey spat. 'Everyone knows you for his whore!'

Before she could stop herself, Jane's hand lashed out and caught him a stinging slap on his cheek. It was little enough punishment compared to some of the beatings he had had, but Geoffrey reeled back, his eyes black and bitter, the imprint of her hand red on his face. 'I hate you! I hate all of you!' he said. 'You will be sorry!'

'Geoffrey, wait!' Jane began, but he ran off, slamming the door behind him so hard the latch rattled and leaving her wracked with guilt and with fear, her palm still tingling where she had struck him.

Jane turned it upwards to look down at it, remembering the viciousness in Geoffrey's eyes. *You will be sorry.* 'Oh God, what have I done?'

'You haven't done anything. It's okay, Roz. Come and sit down.'

He guided her over to the rickety bench where the shop assistants used to hunch over their fags. He remembered how they had huddled into their coats, sucking on their cigarettes with a kind of desperation, not talking. Sad men he had thought them at the time, socially awkward, trapped behind the counter in a model shop. Now he wondered whether their stammers and flickering eyes owed more to the house than their own inadequacies.

Roz's face was eerily blank. She sat obediently but her hands were twisting in her lap. 'I shouldn't have hit him,' she said. 'He will punish me for that. He will bide his time, but he will not forget.'

A coldness breathed on Jeff's back, making his shoulders twitch. He waved a hand in front of her face. 'Wake up,' he said. 'Come on, Roz, wake up!'

Awareness flickered in her eyes, slow at first, and then to his relief her expression cleared. 'Jeff?' she said uncertainly.

He nodded. 'Are you okay?'

She sucked in a long breath and looked around her at the yard. It was an uninspiring sight: wheelie bins, builders' debris, flattened cardboard boxes stacked against the wall. Adrian's car and an electrician's van. Nothing out of the ordinary, but Jeff had the uncanny sense that Roz was seeing something else entirely.

'She's back,' she said, and the strangeness in her voice made the hairs creep up on the back of Jeff's neck. It reminded him of the way she had looked after the séance, but even as he frowned in concern a smile was spreading over her face and she placed a hand wonderingly on her stomach. 'A child,' she said.

Afraid that she might be drifting back into her trance, Jeff snapped his fingers in front of her. 'Hey! Stay with me, Boo,' he said. Was she pregnant? That might explain it. They said pregnant women behaved a bit strangely sometimes. Not that Jeff would know. 'Do you need a doctor?'

Very slowly, Roz turned her head. The breeze was snatching at her hair and blowing it around her face and she held it back with one hand so she could look at him properly for the first time. Her eyes were devastatingly clear once more. 'What did you call me?'

Jeff was caught unawares, pinned by the directness of her gaze. 'What? When?' he blustered. 'Nothing.'

'You called me Boo.'

'Did I?' It had just slipped out. He'd never been able to think of her as Rosalind. 'It doesn't mean nothing.'

There was a long pause. 'You're Mikey,' said Roz.

'I'm Jeff,' he insisted, but even he could hear the lie and she shook her head.

'You're Mikey,' she said again, and at the certainty in her voice he felt something unlock inside him. 'You're my brother.'

'We should talk.' Roz rubbed her arms. 'It's too cold out here, though. Let's go inside.'

'No!' he said without thinking. 'Not in the house.'

'Why do you say that?' she asked but he noted that she didn't sound surprised.

'I don't know,' said Jeff honestly.

They both turned to study the back of the house. The scaffolding was down at last and you could see how the structure

of powerful beams had been restored. The plaster was beautifully rendered, the leaded windows winked in the light. Even
this, the back of the house, was magnificent. No one could deny
that the Holmwood Foundation had done a wonderful job.

'There's something wrong with that house,' Jeff heard himself say, and Roz nodded slowly as if she understood.

'I think so too.'

He looked at her. 'You can feel it? The atmosphere?'

'Oh yes,' she said.

'I can't explain it, but I don't think we should talk in there.'

They went instead to a little cafe near Micklegate Bar. They
sat at a table with a checked plastic tablecloth and plastic
flowers in a little vase. Roz ordered some fancy coffee they
didn't have, so settled for a filter instead. He had tea. 'Strong
and black,' he told the waitress.

Roz pleated a paper napkin while they waited for their
drinks. 'Well, this is awkward,' she said at last, mustering a
smile. 'Where do we begin?'

Jeff shrugged. He didn't have a clue. Calling her Boo had
been a mistake. He should have been more careful. She would
never have known otherwise. He couldn't decide whether he
was glad or sorry now that she did.

'The thing is, I can't believe it really,' said Roz. 'You're my
brother.'

'Half-brother,' he said.

She lifted her head from the napkin and stared at him. 'Why
didn't you tell me who you were?'

Jeff rested his hands on his thighs. He could feel the coarse fabric of the overall under his fingers. On the other side of the table, Roz was looking elegant in soft wool trousers, some kind of silky top and what he was prepared to bet was a cashmere cardigan. Her hair was tousled by the wind, but gold gleamed at her ears and round her throat, and she wore a sapphire and diamond ring next to her wedding ring. She looked classy, sophisticated, *rich*. Nobody looking at them together would guess that she was his sister.

'You live in a different world to me,' he said, nodding at her clothes. 'I wasn't sure you'd want to know. You're the fancy events director from London. I'm the caretaker from prison.'

'You're my brother,' she said again as if that was all that was important and irritation flashed through him at her naivety. Did she really think that made a difference?

'You'd never shown any interest in me before,' he said, unable to keep the resentment from his voice. 'Why would I think you'd be interested in meeting me now?'

'I didn't even know you existed until a few months ago,' Roz protested. 'Aunt Sue told me that my entire family died in a car crash. I knew that I'd had half-sisters but she never said anything about a brother. I'm sorry. It was only when she died that I discovered the truth.'

Jeff felt sick. All those years, waiting for her to remember him, to forgive him, and she hadn't even known of his existence. That bitch, Aunt Sue. She had never liked him.

'That sounds like Aunt Sue,' he said evenly. 'Let's sweep anything difficult under the carpet and pretend nastiness doesn't exist. They told me she'd washed her hands of me, but I didn't think she'd go as far as pretending I'd never existed.'

Roz pinched an end of the pleated napkin and spread the other into a fan. 'Aunt Sue was very good to me.'

'I'm sure she was.' Jeff's mouth twisted with bitterness. 'She always wanted a daughter. She was jealous of our mother. Sue and Keith couldn't have children. I used to hear her crying about it sometimes with Mum. I'll bet she couldn't wait to adopt you.'

'She did want a child,' said Roz. 'She told me that. But she wouldn't have killed her sister to get what she wanted.'

Unlike you. The words throbbed unspoken in the air.

'She should have told you about me.' Jeff could feel the old resentment clogging his throat, making the muscles in his neck bunch.

'Perhaps,' said Roz. 'She was . . . bitter,' she went on carefully, trying to be fair. 'She adored my mother – our mother,' she corrected herself. 'She couldn't forgive you for what happened.'

'And you?' Jeff heard himself ask in a harsh voice.

She smoothed out the napkin she had just pleated so carefully. 'I don't remember,' she said. 'I don't remember my mother, my father, my sisters, *you*. I don't remember anything from before I went to live with Aunt Sue and Uncle Keith.'

'But you were five,' Jeff said. 'You must remember *something*.'

'I don't. Apparently it's quite common for small children to deal with trauma by blocking out memories. All I know about what happened that night is what other people have told me.'

She paused, leaning back in her chair as the waitress brought over their drinks and set them down. When she had gone, Roz lifted her cup and cradled her hands around it without drinking it.

'The other day I went to Millingham Road,' she said. 'I didn't mean to. I didn't even know where it was, but somehow I was there. I didn't recognize the house at all but when I looked at the shed I felt . . . something. Not a proper memory, more of an impression: being cold and frightened, feeling abandoned.'

Jeff's face twitched. He knew how that felt.

Roz set down her cup. 'What happened that night, Mikey?'

'Jeff,' he said automatically. 'I'm not Mikey any more. My name's Jeff.'

'Tell me what happened,' she said.

'I don't *know*!' The words were wrenched out of him. He had been asked that so many times, and nobody ever believed him. He took a sip of tea to steady himself. This, after all, was a familiar story. 'They said I planned it very carefully. They said I stole some petrol from the lawnmower and doused some paper in a wastepaper basket. They said I laid a trail out of the bedroom and set fire to it.' He looked across the checked plastic cloth to Roz. 'They said I burned my mother and the rest of the family to death because I was angry about being smacked for being rude.'

'*They said*? What do *you* say?'

'I remember standing in the garden and watching the house burn.' It had been the strangest sensation, as if he was outside himself, looking at himself with his face lifted to the fire. He had been filled with a sense of exultation. The fire had been beautiful, he remembered that. So pure, so fierce, its flames spearing the darkness.

Another image was coming back to him, dredged up from the depths of his memory. 'You were there. A fireman was carrying you up the garden and I remember feeling puzzled. I didn't understand what he was doing with you or what was happening . . .' He trailed off. 'I'd forgotten that,' he said after a moment. 'The rest of it, laying the fire, all of that . . . I've got no memory of that at all.'

'I read some of the reports,' said Roz carefully. 'They said that when they asked you why you'd done it, all you'd say was that it wasn't you. That someone else had set fire to the house.'

'They decided it was a form of early onset schizophrenia,' Jeff agreed.

'Is that how it felt to you?'

He turned his cup round and round in its saucer. 'What else could it have been?'

Roz didn't answer immediately. She was studying her own coffee, perfectly groomed brows drawn together, working something out in her own mind.

'You said you thought there was something wrong with Holmwood House?'

Jeff was thrown by the change of subject. He'd been expecting her to bang away with the why, why, why questions he could never answer. 'It's just a feeling.'

'You hear the train, don't you?'

He was struggling to keep up with the way her thoughts jumped around. 'Train?'

'The model railway in the great hall.'

'There's no model railway there now.'

'I know, but I hear it anyway,' she said. 'And I think you do too.'

He hesitated. 'What makes you think that?'

'I met someone who used to live in Millingham Road. She remembered us. She said you were a quiet boy until you started spending a lot of time in a model shop. I think it was the model shop that's now part of Holmwood House. You used to come here, didn't you?'

'What if I did?' He felt as if she were prodding him into a corner, into a place he didn't want to go, and he shifted in his chair. His chest felt tight and a headache was jabbing behind his eye.

Roz cast a quick glance and then leant forward over the table. 'I think Holmwood House is haunted,' she said.

Chapter Eighteen

Jeff tried a laugh but it didn't really work. He could feel it dropping away with his smile. He moistened his lips. 'Oh, come on. Is this because of that silly séance?'

'What happened in the model shop, Mi– . . . Jeff?'

'Nothing. It was just a shop.'

'But there was a model railway, wasn't there?'

'Yes,' he said grudgingly. 'There was a big track in the middle of the shop. It had tunnels and bridges and stations, all properly painted. There were fields with animals in them and a little town and a road with toy cars on it.' He stopped himself, embarrassed by the detail of his memory. 'I was fascinated by it,' he admitted, 'but it wasn't creepy or anything.'

The power he had felt in there, the crisp certainty that he could do whatever he wanted, take whatever he wanted . . . that hadn't been *creepy*. That had been cool.

Looking down at that tiny, perfectly functioning world, he had felt like a giant. With one blow of his hands, he could destroy it all. In the model shop, Mikey wasn't a pathetic loser, the way his father had always said he was. In the model shop, he was strong. He could take on every one of the bullies at school. He could look after his mother all by himself so she didn't need Patrick Acclam or his stupid, giggling daughters.

'I used to cycle there on a Saturday morning,' he told Roz. 'I loved it in there. If you went all the way to the back, it was like being in a hidden, secret world. I felt different in there,' he admitted. 'Like I was a different boy altogether.'

'And you became a different boy outside the shop too, didn't you?' said Roz. 'Maggie – the neighbour – told me you started getting into trouble when you'd just been shy before. Our mother was really worried about how you'd changed, she said. They thought it was just a phase. You were jealous of my father and all the attention she gave him and the girls, and then me when I came along.'

'I wasn't jealous of you,' he said quickly. 'You were my sister. But Patrick . . . he was so fucking smug. Always trying to be my friend. Always trying to *understand* me.' Jeff practically spat out the word. 'And the girls used to make my head ache, giggling or screaming, and always making a big fuss about everything. Mum bought into it all. She couldn't do enough for them. She thought Patrick had *rescued* us or something, but I could see they were only using her.' His face darkened. 'There was never any time for just the two of us any more.'

'So you were nasty and set fires to get her attention?'

'Probably.' His face worked suddenly. 'But I didn't want to

374

kill her!' he burst out. 'She was my *mum*. Why would I want to kill her?'

'What if you didn't?' said Roz quietly. 'What if you were possessed? What if you were the one being used, by a spirit or a ghost trapped at that house in Micklegate? What if it was just waiting for a muddled, unhappy boy to come along?'

Jeff stared at her. His mouth was dry. 'What are you talking about?'

'There's something wrong with that house. You said it yourself. It's as if the hall sucks in memories, and then traps them . . . I don't know how to explain it,' she said helplessly. 'As if all the wrongness from the past is still there, somehow, all jumbled up together.' She held her hands apart, making them quiver to illustrate how the atmosphere in the hall felt to her. 'It's like the badness is in the air, looking for a way out. Looking for someone to take the wrongness out of the house.'

'It was a model railway, that's all,' said Jeff, but he could hear the desperation in his denial.

'I don't think so,' said Roz. 'If it had just been a model, I wouldn't hear it now, but I do. You hear it too, don't you? I think something happened to you in that shop. Something changed while you watched those trains, didn't it? Look at me, Jeff,' she said. 'Tell me you don't know what I'm talking about.'

He tried to look at her, but her eyes were too clear, too direct, and his skidded away from them. 'How do you know all this?' he whispered.

'Because it's happening to me too,' she said.

Roz crumpled up the napkin she had been fiddling with ever

since she arrived and put it in her saucer. 'I've been through all the other explanations,' she assured him. 'I've done the whole it-can't-be-happening-to-me thing too, but I've given up fighting it. It *is* happening to me – and I think it's happened to you too.'

She sat at the table with its plastic flowers and its cheery tablecloth, and she told Jeff about coming to York. She told him about her aunt's death, the horrible shock of discovering the truth about her past, and the tensions with Nick over Daniel. And she told him about Jane, right from the start.

It was difficult to judge how Jeff was taking it. He wouldn't look at her but stared fiercely down into his tea. But he was listening and when she had finished, he looked up.

'So today, in the yard . . .? I thought you were pregnant,' he said and she smiled sadly.

'No, not me.' She put a hand on her stomach, remembering how it had felt to know that a child was growing inside her, and longing stabbed at her. 'That was Jane. She's worried about Geoffrey and what he'll do.'

Roz was worried too. A certainty had come to her, like all the pieces of a puzzle falling into place, while she was talking to her brother. But would Jeff accept it?

'Why did you come to work at the Holmwood Foundation?' she asked him carefully.

Jeff shrugged. 'It's not that easy to get jobs when you've been convicted of murder. When I was released on parole, York was the only place I knew. It wasn't like I had any family to go back to,' he said with a grim smile. 'I was happy when the Foundation moved to Micklegate and the restoration began.

The model shop was one of the few places in York that had happy memories for me.'

'So you weren't drawn back to the house itself?'

'A bit.' He paused, thinking about it. 'Maybe. Yes.'

'And when you were given a new identity, did they give you the name Jeff, or did you choose it?'

'I chose it,' he said slowly. 'What are you getting at?'

'I think it's Geoffrey who's haunting Holmwood House,' said Roz in a rush. 'He's just a child but he's evil. He's bound up with what happens to Jane, I can feel it,' she said, leaning over the table, her eyes intent on Jeff's. 'He hates her, but he can't bear to let go of her either. He's conflicted.'

'He *was*,' said Jeff. 'He's dead, right?'

The words were like a slap and Roz shuddered. 'Yes, he's dead. And so is Jane. But don't you see, Jeff, they're trying to live again through us?'

'Say I believe you,' Jeff said, holding up a hand to stop her reply. 'Just *say*,' he warned. 'Why pick us?'

'I don't know,' she said impatiently. Now that she understood what was happening, she was gripped by a sense of urgency. 'Maybe we were both vulnerable because of other things that were happening. Maybe our mother was descended from them in some way. I don't think it matters. What matters is what we're going to do about it.'

Jeff rubbed the back of his hand over his mouth. He was thinking his way through it, she could tell. Not wanting to be rushed into anything. She swallowed her own impatience. The more she pushed, the more he would dig in his heels. Nick was like that too.

The thought of Nick was like a cool balm, and she longed for him suddenly.

'If you're right . . .' said Jeff at last. 'I'm not saying you *are*,' he added quickly when Roz sat up straighter, 'but *if* . . . it would explain how mixed up I've been feeling about you since you arrived. Like, one minute I'd think you were my baby sister and the only family I had, and the next I'd resent you like mad for abandoning me. I knew it wasn't fair. You were only a little kid, you couldn't have stopped them taking me away, but that's what it felt like. Like I was all alone and you had people to love you. Like you had everything and I had nothing.'

'Oh Jeff . . .' Without thinking, Roz reached out and laid her hand over his on the table. Her heart ached for the brother she had never known. If she was right, his fate had been a hard one indeed. Driven by Geoffrey's spirit, he had destroyed his mother and his only chance of a normal future, and she saw something crumple in his eyes at the realization.

He swallowed. 'What are we going to do, Boo?'

'We're going to have to stop them before something terrible happens,' she said, sounding confident, although inside she could hardly believe she was having this conversation. 'I'm calling Charles Denton back. He has some cleansing rituals he uses to get ghosts to depart. I think we should both be there. Can you make sure the house is open if I arrange for him to come? I know the alarms are complicated now.'

'I can do that,' he said. 'But how are you going to keep Sir Adrian away?'

'I'm not going to tell him,' said Roz. 'This is nothing to do with him.'

Here she came, swanning back as if she had all the time in the world! Helen pressed her lips together as Roz walked through the door, brushing her hair back from her face. That Jeff was tagging along behind her, holding the door for her. Another idiot caught up in her spell, Helen thought contemptuously.

'Where have you two been?' she demanded.

Roz favoured her with one of her long, cool stares. 'We've been out,' she said.

'Sir Adrian's called a meeting,' Helen informed her importantly. 'He wants everybody there. You too,' she added to Jeff as he turned to go.

'Me?'

'Everybody, he said. We've all been waiting for you two.'

'Ah, there you are, Roz!' Sir Adrian beamed as she ushered Roz and Jeff into his room. Why could he never be irritable with her for being late? Helen took her seat and opened her notebook.

'I've had an idea,' Sir Adrian announced. 'I think we should all wear Tudor dress to the opening!' He looked around triumphantly, waiting for the applause.

Seated behind him, Helen had a prime view of everybody's expressions. Mark was looking cautious, Lucy dismayed, Roz appalled. That dolt, Jeff, just looked stolid. None of them had any idea of how hard Sir Adrian worked. They didn't appreciate him at all, she thought bitterly.

Lucy looked at Roz, who looked at Mark. It was Roz who spoke first. 'You don't think that might make our guests feel uncomfortable?' Her BBC accent was like nails down a chalkboard to Helen, whose fingers tightened around her pen.

'No,' said Sir Adrian in surprise. 'Why would it?'

'Well . . . I'm just wondering if it might seem a bit odd with some of us in fancy dress and everybody else not.'

'We won't be in fancy dress. We'll be in *authentic* dress,' he insisted. 'And it'll be the perfect opportunity to display the necklace!'

Helen saw Roz's expression slip. Obviously remembering what a fool she had made of herself last time the necklace came out of the safe, she thought with satisfaction.

Sir Adrian went over to the safe and was punching in the code as he talked. 'One five eight zero,' he said. 'Sir Geoffrey's birth date, so it's easy to remember.'

Helen pursed her lips. Only she and Sir Adrian should know the code to the safe. What was he thinking telling the likes of Jeff Wood? The man had been in prison, for heaven's sake! But that was typical of Sir Adrian. He was an innocent in many ways, and far too trusting!

'And here it is . . .' Sir Adrian lifted out the box and carried it over to the desk, where he set it down and took off the lid carefully. 'This is too beautiful not to show off, surely?' he said.

Helen wondered if they realized that they were all staring at the box. It seemed to her as if they were holding their breath and as Sir Adrian pulled it out in a flash and glitter of gold and gems, they let out an instinctive sigh. Her lip curled as she watched them, enthralled by a piece of jewellery. *Some* people were less materialistic, she thought virtuously of herself. Lucy was bad enough, but look at Roz! Miss Superiority herself was staring at the necklace as it dangled from Sir Adrian's hand with naked longing, and as Helen watched in disbelief, a smile suffused Roz's face with such joy that Helen's stomach twisted with envy.

She might look beautiful, but she was well on the way to making a fool of herself too, Helen noted with delight. After all the fuss she had made about the necklace burning last time, Roz seemed to have changed her tune. Not content with looking, she was actually reaching out for the necklace as if she would take it for herself.

'I have brought you a gift,' said Gilbert, bending to kiss Jane as she lay, weary but elated, in the great bed. They had tidied away the bloody sheets, and cleaned her and anointed her belly with some oil of St John's wort and then swathed her in clean linen. She had sipped a decoction of liquorice, raisins and cinnamon and Annis had brought her a nourishing broth with some bread, butter and sugar. And now, at last, Gilbert was allowed into the chamber to see her and inspect his son.

From a purse at his belt he drew a necklace that glittered in the candlelight. 'For you, my bird,' he said, smiling. 'Hold out your hand.' He dropped the necklace into her palm. Exquisite roses made of rubies and pearls were strung together with gold and a delicate pattern of pearl drops, and Jane's eyes stung with tears.

'Oh Gilbert, it is beautiful!'

'As are you, wife,' said Gilbert and she smiled at him.

'I think your delight in your son has addled your brain, sir. Have you forgot I am your plain Jane?'

'You have never been plain to me,' he said, sitting on the edge of the bed. 'You have the clearest, most beautiful eyes I have ever seen, the straightest back, the most gallant set of your head.' He lowered his voice so he could not be heard by the servants bustling around in the background. 'And I have seen you naked, Jane, and I know that you are not plain at all. Your hair is like silk,' he said, lifting a lock from the pillow and rubbing it between his fingers, 'and your skin is soft and smells of gillyflowers – ' He broke off in consternation. 'Now, what have I said to make you cry?'

'Nothing,' she said with a watery smile. 'It is just I do not know what I have done to deserve such happiness.' She glanced at the cradle, where her son, William, lay, his tiny hands curled into fists. He had a smudge of dark hair and his face was red and puckered, and every time she looked at him, happiness squeezed her heart so hard it was painful.

Remembering Juliana's agony, she had been anxious about the birth, but once her labour had started, Jane had forgotten her fears. It was as if her body had taken control, her belly contracting violently whether she willed it or not. Gilbert made sure the best midwife was sent for, and Annis and Bess were on hand to murmur comfortingly that she was doing fine. When they put William on her breast, Jane looked down at his scrunched-up face and tears of joy had leaked from her eyes.

Now it seemed that she could not stop crying. Bess assured her that it was normal. 'I wept scuttlefuls for each of my babes,' she told Jane. 'Did you not cry when Geoffrey was born?'

Jane blinked. She had forgotten that only Annis knew that William was the first child she had borne, although she suspected the midwife had guessed too. She had given Jane some shrewd looks, but Jane did not dare tell Bess the truth. Too many lies rested on the promise she had made to Juliana. Bess was kind but her tongue ran like a fishwife's, and she would be bound to let something slip to Gilbert.

Gilbert, for whom the truth mattered most of all.

Gilbert, whose love for her would shatter if he knew how she had lied to keep Geoffrey safe.

Jane remembered when Geoffrey was born and the relief she had felt that he was alive and a boy, but the joy of his birth and the hopes she had had for him were muddled up with her grief over Juliana's death. Jane had wept then, indeed.

'Not like this,' she said to Bess.

'Well, you have a cry if you need it,' Bess advised. 'You've given my brother a fine son, so you've got thirty days to lie in before you need to be sensible again. I'd make the most of it if I were you.'

So Jane sniffed back the tears as she drew the necklace wonderingly through her fingers again and again in a blur of gold and jewels. She had never owned anything as fine.

'It is beautiful,' she said again.

Gilbert grazed her cheek tenderly with his knuckle. 'Put it on,' he said, and Jane sat up obediently, bending her head down so that he could fasten the necklace around her neck. It settled into place around her throat and she touched it, feeling the warmth of the pearls, the weight of the gold.

Smiling mistily at Gilbert, she tangled her fingers with his. 'Thank you, my heart,' she said. 'I will wear it always, so that every day I will think of this moment when I have everything I could ever want.'

'Are you ready to see the girls? They are clamouring to meet their new brother!'

'Of course.'

But when the girls were hanging over the baby and exclaiming, Jane's eyes met Gilbert's over their heads.

'And Geoffrey?' she asked, knowing what the answer would be.

'He isn't here. He is jealous, Jane. Don't fret. He will be back. Geoffrey likes to be comfortable. Where else does he have to go?'

Sure enough, Geoffrey returned much later, or so Jane was told by Annis, who was keeping her company in childbed.

'It's time he got used to sharing you,' she said briskly. 'A boy like that should be out, not clinging to his mother's skirts.'

'It is hard for him,' Jane said, excusing Geoffrey as she always did.

'How so?'

'You know his story, Annis. He has only had me to care for him.'

'And somewhere comfortable to live and food on the table and a place in a household,' Annis reminded her. 'Geoffrey has more than most boys. He'll come round to William.'

'Of course he will,' said Jane, trying to convince herself, but when the conversation turned to goings-on in the street and Bess came in shaking her head over another fire, Jane couldn't help but wonder.

And worry.

Roz sat at her desk, absently tapping her fingernails against her teeth. It was a habit that drove Nick mad, but at least he wasn't there to complain. She was supposed to be writing the blurb for a new flyer about Holmwood House. *York's most haunted house*, she had written so far, and now the cursor blinked relentlessly at the top of the blank screen, waiting for her to go on.

Would the house still be haunted after tonight? She had arranged for Charles Denton to come after everybody else had left, and Jeff had agreed to be there as well. Charles would be doing a cleansing ritual. If it was successful, Jane would be gone, and Geoffrey too. When she thought about how Jeff had been used by Geoffrey and the terrible price he had paid for being a vulnerable and unhappy boy, Roz was sure that it was the right thing to do. Her brother deserved a chance to be himself, to make his choices unclouded by another's malign spirit.

But when she remembered holding William to her breast,

Roz's certainty evaporated. She ached to go back and feel the warm weight of him in her arms, to stroke his downy head. Her baby, her boy. Roz was afraid that she wouldn't be able to go through with it.

She had been so happy.

Jane had been happy, Nick had pointed out when she told him what had happened, and Roz knew that he was right, and that it hadn't been her experience. But it felt like it was. She remembered the agony of her muscles stretching, stretching, stretching, the feeling of her insides being wrung by pitiless, impersonal hands. The glorious rush as the baby slipped into the midwife's brisk hands. The euphoria even as she sobbed with exhaustion.

She could still feel the weight of the necklace and how comfortably it had fit around her throat. She had glowed with the certainty of being loved, and when Adrian had pulled the necklace from its box, she had reached for it once more, forgetting how it had burned her before. She hadn't been aware of the others' astonished looks, but Jeff had, and he had acted quickly to distract the others and guide her back to her chair, giving her time to come round. He told Roz afterwards that she had only been 'gone' a matter of moments, but the return had been heartbreaking for her. Roz hadn't wanted to leave her baby behind, and she had sat blinking back tears, trying to act normally while yearning to be transported back to the past. Helen's suspicious gaze had bored into her but Roz had barely noticed. How could she when she had just given birth? Her body was aching, her breasts throbbing with the phantom feel of a baby suckling, and her hormones were looping and spiralling out of control. No wonder she hadn't been able to concentrate on the rest of the meeting, and she had barely come round to the present when Adrian carried the day with his idea of dressing them all in Tudor costume.

'Helen will arrange for the costume hire,' he had said, beaming.

'That's you dressed as a maid then,' Jeff muttered in Roz's ear. Helen's jealousy of Roz was obvious to everyone except Adrian.

Roz sighed and forced her attention back to the screen where the cursor was still winking impatiently under *York's most haunted house*. The air in her office was hazy with the smoke that only she could smell. It was familiar now, a constant haunting backdrop to the room.

Should she write about that too? About the necklace? About Jane and how gallantly she had struggled to keep her promises?

No, she couldn't do this. Abruptly Roz deleted the words, banging the backspace key until the screen glared blankly back at her once more. Jane had been real. Her joys were real, her pain was real. Roz didn't want to use her life as a marketing ploy, a jokey idea to pull in the punters.

She didn't want to write anything at all. There was only one thing she wanted right then, Roz realized.

A baby.

'You stay here, sweeting.' Jane kissed William and set him reluctantly on the floor, where he plopped forward onto his hands and immediately started crawling back towards the turned chair. He had just learnt how to pull himself up and make his wobbly way around pieces of furniture. Any day now he would be walking, thought Jane fondly. Her baby was growing all the time.

William was so different from Geoffrey that Jane often felt she had never brought up a child before. Geoffrey had rarely smiled, had hated being held, and seemed to have taught himself to speak and walk in private. It was as if he had deliberately withheld the pleasure of seeing him develop, while William was a sunny-natured child whose face lit up with a delighted smile at the slightest provocation. His chuckle had strangers stopping in the street to pinch his cheeks and exclaim at the brightness of his eyes, and he was happy to be passed around. Everybody, it seemed, loved William – even Catherine, who usually had her head stuck in a book.

Everybody except Geoffrey, of course. Geoffrey wouldn't even say William's name.

'I must go,' Jane said to Catherine, who was sitting in the window. Poppet had been lying with his head on her lap, but as William staggered around the chair, he jumped down and bustled over to the baby, feathery tail whisking gaily backwards and forwards.

'No!' said Jane, starting towards him, but it was too late. Poppet had licked William's face and knocked him off balance. William dropped onto his bottom in a gale of giggles and clutched his fat baby hands towards the spaniel's tail. It was impossible not to laugh with them.

Jane scooped up Poppet and tucked him under her arms. 'You come with me,' she said with mock sternness. Unchastened, he licked her chin.

'Where are you going?' asked Catherine, putting her finger in the book to mark her place.

'Margery Ellis has had a daughter. I must go and give her my good wishes for her lying-in.'

Catherine made a face. 'It's too hot to sit in some stuffy room.'

'I know, but it will be hotter still for Margery. Besides, how else will I know what my neighbours are up to?'

'You could always ask Aunt Bess.'

Jane suppressed a smile. Gilbert's middle daughter had a sharp tongue and was the most like him, and although Jane loved all three of his daughters dearly, it was Catherine who held a special place in her heart. 'Where is Mary?' she asked, smoothing Poppet's silky head so that the dog closed its eyes in bliss.

'She is with Cecily. They're in the kitchen, I think. Cooking or something,' said Catherine without interest. Gilbert despaired of this daughter, who had no desire to learn how to run a house.

'What is to become of her?' he asked Jane sometimes.

'Perhaps she will find a husband who will appreciate her wit and her conversation,' Jane replied. 'Let us hope that it will be so. I fear our Catherine is not meant to be a housekeeper.'

'Will you look after William then?' It was time Catherine had some responsibility, Jane thought. She was overshadowed by the dutiful Mary and the sweet-tempered Cecily, both of whom adored William and never tired of playing with him. Catherine loved her little brother, of course, but she loved reading more. Jane saw the longing glance Catherine cast towards her book. 'I won't be long,' she said in a dry voice.

Catherine closed the book with a long-suffering sigh. 'Of course, Mamma.'

It was stifling in the chamber where Margery Ellis was lying in the big bed. The shutters were closed against unwholesome odours in the air, and a fire burned in the grate so that the women's faces beneath their caps gleamed with sweat. Jane tried to ease her bodice away from her skin as unobtrusively as she could, but she could feel the perspiration trickling between her breasts, down her lower spine and inside her thighs. Poppet lay on her lap and panted. Still, Jane remembered her own lying-in and how it had cheered her to be initiated into the mysteries of motherhood by the other women. She touched the necklace Gilbert had given her that day. She wore it always, a talisman of happiness.

It was good to talk to her neighbours too and to grumble together about the heat, about lazy servants and the incompetence of the local constables. About the latest scandal and their husbands' foibles. When Jane left, she walked slowly back up St Dunstan's Hill and across Tower Street to Minchen Lane with Poppet snuffling along beside her. The whole city seemed to be wrapped in a haze of heat that stung the eyes and thickened the air so that it was like breathing through a rough blanket. The streets were stinking with rotting refuse, and the dogs lay panting in the shade, too hot to snarl over scraps.

Jane put a hand to the back of her neck and made a face at the feel of the dampness there. She wished for a storm to break the suffocating heat. A long spell of hot weather like this was always worrying. The slightest spark could lead to a fire that could ravage a house in no time, and then there was the constant danger of sickness. Praise God, there had been few cases reported so far, but the longer the heat lasted, the sicker folk would get.

She would ask Gilbert if they could go out to the garden house, Jane decided, walking under the sign of the golden lily and down the passage. The door to the kitchen stood open in a vain attempt to let any breeze in. Mary and Cecily were inside, straining the whey from cream boiled with eggs to make a blancmange.

'I see Catherine is not helping you,' Jane said without surprise.

'She's reading.' Mary sounded baffled. She had no more interest in reading than Catherine had in cooking.

'I don't suppose she's got much reading done with William,' said Jane.

'She hasn't got William,' said Cecily. 'She's on her own. I went up to ask her for something and she just told me to go away,' she remembered bitterly.

Jane stiffened. 'Then where is William?'

'Geoffrey's looking after him. Catherine said Geoffrey never does anything to help, and she's right, he should do something, but she never does anything either.'

To Jane, the kitchen was suddenly cold. 'Where did Geoffrey take him?' she asked sharply. 'Did you see where they went?'

'Out into the yard. Didn't you see them when you came in?'

Jane was already picking up her skirts and running back outside. The heat bounced off the dried mud and she held up a hand to shield her eyes. Where would Geoffrey have gone?

Think, Jane, think . . . But she couldn't think. She kept seeing William's trusting smile. He would let himself be picked up by anyone, even Geoffrey, and taken . . . where? There was no time to get the girls to help search and she didn't want to frighten them too soon. Jane was frightened enough for every-one. She had been so careful never to leave Geoffrey and William alone. Why hadn't she ensured Catherine understood that? But how could she have told the girls not to trust her own son?

Jane ran down to the outhouses, opening the doors to the still room, the brew house, the privy to make sure William wasn't shut in. 'Geoffrey!' she called, unable to stop the panic trembling in her voice. 'Geoffrey, where are you?'

It was Poppet who found them. Sensing Jane's distress, he had followed her out into the yard. His ears pricked, he sniffed at the dust, and then he followed his nose to the woodstore, where he stood at the door, tail waving gently.

Snatching open the door, Jane found William sitting round-eyed on the filthy floor. He was watching as Geoffrey carefully laid a faggot on the fire he had laid in the space between the piles of logs. Relief at finding them both unharmed made Jane slump against the doorway.

William's face lit up with a smile at the sight of his mother, and he began to crawl towards her. Geoffrey only glanced up with a peeved expression. 'Oh, it's you,' he said.

Jane picked up the baby while anger rolled over the relief. 'Geoffrey, what are you doing with William?'

Something shifted in the black eyes. 'I'm looking after him.'

'In the *woodstore*?'

Slyness slipped over his face. 'I'm teaching him about fire. Ah!' He sat back with a sigh of pleasure as a flame caught on the dry tinder and flickered into life.

'Put that out!' said Jane. 'It will burn down the whole house, if not the whole street!'

'What if it does?'

Exasperated, she kicked out the little fire he had built herself and stamped on the embers. 'What is *wrong* with you?' she demanded furiously, but Geoffrey only glared back at her, his eyes burning black in his white face. 'Ah, I should have listened to Gilbert when he would have sent you into service,' she said in disgust. 'If it were not for that promise . . .'

'What promise?' he asked sullenly, and Jane let out a sharp sigh. She should not have told him, perhaps, but now that the words were out, she could not call them back.

'I made a promise that I would care for you and keep you safe always.'

Geoffrey's lip curled. 'To my butcher father, I suppose?'

'No, to . . . someone else,' she said. This did not seem the time to tell him the truth about his parentage. 'I am your mother, Geoffrey, and it was a vow any mother would keep for her child.'

'So you keep your vow by marrying a man who despises me and having another child you care for more than me?'

'Geoffrey . . .' Jane sighed and sat on the stump the servants used to split logs. Happily oblivious to the tension, William grabbed at her shoulder so that he could bounce up and down on her lap. Was it possible that all Geoffrey needed was reassurance? 'Geoffrey, I do not love you less because I have another child. Is that what you think?'

'It is what I know,' he said, his face dark with resentment.

'Then you are wrong,' said Jane. She hesitated. Geoffrey was not a boy who let himself be touched but she had to find a way to comfort him somehow. 'Sometimes . . . sometimes you are hard to like,' she said frankly. 'You can be cruel and selfish, and when you light a fire in a woodstore on a hot day . . . well, that is sheer foolishness. But you are my son, Geoffrey, and I love you. Nothing can change that.'

'You will not abandon me?'

'What foolishness is this? Of course I will not abandon you!'

'Promise me,' he said fiercely.

His thin shoulders were hunched, his black eyes blazed. Jane looked at him, this strange, difficult boy who had suddenly given her a glimpse of a much more insecure and vulnerable child inside than she had ever imagined, and she knew that of all the promises she had ever made, this was the one she must keep above all.

'I promise,' she said.

'What's going on in here?' The overhead spotlight stabbed through the dark hall and Jeff jerked back in his chair, throwing up an arm to shield his eyes against the sudden, glaring brightness. Helen was standing with her hand on the switch, her face triumphant. 'I *knew* something was up!'

'For God's sake, woman, think what you're doing!' Charles Denton was on his feet, his face alight with fear. 'Do you have any idea of the danger you're putting Roz in?'

Roz? Danger? Jeff was feeling groggy, disorientated. He rubbed a hand over his forehead as he turned to look at Roz, who was sitting in a chair staring blankly ahead into the shadows.

Helen was unimpressed. 'Oh, this is all such rubbish! She's not in any danger. Any fool can see she's putting it all on!'

'On the contrary, she's possessed by a strong and stubborn spirit. I've been trying to persuade it to leave Roz alone, but now you've broken the connection,' said Charles angrily. 'If I can't re-establish it, she could be lost in the past.'

'What should we do?' asked Jeff, alarmed.

'Get her out of here for a start.' Charles jerked his head at Helen, who visibly swelled with outrage.

'How dare you speak to me like that? You've got no business in here. You're a charlatan, a *nothing*!' Her voice shook with malice. 'I'm going to tell Sir Adrian about the gross abuse of his trust,' she spat and her eyes rested venomously on Roz. 'He'll get rid of *her* at last,' she said with satisfaction.

'And as for you,' she went on, turning on Jeff, 'you can go too! He should never have employed you. You're nothing but a cold-blooded killer. You're a *murderer*.' Her voice dropped, suppurating with spite. 'I know what you did,' she said. 'I'll get even with you yet.'

Chapter Nineteen

Out of nowhere, hatred for her roiled through Jeff. His face darkened and he took a step towards her, but Charles put a hand on his arm.

'Do you know what she's talking about?' he asked in a low voice.

'We never wanted you in the first place,' Helen taunted. 'You were just a means to an end.'

Confused, Jeff hesitated. A moment ago he had been so certain that he knew what Helen was talking about, but now he wasn't so sure. He snatched at the memory, but it was gone. Was she referring to the arson? How would she know about that anyway? His records should show only that he had been released from a secure unit, not any details of his conviction.

'I'm not sure,' he said to Charles. 'Why?'

'I'm just wondering why she's so angry.'

'What are you whispering about?' Helen was pacing in the shadows, as if reluctant to step into the brilliant spotlight. 'I want you all to leave right now,' she said, her voice rising shrilly, 'or I'll call the police.'

'We need to get her out of here.' Charles turned his back on her and focused his attention on Jeff. 'I'm worried about Roz. Jane's hold on her is very deep, and I can't reconnect while Helen is here. She's creating too much negative energy.' He touched Jeff on the arm. 'Can you get her away?'

Jeff glanced at the chair where Roz sat oblivious to what was happening around her. The blankness of her gaze made ice pool in the pit of his stomach, but he was finding it difficult to think clearly. So many emotions were surging and swirling in his head: hate and need, bitterness and anger, loss and longing . . . It was as if she kept shifting, blurring between the sister he had only just found and the woman who coated his vision with resentment. He rubbed the back of his hand over his mouth and tried to focus. At least with Helen, he knew how he felt.

'I'll get rid of her,' he said, and headed purposefully towards her, unaware of the viciousness that twisted his expression.

Helen fell back at his approach. 'Don't you dare touch me!'

'Get out of here!' he snarled.

'You and *her*,' she spat with a glance at the silent Roz. 'You're nothing but trouble. I've known it right from the start. You've always got your heads together, whispering and plotting! You don't care about him. You never have.'

'Care about who?' Charles asked and she seemed to blink and stumble. 'Who doesn't Roz care about?'

'Sir Adrian, of course.' Helen recovered herself, but she touched her head as if dazed. 'She's just using him, and so's he,' she said, jabbing a finger at Jeff. 'I'm not going to let them get away with it. I'm going to go and ring Sir Adrian right now,' she said, backing away as Jeff continued to advance.

'You do that,' said Jeff. 'Just go away.'

'You're going to regret this,' said Helen, whirling around and slamming out of the hall so that the latch on the wooden door clattered, reverberating through the silence she left behind.

'Okay, good. Stay with me, Jeff.' Charles spoke very carefully. He seemed to be speaking from very far away, but Jeff turned and shook his head slightly. 'Can you turn out the light?'

Yes, he could do that. He couldn't make sense of what was going on in his head but he knew where the light switch was. Moving like an automaton, he went over and flicked the switch so that the hall was plunged back into a darkness illuminated only by the three candles Charles had lit earlier. Their flames beckoned him closer.

'That's good,' said Charles soothingly. 'Very good. Why don't you sit down, Jeff?'

Obediently, Jeff sat, his eyes fixed on the candlelight dancing over Roz's face.

'Right.' Charles took a deep breath, his expression worried. He leant towards Roz. 'Jane?' he said. 'Jane, can you hear me?'

'I'm in here,' Jane called from the still room when she heard the new maid asking Catherine if she knew where the mistress was.

She clicked her tongue at the interruption. She was making a distillation of her own recipe for an excellent remedy for all manner of sicknesses, and it needed careful attention. Gilbert suffered sometimes with gout, and it made him irritable, but Jane had found her aqua vitae helped his temper. She had filled a pot with red wine, and was measuring out powdered camomile, gillyflowers, ginger, nutmeg, galingale, spikenard, pepper, cumin, fennel seed, parsley, sage, rue and mint, being careful to weigh each to the same amount.

'What is it, Avis?' she asked when the maid appeared in the doorway, twisting her hands in her apron.

'There's a visitor for the master in the hall, mistress,' Avis whispered.

'Did he say what he wanted?' Jane's mind was on pouring the herbs and seeds into the wine.

Avis shook her head. She was very young and very nervous. 'He just asked for the master.'

Gilbert had gone to do business at the vintners' hall and would not be back for some time. 'Tell him . . . oh, never mind,' said Jane, seeing the terror sweep across Avis's face at the thought of having to remember and relay a message. 'I will go. Do you sweep out the kitchen, Avis, and make sure there are no scraps left for the cats to fight over again.'

Leaving the herbs steeping in the wine, Jane wiped her hands on her apron and made her way to the hall, followed by Poppet, who was growing old and blind and was increasingly dependent on her. The years since her marriage had increased her confidence, and she was smiling and composed as she stepped into the room.

The visitor was standing by the fireplace, talking to Geoffrey. Jane's smile faltered a little at the sight of Geoffrey, who at eleven still had the habit of materializing out of nowhere, and overhearing the most private conversations.

'Geoffrey!' she said a little sharply. 'What are you doing here? You should be at school.'

Irritation flashed over Geoffrey's face, only to be smoothed away as the man turned and put a hand on his shoulder. 'The lad has been keeping me company,' he said. 'He is a fine boy.'

The Yorkshire edge to his voice was the first warning. Jane was already moving across the hall before the realization kicked in and by then it was too late to go back to the shadows. She could see him plainly now, and the floor lurched beneath her feet, the hall tilting alarmingly as dismay raced through her. She had thought herself safe. She had forgotten that fortune was a wheel that kept turning and that a single moment could change everything.

For the past had reared up without warning, and she was facing it across her husband's hall. The last person she had feared to see, and the worst.

Sir Thomas Parker.

Robert's friend, who had been primed to dishonour her. She had last seen him through a drugged haze, kneeling above her with his breeches down. He was stouter now, his nose veined with red, but there was no mistaking him.

She forced her expression to look dull and blank, as if he were just another of her husband's business associates.

'I am sorry, my husband is not here,' she said, hoping that she had changed more than he had. Perhaps he hadn't noticed her in York. She had been invisible then to Robert and his friends.

But Thomas was frowning, staring at her as if trying to place her.

'I do not know how long he will be,' she persevered, keeping the same pleasant smile on her face, but she wasn't sure how successful she was, because Geoffrey's eyes were darting between her and Thomas, sensing something amiss. 'May I tell him who called?'

'Thomas Parker,' said Thomas, still frowning. 'Have we met before, mistress?'

'I do not think so,' she said. 'But you know how London is. We might pass each other a dozen times a day and not know it.'

'Sir Thomas is from York,' Geoffrey offered.

'You have come a long way to see my husband.'

'I have business in London, and your Sir Gilbert was recommended to me for his knowledge of the law.' Thomas paused, shook his head. 'You look mighty familiar, mistress.'

'They say that we all have a double somewhere,' Jane managed. 'I do not know when my husband will be home, but I will—'

'I can run and find him,' said Geoffrey with uncharacteristic eagerness. 'I know where he will be.'

'I don't—' Jane began, but Thomas was already clapping him on the shoulder.

'Good lad. I would be glad if I could see him today.'

Jane was forced to smile and swallow her frustration as Geoffrey beamed. It was typical of Geoffrey to play the bright boy with the one person she didn't want him to impress. 'May I bring you some wine while you wait, Sir Thomas?'

'Thank you,' he said. 'That is a fine boy you have. How old is he?'

'I am almost twelve,' said Geoffrey before she could lie.

'Your father must be proud of you.'

'I do not have a father. Sir Gilbert is my mother's husband.'

'Is that so?'

Jane could feel his eyes on her back as she left. His mind worked slowly, but it was turning. What if he remembered where he had seen her before? What then? Jane's fears scrabbled in her brain and she forced herself to stop and take a breath. She would just deny it. She would tell Thomas he was mistaken. He could not prove anything.

A fine boy . . . almost twelve. Please God he did not remember.

She sent Avis back with wine and some cakes and prayed that Gilbert would stay away. But Geoffrey found him and brought him home, and the next thing Geoffrey was in the kitchen to say that Gilbert had invited Thomas to dine. Too late, Jane remembered her distillation. It had burnt dry, like her luck.

'Ah, wife,' said Gilbert when Jane appeared. 'We have a guest for dinner. This is Sir Thomas Parker from Yorkshire.'

'I know, sir.' She dropped a curtsey, keeping her head down as far as she could. 'You are welcome, Sir Thomas.'

'My wife is from the north as well,' said Gilbert to Thomas. 'She has lost her broad vowels, but I promise you there was a time when we could barely understand her.'

'From the north?' Thomas's eyes sharpened. 'Perhaps that is why you seem familiar, madam.'

'I am from Beverley,' she said, improvising, fingering her necklace desperately for reassurance.

Gilbert looked puzzled. 'I thought you came from York?'

'York*shire*,' said Jane, her mouth dry. 'It is a big place, is it not, Sir Thomas?'

'Aye,' he said slowly. 'How long have you been in London?'

'I hardly remember. A long time.'

'Geoffrey was still a babe,' Gilbert reminded her helpfully.

'So he was.' Jane nodded and picked up a plate. 'Do you care for some mutton, Sir Thomas?' she asked brightly.

The meal seemed to last forever, but finally it was over and Jane excused herself. She was tense from avoiding Thomas's ponderous gaze, from waiting for memory to slide into place. Perhaps he was down with Gilbert even now, telling her husband that she was unlawfully married to him, that Geoffrey was stolen, that everything he thought was true about his wife was a lie.

That William, her dear, sunny-natured William, was base begotten.

Jane paced the chamber, pleating her fingers together, waiting to hear the door close, waiting for Gilbert to come upstairs, his face black with anger.

But when he came in, he was yawning. 'I thought you would be abed,' he said, scratching his hair.

'Did you do good business with Sir Thomas?' she asked after a moment.

Gilbert grunted. 'He seemed very interested in you,' he said. 'I think you have another admirer, my heart. I had to remind him, very politely of course, that you were my wife.'

Jane managed a weak smile. 'I thought he was very curious too.'

'He was taken with Geoffrey, though.' With a resigned sigh, Gilbert bent to acknowledge Poppet's squirming greeting. 'Anyone would think I had been gone for months, dog.' He gave the spaniel's head a pat and absently caressed the silky ears. 'It seems the boy made a good impression, which is encouraging. Perhaps he just needs employment,' said Gilbert as Poppet collapsed with a satisfied sigh and he sat on the bed to pull off his boots. 'I let him come and sit with us in my closet so that he could learn about my business. He seemed interested in Sir Thomas, or pretended to be. We may make a lawyer of him yet!' he said good-humouredly. 'Why don't we send him to Norris? He would teach Geoffrey the law and give him a place if I asked.'

'Perhaps,' said Jane reluctantly.

'My heart, I know you do not want to lose him, but the boy needs to learn a business. And God knows, Geoffrey is tricky enough to make a good lawyer!'

Jane helped her husband unlace his doublet and she brushed it carefully before laying it in the chest, but her mind was on Geoffrey. She had not forgotten the day in the woodstore when she had glimpsed a vulnerability in him, a fear that she would abandon him. *I won't abandon you*, she had said. *I promise.*

Geoffrey had never showed her that side again, but Jane was certain that it was still there, that beneath the sly malice hid a frightened child. So she bit her lip whenever she heard about a fire nearby, and she kept her doubts, and her fears, to herself.

'Will Sir Thomas be back?' She tried to make the question casual. She had to know whether she needed to brace herself for his appearance. If only she had had some warning, she could have disguised herself somehow, or feigned illness. She could have sent one of the maids to tend to him, but it was too late now. Jane kept seeing Geoffrey's face. There had been an alert look in his eye, as if he had somehow sensed that she was afraid of Thomas, and was wondering how to turn her fear to his advantage. Jane had no idea how he could have known that Thomas was the last person she wanted him to meet, but he had, she was sure, and now her mind ran round and round like a trapped mouse, scrabbling for a way out. 'Have you finished your business with him?' she asked hopefully.

'I think so.' Gilbert's voice was muffled as he tugged his shirt over his head. His body was strong and hard still, and Jane longed to go over and lean into him, to wrap her arms around his waist and breathe in the familiar scent of his skin and tell him the truth.

But the truth was that she was too afraid. Gilbert hated pretence, hated untruths. He believed in order and the law of the land. Jane couldn't bear to see his face change at the realization that she had lied, to him, to his children, to their friends, to God. She had stood in the porch of St Dunstan's and sworn that there was no impediment to her marriage. She had said nothing about the husband she knew still lived, to whom she had also sworn obedience till death did them part.

Gilbert might send her away. Jane had been banished by a husband before, she knew it could be done, and few would blame him if they knew the truth. He might send her away and she would never see him again. She would be forbidden William, the girls, Poppet . . . Jane's whole body clenched with panic at the thought. The fear was so sharp that it almost bent her double, and it was only later when she had forced herself to breathe calmly again that she realized to her shame that she hadn't included Geoffrey on the list of those she would miss most.

'Why?' asked Gilbert as he dragged his nightshirt over his head. 'Did you wish me to invite him again?' He lifted his brows teasingly. 'Are you lonely for your friends from the north?'

'No,' said Jane, almost sick with relief at her reprieve. She went over to him and wound her arms around his neck. 'No,' she said again, lifting her mouth to his. 'I do not miss them at all.'

'You met *Mikey*?' Nick stared incredulously at Roz. 'Why didn't you tell me that before?'

'There's been a lot going on.' Wearily, Roz dropped onto the sofa and closed her eyes. She was very glad to be back in London.

When she had come round in the great hall the night before, it had been to find Jeff and Charles watching her with anxious expressions, and she'd been horrified to learn about Helen's interruption. For whatever reason, Helen hadn't, in fact, called the police, which Roz was grateful for. She was tense and vulnerable, still shaken from the shock of suddenly coming face to face with Thomas Parker again, and she would have been in no state to have explained everything to a sceptical constable.

The next day she had slunk into Holmwood House early and had stayed in her office, glad that she had no need to go out and run the gamut of Helen's hostility. She had been desperate to get to London, but now that she was here, she couldn't shake the feeling that she was in the wrong place. The flat felt profoundly alien. The polished floorboards, the Ikea furniture, the oh-so-minimalist white voiles . . . none of it felt like home.

Roz couldn't tell Nick that, though. She couldn't tell him that she hungered to be back in Minchen Lane, where the sign of the golden lily creaked above the shop door.

Nick seemed to be picking up on her sense of disorientation anyway. He was making a stir-fry, talking to her over the counter separating the kitchen from the living room, but his movements were jerky, and his mouth was set in a hard line.

'You met your long-lost brother who just happened to kill your entire family, and that didn't seem worth a mention?' Bang, bang, bang went his knife on the chopping board.

Roz sighed. It was all too hard to explain.

'How did you know it was him, anyway?' asked Nick after a moment.

'He called me Boo.' She told Nick about being in the yard with Jeff, and the certainty that had gripped her when he'd used her family nickname. 'We went and had a coffee.'

'I think I'd have needed a stiff drink rather than a coffee.'

She smiled faintly. 'It was a bit early for that.'

Nick pulled another pepper towards him. 'What was it like? It must have been a bit awkward, wasn't it? I mean, what did you talk about? Hey, sis, remember the time I set fire to the family house?'

'It was weird.' Roz pushed a hand through her hair and rested her head on the back of the sofa, remembering the little cafe with its plastic tablecloths and plastic flowers. 'I've never had a brother before so I'm not sure what it's meant to feel like. Jeff – that's what he calls himself now – is a stranger. We didn't exactly gasp and fall into each other's arms. At the same time, there was . . . I don't know . . . a *connection*. But I don't really know anything about him.'

'You know he's a killer.'

'I'm not so sure about that.' Roz pushed herself up off the cushions and went to the fridge to pour two glasses of wine. She nudged one along the counter towards Nick before pinching a bit of raw pepper. 'I think it's all bound up with the house in Micklegate,' she said. 'I think Mikey was haunted by Geoffrey just like I am by Jane. I felt so sorry for him, Nick,' she said. 'He lost everything, and he was blamed for it all and now he's labelled a murderer, but it was Geoffrey all along. Not that prison psychiatrists would ever have accepted that as an excuse, anyway. They just called him schizophrenic and pumped him full of drugs.'

Nick put down his knife to take a sip of wine. 'Are you sure he's not playing you, Roz?'

'I was the one who made the connection. Jeff didn't think of it until I suggested it. He just knew that he couldn't remember anything about that night, just like I can't remember what happens around me when I'm Jane. I'm sure that Geoffrey was responsible for the fire that killed my parents.'

'Okay, just supposing I buy the fact that Mikey was haunted and not just a disturbed kid,' said Nick, 'why would this Geoffrey, a boy who's apparently been dead for four hundred years, decide to come back to life just to kill your family?'

'I don't think he did,' said Roz. She stole another piece of pepper. 'I think he was in the house all along. When you look at the history of it, it's amazing how many fires there have been there in the past.'

'That doesn't prove anything.'

'No, it doesn't *prove* anything, but it's *suggestive*.' Irritation feathered her voice. 'Geoffrey doesn't care about anyone, but he loves fire. I think Mikey was sad and vulnerable, and he gave Geoffrey a chance to leave the house and make fires somewhere else. I did some reading about it.'

Roz turned and leaned against the counter, holding the cool glass to her cheek. 'Apparently fire setting is relatively common among boys between eleven and fifteen. It's usually just part of a pattern of delinquency, but with Geoffrey it's more than that. He's a psychopath.' Setting down the glass, she rubbed her arms nervously. 'Jane thinks he's a lost boy crying for attention, but I think he's cunning. She's not going to be able to rescue him and make him right, no matter what she does.'

There was a pause. Nick tidied the sliced peppers into a neat pile. 'It sounds to me as if Jane is more of a threat to you than this Geoffrey is,' he said, picking his words with care. 'This cleansing ritual you told me about doesn't seem to have worked at all.'

'It might have done if Helen hadn't interrupted us. Charles said that she's incredibly hostile.' Unaware of it at the time, Roz had still been able to feel Helen's fury jangling in the air long after she had gone.

Nick's expression was serious. 'I think it's time you tried a priest,' he said. 'I'm worried about you, Roz. You're talking about Jane and Geoffrey as if it's normal to be haunted or possessed or whatever is happening to you. Now you tell me you're going into a trance alone in a dark room with some psychic no one knows anything about and a man who turns out to be your brother and, oh yes, the killer of your entire family.'

'I know how it sounds, but I'm sure I'm right about Jeff,' said Roz, 'and if I am, he's suffered far more than I have. He's the only family I've got too. I may not know much about having brothers and sisters, but even I know that you don't turn your back on family when they need you. I'm not going to start treating him like a murderer!'

Nick held up his hands pacifically, knife in one hand. 'Okay, then you *both* need a priest.'

He was right, Roz knew. This had gone on long enough. 'It's just . . . I don't know how to explain it, but I feel Jane needs me,' she said haltingly, knowing even as she spoke that Nick wouldn't understand. How could he?

Sure enough, Nick's face clouded with disbelief. 'You're feeling guilty about a ghost?'

'Well . . .'

He put the knife down again and came over to take her hands in a firm clasp. 'Listen to me, Roz. This is bad stuff.' He shook her hands for emphasis. 'You like sharing Jane's life, and I can see – sort of – why it might be fascinating, but people don't turn into ghosts when they die happily in their beds. I've got a bad feeling about this. You have to get rid of Jane before it's too late.'

In spite of herself, tears prickled behind Roz's eyes at the thought. 'I know, and I will, Nick, I promise. I'll talk to Jeff when I get back to York and we'll find a priest. We'll explain what's happening. But it needs to be in York, in Micklegate. I need to go back.'

'Then I'm coming with you,' said Nick, his face grim. 'I can work just as easily in York.'

'What about Daniel?'

'Daniel managed perfectly well without me for fourteen years. He can cope with me being away for a couple of weeks. I don't want you in York on your own, and that's that.'

Nick was sleeping. Roz listened to his slow, steady breathing, with the slightest hitch at the end. He had never been a snorer.

Her body was loose and warm and woozy with satisfaction, but her mind was full of jagged edges. She cut herself whichever way she turned. Shifting onto her side, she tucked herself into the lovely long, lean length of Nick's body and slid her arm over him. She could feel his chest rising and falling. He felt familiar, he smelt familiar, but there was something missing.

He wasn't Gilbert.

'No,' Roz whispered against his back as the longing rolled through her, a need and an ache that tightened relentless around her chest until she couldn't breathe with the pain of it.

Nick stirred. 'Mmm?'

'Nothing,' she said into the darkness. 'Nothing. Go back to sleep.'

She woke slowly, struggling through a torrent of loss and longing to surface with a gasp. Blinking up at the canopy, she put a hand to her heart to ease the ache that burned there. There was nothing to feel sorrowful about, she told herself as her mind cleared. It had been a bad dream, that was all. She was not lost and alone, Gilbert had not gone. He was lying beside her, sleeping sprawled across the bed as was his wont, and she turned and curled into him for comfort until the tight feeling around her chest lessened and the dreadful churn of distress was soothed by his steady breath.

But she couldn't go back to sleep. Outside the closed shutters, dawn was breaking, and after a while Jane eased herself away from Gilbert so as not to wake him, and swung her bare feet to the rush matting.

Padding over to the window, she opened the shutters as quietly as she could and pushed open the casement. Autumn had always been her favourite season and she sniffed at the cool light. They were far from the country, but she was sure she could smell the harvest on the air, the appley tang of orchards rippling through the breeze and mingling with the mud and the soot and the grime of the city.

Smoke was rising from the chimneys along the street, hanging still in the September dawn as folk started their days. Jane imagined fires being poked in every house, pots being set to boil. Already John the baker had his ovens lit, and his door stood open to let the scent of baking bread drift along the street. Jane saw a maidservant lift her nose hopefully as she laboured back with two buckets of water across her shoulders.

At the sign of the golden lily, life was stirring too. Behind her Gilbert mumbled and grumbled into his pillow. Poppet uncurled from the cushion Jane set out for him, got stiffly to his feet and shook himself awake as he blinked hopefully at Jane. He was old now, and his joints were stiff, his eyes blind, but he knew Jane's step and he followed her around the house, feeling safe when she was there. The stairs creaked as Avis made her way quietly down to the kitchen. William coughed in his sleep, once, twice, three times. He had looked heavy-eyed the night before when Jane put him to bed, and she suspected a rheum was brewing.

She would beat up a spoonful of sugar and drop it into some of her best aqua vitae, Jane decided, and give it to him before the cough got any worse.

It was a month since Thomas Parker had left, and Jane had heard nothing more. It seemed that he hadn't remembered her after all, and surely if he hadn't recognized her straight away, he never would? That was what Jane told herself.

Geoffrey had refused point-blank to go to Mr Norris. 'I am not a servant to be sent away,' he had said, and Gilbert had been so astounded at his impertinence that for a moment he had been unable to say anything.

'You must have some trade or profession,' Jane pointed out. 'Mr Parker did not.'

'Mr Parker was a gentleman.'

'Why can I not be a gentleman?'

'Because you are the son of a butcher,' said Jane as patiently as she could. 'Butchers' sons do not become gentlemen unless they make a lot of money. And they do not make a lot of money unless they train.'

'I do not care,' said Geoffrey. 'I will not go to Mr Norris. He is fat and he smells.'

'He is a clever lawyer, and you, Geoffrey, are not nearly as clever as you think you are,' said Gilbert coldly, less patient than Jane. 'You are an insolent and arrogant puppy, and I will not risk my reputation by sending you to my friends now. Perhaps you will learn some humility when you are starving and need to work for a crust of bread.'

'I will not starve,' said Geoffrey. 'My mother is sworn not to abandon me, are you not, Mamma?'

'I will not let you starve, but you must learn to be useful, Geoffrey.'

His face worked with resentment. 'This is your fault,' he spat at her. 'You must wed a butcher, and then be a servant. You have no ambition! Oh yes, you are comfortable married to Mr Harrison, but what is there for me? You have a new son, your precious William. He will inherit everything and I will have nothing.'

'You deserve nothing,' snapped Gilbert. 'Your mother has sacrificed everything for you. Let us see if a thrashing will remind you of the need for gratitude.'

But Geoffrey wouldn't apologize. He was taut with bitterness, and Jane knew that it was only his promise to her that stopped Gilbert throwing him out into the street. Lately, though, Geoffrey had been different. He was tense, simmering with suppressed excitement, but he would just shrug when Jane asked him what had happened. The day before he had been gone most of the afternoon, and when he came back, the excitement had been lit to a blaze. He had been smiling, and charming, and Jane had reflected wistfully that if only he had been like this all the time, everything would be so very different. But Geoffrey was happy for once, and she was happy for him.

So that morning, Jane was content. She dressed, putting on the necklace Gilbert had given her when William was born, as she did every day. The one that made her feel loved and secure. She stooped over William's cot and brushed his hair back from his forehead as he tossed and coughed again.

'I heard him coughing in the night,' said Mary beside her. 'Is he sick?'

Jane shook her head. 'He will be fine. I will make him something for the cough and we will try to keep him as quiet as we can, but it is hard to keep him out of mischief, I know. Will you watch him for me?'

So the day began like any other. Gilbert was always short-tempered in the mornings. He stomped down the stairs and into

416

his closet without breaking his fast, and Jane poured some ale and put some cheese and bread on a plate, and took it through.

'I'm not hungry,' said Gilbert.

'You will be even crosser if you do not eat,' Jane pointed out serenely, and he glared at her for a moment before he gave in and laughed.

'Jane, what would I do without you?'

'You would be very hungry and very cross.'

He caught her by the waist as she would have passed and pulled her onto his lap. 'I would be wretched indeed,' he said, just as a loud knock sounded at the door.

Jane laughed and disentangled herself. 'You have early visitors today. Are you expecting anyone?'

'Not yet,' said Gilbert, standing up. The door sounded again, loud, arrogant, and something stirred deep inside Jane, not as clear as fear, but akin to it. A knock so demanding rarely brought good news.

Gilbert raised his brows. 'Someone is impatient. Let us see what they want before they break down my door.'

They were at the door of the closet when they saw Geoffrey open the door. Jane saw his face light up before she saw who was standing outside, but something in the way he straightened sent her stomach plummeting.

'Who – ?' she began, and then Geoffrey stood back with a sweep of his arm, and Robert Holmwood and Margaret stepped into the hall.

Jane stopped dead, her head ringing with shock, and for a

moment she thought she would faint. Gilbert didn't seem to notice. He was moving forward politely.

'What can I do for you, sir?' he asked Robert, with a courteous nod at Margaret, whose eyes were fixed on Jane with venom.

'You can give me my son.' Robert looked straight at Jane. 'And my wife.'

Gilbert's head jerked back in surprise. 'I think you must be mistaken.'

'There is no mistake, is there, Jane?' Robert's gaze was triumphant while Jane stood as if turned to stone, unable to think, unable to speak, unable to do anything but stare in horror as her world crumbled around her.

'Jane?' Gilbert was still puzzled, waiting for her to explain the inexplicable.

'I – '

'Yes, let us hear her explanation,' said Robert. 'This woman has played you for a fool, as she did me. She took my son and she ran away. Is there a more heinous crime than to take a child from its father? This is my child.'

'No.' Jane found her voice at last but it seemed to be coming from far away. 'No, he is not your son.'

'I am!' Geoffrey's eyes blazed with hate. 'I am the son of a gentleman and you let me think I was a butcher's brat!'

'Not a butcher's son, a tailor's son,' said Jane. 'My sister lay with John Harper,' she told Robert, horribly aware of Gilbert, rigid as a stone, and of Geoffrey, his face contorted with bitterness. 'You were not capable of begetting a child. We both know this.'

'You lie!' Robert was white with rage.

'Yes, I lied,' she said evenly in the end. 'I pretended her babe was mine. I hoped it would please you to have a child, but you sent me away anyway, and you had no care for Geoffrey. All you wanted was his inheritance.' She glanced at Geoffrey. 'I took you from a soiled cradle. There was no one to sing to you, no one to hold you. I promised Juliana I would look after you, and I had to take you away.'

But Geoffrey wasn't listening. He cared nothing for songs or tenderness. She could see that his mind was closed, that he was seething with resentment at the lies she had told, the injustice he thought she had done him.

'Jane . . .' Gilbert looked as if he was reeling but Jane couldn't comfort him then.

She turned back to Robert. 'I have kept my vow,' she said. 'You did not keep yours, Robert. You vowed before God to honour me with your body, you agreed that marriage was for the procreation of children, and yet you could not touch me. And I know why.' She looked at Margaret. 'I saw what you and your son do together. I could not let Geoffrey be tainted in the same way.'

'You are mad,' Robert blustered, even as Margaret laid a hand on his sleeve.

'Do not waste your breath trying to reason with such a creature, my son,' she told him. 'She will say anything for her own purposes. What matters is that you have found your heir after so many long years.'

Chapter Twenty

'Yes.' Recovering himself, Robert put his arm around Geoffrey's shoulders, and Jane saw Geoffrey stand taller, blossoming in the attention. 'My heir. Geoffrey had known there was something wrong when Thomas Parker saw Jane. He followed Thomas after he left and told him that his mother had lied, that he had never heard her mention Beverley, only York. And he said he would furnish any more information if it was needed. Thomas was back in York before he remembered. He sat in my hall and he looked as if a thunderbolt had struck. By God, he said, I know who she was now. I have seen your wife, Robert, and your son in London. She is naught but a lawyer's drab.'

Gilbert stepped forward, clenching his fists. 'Unsay that, sir! Jane is no drab!'

'Is she not? Has she not been whoring for you, knowing full well that her husband is alive and well?'

'I heard you had married again,' Jane said without expression. 'I thought you had stopped looking.'

'She died. She was no use,' said Margaret. 'There was no child.'

'And so you still have need of a son's inheritance. No wonder you came running to London as soon as you heard Thomas's story!'

'We were anxious to restore my son to his rightful inheritance.'

Geoffrey's face was blazing. 'I knew I was no servant! I knew it!' He turned, sneering, to Gilbert. 'And so it seems dear little William is the bastard!'

Gilbert looked as if he had been beaten around the head. 'I don't believe this,' he said. 'Jane, tell me this is not true,' he pleaded. 'Tell me you have not been lying to me all this time.'

'I had to,' said Jane. 'You are sworn to uphold the law. You would have sent me back to York. And I made a promise. The only way I could keep it was by lying to you.'

'It was all a lie,' Gilbert repeated dully.

'Nothing that mattered was a lie,' said Jane. 'Everything I felt for you was true. Everything I still feel for you.'

His face was blank with shock. 'You are no different from my first wife, then,' he said dazedly. 'At least she was open in her lies. Except, of course, you are not my wife, are you?'

'I am your wife in every way that matters.'

'Not in the eyes of God. Not in the name of the law. What matters more than those?'

'In my heart I am,' said Jane. 'In the truest place of all.'

'You can speak of truth? You who have lied for all these years?'

'What was I to do? Leave Geoffrey to be brutalized and warped as Robert was?'

'More flights of fancy!' Margaret scoffed. 'Come, we have done everything we had to do here,' she went on briskly. 'She does not deny she is your wife, Robert. She does not deny the boy is ours. Sir Gilbert is a man of the law, he must say that we have the right to take them back to York. Is that not so, Sir Gilbert?'

Gilbert said nothing, but his jaw worked. Jane was numb. He was shocked and hurting. How many times had he told her that truth mattered more than anything to him? But how could she have told him without breaking her vow, which mattered more than anything to her?

He was going to send her away, she realized in dull disbelief. He would not be able to stand for the law if he did not give her back to Robert. Jane could see the reality of it hurtling towards her like a stone flung from a catapult. It was going to hurt her, she knew that. It would land with a blow that would send her crashing to the ground, but she could not move to step aside. The pain was coming, and there was nothing she could do to stop it.

'You can keep her if you like,' Robert began dismissively, but Geoffrey stepped forward.

'No,' he said. 'No, she has to come too.' He turned to Jane. 'You said you would not abandon me. You *promised*. You are my mother,' he said, and the expression in his eyes chilled her. 'Will you let me go alone? Do you choose William over me?'

'Do not make me choose, Geoffrey.' Jane's own voice was

unsteady. She glanced at Robert, golden and arrogant, and Margaret beside him, with her cold, cruel, beautiful face. To Geoffrey they must look gilded and glorious, she thought. He had no idea. 'These people are not what they seem,' she told him urgently. 'They are vicious and depraved. They do not care for you. They do not care for anyone but themselves.'

'All the more reason for you to come with me,' he said.

'All the more reason for you to stay here, where you are safe.'

Margaret laughed, a silvery chuckle that scraped over Jane's nerves. 'Stay? The boy has no choice. We will not allow him to stay. He is Robert's son.'

'And I have told you he is not.'

'Can you deny that you came back from Holme Hall and showed us the child in the cradle? "This is your son," you said, did you not?'

Jane said nothing. What could she say?

'Now you want us to believe that was a lie?' Margaret lifted delicate brows and triumph gleamed in her eyes. 'You are an admitted liar, Mistress Jane. You are a liar and a thief. You stole this boy from his father and denied him his inheritance. By rights you should hang. Be glad the boy wants you, for we do not.'

'Geoffrey.' Jane turned to him in desperation. 'I beg of you, do not go with them.'

'But I must go,' he said. 'They offer me a future. I will inherit a house, a hall of my own. What can you offer me here? Apprenticeship to a fat lawyer?'

'A decent life,' said Jane, but Geoffrey only looked contemptuous. Indeed, perhaps to him it seemed a poor exchange for wealth and status.

'If the boy wants you, then you will come too,' said Robert, as ever acting the grand gentleman while manipulated by others. Geoffrey had the measure of him already, Jane could see that.

'No!' she protested but Geoffrey was by her side, tugging at her arm.

'You promised,' he said, triumph in his eyes. 'You cannot deny me now.'

Over his head, Jane met Gilbert's eyes. He was stony-faced. 'Gilbert,' she said. 'Don't let this happen.'

'What can I do?' he said furiously. 'You have lied. You are this man's wife, and Geoffrey is this man's son. There is no court in the land that would say you should stay with me.'

'You are sending me away?'

'I have no choice.'

'There is always a choice,' said Jane bitterly. 'What of William? What of my son?'

'You will not take another son from his father,' said Gilbert, very white about the mouth.

'No, I would not take him to the hell that is the Holmwoods' house,' she agreed. 'But how will he manage without a mother?'

'Mary is old enough to care for him.'

'Mary is not a mother.'

'What would you have me do?' Gilbert lashed out at her. 'It

has always been Geoffrey, Geoffrey, Geoffrey. You said you promised to put him first. Well then, do it. You cannot now pretend that William is first, or that I am, or the girls. If your vow is so important to you, keep it.'

Robert and Geoffrey were looking delighted, Margaret contemptuous.

Jane was starting to shake, but she did not dare show it. 'So be it,' she said, quite as though her heart was not splintering into a thousand bitter shards. 'May I say goodbye?'

'Be quick about it,' said Robert. 'I am anxious to be gone. London is unwholesome. I would have my son back in York where he belongs.'

So Jane climbed the stairs for the last time. *The last time*, she kept saying to herself in disbelief. *This is the last time I will walk along here. The last time I will pass the parlour door. The last time I will see that crack in the plaster.*

The last time I will hold my son.

Cecily and Mary were keeping watch over William, who was coughing still but watching big-eyed as they vied to entertain him.

'What is it?' Mary asked sharply, seeing Jane's face.

'I have to go away,' said Jane.

'For how long?'

'I . . . don't know.' Somehow she summoned a smile. 'But you must be good girls and look after the house for your father. And care for William for me. Will you do that?'

She bent to pick up William, who nestled trustingly into her, his fat hands clutching her hair. 'My heart,' she whispered to him. 'Your mamma will always love you.'

The girls clung to her, until she had to prise their hands from her waist. 'I must go,' she said, her heart cracking, crumbling.

She lay William back down, and he gurgled happily up at her, reaching his arms to be held again.

Never again. Jane wanted to lie down and howl, but the girls were distressed enough. She couldn't let them witness Robert dragging her away. Witness their father letting her go.

Catherine was in bewildered tears in the hall. 'I don't understand, Pappa,' she was saying to Gilbert, whose face seemed carved from a rock.

'I don't either,' he said. 'We must accept it anyway.'

'Catherine.' Jane held her tightly, unable to say more than her name.

'Come back,' Catherine whispered. 'Come back soon. We need you. Pappa needs you.'

'This is all very touching, but it is time to be gone,' said Margaret, bored.

Jane turned to Gilbert at last. His expression was as stark as hers must be. 'I love you,' she said. 'I'll always love you. *That* is the truth.'

His throat worked, but he couldn't speak, and after a moment, Jane nodded and turned. She had put on her warm gown but her hands were empty.

'Is that it?' said Robert in surprise. 'Aren't you taking anything with you?'

Geoffrey, she saw, had packed a bag. He must have prepared it earlier.

'Everything I need belongs in this house,' said Jane without looking at Gilbert.

'Then let us be off.'

Robert and Geoffrey were already at the door, and Margaret swept before them out into the yard and up the passage to where a carriage waited, blocking the street, judging by the cursing that could be heard even behind the shop.

Jane made her legs move. One step towards the door, and then another. Then a wheezy bark stopped her in her tracks. Poppet had sensed she was going without him and was struggling to catch up.

A sob tore from Jane's throat as she bent to pick him up. 'You can't come with me, old boy,' she said brokenly. 'You must stay here. Stay!' Thrusting him into Gilbert's arms, she turned and ran blindly for the door, clapping her hands over her ears as he lifted his muzzle and howled and howled and howled for her to come back.

'It's all right. Shh, come on, it's okay now.' There were strong arms around her, a hand smoothing gentle circles on her back. She couldn't make sense of the words through her wrenching sobs, but she could feel the comfort of them, and she clung to a warm, solid body, until gradually reality seeped back and she remembered where she was, who she was. She was Roz, and this was Nick, and she didn't have to leave him if she didn't want to.

'Oh Nick . . . Nick, I don't want to lose you,' she sobbed.

'Hey, come on, I'm not going anywhere,' he said, the comforting circles turning to pats. 'You've been having a terrible dream.'

If only it were true. Roz clutched at him in her distress. She could feel only too clearly the churn of Jane's grief, the desperation at having to say goodbye to everything and everyone she had loved.

'It's Jane,' she said brokenly. 'She's so unhappy.'

Nick muttered under his breath, but he was very patient as he stroked her hair and held her close against the comfort of his body. 'Jane's not here, Roz. I'm sorry she was unhappy, but she's gone and you're here and I'm here.'

'I know.' Roz pressed closer. She was fully awake now, still wretched but aware of the present: the clean, soft sheets, the street light casting an orange glow through the window, the distant whoop and wail of a siren. And Nick, lean and muscled, holding her, soothing her.

'I came so close to losing you,' she said quietly. 'When you told me about Daniel, I lost you, and I lost myself. I was so angry and so disappointed, and now I can't understand why it mattered so much.'

'I know why,' said Nick. 'You'd just discovered your aunt had kept a huge secret from you, and that everything you'd always believed to be true had been turned upside down. And then I kept something from you too, and it must have felt as though nothing was certain any more and you couldn't trust anyone. I didn't mean to hurt you, Roz,' he said, 'but I know that I did, and I'm so, so sorry.'

'But you're here,' said Roz, clinging to him. 'I keep thinking about Jane, and how wretched she is, and I can feel you right here, and I'm so relieved and so lucky. It's like waking from a terrible dream. That could have been me,' she told Nick. 'I could have driven you away. I could have gone to York and refused to forgive you and that would have been that.'

'You could have done,' said Nick, 'but I wouldn't have let that be that. I would have followed you to York. I would have made you forgive me. I wouldn't have accepted it was over.'

'Nick.' Roz pressed her face into his throat. 'Nick, I love you.'

'And I love you,' he whispered against her hair. 'I don't want to lose you, Roz. I won't let you go.'

Roz shifted closer. Her mouth was urgent, her hands streaking over him. 'Nick,' she said, 'I don't want to waste any more time. I want a baby.'

'What, right now?' he said, and she smiled against his skin.

'Maybe not *right* now, but soon. Can we try soon?'

Nick tangled his fingers in her hair, held her head between his hands. 'Let's try now,' he said.

'Oh God, I don't really have to wear a tie, do I?' Nick grumbled when Roz reminded him of the launch that evening, and the need to look smart.

'Think yourself lucky you're not expected to be in a doublet and hose,' said Roz, rolling her eyes. 'We're all going to be in full costume!'

'I'll be glad when tonight is over,' said Nick. 'And not just because I can take my tie off.'

'I know,' she said. She would be glad too. The atmosphere in Holmwood House was taut with tension, and the sense of waiting for something to happen was wearing on her nerves. Everyone had been busy preparing for the launch, but Roz knew that the queasy sense of dread simmering in her belly was due to more than worry about press coverage or whether or not the caterers would turn up.

It had been good to have Nick around, though. She felt safer with him there. If nothing else, Jane's wretchedness had made Roz appreciate what she had, and she and Nick were working hard to rekindle their relationship. Having someone to go home to at the end of the day made all the difference too. Roz hadn't realized how lonely she had felt in York until Nick was there, a blessed distraction from the oppressive atmosphere in Micklegate, where sadness gathered, dense and heavy as a stone inside her, and the smell of smoke in her office was growing day by day, so strong that she had to keep the window open in spite of the fog that had been hanging cold and clammy over the city for days now.

The fog muffled everything. It slumped thick and grey over the rooftops, pressing down on the streets. For Roz, it was like walking through a different world where the usual points of reference had disappeared. Every morning when she walked to Micklegate she would stop in King's Square, where Jane's church had once stood, and look up Petergate to orientate herself by the Minster that loomed over the city. But now the fog had gulped even the cathedral, and all she could see were the shops, their tiled roofs indistinct in the blurry light.

Sometimes she thought she saw a figure in doublet and hose disappearing down an alley, or the end of a cart just rounding a corner. Sometimes she was sure she heard the bells ringing the opening of the market, or smelt the hot pastry on the pie seller's tray, but a turn of the head, a blink of the eye, and all were gone and a van was tooting its horn behind her, or a burglar alarm was jangling above a shop. On Ouse Bridge, Roz paused and peered down at the river. Sometimes she could have sworn she saw the keelboats pulled up against the King's Staith, but the next moment their ghostly shapes would be gone and there would just be the tourist boats tied up together, waiting for the weather to clear.

In Holmwood House, there seemed to be an unspoken agreement that no mention would be made of the séance Helen had interrupted until after the launch. If Helen had said anything to Adrian, he gave no sign of it. He was as unctuous as ever, and was determined to get involved in every aspect of the launch. His constant questions and suggestions drove Roz mad, but she gritted her teeth and was grateful that she still had a job at all. She avoided Helen as much as possible, which clearly suited Helen herself just fine.

Jeff, too, was keeping a low profile. Roz had invited him round for supper to meet Nick, which hadn't been an entirely comfortable occasion, although they had all done their best. Her brother and her husband had nothing in common, except for their insistence that Roz call in a priest to exorcize Jane as soon as possible.

'All *right*,' said Roz in the end, exasperated by the way they wouldn't let it go, and unwilling to admit how reluctant she still was to sever Jane from her life. 'You find one, Jeff, if you think it's that important, but can we just get the launch out of the way first?'

Now they were almost ready. The caterers were already in the kitchen, and the waiting staff were setting out glasses in the great hall. The costumes had arrived, and Jeff had delivered them to everyone on the team. Roz's was hanging behind her door. Helen had chosen a plain blue gown for Roz with a roll at her waist to spread out her skirts, and a tight bodice.

'I think I'm supposed to be a craftsman's wife,' she said to Lucy, inspecting the gown as they helped each other to dress. There was less lacing and pinning than she remembered, but the fabric hung beautifully and swished satisfactorily from side to side when she swung her hips.

Lucy's gown was more elaborate, with a modest farthingale. 'You're higher up the social scale,' Roz told her. 'Perhaps your husband is Lord Mayor.'

Lucy rolled her eyes. 'Helen really doesn't like you, does she? She's given you the dullest dress.'

'I don't mind,' said Roz, and it was true. The dress felt comfortingly familiar, and when she patted the little ruff at her collar into place and smoothed down her skirts, a shiver of recognition raced through her.

Jane sat on the edge of her bed and smoothed her skirts. The fabric was familiar, a blue broadcloth she had had made up by a tailor in Fenchurch Street earlier that year. Jane remembered quite clearly being measured for the gown. It was a serviceable dress, warm and comfortable. Gilbert had shaken his head when he saw it. 'We will never make a fashionable lady of you, sweeting,' he had said, smiling, but Jane hadn't minded.

'What use do I have for fashion?' she'd replied. 'A court dress would be little use to me when I am in the kitchen!'

She had been wearing the blue gown the day the Holmwoods came, and she was wearing it still. Jane fingered the broadcloth, marvelling that it could be the same gown, that she could be the same person. Her life was cleaved in two. There had been before, at the sign of the golden lily in Minchen Lane, when she had been happy, and there was now, wretched and alone in the house on Micklegate. It was as if she had never been away. Sometimes she wondered if the years in London had been no more than a wonderful dream, but then she would hold on to the necklace Gilbert had given her, and the memories would crash over her, bittersweet: William, staggering towards her, his arms outstretched; Catherine, curled up with a book; Poppet, closing his eyes in bliss as she caressed his silky ears; Gilbert, his hands gentling down her spine.

Jane's heart cracked and curled at the memories. No, they hurt too much to be imaginary.

She had been given one of the servants' chambers at the top of Holmwood House, a bare, mean room with a straw mattress on the bed and a thin coverlet. And a bar on the door.

Margaret told her she should consider herself fortunate to have a chamber to herself, but Jane would have welcomed the company. She might have found an ally then, but as it was, all the servants clearly had orders not to befriend her. She had wondered if she might be banished to Holme Hall again, but that would have been too kind.

Since she had been back in York, Jane had been out only to go to church, where she was sat next to Margaret and unable to talk to anyone else. They had told everyone that she was mad, but made sure to parade her anyway so that folk could see that she really had returned, and that Geoffrey was lawfully Robert's son. Nobody mentioned Anne, who had been Robert's wife while Jane was in London. Poor Anne, who had died childless and, Jane was sure, unwanted. If she had lived, if she had had a son, how different would things have been? Margaret and Robert would have had no use for Geoffrey then. Jane and Geoffrey would have been safe.

As it was, the Holmwoods were enjoying the chance to exact revenge on Jane. She was not locked in her room. She was not a prisoner, no, but they all knew that there was nowhere else she could go. Henry Birkby, they told her, had died only a month or so earlier. No one would aid Jane in her disgrace, they said. She could earn her board and her keep, and her place with Geoffrey, by running the house as she had done before, but she would be no mistress. She was a servant, to be isolated and humiliated at every opportunity.

For the first few weeks Jane was too wretched to care. She ached for the house in Minchen Lane, for her son, for the girls, for the dog, and for Gilbert most of all. It had all happened too quickly, like a thunderbolt out of the blue, smashing her life apart, and at first she was too shocked and numb to react. She had sat dully in the carriage with Margaret as it jolted up the long road to York, and the only thing she had been able to think was that Gilbert had let her go.

But now she was thinking again. She should have resisted, she realized, slowly brushing the fabric of her gown, feeling the nap beneath her palms, slowly starting to *feel* again. She should have fought harder to stay. She should have explained more clearly why she had done what she did, and made Gilbert listen.

She had made a mistake, Jane knew that now. She had kept the wrong promise.

Geoffrey didn't need her. Why had she ever believed that he would? He had wanted to punish her, that was all. He was in his element in York, strutting around behind Robert, revelling in the vicious atmosphere, blooming in the unkindness that warped the very air in the house. Jane didn't know whether he was aware of the depraved relationship between Robert and his mother, but she knew that if he was, he wouldn't be shocked. There was a wrongness in him that no amount of love or attention could change, she had come to realize. She had tried her best, but all her efforts were pointless, Jane could see that now.

Her life, her love, had been lost for a promise that had mattered to no one but herself.

Jane looked up at the tiny square of grey sky she could see through the window. She wanted to go home. She had done all she could for Geoffrey, and now she could do no more.

The house was empty. She had heard them all go out earlier. She might not have a better chance. Making up her mind, she went down to Robert's closet, closing her mind against the horrible memories that room held. She found paper, a pen, some ink. Trying not to think what would happen if Robert came home and found her there, she scrawled a quick note to Gilbert, and sealed it. Then she went to find Sibylla, the shy servant who blushed and stuttered whenever Jane was in the room. Nan and the other servants she remembered were long gone. The servants now were poorly trained, Jane had noted. They were slapdash and insolent, and taking their cue from Margaret and Robert, they treated her with thinly veiled contempt. Only Sibylla was young enough to be thrown into confusion by Jane's presence.

Jane had not managed a house for years without learning how to overawe a little maid. 'Take this and find a carter,' she said. 'I need the letter to get to London as soon as possible.' She pulled off a ring. 'Give him this in payment.'

Sibylla took the letter after a moment's hesitation. 'Go now,' said Jane, 'and then you may get back to your work.'

'Yes, mistress,' she whispered.

It would take some time for the letter to reach London, but Jane could endure it if she knew Gilbert was coming. And he would come, she knew that. He loved her. He would have had time now to think, as she had done, and he would know that she had had no choice. Jane knew this in her heart.

So she would sit, and she would wait, until he came.

It was a day like all the others then, short and dark and dank, and the light faded barely halfway through the afternoon. Jane ate a simple meal in her room. She had no one to talk to, no one to share the long night with, but she was full of hope. It would not be long, she told herself. Gilbert would come for her.

'Ready?'

Ah, yes, she was ready! She smiled fiercely, only to realize that there was someone else in the room after all, a young woman in an elaborate dress but with strange, wild hair, and her smile faded before her perception stumbled and righted itself and the world slotted jarringly back into place.

Not a strange woman, but Lucy. Lucy in costume. The launch at Holmwood House.

Roz felt nauseous but she recovered her smile. 'Yes, I'm ready,' she said.

'Are you nervous?' Lucy asked as they made their way carefully down the stairs.

'I am a little,' said Roz, but she wasn't thinking of the launch. She was thinking of Jane, waiting alone in the attic room, and foreboding tickled between her shoulders.

'Ooh, look at Mark!' Lucy hooted with laughter as she caught sight of the front-of-house manager looking uncomfortable in a blue velvet doublet and hose, but he took her teasing in good part, taking off his cap to flourish a bow.

Adrian was bustling around in a white silk damask doublet and white satin trunkhose, but it was Helen who made Lucy's jaw sag. She was wearing a magnificent farthingale covered in red satin with white sleeves and an enormous ruff pinned open around her collar, and her usual dour expression had hardened to an hauteur that was clearly intimidating the guests who were starting to trickle into the hall.

'Wow! Helen looks absolutely amazing, doesn't she?' said Lucy. 'It's a bit obvious to keep the best dress for herself, though,' she grumbled, but Roz didn't answer. The warning tickle just below the nape of her neck was turning into an insistent pinch and she wriggled her shoulders to try and shift it, but the sense of unease only deepened as she looked around the hall.

Everything was in place. The great hall looked magnificent now that the furniture lovingly sourced by Lucy was set up: a vast oak table, chests covered with Turkey-work carpets, a cupboard with a splendid display of silver, a fine chair by the fireplace. There were flamboyant hangings on the wainscot walls, colourful cushions in the window embrasures. Artificial candles flickered convincingly. It wasn't quite as it had looked in Jane's day, of course, but it was close enough to account for Roz's unease.

She hoped that was all it was.

A team of waiters and waitresses, also in costume, were already circulating with glasses of champagne and trays of canapés. A musician was playing Elizabethan tunes on a lute in one corner. To Roz, the haunting notes seemed to accentuate the tension thrumming in the air, but nobody else appeared to notice anything amiss. She was just projecting her distress at poor Jane's fate, Roz tried to convince herself. All she had to do was get through tonight and everything would be fine.

Still, she wished Nick would arrive. She sneaked a glance at the mobile she had secreted in the purse hanging from her girdle to see if Nick had sent her a text to say that he'd be late, and frowned when she saw that the screen was lit up but blank. Odd, there was usually good reception in the house.

The trickle of guests had turned into a flood. One moment the hall was almost empty, with a handful of people standing in self-conscious groups, the next it was heaving, and the noise of conversation swamped Roz's sense of unease. Besides, she was too busy to think about that as she circulated, and she even missed Nick's arrival.

When Nick touched her arm, she turned in relief and kissed him. 'There you are! Where have you been?'

'Martin rang just as I was about to leave and offered me a travel piece,' Nick said. 'You know what he's like. I couldn't get him off the phone. Didn't you get my text?'

'My phone doesn't seem to be working.' Roz showed him the blank screen.

'Hmm, that's odd,' he said, shaking it experimentally. 'Must be a dead zone here.'

A dead zone. An icy finger skimmed down Roz's spine, and she shivered.

Nick looked around the hall as he snagged a glass from a passing waitress. 'It all seems to be going with a swing so far.'

'Yes,' said Roz, but foreboding was gathering, bunching its muscles at the back of her mind, ready to spring.

'Is Jeff around?'

'I haven't seen him for a while.' Come to think of it, she hadn't seen Adrian or Helen for a while either. But she could hardly go chasing after them, Roz told herself. She shook off the feeling. 'Come on,' she said to Nick, 'I'll introduce you to some people.'

It was some time before she saw Adrian again. He appeared at her elbow, looking uneasy. 'Roz, could I have a word?' he said.

Roz glanced around at the hall, which was buzzing with conversation. It seemed an odd time to have a heart-to-heart. Adrian should be circulating. They both should, in fact. 'Now?' she said in surprise.

'If you don't mind. It's a little difficult . . .'

'Well . . . sure.' Roz smiled an apology at the guests she had been talking to. Nick was nearby, deep in discussion with a journalist from the local press. 'Are you okay?' she asked him in an undertone as she followed Adrian past him, and he nodded.

'Where are you off to?'

'Adrian wants to talk to me about something. Not sure what can't wait, but I'll come and find you later.'

'All right,' said Nick absently, already turning back to his conversation, and Roz hurried after Adrian, who was threading his way through the crowd, barely noticing the guests who were trying to catch his attention. Adrian's usual urbane manner had vanished, she noticed uneasily.

'What's this about, Adrian?' she asked when they reached the passage. 'Is everything okay?'

'Could we go to your office?'

'My office?'

'You'll see why,' he said.

Away from the noise and company, disquiet clawed at her once more. Roz hesitated and glanced up the stairs, searching desperately for an excuse. She really didn't want to go back up there, not right then. Jane was up there, waiting, she knew it. She could smell the smoke drifting down the stairwell. The smoke that no one else could smell and no smoke alarm detected. The air was heavy with the foreboding that had been dogging her all week, and every instinct told her to run back into the hall and find Nick, but she could hardly refuse to go with her boss, could she? The house was full of people. Nothing was going to happen to her. And besides, it was just Adrian.

So in the end she shrugged and led the way back up the stairs, up to the first floor, and then up the second, smaller staircase that led up to the attics. The further they climbed, the more the sound of the party below receded and the louder their footsteps echoed in the dim stairwell. Roz's heart was thudding by the time she reached the top floor, and the smell of smoke was very strong. She had to force herself along the corridor to her office, only to falter in the doorway.

Helen was sitting behind her desk, her expression gloating. She made such a bizarre picture in the elaborate gown and ruff beside Roz's desktop computer and shiny phone that for a moment Roz could only blink.

'Helen! What are you doing in here?'

'Haven't you told her yet?' Helen demanded, looking at Adrian. All at once she seemed taller and more commanding, her personality unfurling and swelling to fill the space while Adrian was oddly diminished in comparison.

'Well, I . . .'

'Told me what?' said Roz.

'The necklace is missing,' he said in a rush.

'Stolen,' Helen corrected sharply.

Jane's necklace. Roz felt sick. She hadn't expected that. 'That's awful! Have you called the police?'

'Not yet.' Adrian shifted, clearly ill at ease. 'The necklace was taken from the safe, so it has to have been someone who knew the code. I don't want to involve the police unless I have to. We only discovered it when Helen suggested the gown she's wearing would make a fitting setting for the necklace.'

The thought of Helen wearing Jane's necklace made Roz recoil. 'It's not her necklace!' she said instinctively.

'No, and it's not yours either,' Helen snapped back as if Adrian wasn't in the room. 'So how does it come to be in your desk?' She pulled open the top drawer where Roz kept pens, Post-it notes and other messy stationery items neatly stashed away, and slowly drew out the necklace until it dangled, glittering with a kind of menace, from her hand.

Roz's first reaction was relief that the necklace was safe. Her second a desire to snatch it from Helen's hand. It was easy enough to see where this was going now.

'You think I stole it?' She couldn't help it. She laughed. 'If

I had, I'd hardly be silly enough to hide it in my own desk, would I?' She looked at Adrian. 'You don't believe this, do you?'

Adrian's eyes flickered between Roz and Helen. 'It does seem unlikely,' he admitted.

'Unlikely?' Helen surged to her feet, fury contorting her features, her finger shaking as she pointed at Roz. 'She knows the code for the safe!'

'So do several people.' But Roz was distracted by the way the jewels swung, glinting, from Helen's other hand, and she was struggling to concentrate.

'We all know you want it,' spat Helen. 'You practically grabbed it out of Sir Adrian's hand the other week.'

The winking jewels were blurring in front of Roz's eyes. There were footsteps approaching along the corridor outside. She could hear them clearly, but when she looked at Helen all she could see was her mouth opening and closing, with no words coming out.

Even as she realized that she couldn't hear what Helen was saying, the world began to tilt and slide, and she grabbed desperately at the edge of the desk for support.

Chapter Twenty-one

She looked up at the sound of footsteps on the wooden stairs. It was early still for the servants to be going to bed. And there was something about the carefulness of the steps that made Jane pause, and a warning slithered down her spine. Without knowing quite why she did it, she braced her hands on the coverlet for support.

Then the door creaked as it swung open, and there stood Geoffrey with a candle.

'Sitting in the dark, Mother dear?'

'I have a candle,' she said, pointing to the tallow candle that guttered on the chest. 'It is enough.'

'Enough to write by?'

Jane went still. 'I think not,' she said slowly.

'Oh, then you must have written this this morning,' said Geoffrey, drawing her letter to Gilbert out of his doublet. 'It was so touching!'

'That was not a letter to you,' said Jane. 'Where did you get it?'

'I saw that little servant scuttle out with it. It was easy enough to take it from her. And by the way, she will not be back in case you were tempted to try to write again. Your little rebellion has cost her a position in a good household.'

The coverlet crumpled as Jane clenched it between her fingers. 'What happened to you, Geoffrey?' she asked. 'What made you so cruel?'

'Well, it seems I must just be made that way,' he said. 'Better than being mawkish like you.' He unfolded the letter. 'Mine own husband,' he read mockingly. 'I yearn for you . . . Do not forsake me, I beg of you, and send for me as soon as you may . . . You have my heart till death depart, your faithful wife, Jane. Ahh . . .' Geoffrey pretended to be moved as he folded the letter. 'What a shame Mr Harrison will never know how sorry you are!'

'Why do you not let me go?' Jane asked after a moment. 'I am nothing to you. You do not heed me and you do not care for me. What matters it to you if I go back to London?'

'I do not choose for you to go back to hang over that brat.'

'William is a *baby*. I hung over you too, Geoffrey, when you were that age.'

'He will not have what I cannot have.'

'But you do not want me!' said Jane, lifting her hands in despair.

'You swore to look after me,' he said.

'Then I break my vow.' She got to her feet. 'I will go back to

London, Geoffrey, with or without you. The Holmwoods do not care for you. They care only for themselves, and the money you bring.'

'Do you think I cannot see that for myself?' asked Geoffrey contemptuously. 'I will deal with them in my good time, when I come into my estate. For now they are easily enough manipulated.'

'Then come with me,' she said urgently.

'And leave my inheritance? I think not!'

'They are depraved people,' Jane said in a low voice. 'I fear for you being near them on your own.'

'I will not be on my own. You will be here to keep my thoughts pure.'

Jane shook her head. 'No. I have given up enough of my life for you, Geoffrey. I am going home.'

'You have no money.'

'I have this necklace.' Her hand went to her throat, where the necklace lay warm and comforting, a reminder of Gilbert's love for her. 'I will sell it. I will go home, to my husband, to my son, to my family, whatever it takes.'

'No,' said Geoffrey, a darkness in his face. 'No, you are not going to leave me. My father told me you abandoned me once before, and you will not abandon me again.'

'I had no choice. I was banished, and I came to fetch you as soon as I could.'

'And kept me as little better than a vagabond!'

'That is enough, Geoffrey,' said Jane. 'You speak like a child!'

That was a mistake. Geoffrey advanced on her, still carrying the candle.

'Give me that necklace now!' he ordered.

'No, it is mine.' She put up her hands to ward him away, but he kept on coming, reaching for her throat. 'I said no!'

Wrestling him away, she knocked the letter and the candle to the ground. Geoffrey twisted his fingers around the necklace and wrenched, making her cry out as the catch came free and it slithered to the floorboards.

She bent to retrieve it but Geoffrey grabbed her by the arm and pulled her round, and only then did Jane see how flames were gobbling up the letter. She could see two words quite clearly before they shrivelled and curled up. *Dear heart.*

'Fire!' she gasped. 'Quick, stamp it out, Geoffrey!'

But Geoffrey only stood there, watching the flames, his hand tight around her arm. 'See how the flames reach out,' he said. 'See how they lick along the floor, eager for more.'

'Geoffrey!' Jane struggled to get free so that she could batter the flames herself. 'Let me go! We must put it out before it spreads. You do not wish your own house to burn, surely?'

'I have told you before, fire burns upwards,' he chided her. 'They may need a new roof, perhaps, but we can afford that.'

He was surprisingly strong for a boy not yet twelve. Jane gave up trying to argue with him, and pulled at his hand instead, but viciousness raced across his face and he shoved at her, sending her stumbling back over the fire to fall and knock her head against the corner of the chest, and the world was wiped out in one savage blow.

There was a terrible pain in her head, but when she opened her eyes, the first thing she saw was her necklace, dangling tauntingly in front of her.

'That is mine,' she said, straightening and reaching for it with fierce determination. She would not let it go again.

'You see?' Helen was triumphant as she swung the necklace out of Roz's reach. 'I told you we should have called the police!'

When Jeff paused in the doorway, the office seemed crowded, but there was only Helen, face ablaze with dislike, and Roz, looking uncertain. Sir Adrian appeared overwhelmed between them.

For a moment Jeff hesitated, frowning, confused about what was happening and what he had come for, but then his mind cleared and he strode forward towards the meddling women.

'I will take that,' he said, grasping Margaret's wrist and taking the necklace forcibly from her.

She gaped at him. 'What do you think you're doing?'

'Taking what is mine. It were an insult to drape jewels like these around your scrawny harridan neck.' He smiled cruelly at her expression.

She went red and then white and then red again. 'How dare you speak to me like that?'

'Dare?' He laughed in her face. 'It is not a question of dare. This is my house and everything in it belongs to me. You have ruled the roost long enough, madam. I do what I like now, and there is nothing you can do to stop me.'

'This is most certainly *not* your house!' Gobbling with outrage, Adrian stepped forward but Jeff swatted him back with ease.

'It is now. You do not deserve the name of Holmwood, neither you nor your filthy paramour there,' he said, jerking his head contemptuously towards Margaret. 'You are nothing but her creature.'

'Jeff.' A voice cut across Adrian's spluttering. 'Jeff,' she said clearly as he turned on her. 'This isn't you. I know it isn't. Don't let Geoffrey do this to you.'

'What are you talking about, Roz?' That was Margaret, shrill as ever.

Roz? Something needle-fine darted through him at the name and his concentration flickered for a moment before anger came surging back, stronger than ever.

'Do not look at me like that!' he roared at her. He hated the way she watched him with those clear eyes of hers, this woman who had calmly told him she was not his mother after all. He hated how she seemed to be able to look right at him and see everything that squirmed and seethed inside him. He'd had enough of her disapproval, of her understanding, of her constancy. He hated the way she held her shining honesty up to him like a looking glass and made him look at his own reflection.

He hated her and her pompous lover and her puling, puking son. She didn't love him, she never had. She had only ever pretended.

Taking advantage of his momentary hesitation, Adrian leapt onto him, but Jeff's fury lent extra power to his arm as he swung to meet him and he hit him with a savagery that sent him crashing to the floor.

'Oh my God!' Helen shrieked and stumbled over to throw herself onto Adrian's prone body, covering his face with kisses. 'Are you all right, my darling?'

'*Darling?* For heaven's sake, Helen! What are you talking about?' Adrian pushed Helen away with such an expression of disgust that Roz bit her lip and Helen's face stiffened as if he had slapped her. 'Has everyone gone quite mad?' Adrian struggled to his feet, angrily wiping Helen's kisses off his cheeks. 'Jeff, this has gone far enough.'

'It's not Jeff,' said Roz as calmly as she could, and Adrian stared at her.

'What do you mean?'

'Look into his eyes. That's not Jeff.' Roz kept her voice quiet. She was very frightened but trying not to show it. Jeff had his head lowered like a bull, and he was shaking it slowly from side to side, and she didn't want to do anything to draw his attention to her again. When he had glared at her she had seen the emptiness and the loathing in him and it had been like standing on the edge of a black, sickening chasm, terrified by the pull of it, the remorseless drag into its depths.

Adrian wasn't going to listen. 'Of course it's Jeff. I've had enough of this. Have you all been drinking?' he blustered. He brushed down his doublet impatiently and held out his hand. 'Jeff, give me back the necklace at once,' he ordered, but Jeff only curled his lip and held the necklace out of Adrian's reach.

'This is outrageous!' Adrian was very red in the face, having obviously decided not to make a fool of himself leaping at Jeff's hand. 'Outrageous! I'll be having a word with your parole officer first thing in the morning!'

Helen laid a hand on his arm. 'Calm yourself, my love,' she said, but Adrian brushed her hand away irritably.

'For God's sake, stop pawing at me! What's got into you, Helen? I suggest we forget this extraordinary display as soon as possible.'

'Forget it?' Helen was uncurling, unfurling, rearing back like a snake about to strike. Roz could almost hear her hissing. She put her face close to Adrian's. 'Do you think to forget me? I am your one and only love!'

'Helen!' Adrian looked as if he couldn't decide whether to be disgusted, furious or embarrassed. 'You're making an exhibition of yourself! Stop it at once!'

Dear God, Helen is Margaret! Roz backed against the wall, swallowing. Why hadn't she guessed before? Margaret, who was looking for a substitute for Robert in Adrian.

'You love me!' Helen cried, twining her arms around a horrified Adrian, apparently oblivious to his attempts to wriggle out of her grip. 'He loves me,' she insisted to Roz and Jeff, who curled his lip back at her.

'He did not love you at the end,' he said, and Helen jerked backwards as if he had slapped her.

'You lie!'

'All right, that's enough!' Adrian made a brave attempt to

take control, but his bluster was shaken. 'You're both behaving inappropriately. I'm going to call the police!' he said, pulling out his mobile phone.

'The police!' Jeff snickered as Adrian shook the phone frantically, realizing as Roz had done earlier that the screen was blank and useless. 'I think not.'

Adrian snatched up the receiver on Roz's desk instead, but it was clear from his expression that the line there was dead too. 'I don't know what's going on here, but I've had enough,' he said, and made for the door only to find his way blocked by Jeff.

Funny, Roz hadn't realized until then how big her brother was. He loomed over Adrian, the sheer size of him threatening, and she saw Adrian hesitate and take an instinctive step back.

'That's better,' said Jeff in Geoffrey's voice. Tauntingly he tossed the necklace in the air, once, twice, three times, and in spite of themselves, they watched it rise and fall into his hands in a ripple and a glitter of jewels, their heads nodding up and down like dogs.

'You cannot keep us here.' The hostile energy emanating from Helen surged and crackled around the room. All it would take was the smallest spark and the air would erupt.

And as if Roz had conjured up the thought, Jeff closed his fingers round the necklace, slid it into his doublet and in one smooth movement drew out a lighter. One click, and the flame burned small and steady in front of his face.

'I can and I will,' he told Helen, and he glanced contemptuously at Adrian. 'This time I will let you die with your creature, hmm? Last time he cried for you, but not before he had disowned you. He crawled at my feet and clutched at my knees, begging me to spare him. Pah, you unmanned him from the start.'

'Oh God, no!' breathed Roz as the blood drained from Adrian's face. What had Geoffrey done to Robert?

Helen's fingers curled into claws. 'You will not better us this time,' she snarled.

'Will I not?' Snagging a piece of paper from the pile on Roz's coffee table, Jeff set light to it almost tenderly. 'See how it burns,' he said as he let it burn almost to his fingertips before lighting a flyer from it and letting the first one fall unnoticed to the floor. 'Do you care to wager on that, madam?'

Roz's eyes skittered frantically around the room, looking for a way out. She had to get help, but how? Jeff was blocking the door, but if she could sidle closer, she might be able to get past him if he was distracted.

'*You* did not succumb, did you?' Jeff said almost admiringly to Helen. 'You cursed me to the end. What a shame I had to burn down Holme Hall to rid the world of you, but it made a splendid blaze. Now that was a fire! And a fine hall that I built in its place,' he congratulated himself.

He let another burning paper drift to the floor, where it rekindled the others. Roz took a cautious step sideways. She didn't think the fire was dangerous yet. The flames were small still, and could be easily stamped to ashes, but Jeff – Geoffrey – was intent on feeding the fire, dropping more and more papers. Surely the smoke alarms would start to go off soon?

She could see Adrian belatedly realizing that he wasn't dealing with Helen or Jeff any more. He was standing frozen in disbelief. Helen gripped his arm, her face contorted with hate, while Geoffrey had consumed Jeff so completely that Roz barely recognized her brother.

Very cautiously, she slid her foot sideways. She'd hoped that Adrian might realize what she was doing and cause a distraction, but instead he stared at her so obviously that Jeff swung round just as she took another tentative step.

'Where are you going?'

Her mouth was dry with fear but she moistened her lips. 'That is not much of a fire,' she managed. 'I will fetch you something to make the flames burn higher.'

His eyes gleamed with interest but Helen interrupted him before he could speak. 'Don't be a fool! She's not going to bring you anything. You can't trust her.' She let go of Adrian to pace, her skirts rustling dangerously close to the fire. 'This is all your fault,' she told Roz fretfully. 'If you hadn't taken him away, we would have brought him up as one of us. He would have been a true Holmwood.'

'I am a true Holmwood!' Jeff's face darkened. 'No more lies about your sister and that tailor! I am a Holmwood through and through, and *you*,' he said, turning on Roz, 'you denied it. You denied me my inheritance!' he accused her, kicking petulantly at the little pile of burning papers, so that they tumbled like burning autumn leaves over the carpet. Roz prayed that it was fire retardant. 'You abandoned me,' he remembered, resentment thick in his voice.

'No.' Roz couldn't take her eyes off the flames. They were starting to catch together, and the smoke was rising slyly. She fought to stop her voice shaking. 'I never abandoned you. I came with you, Geoffrey. Do you not remember?'

Confusion clouded his face. 'No . . . no, you left me alone. I was alone. I remember that.'

Roz tensed. All at once there was a lost look in his eyes. If she could just reach him . . . 'Mikey? Mikey, I didn't mean to leave you. I was just a little girl, Mikey. I couldn't save you.' If she kept saying his name, he might fight through, but she knew from her own experience how hard it was to blot out another voice in your head. 'Our mother tried to save you. She didn't abandon you.'

'What?' His brows snapped together but she took courage from the fact that he was at least listening. 'What mother? I don't know what you're talking about.'

'I spoke to a fire officer,' Roz persevered. The smoke was making her eyes sting. 'He was there that night. He said she hadn't called the fire brigade. She'd gone back to the house to look for you.'

'No,' said Jeff, but there was a thread of uncertainty in his voice. 'You're my mother.'

'I'm Rosalind,' she said. 'I'm your sister, Mikey.' Roz coughed and covered her nose and mouth with the back of her hand. The flames had died but the smoke was gathering into a dense cloud. 'Jeff, I know the fire wasn't your fault,' she said urgently. 'I know it was Geoffrey, and he's here again now, but you can beat him this time. You were just a little boy before,

455

but you're a man now. You don't need to do what he tells you. Put out the fire and let us all go. We can sort it out.'

Roz kept her eyes fixed on Jeff, although it was getting hard to breathe. What had happened to the smoke alarm? She had personally arranged for the fire service to install a state-of-the-art system. It was supposed to alert the fire station at the first hint of smoke, but she couldn't hear any sirens.

She didn't dare look at Adrian but she hoped that he was making his way to the door behind Jeff's back. Out of the corner of her eye she could see Helen watching with a sneer. She didn't seem to have any notion of the danger she was in.

'Come on, Mikey,' said Roz, holding out her hand. 'Let's get out of here.'

He hesitated, looking between her hand and the fire with a mixture of longing and fear. 'Jeff,' she said urgently, between coughs. 'It's time to go.'

And then everything seemed to happen at once. Roz didn't see Adrian move but he must have been waiting for his chance, for he tried to plunge past Jeff, who dropped the lighter as he was startled into a roar. At almost the same moment, Helen grabbed Roz and pushed her hard. 'We're going,' she said, her eyes wild. 'This time you two can burn!'

Roz was sent reeling backwards, as Jeff punched Adrian, who dropped cold. Helen let out a blood-curdling shriek and threw herself on him. 'No, no, no!'

Desperately, Roz tried to recover her footing, but the smoke was making her dizzy and she tripped. As if in slow motion, she saw Jeff starting for her through the choking air. There was a moment of utter stillness. Roz was frozen in mid-fall and as the smoke cleared she saw his face. Not Geoffrey, but Jeff. Her brother, coming for her. Then time moved on, and she kept on falling until her head hit the edge of the coffee table and she crumpled into darkness.

Little lights were flickering blurrily in front of her vision. She blinked in an effort to focus. There was something wrong with what she was looking at, but it took a long time to realize that she was lying on the floorboards and watching tiny flames dance across the floor towards her. The necklace was right by her fingers, and she touched it wonderingly, unsure of what had happened. She was sick and dizzy, and there was a pain in her head that made it hard to see. The smell of burning was very strong. Blearily, she pulled herself up to a sitting position, gathering the necklace as she went, horrified to realize that the guards of her skirts were already smouldering. She pulled them away from the flames. The fire was spreading fast, gobbling up the air as it went, and the flames stretched right across the room. Already it would be hard to step over them without getting burnt. The smoke was gathering itself into sly clouds and she coughed.

'Geoffrey,' she said, looking at him across the flames. 'Help me.'

'You were going to leave me. You were going to go back to *him*.'

'I won't. I'll stay here with you.'

'I don't believe you. You were going to break your vow. You will break it if I give you the chance.'

'Geoffrey, help me,' she said again, trying to keep her voice steady. The necklace was hot. It burned against her palm, but she closed her fingers tightly around it. The necklace meant Gilbert. It meant love. It meant hope.

'No,' said Geoffrey. 'You must stay. I will go outside and watch the fire from the street. I will tell everyone that you were talking wildly, that you were careless with a candle. By the time we can stop the spread of the fire, it will be too late for you. My father and grandmother won't care. And perhaps I will send a letter to Mr Harrison to tell him that you are dead, and remind him that you chose me.'

The flames weren't growing, Jane realized, but the smoke was thickening. Her eyes stung and her throat was raw. Geoffrey must have felt the same, but he was just standing there by the door, smiling at the fire. She had to get out of there. Summoning her courage, she threw herself over the flames, but before she had finished her leap, Geoffrey had slipped out of the door, and even as Jane reached for it, she heard the bar drop into place.

'No,' she whispered. 'Geoffrey, open the door!'

But she could hear him running down the stairs. She beat on the door anyway, but the smoke was making it too hard to breathe. Coughing, she slid down against the door. Just to get her breath. Just to decide what to do next. The necklace was still clutched in one hand, and she held it close to her face so that she could see it through the smoke.

The gleam of its gold burned through the thick air like sunshine through the fog that hung over the Ouse, dispersing the foulness in a dazzle of light so bright that it hurt her eyes, illuminating a radiant path through the swirling darkness that pressed on either side. And there, at the end, was a figure, beckoning.

'Gilbert,' she whispered, lifting her arms towards him. He was there at last. The relief was so intense that it seared through Jane like a sharp pain, but she was smiling as she closed her eyes against it, knowing that when she opened them again, Gilbert would be there. He would take her home, and keep her safe, and never let her go again.

'Jesus, what's been going on? Come on, come on, wake up, Roz!' Nick's voice was rough with panic. 'Wake up, wake up! We've got to get out of here.'

Roz coughed and choked, struggling her way up through the blackness. 'Thank Christ,' she heard Nick say quite clearly. 'Roz, can you hear me?'

'I'm okay,' she managed hoarsely, and she clutched blindly at him as she tried to drag herself up. 'What . . . what's happening?'

'Your office is on fire. Why aren't the fire alarms going off?'

'I don't—' Roz began before Jeff's voice cut in and she realized the question hadn't been meant for her.

'I think . . . I remember switching them off on my way upstairs.'

'*What?* What the fuck did you do that for?'

'It was Geoffrey,' said Jeff wretchedly. 'He loves fire. He wants the house to burn again and again and again.'

'Jesus . . .' Nick was fumbling frantically with his mobile.

'There's no signal.' Jeff made a helpless gesture with his hand. 'The landlines are out too.'

As Roz's vision cleared she could see that she was half kneeling in the corridor outside her office. Smoke was billowing through the door, thick and murky. Her head was throbbing and she put a hand to it. 'What happened?'

'There's no time for that now,' said Nick curtly as he hauled her to her feet, ignoring her wince of pain. 'We need to get everybody out and call the fire brigade. Jeff, take Roz's other arm.'

'Helen and Adrian are still in there.'

'No!' coughed Roz as Jeff turned back for the door. 'No, Jeff,' she begged. 'We'll get the fire engines here. They know what they're doing.'

'This is my fault, Roz,' said Jeff. 'Everything's my fault. I can't leave them. Nick, get her out of here. Call the fire service. Tell everyone to leave.'

Nick hesitated, then nodded briefly. 'We'll get help.' Putting his arm around Roz, he urged her towards the stairs, but she held back. 'Jeff!' she pleaded and stretched her hand out to him. 'I don't want to lose you. Not now.'

Jeff's fingers closed around hers in a warm clasp. 'I have to do this,' he said, and he let go of her hand so that he could turn and head back into the smoke.

Blue lights revolved frantically, and the night throbbed with activity. The guests huddled on the pavement across the road, watching the firefighters moving purposefully around. An extending ladder stretched up from one of the appliances to the attic rooms. The firefighters had come with incredible speed once Nick had reconnected the fire alarm. As far as Roz could tell, most of the guests seemed to regard the fire engines as part of the evening's entertainment and there was no panic as people filed outside. There were police cars and ambulances blocking the road and a couple of police officers were posted to keep gawpers at bay.

Roz felt sick as she clung to Nick. Every time someone came out of the house, her heart would leap, but it was never Jeff. Tears trickled down her grimy face. 'Where is he?' she kept asking, but Nick's face was very grim and he didn't answer.

The blue lights and the silent figures of the firefighters moving through the dark were tugging at Roz's mind, and when the senior officer looked round and headed for her, she felt her brain unlock and a memory slide into place with an almost audible click.

She was standing on the blanket in the shed, clutching her toy dog, the one she called Pook, when the door opened, and the fireman loomed above her. He wore a helmet and big trousers and a big yellow jacket that crackled as he bent down. 'Hello,' he said. 'What's your name?'

She hadn't been able to speak, but when he lifted her up in his arms, she had felt safe, and she let him carry her up the garden. There were blue lights flashing and a strange orange flicker in the upstairs window.

'I remember,' she said to Nick slowly. Her mother jolting her as she stumbled through the kitchen. *Promise me you'll stay here*. The damp and the cold and the fear of being left alone. 'I remember it all.'

It was so vivid now, Roz couldn't believe that she had been able to wipe it from her memory.

The fire officer's face was sombre. Nick put his hand on Roz's shoulder. 'I'll talk to him,' he said, and Roz was glad to put her head on her knees. Geoffrey's words kept echoing in her head. *You abandoned me*. Was that what she had done? She had left Jeff alone all over again.

When Nick came back, he crouched down beside her and took her hands between his. 'They found Adrian in the corridor. He's on his way to hospital. Jeff must have dragged him out and then gone in again for Helen.'

Roz's eyes filled with tears. She knew what Nick was going to say. 'And Jeff?'

'I'm sorry, Roz.' Nick gathered her into his arms, and held her while she sobbed out her shock and fear and grief for the brother she had never had the chance to know properly.

'Are you up to answering some questions?' he asked after a while and Roz nodded, knuckling the tears from under her eyes as Nick beckoned the officer over. Behind him, firefighters were manoeuvring two stretchers out of the door and handing them carefully into an ambulance.

'Your husband tells us that you were unconscious when he found you, but that he and your brother managed to get you out before the fire really took hold,' the officer said after he'd commiserated with Roz. 'Then it seems that your brother went back in to rescue the two other people in the room. He was a brave man,' he told Roz, and she nodded slowly.

'He wouldn't have thought so.'

'We found this in his hand.' The officer produced a blackened chain, dully gleaming, and Roz drew an unsteady breath.

'My necklace,' she said.

'Would you like to look after it? We've included it on the inventory.' He handed Roz the necklace and she took it without thinking. Jane's necklace. She held it wonderingly. There was no burning this time, no throb of fear. Instead the jewels nestled comfortably in her palm, warm and safe, and she felt a sigh of peace brush past her ear like a blessing.

Jane had gone.

It was too hard to explain about the necklace. She would give it back to Adrian, but for now it was enough to hold it in her hand and feel alive. Roz looked at Nick, who had come for her as Gilbert hadn't been able to, and she smiled unsteadily.

'It does seem to have been a particularly intense fire,' the officer went on, 'but all the damage is confined to that one room. Can you tell me what happened?' he asked Roz. 'How did it start?'

When *had* it started? With Mikey's father, whose violence had left Mikey himself vulnerable to Geoffrey's malign influence? Perhaps it had been her own refusal to accept Daniel straight away or to confront the past that had set her on a collision course with Helen's secret and obsessive love for Adrian.

Or perhaps it went back further than that. If Jane's mother hadn't made her promise to care for Juliana. If Juliana hadn't turned away from Geoffrey as soon as he was born. If Margaret's love for Robert hadn't taken such a warped direction. If she hadn't been abused in her turn, might she have had the chance to be a loving mother like any other? So many ifs, so many choices, so many turnings taken or ignored. Roz could follow the thread of every reason back and back and never find the end.

The fire officer was waiting expectantly. How had it started? 'I don't know,' said Roz. 'It was very confused. I don't remember.'

'A boy.' A wide grin cracked Nick's face as the reality hit. He picked Roz up and swung her in an exuberant circle. 'We're going to have a boy! I'm going to have a *son*!'

'Another son,' Roz reminded him, smiling. She had grown fond of Daniel, who they still saw regularly, although he was more settled at home.

Seeing the baby on the scan had been extraordinary. Roz's throat had closed as she and Nick held hands tightly and watched their child touch his face as if in equal wonder.

The nurse had smiled at their expressions. 'Is this your first baby?'

No. Roz almost said it out loud. The memory of William was still imprinted on her heart. Her medical records might not show it, but she knew what it was like to give birth. She remembered the twist and rip of her muscles, the certainty that she was going to split open, the flood of love as William snuffled into her, his tiny hands kneading her breast.

William, her boykin, her dearest dear. Roz couldn't think of this new child without a pang for the one she had lost and missed so terribly still.

She summoned a smile for the nurse. 'Yes, my first,' she said, but she touched the necklace with her fingers, a fleeting apology for the lie.

It was over a year since that terrible night in Holmwood House. Adrian had recovered, and although they were all shaken and distressed, they had agreed to press ahead with the opening. Apart from Roz's office, there was very little damage to the house itself, and once the repairs had been done, there seemed no reason not to open the house to the public as originally planned. So much work had gone into it, Adrian argued, that it would be a tragedy to shut it away.

Roz had agreed. While Adrian was still in hospital she had quietly arranged for a service of deliverance to exorcize any lingering spirits, but in her heart she knew that Jane and Geoffrey and Margaret were already gone. The fire in her office had purged the house and now when she walked through the great hall, she heard only the sound of her own footsteps and the Elizabethan music playing on a loop through the hidden speakers. The air was lighter now, the shadows less dense.

Inevitably news of the dramatic fire on the night of the launch had spawned much speculation about the cause, and Jeff and Helen's tragic deaths only fuelled rumours that the house was haunted. Mark's prediction that a reputation for ghosts would be good for business proved correct, and visitor numbers were staggering. Roz was pleased that Holmwood House was so popular for Adrian's sake. Since the fire she had got to know him better. The tragedy had changed him. He was less pompous and more likeable, and she wondered sometimes just how much he remembered about that night.

'You keep it,' he had said when she tried to return Jane's necklace to him.

'Adrian, I can't, it's too valuable.'

'It's yours,' he insisted, and just for a moment there had been something in his eyes that reminded her of Robert. 'I'm sorry,' he said. 'I'm sorry for everything.'

'Adrian . . .'

'I'm not going to have any children,' he said a little painfully. 'When I die, the Holmwood name will die with me, and the house and Holme Hall will be broken up. Perhaps that's as it should be, but I'd like to know the necklace is cared for and worn.'

Roz swallowed. 'It should really be in a museum,' she made herself say, but Adrian shook his head.

'No, I want you to have it.'

So Roz wore the necklace, and every time she touched it she remembered Jane, who had tried so hard to keep her promises, but never again did she slip back to the past. The world stayed firm beneath her feet now, and if she sometimes caught a glimpse of a farthingale or a figure in a fine doublet out of the corner of her eye, by the time she had turned her head to look closer it had whisked away, swallowed into the past once more and leaving only a shimmer in the air. Roz was glad of it, but sometimes, it was true, she missed the house at the sign of the golden lily. Sometimes she would remember Gilbert, and William, and the girls, or she'd see a little spaniel in the street, and the yearning was so sharp she would suck in a breath to stop herself crying out.

Jane was part of her now, her memories entwined with Roz's own, but Roz didn't want to live that life again. Jane was the past, and she had a present, and a future with Nick, and the child still to be born.

Now Nick set her back on her feet and held her face between his hands. He seemed to know when she was thinking about Jane, and he sensed that Roz was remembering the baby she had borne in the past.

'Do you want to call him William?' he asked gently and Roz was so touched by the thought that for a moment she couldn't speak.

'No,' she said eventually. 'No, William would have had a good life, I think. He would have been loved.' She thought about another boy who had been less fortunate, the brother she had found too late, but who had redeemed himself at the end. Poor Mikey, who lay next to his mother now, and the family he had never meant to kill. 'I think I'd like to call him Michael,' she said.

Nick nodded his understanding. 'We'll do better by our Michael, Roz, I promise.'

Roz wrapped her arms around his waist and leant into him, glad and grateful. 'Let's not make promises we might not be able to keep,' she said. 'Let's just do the best we can.'

Acknowledgements

Turning a nebulous idea into a published book is a long and tortuous process that involves many people, and it wouldn't happen at all without Louise Buckley and the whole team at Pan Macmillan. I am so grateful to them, as I am to my agent, Caroline Sheldon.

For their help with *The Edge of Dark*, I'd like to thank particularly: John Mackenzie for telling me about his experience as a firefighter; Steve Hodgson, always helpful on police procedure and obscure points of the law; and Lauren Marshall of the Merchant Adventurers' Hall and Chris Tuckley of the York Archaeological Trust, who gave up their time to explain some of the practical challenges of opening a historic building to the public. Deana Naraparaju told me about working in a museum, and Laura Mason about 'the edge of dark', a phrase I'd never come across before. As fiction writers will, I took the knowledge and experience they all so generously shared and pillaged them for my own purposes; needless to say, any mistakes in the book are all mine.

I'm running out of ways to thank those friends who patiently point out inconsistencies or thrash out knotty plot problems, most especially Diana Nelson, Julia Pokora and Stella Hobbs – and John Harding, who makes me stick to my schedule when I least feel like it. I couldn't do it without them.